The
Reluctant
Queen

THE RELUCTANT QUEEN

The Story of Anne of York

JEAN PLAIDY

 THREE RIVERS PRESS · NEW YORK

Copyright © 1990 by Jean Plaidy

Reader's Group Guide copyright © 2007 by Three Rivers Press, a division of Random House, Inc.

Originally published in hardcover in the United States by G. P. Putnam & Sons, New York, in 1991.

Library of Congress Cataloging-in-Publication Data
Plaidy, Jean, 1906–1993.
The reluctant queen : the story of Anne of York / Jean Plaidy—1st pbk. ed.
Includes bibliographical references.
1. Anne, Queen, consort of Richard III, King of England, 1456–1485—
Fiction.   2. Richard III, King of England, 1452–1485—Fiction.
3. Great Britain—History—Richard III, 1483–1485—Fiction.
4. Queens—Great Britain—Fiction.   I. Title.
PR6015.13R44   2007
823'.914—dc22   2006026749

ISBN 978-0-307-34615-5
Printed in the United States of America

Design by Maria Elias
10 9 8 7 6 5 4 3 2 1
First Three Rivers Press Edition

CONTENTS

THE ECLIPSE

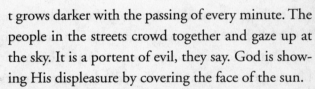

It grows darker with the passing of every minute. The people in the streets crowd together and gaze up at the sky. It is a portent of evil, they say. God is showing His displeasure by covering the face of the sun.

Very soon I shall lay down my pen. I am too tired to write more. My strength is slowly ebbing away and I feel Death close.

It is an unhappy time to leave this world. Suspicion and treachery are all around us. There are rumors to which I try to shut my ears. They frighten me. I tell myself I do not believe them. I do not want to hear the things people are saying—yet I must know.

"Tell me . . . tell me everything," I beg my ladies.

They shake their heads. They say, "There is nothing, your Grace."

That is not true. They know but they will not tell me.

We were happy at Middleham before Richard took the throne. Middleham will always be home to me . . . and, I believe, to him. It meant something very special to us both. It was there that we first knew each other. I always said it was there that love between us first began. The people there understood him. They knew his worth. They do not like him here. In their hearts they do not accept him as their king. He is not tall and handsome as his brother was. He lacks the gift of charm that Edward had in such abundance. How perverse human nature is! Richard would be a good king; he would serve his country faithfully; but it was Edward whom they loved because he was good to look upon; he was a giant among men; he smiled his way through his reign, beguiling rich and poor alike. His profligacy, his self-indulgence mattered not. He looked like a king and they had adored him. It was perhaps natural that they should resent his successor. Richard is not tall; he lacks the golden beauty of his brother; he is dark and serious and does not smile easily; he serves his country with zeal; but the people remember Edward's charm and mourn for him.

And in the streets they are whispering that I am dying on my husband's orders. The rumor is that he is having me slowly poisoned. How cruel they are! They cannot think of anything vile enough to say of him. It is his enemies of course—and they are all about us. They would make a monster of him. But who should know him better than I? And I know he is a good man. He would be a great king and good to them, greater than his self-indulgent brother—if they would let him.

It is true that I am dying—but not at his hands. He knows that I cannot live long and he is heartbroken. I can see the misery in his eyes. I am the only one whom he can trust. How could anyone think that he would want to be rid of me? I know I am sick, unable to bear the sons all kings want, but there has been a special bond between us since he came to my father's castle when we were children. If only he could cast away his crown! If only we could go back to Middleham and the North where the people love and understand us. Richard is paying too highly for his crown.

I try to comfort him. More than any I know his feelings.

"Whom can I trust?" he asks. "Who in this sad court can trust whom?"

I know he is thinking of Buckingham—his one-time friend, or so he thought—now turned traitor.

Sometimes when he looks hurt and bewildered he reminds me so much of the boy I knew all those years ago. I alone am able to see the real Richard; to others he is cold, aloof, a stern king, determined to hold what he believes to be his by right, dedicated, determined to do his duty.

Throughout the court there is a rumor that he wants to marry his niece, Elizabeth, when he has rid himself of me. I think this has grieved him more than anything.

"They hate me so much," he said. "They bring the most harmful accusations against me. They compare me with my brother. They say I have usurped the throne from young Edward. They do not believe he is a bastard. Oh, if only my brother had not died! How they loved him! He could do no wrong in their eyes and I can do no right."

I said, "Your brother was an unfaithful husband; he was profligate. He loved luxurious living. He cared more for his own pleasure than for the good of the country. You are a good man, Richard. You will be a good king; and in time the people will come to realize that."

He smiled at me sadly, fondly. I remember that, from the time he was a boy, he would not listen to criticism of his brother. Edward had been a god in his eyes. It had always been so. Like the rest of the country, he had succumbed to that charm.

"They are silent when I pass," he said. "Do you remember how they used to cheer Edward?"

"They will cheer you one day."

He shook his head. "And now they say I would remove you that I might marry Edward's daughter—my own niece! Anne, you could never think for one moment . . ."

I took his face in my hands and kissed it. I wanted to assure him of the contempt in which I held such gossip.

But secretly there were moments when I thought with some apprehension of Elizabeth of York. The eldest daughter of hand-some Edward and his beautiful Queen. It was natural that she also should be beautiful—sparkling, radiant, healthy. If she were like her mother she would bear many children.

Before I was so ill I would see her at court. Did I fancy she watched Richard with speculation in her eyes? Did she flaunt her beauty, her radiant charm? Was she implying: "Look at me. How different I am from the poor, sickly queen." I did not believe for one moment that she was in love with Richard; but she was her mother's daughter and she would dearly love a crown.

And even I, knowing him as I did and understanding full well the venom of his enemies, was sometimes overtaken by cruel

doubts. I am ill. I am barren, I would say. And is it not the duty
of kings to get sons?

Common sense returns and I remind myself that it is I whom
he has always loved; and then how I long for the days of peace at
Middleham and I say, "If only Edward were back on the throne
and we could return to the North—our true home, where we are
known and loved and the people do not murmur evil slander
against us."

Here there are enemies everywhere. There are sly rumors . . .
ridiculous rumors, but the people accept them as truth because
that is what they want to do.

Richard's enemies are all about us. They are whispering of a
certain Henry Tudor, now sheltered by our enemies of France,
waiting until that day when he is ready to make his spurious
claim to the throne.

Yes, there is treachery all around us.

The light is fading. The face of the sun is almost obscured
now and for me the end is near. What will become of Richard?
What will become of the country? I shall never know.

My life is fading as the light is. Someone approaches. It is one
of my women.

"My lady, the King is on his way to you."

I shall write no more. Richard is coming and something tells
me this is the last time I shall look upon his face.

MÉSALLIANCE

L ooking back over my life I often think how strange it is that a woman such as myself should have so little control over her own destiny. I was the daughter of a man who at the time of my birth was one of the most important men in the country. In truth I might even say *the* most important for he was even greater than the king. He was indeed known as the Kingmaker. Then I was the affianced wife of a Prince of Wales and later a queen. What a glittering fate that would appear to be, yet now that my life is coming to an end, I realize that it was lived in the shadows. I moved—or perhaps it would be more correct to say I was moved—into important positions, but always for the benefit of others—except, I like to think, in marriage to the man who became King of England. It was certainly my wish and I hope his that I should become his queen. And now I have come to the time when I must ask myself for how long?

But I must go back to the very beginning. Who would have believed that a man such as my father could fail to beget the son he so ardently desired and had only been able to produce two girls—my sister, Isabel, and myself? His grandfather, Richard, Earl of Westmorland, had had twenty-three children from his two marriages. But perhaps my father found consolation in the fact that even girls have their uses. They can form alliances that can be of inestimable value. My father was a man to make the most of his advantages.

It was different with my mother. I believe she was very satis-fied with her two daughters, as is often the way with mothers who come to believe that the offspring they have are just what they wanted. At least my father could not have been disappointed in his marriage, for through my mother had come the greater part of his wealth; she had been Anne Beauchamp, heiress to vast lands and fortune, and she had brought him the earldom of Warwick.

She lavished great care on Isabel and me, which was necessary, I suppose, because neither of us was robust. The three of us were very happy together, whether we were at Middleham Castle, War-wick Castle, Cawood, or Warwick Court in London.

We saw our father infrequently, but when he did come the atmosphere changed completely. Bustle, excitement, apprehen-sion prevailed. Men wearing the emblem of the Ragged Staff were everywhere, and, of course, there was my father's dominating presence. He took some interest in us girls, which was surprising. I sometimes thought he might have been a family man if he had not been so ambitious to rule the country, through the king of his making. My childhood memories are of comings and goings, some of which affected us and then we could be off to other family residences at a moment's notice.

Isabel was my senior by nearly five years and she often tried to explain to me what was going on, but when she herself did not understand she refused to admit it and relied on her invention. When my father departed with his followers, we would be at peace again.

Of all our homes I loved Middleham best. It was situated in the heart of wild and open country in the North Riding of Yorkshire—and it will always be home to me.

It was at Middleham Castle that I first met Richard of Gloucester, when he was sent to my father to learn the arts of war and chivalry; and it was there that the bonds of something deeper than friendship were forged between us.

I was five years old when a momentous event occurred. Isabel, then ten, told me about it.

"There is a new king on the throne," she said. "It is all because of the War of the Roses. The White Rose is for York . . . that is the good one. That's us. Then there is the Red Rose of Lancaster. That is the wicked one for silly old Henry and his horrible Queen Margaret. They are not King and Queen anymore because our father does not like them. So he has made our cousin Edward king and he is now called Edward the Fourth."

"Does our father say who is to be king then?" I asked.

"Of course. He is the Kingmaker. Wicked Queen Margaret killed King Edward's father at Wakefield. She cut off his head and put a paper crown on it to mock him because he had wanted to be king instead of silly Henry, and she stuck his head on the walls of York. Our father was very cross about it and he would not let her be queen anymore—so Edward is king instead."

This was in a way a version of what had happened at Wakefield, for the battle had been a decisive one in the War of the Roses. Edward, however, had not such a strong claim to the throne as Henry, who was the son of King Henry the Fifth and therefore in the direct line; but Edward's father was descended from King Edward the Third through both his father and mother—through Lionel, Duke of Clarence, who was the old king's second son, and Edmund, Duke of York, who was his fifth. Richard told me all this during one of our talks when I was a little older.

Most people, except those absolutely dedicated to the cause of Lancaster, must have thought it preferable to have a king like Edward than one such as Henry. Edward was young, strong, and outstandingly handsome—he was a giant among men and a king the people could admire and be proud of.

He was also Richard's brother and because of the deep bonds of friendship between King Edward and the man who had put him on the throne—my father—it was decided that Richard should be sent to Middleham to be brought up under the guidance of the Earl of Warwick. Thus it was we met.

I remember the first time I saw him. He was sitting alone and despondent. He was very pale; he looked tired and was staring rather gloomily straight ahead.

I said, "Hello. I know who you are. You are the king's brother."

He turned to look at me. I could see that he was not very pleased by the intrusion and was wishing that I would go away.

"Yes," he answered. "I am, and you are the earl's daughter— the younger one."

"How long are you going to live with us?"

"Until I have learned all that I have to learn."

"There are always people here learning what my father can teach them."

He nodded.

"I know Francis Lovell and Robert Percy," I said. "Do you?"

"Yes. I know them."

"Sometimes I watch you all riding in the mock tournaments. There must be a lot to learn."

"There is a great deal to learn."

"It must make you very tired."

"*I* am not tired," he said firmly.

I knew he was, so I said nothing and we were silent, he staring ahead, I think, willing me to go away.

I watched him, thinking of his father's head being cut off and stuck on the walls of York City.

He stood up suddenly and said, "I have to go. Good-bye."

"Good-bye," I said; and he went away.

After that I was more interested in the boys who came to be brought up at Middleham. They were all highly born, of course, and they were made to work very hard and continually. It was necessary, Isabel told me, because they had to become knights and fight in the war—and there were always wars, so there had to be men trained to fight in them. These boys who were learning would all have to go to war and probably have their heads cut off and stuck up somewhere.

The boys lived like the soldiers my father always had with him wherever he went. They slept together and ate together; and there was a comptroller of the household whom they must obey. They had so much to learn; not only must they be proficient in the arts of war but they had to learn how to behave in the presence of ladies, so there were times when they came to the solarium or the great hall where we were assembled at that time to converse with my mother, Isabel, and myself. They might play chess or some musical instrument, or dance.

I would look for the small dark boy who, I believed, preferred even the strenuous exercises of the fields and moors to those social occasions. It was different with Francis Lovell. He was very good-looking and merry, so Isabel usually made sure that she talked to him. I did not feel in the least envious. I had a great desire to learn more about Richard.

My mother smiled to see us together. "He is a strange boy," she said. "He is not easy to know. But at least he is the king's brother."

I said I thought Richard did not really want to talk to anyone.

"No," she said. "That's true. But I think if he has to talk to someone he would rather it were you."

I felt a surge of pleasure at that until Isabel told me that it was because I was the youngest and did not count for much.

Poor Richard! He was often very tired. When I saw him coming in wearing his heavy armor, I was very sorry for him. He was different from the other boys; they had more sturdy bodies. Richard never complained; he would have fiercely denied his fatigue, but I noticed it, and I liked him the more because of his stoical attitude.

I knew by that time that he wanted to be strong and learn everything that would make him of use to the brother whom he adored. It was a hard life these boys were expected to live. I supposed it was necessary if they were to be prepared for arduous battle; but perhaps now that we had the wonderful Edward on the throne he would keep the peace. But of course they must always be prepared.

Sometimes, if the exercises were taking place in the castle grounds, we would watch. We saw the mock battles when the boys fought each other in the field with swords or even battle axes; sometimes they rode out in heavy armor for some exercise on the moors. It was all part of the training. And when they came back they must clean themselves, take supper, and in the early evening join the ladies for conversation, singing, or dancing.

I often thought what a brave spirit Richard had; and what a tragedy it was that he had been given such a frail body.

In the beginning I knew he hoped that I would not seek him out, but after a while I fancied he used to look for me. My mother, who had a kindly heart and felt deeply for the young and all the trials they had to face in life, was somewhat pleased.

"I think they overwork him," she said. "He is smaller than the other boys. Perhaps he will shoot up with the years. Some do. It is strange as his brothers are such fine tall men. As for the king, he stands head and shoulders above most." She smiled in that indulgent way people did when they spoke of the king. "But I like to see you two friendly."

He used to dance with me. He was not very good and I pretended not to notice. I think he appreciated that.

I said, "I believe men should not dance well. It is not quite manly to do so."

"My brother dances well," he said. "When he takes to the floor everyone is captivated by his performance. And he is the most manly man that ever lived."

He glowed when he talked of his brother. When he was tired and obviously so relieved to take off his heavy armor, I would ask him questions about his brother and the tiredness would disappear. King Edward was his ideal. According to Richard, he was perfect in every way. I soon discovered that Richard's dearest wish was to be exactly like this brother. That wish was futile. Edward, it seemed, was all that Richard was not. I thought later that it was an indication of something unusual in his nature that he should so admire someone who was the absolute antithesis to himself.

There was a special seat at Middleham; it was cut out of the stone wall; shrubs grew around it so that it was comparatively secluded. He made it his special refuge; he would go there to recover from those exhausting exercises. He wanted to be apart from the other boys who naturally looked down on one who was not as strong as they were; and after the manner of the young they would not hesitate to call attention to this.

I used to join him there. At first good manners prevented him from asking me to leave, and he tolerated me; after a while I think he was sometimes glad of my company, for there was one day when I was unable to go to him and the next time he mentioned the fact with something like reproach in his voice. Then I knew he was pleased to be with me.

It was from him that I learned something of what was going on in the country.

"Tell me about the Wars of the Roses . . . about mad Henry and fierce Margaret and how it all came about," I said; and I settled back to listen.

"The trouble is between the Houses of York and Lancaster," he explained. "It would never have arisen if Henry the Sixth had been a real king. Kings must be strong like my brother. Henry is mad. It is not surprising. His French grandfather was mad and had to be put away for long periods. And the worst thing was that he married Margaret of Anjou. She is haughty, domineering and the people hate her. They do not like her two chief ministers—Suffolk and Somerset—either. And in '53, when Henry and Margaret had a son, it looked as though the Lancastrians would be on the throne for a very long time. It was not good. A mad king, an arrogant foreigner for a queen—and a child heir. Your father was against them. He was for the House of York. After all, we are related. Our mother is your father's aunt. She was one of twenty-three children . . . the youngest, you see. There is a family bond. It was natural that he should support the House of York. The Percys are for Lancaster and the Nevilles do not like the Percys. They both regard themselves as Lord of the North."

"I am glad we are on your side, Richard," I said. "I should not have liked to be with mad Henry and fierce Margaret."

"It would have been the wrong side to be on, for we are the winners, and once the people realize what it is like to have Edward for a king they will want no other."

"Sometimes the people cannot judge what is best for them, and sometimes they have to accept what king they are given."

"That is true, but my brother and your father will see that they will accept the king they are given."

"It is most exciting. I can see why you want to excel at all the things you have to do. They will be necessary if you have to go to war for your brother."

He smiled. I had said exactly what was in his mind.

He grew animated talking about the battles. St. Albans, Blore Heath, Northampton. Wakefield made him both sad and angry. I ventured to put out a hand and touch his because I knew he was thinking of his father's death and the ignoble treatment he had received.

"Wakefield has been avenged," he said. "And then . . . St. Albans."

"Tell me about St. Albans."

"This was the second battle that had taken place at St. Albans. It was truly brilliant strategy on the part of your father. His army was beaten in the field. Margaret thought she was secure. But your father joined up with my brother, and they decided that they would not accept defeat and would march to London and there proclaim my brother king."

"But you said they had been beaten."

"That was at St. Albans. But the Lancastrians were unpopular. It was not Henry whom they hated. He was a poor sad creature. It was his overbearing wife. And when the news of the defeat of St. Albans reached London the people were afraid of being in the hands of the Lancastrians. They knew what it would mean if the rough soldiers came to London. There would be trouble in the streets—houses would be ransacked, wives and daughters of the citizens misused. They were burying their valuables and were in a state of great anxiety. So your father decided to get to London first to save the city from the Lancastrian soldiers—many of whom were mercenaries intent on gaining spoils for their efforts. It was a clever idea. Your father with my brother marched on the capital. They persuaded the people that they came in peace to save them from inevitable pillage and to ask them if they would accept Edward of York as their king."

"And they were welcomed," I cried, having heard something of this from Isabel.

"It is true. The important citizens were called together and asked if they thought Henry and Margaret fit to rule them. At this there was an immediate response in the negative. And would they take Edward of York to be their king? They cried, 'Yea, yea, yea.' Oh, how I wish I had been there!"

"Where were you?" I asked.

"I, with my mother and my brother George and sister Margaret, were all on a ship bound for the Low Countries. When my mother heard about the defeat at St. Albans she had thought she must get us out of the country. Of course, I was not old enough then to fight for my brother, but now I am older I shall soon be able to. As soon as we heard the news that my brother was the accepted king we returned home."

I listened enthralled—proud that I was the daughter of the man who had made this glorious victory possible. My father and Richard's brother stood together. No wonder Richard and I were friends.

He seemed to share that thought for he turned to me and smiled warmly.

"Of course," he went on, "there had to be a lot of fighting after that. Margaret had really won the battle of St. Albans. It was just clever strategy that had won the day for us. There had to be the battle of Towton where we finally beat them and after that there was no doubt that my brother was truly king."

"With my father helping him to rule."

"They are kinsmen and allies."

"As we are. Let us always remember that."

"Yes," he said. "Let us always remember."

It was October. The leaves of the trees were already turned to bronze and there was a strong smell of autumn in the air.

I loved such days. Isabel and I often rode out with some of the boys and I usually found myself with Richard. He was looking better; he was becoming very skillful in all the martial arts, and I admired him more than ever because I knew he had to make an extra effort to equal the others. He did tell me once, in a rare moment of confidence, that sometimes his shoulder was painful after the exercises. But when I asked afterward if it were better, he frowned and I knew he did not like me to refer to it, so I did not ask again. I knew he was regretting mentioning it to me in the first place.

Returning to the castle one day, we found great activity. I knew at once by the number of men in the courtyard and about the castle that my father had come home.

My mother hurried to us as we arrived.

She said, "Your father is here. There is bad news. The enemy has landed at Bamborough."

She looked very grave.

"There will be fighting," she went on. "We have had a comparatively long respite but it seems that is over and we are to start again. Is there to be no end of it?"

But it was no time to brood on such a question. We were surrounded by my father's followers. When he was home the number of people in the castle was great. When I was older I understood how he boosted his popularity with his extreme wealth. He used his money to create an image of power wherever he went. When we were in Warwick Court in London his followers thronged the streets; they were in all the taverns and market places so that everyone should know great Warwick was in town. In the kitchens of Warwick Court oxen, pigs, and lambs were roasted whole, and any man was welcome to take away as much meat as he could carry on his knife. So it was not surprising that people rejoiced to see Warwick in town, and my father evidently considered it a small price to pay for his popularity and to hear the shouts of "A Warwick" every time the emblem of the Ragged Staff was seen; and whenever the great man himself appeared, it was as though he were indeed the king. My father was a vain man. His great ambition was to rule the country, and as this could never be acceptable because he was not royal, he would do it through the king of his choice. He appeared not to realize that his power came through his vast wealth—much of which had been brought to him by his wife—and not because of his wisdom and achievement.

But at this time he was at the height of his glory. The king he had made was on the throne and there seemed every indication that, pleasure-loving as the young king was, my father had every chance of fulfilling his ambitions.

Now he must bring all his efforts to defeating the invading forces of Margaret. Henry did not count; he was a poor, half-mad puppet. Margaret was the enemy. It was a pity Henry had married such a forceful woman.

The great news was that the king would be coming to Middleham to join my father for the march to Bamborough.

I had never seen Richard so excited.

I said to him, "I am longing to see the king. I want to see for myself that he is all you say he is."

"He is all of that—and more. Whatever I said of him could not be praise enough. He will be going into battle. How I wish I could go with him."

"One day you will," I replied, and he nodded happily.

My father wanted the most lavish feast prepared—something to outshine even Warwick's standards. The king would be at the castle only one night, for the next day at dawn he and my father, with their armies, would be marching to Bamborough.

Servants dashed hither and thither; my mother gave orders in the kitchens; and Isabel and I were instructed how to behave. We must be a credit to our father.

"I long to see the king," said Isabel. "They say he is the most handsome man in the kingdom."

We heard his approach when he must have been some distance away, and Isabel and I were in the turret with some of the ladies waiting. And then we saw the cavalcade and the king was riding at the head of it.

Reports of him had not been exaggerated. He was magnificent. Our mother, who joined us, said, "We must go down there to greet the king," and with her we went down to the courtyard. Our father was at the gate of the castle and we joined him there.

The king had leaped from his horse and advanced toward us. I had never seen such a good-looking man. He was very tall and there was an immense vitality about him; his features were clear cut and perfectly formed; but his greatest charm was that air of affability, his warm, friendly smile—and I discovered that was for everyone, even the humblest; he looked on all men as though they were his friends and all women as though he longed to be their lover. It was what is called charm, and it would always bring people to his side.

"Ah, friend Warwick!" He beamed on my father and I glowed with pride. That look conveyed love and reliance; and I could see that my father was greatly gratified. Later I realized that he regarded the king as his creature, the puppet to do his will; handsome, gracious, made to be loved by the people; the façade behind which lurked the true ruler of the country, for the king, given what he wanted—a life of luxury, easy living, and above all women—would be content for the Earl of Warwick to rule England. That was what my father thought at the time.

"My gracious lord," he said, "may I present my lady wife."

"Countess," murmured the king.

My mother was about to kneel but he had caught her and, putting his hands on her shoulders, kissed her on the lips.

"Your pardon, Warwick," went on the king. "Temptation was too great."

And there was my mother blushing, smiling, a victim of his enchantment.

"My daughters, Isabel and Anne, my lord."

"Charming, charming." And before Isabel could kneel, he had taken her hand and was kissing it. Then he turned and did the same to me.

He said something about my father's being the most fortunate of men and from that moment we were all caught up in his spell. I understood how he had enslaved Richard.

There was feasting in the great hall, but my father was grave, no doubt thinking of Queen Margaret and wondering how many men had landed with her and whether they should leave immediately for Bamborough. The king showed little concern and none would have believed from his demeanor that he might be on the point of losing his kingdom.

When the meal was over my father conducted the king to the bedchamber that had been prepared for him. They would be leaving at dawn for Bamborough.

I was awakened in the early morning by the clattering of horses' hoofs and voices below. And then all was quiet.

They were anxious days. My mother talked to us about the state of affairs in the country more than she ever had before. I think it was because she was afraid. With a Yorkist king on the throne we were all safe, but that could change suddenly. When I was very young, there had been an occasion when we had all had to leave with great speed for Calais, of which town my father held the captaincy. That was when, briefly, Henry was king again.

Now I was eight years old and Isabel thirteen—of an age, I suppose, to understand a little of what was going on around us. Perhaps my mother thought that she should prepare us for a possible change in our fortunes.

"It is Margaret," she said, as we sat over our needlework. "She is a persistent woman, and now she has a son who, she hopes, will inherit the throne one day and she is determined that he should do so."

"My father will never allow that," said Isabel.

"It might be beyond his control. There will be battles . . . and if it should go against him . . . oh, how I wish we could all be at peace!"

"We were until this woman landed," said Isabel.

"She is the kind of woman who will never give up. She knows what she wants and is determined to get it—and that is the throne of England."

"To get it she will have to beat our father and that she can never do," said Isabel firmly.

"It has been done before," our mother reminded her.

"But my father soon changed it."

"He would be pleased to hear your confidence in him."

"He is the king, really."

"Hush, child! You should not say such a thing."

"But one must speak the truth."

"One must adhere to the truth but when it is dangerous to mention it it is better not to do so."

"My father will soon have won," said Isabel stoutly. "I do not want to go to Calais again."

"Alas, Isabel, it might not be what we want but what is thrust upon us."

I wondered why my mother was so apprehensive, and it occurred to me that it was because she was so much wiser than Isabel.

"So," she went on. "We must pray for victory while we prepare for defeat."

After that she talked to us often about the situation.

"It was a pity Edward the Third had so many sons," she said. "It makes too many claimants to the throne. Strange, is it not, that men crave for sons." She looked a little sad and I felt I ought to apologize for being a daughter as well as Isabel, but I was glad to be reminded that some men could have too many.

Poor Henry. She felt sorry for him. She was sure he did not want the crown. He would have been happy with religion, a life of contemplation. She had heard it said of him that he wished to be a monk or enter the Church. Perhaps if he had done that he would not have gone mad in the first place. And now he suffered from periodic attacks of insanity. It was the case of his grandfather, Charles the Mad of France, all over again. She wondered whether his madness had come to him through his mother, the family that lady was reputed to have had with Owen Tudor was equally affected.

She ended up by telling us that our father was a very clever man; he was the most important and powerful man in England and while he was in control England would be safe. On the other hand, we must not think it would be too easy. There were enemies all around us and we must be prepared.

But on this occasion we were saved from disaster. Messengers arrived at the castle. When news had reached Margaret that the Earl of Warwick, with the king, was marching on Bamborough, she immediately abandoned all thought of fighting and took to her ships. God must be looking after the Yorkists, for He sent a storm that shattered her fleet.

It was victory. But not entirely. More news came. Margaret had escaped and had arrived at Berwick with her son: she was well and ready to fight another day.

Having seen the magnificent Edward, I wanted to know more of him and his family, and Richard was not averse to telling me about them, which surprised me, he being so reticent about most things. But he was very proud of his family.

I said, "I thought your brother, the king, was all that you said of him."

That pleased him, of course, and put him into a communicative mood.

"I have another brother, too," he said. "George. He is almost as wonderful as Edward . . . only just not quite. And I have a sister Margaret. She is a wonderful person."

"How lucky to have so many brothers and a sister when I only have Isabel."

"There were seven of us," he said. "Four boys and three girls."

"Seven! Quite a large family."

"Large families are good to have."

"Sometimes there can be too many sons who claim the throne," I said, remembering my mother's words.

He ignored that and went on: "It is those about my own age whom I saw most of. My brother Edmund was with my father when he was killed at Wakefield." His voice shook a little. I doubted he would ever forget that terrible event. "Then I had two sisters, Anne and Elizabeth. They were sent away to be brought up in some other noble house. Edward and Edmund were at Ludlow. I stayed at Fotheringay with the younger ones George and Margaret. George is three years older than I. My brother made him Duke of Clarence when he made me Duke of Gloucester."

"Tell me about George and Margaret."

"George is very handsome and everybody loves him."

"As tall and handsome as Edward?"

"Oh, not quite. Nobody could be. But he is very good-looking and clever."

"And Margaret?"

"She is three years older than George."

"And beautiful, I suppose."

"Yes, she is very beautiful."

"But not as beautiful as Edward."

"Not quite."

I laughed. "It is always 'not quite.'"

"Well, although they are very handsome, they are . . ."

" . . . not quite as perfect as the king."

"If you are going to laugh at my family, I shall not tell you any more about them."

"I was not laughing. I was only admiring. Please tell me some more."

"Well, what do you want to know?"

"I want to hear about when you were a very little boy."

"My father was always away from home fighting."

"Fathers always are."

"My mother was often with him."

"What is your mother like?" I stopped myself from saying, "Beautiful, of course, though not quite so beautiful as Edward." But I restrained myself. I did not want to anger him. He was rational about most things, though perhaps taking a somewhat morose view of life, he was fanatically devoted to his family and appeared to consider all the members of it far above ordinary mortals.

"My mother is truly beautiful," he said. "When she was young she was known as the Rose of Raby. She and my father were devoted to each other and she traveled with him whenever it was possible. She could not be with him in battle, naturally, but often when he was fighting, she would be somewhere near, so that she could see him often."

"And she had all those children?"

He nodded. "We were all in awe of her . . . more so than we were of our father. Edward is very like her . . . in looks, and George perhaps more so. He was Margaret's favorite. I used to wish that I were. Margaret was very kind to us both but it was clear that she loved George best. He was always doing something that was forbidden and although she used to scold him she would make excuses for him and she always told him that, however wicked he was, she loved him just the same. She was good to me. Oh, but it was different with George. Well, he was tall and strong and golden-haired. I was never like that . . . not like him and Edward . . . Margaret did not mean it to show . . . but it did."

Poor Richard, I thought.

"Well, you were lucky to have a big family," I said. "I wish I had some brothers."

He admitted that it was good. "Especially in war," he added. "Families stand together."

"Not always. Brothers fight over crowns and things."

"We never would. We are a united family. Oh, how I wish I were old enough to go and fight with Edward!"

"Well, you will one day."

I used to think a lot about Richard. What a pity he was not tall and handsome. It must be particularly galling, having been born into such a perfect family. I wanted to see them all . . . George, Margaret, and the Rose of Raby. It all sounded so romantic and exciting.

Christmas was on the way. My father was absent most of the time, for although Margaret had eluded capture at Bamborough she was still around to make trouble, and there were several castles in the North that were still in Lancastrian hands. My father and the king were making war on these.

A messenger came to the castle with news from the king. He was ill and at Durham Castle. It was not a serious illness but his physicians said he should take a short rest. He wanted his brother, Richard, to come to Durham and spend Christmas with him.

To my chagrin and Richard's great joy, he left Middleham to spend the festive season with his brother.

My mother was growing less apprehensive. The storm had passed, but she was ever on the alert for danger.

I said to Isabel, "I suppose there could be times when people do not have to worry and the king who is on the throne is left in peace."

"That would be rather dull," she replied. "And what about our father? How could he be a kingmaker if there was not any need to make a king and keep him on the throne?"

"I think our mother would like it better."

"And every day would be the same. Lessons, needlework, riding, walking. Whereas now people come here. One never knows when the soldiers will come . . . and you can wonder what will happen next."

"I still think it would be rather pleasant," I said.

"That's because you are so young," she said in her usual contempt for my youth.

I missed Richard. He had not returned after spending Christmas with his brother. Our father came home for periods and there would be the usual activity: entertaining went on and there were often a great many people at the castle for whom lavish meals were provided. I often wondered how many of these people who paid such homage to my father would have done so without the benefits they received.

Many of them came to the castle from France.

This made Isabel very excited. She was always reminding me of her age, for she was very proud of being nearly five years older than I. I was ten at this time so she must have been nearly fifteen. It was an age when the daughters of powerful men were found husbands.

Desperately Isabel longed for a husband. There was no one else to talk to about this except her little sister; so it was to me that she talked.

"You realize, do you not, that our father is the most powerful man in the kingdom. He is also the richest. What does that mean?"

"That he is the most powerful and richest man in the kingdom, I suppose."

"Idiot! It means that we are great heiresses. I more than you because I'm the elder. I suppose there will be something for you, too . . . quite a lot, as a matter of fact. Our parents have no sons. So it will come to us."

"I had not thought of that."

"You don't think of anything but being with Richard of Gloucester. Mind you, he is the brother of the king. But *I* wouldn't want a brother. I would want a king. And why shouldn't I? After all, I am great Warwick's daughter . . . his elder daughter . . . so what if . . . ?"

"What?"

"Didn't you think the king was the most handsome man you ever saw?"

"Why yes, I suppose he is. I cannot think of anyone else . . ."

"Well, just suppose . . ."

"Do you mean . . . ?"

Her eyes were sparkling. Then she said, "After all, who made him king? If my father didn't like what he did, he could say, 'You are no longer king. I'll put Henry back.'"

"Henry already has a wife . . . Margaret . . . the one they all hate."

"I was not thinking of marrying Henry, stupid. Oh, I do wish you had a little more sense."

"But you are thinking of marrying Richard's brother."

"Do not tell anyone. It would not do to talk."

"Has our mother said . . . ?"

"Nobody has said anything. I'm just telling you. I am just saying it could be."

"Richard would be your brother-in-law."

"Richard is not important. He is too young and too small. He might do for you."

"What do you mean—do for me?"

"Well, if I married the king it would be rather nice if you married his brother. Particularly as I think you like him better than anyone else. And I think he likes you, too, because he talks to you."

I was pleased. "Yes," I agreed. "He does. I wonder when he will be coming back."

Isabel was not interested in that. She was dreaming of herself as Queen of England.

Our father came home for a while and there were more visitors from France, and it was obvious that he was very pleased to have them in the castle. They brought letters for him. Isabel and I wondered whether my father might be arranging a match for her in France.

"Poor Edward will be disappointed," I said.

She glowered at me. "I might be Queen of France."

"I believe the King of France is an old man and already has a wife."

"Well, he'll have a son, won't he? I expect I'm for him."

She was certain that that was what the messengers were arranging. It was a bitter blow when she discovered how wrong she was.

My mother talked to us often while we did our needlework. Isabel was old enough to know what was going on, and it could be true that they were trying to find a suitable husband for her. My turn for that was a little way ahead, for which I was thankful. I often saw my mother looking at Isabel anxiously and I knew she was thinking of the fate of young girls who were thrust into marriage before they knew what it was all about, and with her daughter it would have to be a marriage of state.

One day Isabel said to our mother, "Why are there so many French at the castle these days, my lady?"

My mother looked up from the altar cloth that she was embroidering and said, "The King of France is very anxious to be friends with your father."

"I know." Isabel smirked. "Is there some special reason?"

"I believe that the King of France is a very wily man," went on my mother. "They call him the Spider King."

"Are spiders wily?" I asked.

"So many people are afraid of him," said my mother. "Many people have a fear of spiders. I suppose it is because they lie in wait for their prey and watch them being caught in the sticky web and then the spider comes out and makes his victim powerless."

"It sounds horrible," I said, looking at Isabel. She was thinking of marriage, of course. How would she like to be in a family at the head of which was such a man?

"The King of France," went on my mother, "likes to be on good terms with the important men in all countries that might affect him, so that he can have good friends all around him. That is why he seeks your father. He has only been on the throne for three years. He became King of France at very much the same time as your father made Edward King of England. He is full of admiration for your father's management of this country. That is gratifying and pleases your father mightily. Not only is he pleased to be on good terms with such an important country as France, but France is the country where Margaret takes shelter. Your father is always hoping that out of friendship for him, Louis may agree to a treaty that would prevent Margaret's taking refuge in his country."

Isabel yawned slightly. Then she said with animation, "I was wondering whether my father is trying to arrange a marriage."

My mother looked at her sharply. "Have you been listening at doors, Isabel?" she asked, for Isabel had occasionally been discovered in such situations.

"No, no, my lady. I just wondered."

"Well, I will tell you, but you must speak of this to no one. Your father *is* trying to arrange a marriage." I was aware of Isabel:

she was leaning forward, her hands clenched. "For the king," my mother went on.

Isabel looked blank. What could the king's marriage have to do with France? Her eyes were already darkening with disappointment.

"Yes, the King of France is eager that his sister-in-law, Bona of Savoy, should be Queen of England, and whom should he ask to arrange this but your father?"

Poor Isabel! My mother did not notice how shocked she was and went on: "It is time the king was married. We need heirs to the throne. It is always good for kings to have their children when they are young. One never knows what is going to happen, particularly in these terrible times. Who would have thought that Henry the Fifth would have died when he did—a young man, so strong, so brave, the conqueror of France? Oh, if only he had lived! And then he left poor Henry, his only son. Sometimes I feel sorry for that poor man. Only don't tell anyone I said so. However, the point is that the king should marry. I am sure the marriage will be fruitful and everyone will be happier to know there are little heirs to the throne. So that is what your father is so eager to arrange with the French visitors."

We went on with our needlework and Isabel was very silent.

But when we were alone, I could not resist saying, "So, you were wrong. The marriage was for the king, but not with you."

"All this stupid war," said Isabel. "All this looking after Edward. Our father made him king. It is time he gave some thought to his daughters."

Poor Isabel! It was a great disappointment. She had so looked forward to being Queen of England, or at least Dauphine of France.

A few weeks after Christmas our father left home to attend the funeral of our kinswoman, the Countess of Salisbury. This was to take place in Bisham Abbey in Buckinghamshire, and all the greatest nobles of the land would be there to pay tribute to her, or perhaps it would be more correct to say to the Earl of Warwick. I was not sure whether the king would attend but I guessed that Richard would be there.

And when my father returned to Middleham, to my delight Richard came with him. His brother George, Duke of Clarence, was also a member of the party.

It was our first meeting with George who was to play such an important part in our lives.

Richard introduced him proudly and it was obvious that he had great respect for his brother. It did not match the admiration he had for Edward, but it was a deep affection. Knowing Richard, I could understand why. George bore a certain resemblance to Edward. He was tall and extremely handsome; he had that easy charm that I had recognized in his brother. He was affable to everyone, easy-going, laughing a great deal and giving the impression of enjoying life in every way.

I soon discovered though that he had a grudge against fate, which was that he had not been born the eldest son. I believe that sentiment was common enough among the sons of great men: they all wanted to be heir to the title, lands, and wealth that their father had enjoyed. And, of course, in addition to all that in this case there was the crown.

Isabel was attracted to him from the beginning and he was very attentive to her. If he resembled his brother Edward, he would be like that with all girls, of course; but I was glad, for his coming made up for the disappointment she had recently received about marriage. Isabel was longing for that state. She wanted a grand title, riches and power perhaps. That would not be surprising, considering her father's veneration for these assets, and George was the brother of the king.

Richard seemed to have grown much older during that Christmas he had spent with the king. His brother had talked to him often and Richard had learned a great deal about the state of the country, and some of this Richard passed on to me. He had an even greater desire to serve his brother. I had no doubt that the king had promised him it should not be long before he did so. He must spend just a few more months under the guidance of the king's good friend, the Earl of Warwick, and then he would be ready.

My father was determined to show the Duke of Clarence that he was very welcome at Middleham. Or perhaps he wanted to remind him of his wealth and power. I was just beginning to realize how important it was to my father that people should be made aware of this.

I believe the hospitality shown to the Duke of Clarence was no less grand than that set before the king himself; there was feasting, dancing, and great merriment every evening; and mock tournaments had been arranged to take place in the tilt yard for their pleasure. Clarence enjoyed this as he was very skilled and usually came out the victor. This may have been arranged, for my father would want to show his distinguished visitor that he was an honored guest—which would include allowing him to win. But perhaps it was rarely that this had to be maneuvered, for Clarence was very skilled, a superb horseman, and adroit with the sword—achieving all his triumphs with an effortlessness that won the admiration of the ladies, and in particular Isabel.

In fact, Clarence was remarkably like his elder brother, winning people to his side with charm, only—as Richard said—not quite as perfect. But of course, in Richard's eyes nobody could be.

Richard was obliged to join in the displays. I used to sit with my mother, Isabel, and the ladies watching, and while I did so, I would pray that he would win and not show the fatigue he must be feeling.

We talked now and then together, but not so much as we had now that his brother was there to spend a good deal of time with him.

I asked him about Christmas and learned that it had been very enjoyable and that he and the king had been together most of the time.

He told me what a moving ceremony there had been at Fotheringay whither he and the king had gone immediately after Christmas.

"Both my father and brother were murdered on December the thirtieth, three years before, and we have a ceremony to remember their deaths every thirtieth of January, just one month by calendar after the date of their deaths. It is a very solemn occasion in which the entire family joins."

"Does that not bring it all back too bitterly?"

"It is important that we do not forget."

"But you could not forget. I know it is always in your mind."

He nodded gravely. "I wish you could have been there, Anne," he went on. "We had a hearse covered in golden suns. The sun is our emblem, you know . . . the Sun of York. There were silver roses and banners showing Christ seated on a rainbow and others with angels in gold. It was wonderful."

"And your mother? Does this not make her very sad?"

"It makes her very sad but she insists on being present. She is very proud of our family—especially now that Edward is king. She knows it is what our father would have wished. He did not get the crown for himself—but it came to Edward."

He paused and I knew he was thinking, as I was, of that head on the walls of York wearing the paper crown, which had meant the temporary triumph of the House of Lancaster. A short-lived one, it was true. But now here was glorious Edward—the incomparable King of England.

There were tears in Richard's eyes and I was happy because he did not mind that I saw them. I knew he would have been ashamed and angry if anyone else had.

During that spring and summer Richard was often away from Middleham. The king would send for him and most joyfully he went. I was continually hoping that he would come back and was always quietly happy when he did. He would tell me of his exploits with the king; how Edward had given him his own company of followers; how good his brother was to him; how honored he was to be the brother of such a king.

Isabel told me that the king was more fond of Richard than he was of George, which was not fair to George, he being the elder.

Richard, was, after all, only a boy, and small for his age—not in the least like his brothers. But Edward liked his adoration, for really Richard was quite blatant about it. As a matter of fact the king had given more honors to Richard than he had to George.

"Who told you that?" I asked.

"George, of course."

"You seem to have become very friendly with him," I replied.

She smiled secretively and I went on: "The king gives honors to Richard because he is so loyal."

"George is clever and handsome and if Richard were not the king's brother no one would take any notice of him."

"You don't know Richard."

"You're so young," retorted Isabel contemptuously. "*I* think George is very attractive. It is a pity he is not the eldest. Then he would be king."

There were dreams in her eyes. I thought, she is thinking of George as a future husband.

That was an uneasy spring followed by an uneasy summer. I supposed it would always be like that until Margaret was completely defeated. There were Lancastrian risings throughout the country and my father would be away for long periods of time, and when there were arrivals at the castle my mother would be fearful of what news they might bring. With good reason. Fortunately there were more Yorkist victories than setbacks and a great deal of the credit must be given to our family.

At Hedgeley Moor my uncle John Neville, Lord Montagu, greatly outnumbered by the Lancastrians, defeated them and shortly afterward at Hexham delivered the final blow. It was a great success for the House of Neville and it was generally accepted that the Earl of Warwick was making the throne safe for Edward.

I had never seen my father so contented. He had achieved the very pinnacle of power; his dream had come true. He had made Edward king and—so he thought—he could not have chosen a better man to suit his plans. Edward was the perfect king: affable to the people, greatly loved by them: he had all the charm and grace a king should have. Moreover he was pleasure-loving, which would prevent his meddling in state affairs, which was exactly what my father wanted. The king should be amused while, in his name, the Earl of Warwick ruled the country.

It was late September. We had come to a period of comparative peace. After the defeat at Hedgeley Moor and Hexham, Margaret fled the country; the Lancastrians were in disarray.

My father returned to us contentedly. His family were receiving the honors they deserved. After his magnificent performance at Hedgeley Moor, John was given the Earldom of Northumberland. George Neville, at that time Chancellor and Bishop of Exeter, was to be made Archbishop of York. This was what my father wanted—his family in high places with himself at the head of the state to be called on should his help be needed, while Edward remained the charming representative, doing Warwick's will as though it were his own with the grace and charm of which he was capable.

It was a dream come true.

Then came the awakening.

It was a late September day. How well I remember it! We had arisen as usual and Isabel and I had spent the morning at our lessons and in the afternoon ridden out with the grooms for a short period of exercise.

We were in the solarium with our mother and some of the ladies when there were sounds of arrival from below. My mother rose from her chair and went toward the door, but before she could reach it my father strode into the solarium.

I had never seen him look as he did. He had apparently come straight from a long journey, but where were his followers? Even as the thought entered my mind I heard the sounds of their arrival below. He must have ridden on ahead of them.

My mother immediately dismissed the ladies. They left their needlework where it was and went swiftly out. She signed for us to follow them. We went to the door and Isabel caught my hand. She stood in a corner behind a screen and I stood with her.

Both my parents were so agitated that they did not notice we were there.

My mother stammered: "You have come from Reading?"

"Aye . . . from Reading."

"Richard, what has happened?"

"Disaster," he said.

"Margaret?" whispered my mother.

"Worse," he said. "Worse. The king has married."

"But it was his wedding you were going to discuss. You were arranging it."

"I know. I know. The effrontery! He is not what I thought. This has changed everything. The truth is, Anne, I did not know

this man I set up. I have worked for him. I have made him what
he is . . . and what do I get in return? Ingratitude. Defiance. The
Council is outraged, but of what avail? The deed is done. I should
never have made him king."

Isabel and I were as still as statues. We *had* to stay and hear more.

The king married! He was to marry Bona of Savoy. Our father
had arranged it.

My mother said, "Richard, what does this mean?"

My father was silent for a few seconds. Then he said slowly, "It
means that all my work has been in vain. I have given my support
to the wrong man. I have put him where he is, guiding him,
shielding him. I have made him the king. And what does he do?
He flouts me. He has married that woman while he was allowing
me to negotiate with the King of France. He has made a fool of
me. After I have put the crown on his head, he is showing me
quite clearly that he intends to go his own foolish way."

"My dear," said my mother, "this has been a terrible blow. You
have ridden far. You need rest. Then we can talk of it calmly.
Please rest now, Richard."

He put his hand to his head. "Everything that I have done,"
he murmured. "Useless. I have put him there . . . and now I see
that I made the wrong choice!"

"He will regret it. He will soon be back with you."

"Aye!" said my father fiercely. "He shall regret it."

"Now you need to wash off the stains of your long ride," said
my mother soothingly. "You need food . . . time to think." She
put her arms around him and he embraced her.

Isabel looked at me. I nodded and we crept silently away.

THE RIFT

veryone at Middleham was talking about the king's marriage and I guessed it was being discussed all over the country. There was a great deal I did not know at the time but I learned later, little by little.

To my father's chagrin, the people were on the king's side. Was it not just what the handsome boy would do? And, like the romantic lover that he was, he snapped his fingers at conventions and married the object of his devotion.

"God bless him," said the people. "He may be a king but he is a gallant boy at heart."

It was indeed a romantic story. He had met Elizabeth Woodville in the forest by chance, it was said; but there were some who laughed that to scorn. Who was this woman? She was older than he was and already a mother with two children by her first marriage. She, with her mother, had planned the whole episode. She had stood there, her golden hair loose about her shoulders, holding her two boys by the hand, and when the king had appeared she had knelt and begged him to restore her late husband's estates; and, so attracted was he by her outstanding beauty that she was able to trap him into marriage.

Isabel was obsessed with the subject; she was a little piqued because the king had come to Middleham and seen her. Yet he had not fallen madly in love with her. How she envied Elizabeth Woodville!

"It is witchcraft, of course," she said. "Elizabeth Woodville's mother is said to be a witch. And who is Elizabeth Woodville? There are ladies of higher birth than she is who would have been far more suitable. Oh yes, it was certainly witchcraft."

"Ladies of high birth such as the daughter of the Earl of Warwick?" I asked rather maliciously.

"I feel sure that if I had been older . . ."

I studied her. She really was very pretty—and well aware of it. Yes, I thought, perhaps if she had been older . . . how differently my father would have felt about that! Then he would not be regretting the cancellation of the plans for marrying the king to Bona of Savoy. It was hard to imagine Isabel, my sister, Queen of England.

"Of course," I said, "the new Queen's mother *was* the widow of the Duke of Bedford—so she is connected with royalty. Was not the Duke of Bedford brother of King Henry the Fifth?"

"Yes, but when he died, she married Sir Richard Woodville,

Lord Rivers, and he was killed in battle . . . fighting against the king!"

"That's what makes it all so romantic!"

"Everyone expected she would be his mistress, but she said, 'No, I will not have you unless you marry me.' Had I been her, that is what I should have said."

"If he had wanted to marry you he could have done so without any fuss. Our father would have liked that, surely. In fact, I wonder he did not arrange it."

"He should have done so," she said almost tearfully. "But it is too late now."

"Isabel, have you thought what this is going to mean to us?"

"We shall not be Yorkists anymore."

"Then what shall we be?"

"I suppose," she said, "we shall have to wait and see."

"Does this mean that they are our enemies . . . Richard . . . George . . . ?"

She looked grave at the suggestion.

"I do not think," I went on, "that I would ever be Richard's enemy . . . certainly not just because his brother had married Elizabeth Woodville."

"Our father is very angry."

"I know. He shuts himself away and does not talk to anyone but our mother."

"He is so shocked by all this. He thought that, as he had made Edward king, he could make him do exactly what he wanted. What has upset him so much is to find he cannot."

And so we talked—and scarcely of anything else. We heard

rumors of the king's besotted love for his new wife. He had given her everything she wanted and her family were already filling most of the important posts in the country. It seemed that we were in danger of being ruled no longer by the Earl of Warwick, but by the Woodvilles.

There was tension throughout the castle. We all knew that the storm must break soon.

And so we waited for it.

Eventually my father began to look like his old self, but his anger still burned within him, and, as was proved later, he was making plans.

As Premier Earl of the Kingdom, it would naturally fall to him to present the new queen to the Lords in Reading Abbey. For a few hours he raged and stormed in my mother's presence and declared it would be an added insult for him to do this and he would not endure it; but she managed to persuade him that to decline would mean an open rift with the king himself and this was not the time for that. He saw the good sense of this.

There was so much talk about the situation between the king and the earl that I could not help hearing it and, although at that time I was not old enough to understand it all, I did later, for this quarrel was one that was talked of for years to come.

My father did go to Reading to the ceremony and stood on one side of Queen Elizabeth, while George of Clarence stood on the other and they presented her to the Lords and listened to their acceptance of her as Queen Elizabeth.

I can picture that cold and beautiful woman—the poor

widow of a man killed in action fighting against the king whom she had now married. I can picture the triumph in her eyes, for she had reached the height of her ambition and, being shrewd, as she proved in later years, she must have been amused to be presented to the Lords of the Realm by the man who, she knew, disapproved with all his heart of her marriage and was now, for the sake of expediency, being forced to accept it.

There was something very significant that came out of that ceremony, for my father's companion in this distasteful office, George, Duke of Clarence, shared the resentment of his brother's marriage as fervently as my father did. It was the beginning of that alliance between Warwick and Clarence.

My father soon began to realize that the marriage was even more disastrous than he had first thought. It was not merely an instance of the king's showing that he had a will of his own and was determined to make his own decisions. The queen had a rapacious and ambitious family, all eager to exploit the amazing good luck that had come to them. The king was under the spell of his wife and that meant grand marriages for members of her family— and there were many of them. My father could see that through these alliances with the richest and most powerful men in the land and the taking over of important posts, before long there would be another family ruling England and taking over from the Nevilles. As he and his family had risen to great power through advantageous marriages, none knew better how this could be achieved.

I learned that it was when my father heard that the queen's sister was betrothed to the Earl of Arundel's heir, Lord Maltravers, that his rage broke forth.

Without my mother to restrain him, he took an unprecedented action. He went to the king's chambers and confronted Edward and there gave vent to his anger.

He told the king that it was an act of folly to have married a woman of no standing in the realm, one who had already had a husband and had two sons as old as the king's own brothers, and who came of a family who had actually fought with the enemy. Moreover, he had placed him, Warwick, his loyal friend and ally, in an invidious position by allowing him to parley with the King of France for a marriage with Bona of Savoy while he was already married. So he had insulted the man who, more than any other, had helped him to the throne.

I see now how clearly that encounter reveals the character of those two men. My father was ambitious in the extreme; he was single-minded, possessed of certain gifts, but he showed a lack of wisdom in some ways. His great rise to power had been largely through the accumulation of wealth—and luck; of course, he had made the most of his opportunities, but I have come to wonder whether he lacked the essential qualities for greatness.

Edward was a man of easy temper, it was true. But my father had miscalculated in summing up his character. Edward *was* luxury-loving, a man who wanted to be on good terms with those about him; he disliked quarrels, I think, partly because he thought they were a waste of time and energy; he saw himself as the benign monarch; he went about the countryside bestowing his smiles on all his people—and particularly the female section. He knew that he had behaved badly to my father, but the earl would never understand the sensual nature of a man like the king. Edward had seen Elizabeth Woodville; she had refused to become his mistress, and therefore, because of his insuppressible desire for her, he had been forced to marry her. How could he explain that to a man like Warwick? On the other hand, he was grateful to Warwick, and it grieved him to disappoint him. Perhaps it would have occurred to him that the king should not tolerate a subject's insolence and he should order his arrest. But Edward was not impulsive. Some might think so because of his marriage to Elizabeth Woodville, but that had been a calculated act; simply, he had had to marry Elizabeth because his desire could not be slaked in any other way.

He would realize, too, that if he ordered Warwick's arrest a civil war might be provoked. He might have seen Warwick joining with the Lancastrians and that would certainly mean disaster for the House of York. So he did what was typical of him. He set aside his kingship and talked to Warwick as though he were still his friend.

The queen's mother was the widow of the Duke of Bedford, he explained gently. She was of the noble house of Luxembourg. There were royal connections on her mother's side. It was unfortunate that she had married a Lancastrian, but that was no fault of hers. Young girls could not choose their husbands. She was beautiful and had already shown herself capable of bearing strong, healthy children. If the Earl of Warwick would set aside his disappointment about the marriage to Bona of Savoy, he would realize there was nothing to regret. And such a matter should not come between old friends.

Edward, as everyone knew, was one of the most charming of men, and he did manage to some extent to soothe my father's wounds. There was a reconciliation of a kind. The king embraced the earl and said, "There has been too much friendship between us two, Warwick, for this matter to spoil it."

My father's anger must have cooled sufficiently for him to realize that it would be folly for him to indulge in more outbursts, and common sense got the better of anger. He appeared to agree with the king.

But whatever was said, danger was looming. The Woodvilles were trying to oust the Nevilles and that was quite unacceptable.

My father returned to Middleham.

Richard, naturally, was no longer at Middleham, and I wondered if he would ever come back. But I did see him not very long after the quarrel.

One day my mother called Isabel and me to come to her and she told us we were going on a journey. She looked happier than she had for some time.

"Your uncle George is to be made Archbishop of York, and there will be a grand banquet afterward. All the nobility will be there and your father wants every member of the family to be present if possible."

Isabel was very excited. "Will the king be there?" she asked.

"Oh no. I don't expect the king will be there. But he will surely send someone to represent him. We shall see."

I was thinking, could it be that Richard would be there? The prospect of seeing him made me very happy. Moreover if he were, it might be an indication that this feud between the king and my father was coming to an end.

"We shall go to Cawood Castle," went on my mother. "It is very pleasant there on the south bank of the Ouse. We shall have the river and it is only ten miles from York, so after the ceremony the company will, with your father and the archbishop, join us there for the feast."

In due course we set out for Cawood and as soon as we arrived, if we had not been aware of it before, we would have realized what an important occasion this was. The castle was swarming with retainers. There were fifty cooks at work in the kitchens and the carcasses of sheep, cattle, pigs, swans, and geese were being prepared for the table, together with artistically fashioned pastry commemorating the archbishop's elevation and the power of the Nevilles. It was borne home to me that there was something significant about this occasion.

The party arrived from York and, to my great joy, riding with my father and uncle was Richard.

In the great hall I was seated at the long table with my mother and Isabel, and Richard was with us. He gave me his rare smile and I knew that meant that he was glad to see me.

All the feasting ... the drinking ... the dancing ... the splendor indicated one thing: the power of the Nevilles was by no means diminished. The local peasantry had the earl's permission to go to the kitchens and take as much meat as they could carry off on their knives; and for that they were ready to throw their caps in the air at any time and shout "A Warwick" as often and as enthusiastically as the great earl wished.

It was a reminder to all that the Nevilles were not to be treated with disdain. The king might travel about the south, smiling and courteous, winning the approbation of the people, but this was the north and the Nevilles were the lords of the north. They had wrested the title from the Percys; and these sturdy, down-to-earth people were not the sort to be seduced by a few superficial smiles.

I could see that Richard was not happy. I longed to talk to him, but I could not do so at the table before my mother, Isabel, and the guests who sat with us. But I determined to find an opportunity of doing so before he went away.

It had always been a habit of his to go off alone somewhere and eventually I found him. He was walking in the castle grounds and I called to him.

"Richard, I'm here. Or do you want to be left alone?"

"I don't mind you," he said.

"I was hoping to have a talk with you. Oh, Richard, how deep is this trouble between the king and my father?"

"Your father is making it deep."

"Has he no reason?"

"I suppose there are some who would say he has." He turned anxious eyes to me. "You know of my brother's marriage?"

"Everyone knows."

"A man must marry where he will."

"Must not a king think of his country?"

"My brother thinks of his country. They are demanding that he get an heir. That is what he is preparing to give them."

"But I have heard that my father was negotiating with the King of France for a suitable marriage. The king allowed him to do so while he was already married."

"I know. Perhaps the king should have told your father. But it is more than that, Anne. The king does not wish others to tell him what he must do. He decides for himself. That is what he means your father to understand. He is sorry to be on ill terms. He does not forget the good service your father has given him in the past and the friendship between them. But he will make his own choice and he has chosen this queen."

"So you, too, are against my father?"

He shook his head. "I have admired your father more than any man except my brother. They have both been ideals to me. I have often wished that I could be like them. But your father must remember that it is my brother who is the king. The people shout for Warwick in the streets, it is true. I believe that, next to my brother, they respect him more than any other man. It grieves me as much as it does you that they should not be good friends."

"What does George say?"

He was silent for a few seconds. Then he said slowly, "George does not like the queen. George is always . . . a little critical. Secretly, I think he would like to be king himself. He is handsome and clever . . . and people like him. But he should know that not he nor anyone . . . could compete with Edward."

"How loyal you are to the king!"

"I would die rather than fail him. I have taken for my motto 'Loyaulte me lie!' I think loyalty is the most important virtue and that is what I have for Edward."

"He is fortunate to have such a brother."

"Nay. It is I who am the fortunate one."

"Tell me. Why does George not like the queen?"

"George would not like any queen my brother had, for if she produces a son, George would be a step backwards from the throne. Now, you see, he is next in line. I believe that is at the heart of George's dislike. Besides . . ."

"Besides, what?"

"Well, the queen is haughty. People have to kneel before her all the time. It is what happens. She was of no importance before her marriage. Now she is the queen and she wants no one to forget it."

"That will not make her very popular."

"I believe she does not crave popularity. She just wants to be the Queen of England. Surely that is ambition enough."

"Richard, I believe you do not like her either."

"Have I shown that?"

"Yes, you have."

He hesitated for a moment, then he said, "The Woodvilles are arrogant. They have come too high too quickly. They are pushing themselves into the highest positions in the land; and the queen is seeking great marriages for all her relations . . . her sons . . . her brothers. There are many of them. People are saying that before long we shall have the Woodville clan ousting . . ."

". . . ousting the Nevilles," I finished.

"Yes, they are saying that. We shall be ruled by the Woodvilles and the Woodvilles are unfit for high office."

"So you see why my father is so upset."

"I understand, and it grieves me. My brother has been kind to your father. He stormed into the king's chambers and actually dared berate him. My brother was so calm . . . so reasonable!

'Poor Warwick!' he said. 'I should have told him I was married and not let him go on making plans with the old Spider. Yes, I understand his wrath. He has been of good service to me and I am ready to forget that outburst. I am ready to be his good friend again.' There! You see how forgiving he can be. He does not want conflict with his old friend. If only your father would be friends again, my brother would be ready."

"He will, I am sure."

"He must be."

"And in the meantime, does that mean that you will not be staying at Middleham?"

"I am here now only for this celebration."

"I am so glad you came, Richard. Oh, how I wish for a return to the old days before there was this trouble."

"We were always good friends, you and I, Anne," he said. "Let us always be."

"That is what I want. Very much I want it."

"We will agree then that, whatever happens, you and I will always be friends."

How readily I agreed to that.

We returned to Middleham and Richard said good-bye to me and went to join his brother.

Life settled down to what it had been. There were boys in the tiltyard and in the fields doing their martial exercises, but I was not interested because Richard was not among them.

I was learning more about what was going on. The quarrel between my father and the king had made me more aware. There were times when there was no sign of the rift, but it was there, and occasionally it was brought to our notice.

When there was a visiting embassy—from Bohemia, I think—and the king was anxious to entertain the emissaries lavishly, we heard that he had offered them a banquet with fifty different courses of the finest foods. Everyone gasped with wonder until they heard that the Earl of Warwick had invited the visitors to Warwick Court where sixty courses were offered; and that because of the earl's generous gesture in allowing the people to come to the kitchens and take away the surplus food, there was rejoicing in the streets because Warwick was in town. The cries of "A Warwick!" "Long live the great earl!" were heard far into the night. A reminder to the king that, although he wore the crown—put on his head by Warwick—the earl was still to be reckoned with and the quarrel with the king had not diminished his popularity with the people; and they were of paramount importance when it came to keeping a king on the throne.

In spite of his half-hidden rancour, my father stood sponsor when Elizabeth Woodville produced her first child—a daughter, named Elizabeth after her mother; and George, Archbishop of York, performed the ceremony.

When it was suggested that Charles, Count of Charolais, heir to Philip, Duke of Burgundy, might marry the king's sister, Margaret, it was the Earl of Warwick who was the natural emissary sent to arrange the match. He was the best of ambassadors, on good terms with the King of France and not on ill ones with Burgundy. The king must be aware that it would not be good for him if there was warfare between him and his old friend.

My mother now talked to us more freely. Isabel was growing up and, as her sister, constantly in her company, I might have appeared older than my years. In any case, I was present at some of these conversations.

"I do wish this trouble between them was over," said my mother. "They really cannot do without each other. Sometimes I think your father is on the point of forgiving the king, and beginning to see that the marriage was the impetuous act of a young man in love."

Isabel sighed. She could not forget that the king had seen her and he had looked at her in what she thought was a special way for her alone. I hoped she was now realizing that there was nothing special about it; it was his way of looking at all women, young or old. It was the secret of his charm, for what woman could resist such looks that implied that she was desirable above all others— until she realized they were given to all members of her sex.

We were all hoping that my mother was right; and indeed, when my father was away from home on a mission for the king, it seemed that she might be.

Two events took place that brought my father's scheme out into the open, and after that even I knew that there was little hope of reconciliation.

My cousin George, son of John Neville, was betrothed to the heiress of the Duke of Exeter—a match that had my father's complete approval. However, the queen had other ideas for the Exeter fortune and thought it would do very well for the elder of her two sons—at that time Sir Thomas Grey. As the king gave in to the queen in almost everything she demanded, she succeeded in this matter; and my father's wrath was great.

He was at Middleham when he heard the news from his brother, and he did not have to hide his rage from his wife and family.

"What are we coming to?" he demanded. "It is only a short time ago when the queen's father was appointed Treasurer of England and made Earl Rivers. Whatever that rapacious witch asks for is given her!"

But the real cause of my father's disquiet, and what made him give up trying to hide his real motives, was that the king was planning to find a bride for his brother George, Duke of Clarence, and he had settled on Mary, daughter of Charles of Burgundy.

My father had other plans for Clarence.

George, Duke of Clarence, came to Middleham. His reception was as grand as that given to the king when he had visited us.

"Well," said Isabel, smiling secretly, "is he not the king's brother?"

There was feasting and revelry with the usual entertainments, but what struck me most was the show of affection between my father and the duke. They were cloistered together: one saw them walking arm in arm in the gardens and they were always deep in discussion.

This meant something, I was sure, and I was soon to discover what. It was through Isabel, as usual.

I had retired for the night and my woman had just left me when Isabel came in. She looked very pretty, radiant in fact.

"The most wonderful thing has happened," she announced. "I am going to be married."

"Well," I said. "It was certain to come sooner or later. You are no longer *very* young."

"Why don't you ask who my bridegroom is to be?"

"You know you are longing to tell me."

"It is George."

"So that is what all this is about."

"Yes. He came here to ask me. Our father is delighted. So everything is just as it should be."

"And the king is pleased?"

She looked at me blankly. "The king . . . ?"

"Wouldn't he have to give his consent? George is his brother."

"Of course the king will be pleased, and if my father wants it, it will be."

"It is all very mysterious. What is going on between our father and the king, I mean. They are not the friends they once were."

"Oh, be silent. You are jealous."

"I'm not. I'm just hoping it is going to be all right."

She sat on my bed. "I shall go to court. I shall wear wonderful gowns. George is so good-looking, is he not? They say he is remarkably like the king. Just suppose the king did not have any heirs . . ."

"He already has a daughter. You are going too fast. Let us get you married first. When is the wedding to be?"

"Hush. It is not to be generally known at first. You forget who George is."

"I certainly do not."

"There are all sorts of things that have to be arranged. It is a secret so far."

"So you immediately tell me!"

"You don't count."

"Thank you."

"I mean you are my little sister, and haven't I always told you things?"

"You have . . . now and then."

She flung her arms around me and hugged me. "I'm so happy, Anne. I always loved George, you know. He is rather wonderful, is he not? He's always so merry and good at things . . . just everything." She sighed. "He would make a very good king."

I could not help feeling a little uneasy—not only because of my father's strained relations with the king, but there was something else. I confessed it to myself now. There was something I did not like about George. He was not exactly shifty but watchful. He had too much charm and it was not like the king's, which appeared to be so spontaneous. There had always seemed to me to be something calculating about George. I had noticed a rather petulant look when his brother Edward's name was mentioned. I had a feeling that he was furious with a fate that had not made him the first born. But then, perhaps I was comparing him with Richard.

But I had to rejoice with Isabel. She was so pleased with life. She had wanted to be married for some time, but it had to be to the right person. It seemed to her now that George was that person. Brother to the king! She was thinking that a glorious future awaited him . . . and her.

When my mother heard that Isabel had told me the news she sent for me.

"Anne," she said. "I want to talk to you. Isabel has spoken to you, I believe."

"You mean about her betrothal, my lady?"

"I mean that. She is so happy that she must talk of it, but your father does not wish it to be announced just yet. There are one or two little matters that have to be arranged first."

"Yes, my lady."

"Your father did not know that George would ask Isabel yet. He meant there to be certain negotiations . . . then we could have been sure that all would be well."

"Is all . . . not well, my lady?"

"Oh yes . . . it will be. George, of course, will have to have the king's consent."

"And you think the king may not give it?"

"Your father thinks it an excellent match and the king will think so, too."

I looked at her disbelievingly. Even I knew that those days had gone when the will of the Earl of Warwick was the king's.

"Isabel is one of the greatest heiresses in the country, as you will be, my child. Your father is, after all, the great Earl of Warwick. Most young men would find that irresistible, but this is particularly agreeable, for it is not as though George and Isabel were strangers. They were drawn to each other from the first, so it is an ideal match. But we have to keep quiet about it."

She paused and sighed. I guessed she was wondering how much it would be necessary to tell me. I know I appeared older than my years and, being my father's daughter, although leading a sheltered life at Middleham, I had been aware of events.

She went on: "You will have heard that the Woodvilles have taken over the court . . . more or less. There are so many of them.

Your father might have been reconciled even to the queen if she had not brought in her numerous relations to take charge of everything. As I said, Isabel is an heiress. It may well be that one of the Woodvilles would seek to marry her and the queen would wheedle the king into allowing this."

"Against his own brother's wishes?"

"The queen has her methods of getting her own way. But enough of that. Suffice it that your father and I do not wish this proposed marriage to be discussed until it is ripe to do so. There is another matter that could mean delay. There is a blood relationship, between Isabel and George, so there will have to be a dispensation from the Pope."

"I had not thought of that."

She smiled at me. "Well, I have made the point. Do not mention this to anyone. It is a secret just as yet. Isabel was very indiscreet to tell you but, dear child, she was so happy. So . . . let us rejoice with her and pray all goes well and that soon she will be George's happy wife. You understand?"

"Yes, my lady," I said meekly.

My uncle George Neville, Archbishop of York, arrived at Middleham. He was the most important of my father's brothers and completely dedicated to the advancement of the Nevilles; thus he worked in close contact with my father.

Uncle John, who had recently been so uneasy about the relationship between the king and my father, was torn between his loyalty to the crown and to his family. Not so with Uncle George. He was wholeheartedly for the restoration of power to the Nevilles.

As Chancellor and Archbishop, Uncle George was a very powerful man and he had been asked to Middleham for a purpose.

At the time I was not sure what that purpose was but later I learned that he had come to discuss the dispensation that would be required from Rome before the marriage of George and Isabel could take place.

My uncle was involved in two missions in Rome: one the dispensation and the other his hope of receiving a cardinal's hat. Both must be kept secret from the king, of course, because it seemed likely he would approve of neither.

So during my uncle's stay at Middleham, there were many secret meetings between him, my father, and the Duke of Clarence.

I was rather disturbed. I could not help wondering what Richard would think of all this. That he would deplore it, I was sure, but it would mean that these three were not working in unison with his brother Edward.

Isabel, however, thought it was immensely exciting. Whether she was in love with George or the prospect of making a brilliant marriage, I was not sure. Certainly she and George seemed very happy together; and there was no doubt of his charm, but for some reason I could not entirely trust him and I wondered how deep his feelings went.

During that visit there was a great deal of talk about the Woodvilles and their influence at court. George was less discreet than my father and uncle. He told Isabel and Isabel told me that the main trouble with the queen's family was that they flattered the king and fell in with everything he said. He liked that. It made life easy. And then that woman would come along with her request for this and that . . . and it was the simplest way to give it to her.

"George says that the king is not faithful to the queen," said Isabel. "She knows it but she never reproaches him. She just treats it as though it is natural. I told George I would never be like that so he will have to be a good husband when he marries me. He says Elizabeth is very clever. All she cares about is having children and getting her family into high places and rich marriages. He says she will think of one for him and one for me . . . and it won't be for us to be married to each other but to a Woodville for each of us. That makes us laugh, because we are going to marry each other, says George, and nothing is going to prevent us."

"Oh, Isabel," I cried. "I hope it all comes right for you."

"Of course it will come right. Our father will see to that."

When I look back over that time, I can follow step by step how everything fell into place and how gradually we approached disaster.

Now that I see it all so much more clearly and with the advantage of hindsight, I cannot blame my father. He had worked hard to attain his power but he had simply misjudged his puppet. He had found it difficult to understand the nature of Edward and it was imperative for him to do so if he were to succeed in his schemes. He had dismissed Edward as a light-living luxury-loving young man—which he was—but there was another side to his nature.

From the beginning Edward had the making of a king who was determined to become one and remain one. This my father failed to see. Edward was a great soldier and so far had never been beaten on the battlefield. He had avoided conflict, was not in the least vindictive, and was inclined to forgive his enemies and bear few grudges, and this, in some ways, added to his strength. He knew what he owed to my father; he realized he could be a powerful enemy; but Edward was determined to rule in his way and no other man's. When he had sought the crown and Warwick had helped him attain it, he had listened and obeyed his mentor the earl because he recognized his power at the time to make or break him; but he was now made; he was the king and all must be made aware of it.

I think that was the true state of affairs, and who could blame Edward? My father had agreed to accept him as king, to work for him and serve him. The quarrel over Edward's marriage could have been forgotten and the king would have borne no rancor. They could have resumed their normal relationship and have been of inestimable help to each other. It was my father's pride—and that only—that stood in the way of a reconciliation.

There was a difference of opinion between them on foreign policy. My father had been wooed by the King of France, who had seen in him the real ruler of England, which had been true in the first period of Edward's reign. My father greatly valued the friendship of France. For many years there had been conflict between the royal house of France and that of Burgundy; and both the French and the Burgundians would be watching what was happening in England and would be aware of the coolness between the king and the Earl of Warwick. Therefore Burgundy decided to woo Edward.

Since he had come to the throne, Edward had matured considerably and he would have realized that my father's power was increased by the support of the King of France. He had given my father the chance to patch up their quarrel, but Edward would know that the resentment still smoldered and would grow when Warwick fully understood that Edward was no longer prepared to be led.

He may well, at this time, have come to think of my father as an enemy. My father was a little careless—and so was the archbishop, for when the Pope's emissary came to England, he did not present himself to the court in the customary manner, but went straight to the Moor in Hertfordshire, which was the archbishop's residence in the South of England.

It was natural that the king should want to know what business was taking place between Rome and the archbishop and he must have discovered that he was seeking not only to become a cardinal but also a dispensation for the marriage of George and Isabel.

This would have made Edward highly suspicious, for neither of these projects had his approval.

Poor Isabel! I was glad she did not know at that time of all the difficulties that were being put in her way. She was too blissfully happy to accept the fact that she was just a pawn in the game—to be moved whichever way was most advantageous to the players.

My father managed to persuade the king that it was necessary for him to accept an invitation to the court of France.

I remember his departure at the head of a cavalcade, and heard the shouts of "A Warwick!" and "Long live the earl!" It was very heartening. When we saw him thus we could believe he really was mightier than the king and that Edward must soon realize this and it would all be as it had been before.

It was unfortunate that no sooner had my father left for France than emissaries from the Duke of Burgundy arrived. We heard about the magnificent reception they had received at court and how feasting and jousting had been arranged to make the visitors understand how welcome they were. It was a situation that needed my father's attention and he should not have been out of England at such a time.

But how were we, at Middleham, to know that momentous events were building up to a climax that would change our lives?

We heard vague rumors and we did know that the Burgundians were in England and being well received by the king while my father was being fêted by the enemy of Burgundy in France—which was a strange situation.

Visitors to Middleham told us how the Woodvilles were very much to the fore, making sure that the visitors from Burgundy noticed them; and they made it clear that they had the friendship of this powerful family that had so recently come into evidence. Meanwhile the king showed his regard for the Burgundians by inviting them to the opening of Parliament.

My mother was worried, I knew, though she said nothing.

"Who cares about the Burgundians!" said Isabel. "As soon as we get the dispensation, George and I will be married. And once we are, nobody can stop us."

"Do you think it will be easy to get the dispensation?" I asked.

"Of course."

"I think what our mother is worried about is that the king has all these people at court while our father is a guest of the King of France and he is not friendly with Burgundy."

"What do you know about it?"

"Very little. But then, what do you know?"

"I know I am going to marry George and that is all that matters to me."

I knew Isabel well, so I was fully aware that she did not want to think of all these conflicts because in her heart she knew that her fate was not in her own hands—or even those of George; but in those of my father and the King of England.

Then something rather alarming did happen. If my father had been in England, it might not have come to pass, but he was away and, although Uncle George was determined to fight for the family of Neville, he was not sure how to do it. We learned of this through a visitor to the castle.

It was some distant cousin who had called to tell my mother the news and I suppose to assure us that our most humble connections never forgot that they belonged to the House of Neville.

My mother sent for refreshments for him, but before they were brought, he blurted out, "The Archbishop of York is no longer Chancellor, my lady."

"What?" cried my mother. She had turned so pale I thought she was going to faint.

"My lady, when the archbishop knew that the Burgundians were going to attend the opening of Parliament, he sent a message to say he was too ill to deliver the Chancellor's address."

"But it is the custom," stammered my mother. "Yet . . . if he were ill . . ."

"My lady, they say that the king did not believe he was ill and looked upon it as an insult to Burgundy."

My mother put her hand to her head. "And . . . so the king has taken the Great Seal?"

"Yes, my lady. My Lord Herbert rode with the king to the archbishop's palace and asked him to give it up."

"The earl will be . . . angry."

"Yes, my lady."

"And what of the Great Seal?"

"It has been given to the Bishop of Bath and Wells, my lady."

"Is that all?"

"My lady, it is enough."

"What does this mean?" I asked my mother later.

"It is a slight on the family."

"If my father were here . . ."

"I don't know of anything that he could have done. It is another instance of the king's declaring that he will go his own way."

"But to take the Chancellorship from Uncle George . . ." I said.

"Your father will regret leaving England."

Isabel had not spoken. I knew she was wondering what effect this would have on the dispensation.

I think that incident, more than any other, brought home to us the fact that our father was no longer the most powerful man in England.

The entertaining of the Burgundians came to an abrupt end when news reached England of the death of Duke Philip of Burgundy and the emissaries prepared to leave. Duke Philip was succeeded by his son, Charles, which made the proposed match with Margaret of York, the king's sister, even more desirable, for now she would be marrying the duke himself instead of his heir.

My father returned from France.

At Middleham we waited in some trepidation to see what would happen next. I know my mother wished we were at Warwick Court in London rather than Middleham, so that she would have been closer to events. As it was, we had to wait until news was brought to us, which was very frustrating.

It seemed a long time before my father arrived at Middleham and when he did, none could help but be aware of his smoldering rage; and in the heart of his family he let it burst forth.

"The King has chosen Burgundy!" he said. "He will now be the enemy of France. Everything I have worked for has been thrown away at the instigation of these traitors."

We all knew that the traitors were the Woodvilles, for all the troubles dated back to the king's marriage. If only it had ended there. But the woman whom the king had married was surrounded by scheming relations and they had determined to set themselves up and rule England in place of the Nevilles.

The great disaster was that they were succeeding.

I learned what had happened later. It seemed certain that the king's sister was destined to become the Duchess of Burgundy. Moreover, when an embassy from the King of France arrived in England its members were coldly received.

"There was no one to meet them," said my father, "except myself and Clarence! Clarence has been my friend in this."

That pleased Isabel.

"Of course, he would be father's friend," she said. "He is going to be his son-in-law."

I looked at her sadly and prayed she would not be disappointed. She would be miserable if anything stopped the marriage she had set her heart on.

"I asked the king to see them and he agreed," I heard my father tell my mother. "He was reluctant, but it was less trouble to see them than make an issue of it by refusing. But all the time he was listening to them he appeared bored and inattentive. Clarence was a great help with them. They thought him charming but, of course, it could not make up for the king's manner. I apologized to them. I told them I was ashamed. Do you know what they said to me? 'Do not distress yourself, my lord earl. You will be avenged.'"

My mother tried to soothe him, but there was little she could do.

"Our enemies have taken the Great Seal from my brother," went on my father. "Do you realize what this means? The king has declared for Burgundy and most blatantly has he done this while I was on a mission to France."

"It is very upsetting," replied my mother. "If you had been here it could not have happened."

"It is war," cried my father. "Yes, this is war between the Nevilles and the Woodvilles—and that means war between Warwick and the king."

It was rarely that my father spent so much time at home, but these were days of activity. There was much coming and going at the castle. One of the first to arrive was Uncle George—one-time Chancellor and now only Archbishop of York.

His anger was as fierce as that of my father—but perhaps, I thought, that was because he was less able to control it. For my father there had been only hints and signs; for the archbishop there had been an unmistakable blow. He would never forget the insult of the king's arrival at his London palace to demand the return of the Seal; and at this time he was obsessed by the thought of revenge.

His rage had been exacerbated by a definite insult from the king. When Edward had discovered that Uncle George was in secret negotiations not only for the dispensation needed by Clarence and Isabel, but for the support of his election to the College of Cardinals, the king himself had put forward a candidate—Thomas Bourchier, who was the Archbishop of Canterbury. What made this so intolerable was that Bourchier was elected and Edward sent a personal message to Uncle George telling him so.

Uncle George said, "It is time the king was taught a lesson."

"That is so," agreed my father. "But we should have to be very sure of success before we undertook the task of doing it."

Members of the family were gathering at Middleham. Even the most obscure were making their way to us to assure my father of their loyalty to the family.

Clarence came and, to my great delight, Richard was with him.

Richard was bewildered. I was sure he did not know what this was all about. His brother had brought him with him and Richard at first had clearly expected this to be a friendly call on the man whom, next to his brother, he admired more than any other in the kingdom.

Isabel said to me when we were alone, "It is because of our marriage that they have come. I think the king may try to stop it now that he is not on friendly terms with our father."

"Oh, Isabel, I do hope it does not go as far as that."

"Think of the way the king has treated Uncle George! My George is very angry with his brother. He says the Woodvilles have ruined him and he is too weak to resist them. What sort of a king is that?"

"Be careful what you say."

She shrugged her shoulders. "George says that Edward is showing himself unworthy to be king. George says . . ."

I turned away. George was a very indiscreet young man. I had always suspected that, and now I knew it was true.

When Isabel and I were alone with our mother, she said, "I want to talk to you girls very seriously. You know there is trouble between the king and our family. You must not listen to gossip and you must guard your tongues. You must not be tempted to say anything that could be construed as treason."

"Is my father going to war with the king?" asked Isabel.

"Hush, hush! I never heard such nonsense. Of course not. It is just a difference of opinion. Your father is the king's most loyal subject, as he always was."

Isabel pursed her lips and smiled. She had her own views and I could see that my mother was very disturbed.

Isabel talked indiscreetly but—I hoped—only to me, which did not count. George was evidently equally indiscreet if what she told me was true.

"George says his brother is ruining the realm," she said. "He

spends most of his time with women . . . not the queen . . .
though she knows about it and says nothing. She never protests as
long as he lets her family have all the best positions in the country. That's no way to rule a kingdom. So . . . well . . . what if he
were no longer king . . . ?"

"What do you mean?" I cried.

"There are others who could take the crown."

"You mean . . . ?"

She smiled and I followed her reasoning. She was seeing herself in a crown, receiving the homage of her husband's subjects.
Isabel, Queen of England.

"And you . . . well, after all, you *are* my sister. George has a
brother and I think you do not exactly dislike him."

"Richard!"

"Why not? With our father and all the Nevilles . . . and the
brothers of the ex-king . . . his sons-in-law. Well, you see . . ."

"It is not possible."

"I tell you, it is . . . and we are going to see that it is."

"Who?"

"George . . . my father . . . ," she answered.

That was wild talk, but I was not entirely dismayed to hear it. I
was of an age when many girls in my position would find themselves betrothed to men whom they had never seen before—yet so
far nothing had been said about a husband for me. If Isabel was
suitable for the Duke of Clarence then I could be for the Duke of
Gloucester. In the old days it might have been a possibility but that
was before this unhappy state had arisen bringing strife between

my father and the king. Richard would have to marry where his brother, the king, wished him to, and so would Clarence.

I did have an opportunity of talking to Richard, and I felt a little embarrassed when I did so.

"What is going on?" he asked. "Everything seems different."

"There has been trouble. You know my Uncle George is no longer Chancellor."

"Yes, but it is the earl, your father, who has changed."

"He has much on his mind."

"He is constantly in the company of my brother George."

"Well, they were always good friends."

"But I was brought up here. I feel sure that the earl wants to tell me something. I am not sure what."

"I think he probably wants to explain his side of the question."

"Side of what question?"

"You must have seen the king and my father have not been quite on the old terms for some time."

"Not since Edward's marriage, you mean. Your father did not like that, I know. But it is for a man—and in particular a king— to say whom he will and will not marry."

"Kings are in very important positions."

"Certainly, but it is not the duty of subjects to show displeasure at their choice."

Richard would always support his brother. He might imply that he would have preferred his brother to have married more suitably, and that he deplored the manner in which the

Woodvilles were seizing power, but his brother had given them what they had and that was an end of the matter.

I realized that I could not tell Richard of my fears and I tried to assure myself that they were unfounded.

I said no more on the subject and tried to behave exactly as I had in the days of that deep friendship between the king and my father.

It was soon after that talk when guards riding at the head of a company of men-at-arms arrived at the castle.

They had come, they announced, to conduct the Dukes of Clarence and Gloucester to the king who had need of their company.

Clarence hesitated and was about to refuse to go, but on my father's advice he left with his brother.

Isabel was very upset at their departure. She shut herself in her room and when I went to her I found her weeping bitterly.

"You know what this means," she said. "The king has heard that we are arranging to get married. Oh, Anne, he is going to try to stop us."

"Perhaps he will agree when the dispensation comes."

She could not be comforted. She was sure this sudden and peremptory call meant that the king had heard of the arrangements and was determined to put a stop to them.

It was more than a month later when Clarence came to see my father. He looked very serious and determined. My father greeted him as though he were indeed his son and then took him away to his apartments where they were in conference for a long time.

Isabel eventually learned what had happened and told me about it.

She was more cheerful now. She had been right, she said. The king did want to stop the marriage, but her gallant and faithful lover was determined to snap his fingers at his brother if need be.

"George is wonderful," she said. "He is so much in love with me. He said twenty kings could not keep us apart. All we want is that wretched dispensation. Otherwise, of course, they would say it was no true marriage. Let me tell you what happened."

She proceeded to do so.

"Your poor little Richard was in a fine state, because he thought his brother Edward was angry with him. George did not care if he were. But Richard was right. Edward was angry. He had them both brought before him and he wanted to know why they had arranged to leave court without his permission. Who had suggested they do it and so on. They said no one had. They had decided they would go and visit their old friend, the Earl of Warwick. Then Edward said, 'Have either of you been contemplating marriage with one of Warwick's daughters?' And he reminded them that they could not marry without his consent. Richard was silent but George would not be bullied. He said why should he not marry the daughter of the Earl of Warwick? I was the best match in the kingdom! Edward lost his temper with George, which was rare for him, so he must feel strongly about this. He's usually all smiles and waving awkward things aside. He put both George and Richard in a room with

guards at the door. Not for long, of course. He soon let them out
and was jolly with them. But George said he was quite serious
when he impressed on them that they could not marry without his
consent."

"What does this mean, Isabel?"

"George says it means that as soon as the dispensation arrives
we shall be married, whatever the king says."

"It could cause terrible trouble."

"It is what our father wants."

"Has it occurred to you that our father no longer has the
power he once had?"

"Don't talk so about our father. It's disloyal."

"It's the truth."

She laughed at me. "I should not be afraid to marry without
the king's consent, even if you would."

"Oh, Isabel," I said. "I hope it will not come to that."

"I can tell you this," she said. "We have seen the last of
Richard. George says he will stand by Edward. He will do nothing of which the king does not approve. So he will not be coming
to Middleham again."

"I know."

"How different George is! George is bold and adventurous.
When George makes up his mind, no one is going to stop him,
and he is determined to marry me."

I had seen the look in George's eyes, and I feared he was determined to do many things besides marry Isabel.

ISABEL'S WEDDING

The shadows deepened. My mother was constantly apprehensive of what would happen next; and I shared her feelings.

Isabel was living in a world of dreams, I believed. George was often with her. They would talk, laugh, ride together, and plan for the future. I did wonder whether George was in love with her or her fortune and what my father could do for him.

It sobered me a little to remember that I, too, was a great heiress. Our father must be the richest man in the country and to whom could he leave his wealth but to his two daughters? Yet Richard did not seek me in spite of my fortune. He was above all loyal to the king.

There came an alarming day when guards arrived at the castle.

There was shocked tension throughout the place when we heard
they had come to conduct my father to the king. Certain charges
had been made against him and he must answer them.

My father was furious. This was the greatest insult. He
demanded to know what the charges were.

He was told that, when the army was storming one of the
Lancastrian castles, a man had been captured and, probably
under threat, had declared that my father was scheming to bring
Henry back to the throne after he had deposed Edward.

At this time this was an absurd accusation, for although my
father had decided to withdraw his support from Edward, he had
no intention of restoring Henry, for if he did there would be
Margaret of Anjou to contend with, and she would be more difficult to handle than Edward could ever be.

I realized then that at the back of his mind was an idea of
replacing Edward with George, Duke of Clarence who, by that
time, would be his son-in-law.

However, that plan was in its early stages and my father was
incensed that he should be accused of something of which he was
not guilty.

It amazes me, looking back, how easy-going Edward was and
always had been. I suppose he could have arrested my father, but,
in view of my father's power—particularly in the north—that
could have meant the starting of a civil war; but Edward was
forever placatory.

When my father refused to leave, the king sent back a messenger this time. Would the Earl of Warwick be kind enough to
confront his accuser, just to show those who might be ignorant

enough to believe there might be truth in the rumors, that they were utterly false?

When this request was made my father graciously acceded to it. He saw his accuser, completely confounded him, and outwardly it now seemed that he and Edward were on better terms.

This was emphasized when my father agreed to accompany the king's sister Margaret to Burgundy where she was to marry Charles who, on the death of his father, had become the Duke of Burgundy.

We heard about that ceremonious journey. The people of London cheered the procession rapturously, for my father was at the head of it and they thought this implied peace between him and the king.

I think my mother was hopeful of complete reconciliation. She understood far more than we could what a rift between our father and the king could mean; she had seen enough war in her lifetime and I knew she prayed each night that that would not come back.

Alas for her prayers!

Our father returned from the journey with plans in his mind.

I heard, from our mother, about Margaret's wedding and I knew that, though our father made a show of affability, he was far from pleased.

He was in favor of friendship with France and for him to be on terms of amity with Louis's enemy Charles of Burgundy would certainly not please the King of France; and if he decided to depose Edward, help from France would be very necessary.

We listened avidly to our mother's account of the wedding

festivities, gleaned from our father, of course. How the feasting had lasted for days. But what interested us most was the account of the great fire in a castle near Bruges when the new duchess and her husband were almost burned to death in their bridal bed. It must have been caused by some enemy who was not discovered.

My mother said, "How thankful I am that your father was not involved in the fire."

But there were other matters in which he was involved.

Clarence came to Middleham, which delighted Isabel although she was a little petulant because he spent so much time with our father. And while he was there we had another visitor: our Uncle George. Isabel was truly in a state of bliss. She was soon telling me why. She could never keep news to herself, although I believe she had been sworn to secrecy.

"Uncle George has the dispensation from Rome," she told me. "There is now no longer any reason why we should not be married."

"Only that you haven't the king's consent," I reminded her.

Isabel snapped her fingers—a gesture learned from George. She looked smug. "What do we care about that?" she replied.

She was smiling secretly. I wondered what that meant.

We were to prepare to leave. We were going to Calais. My father, who was Captain of Calais, wanted to test the defenses there. It was a perfectly legitimate reason. Why should he not take his family with him? A man liked to have his family about him and there were so many occasions when it was necessary to leave them.

Uncle George accompanied us, which was significant.

We were excited at the prospect of going on such a journey, but all of us were dreading the sea crossing.

We came south, attracting as little attention as possible, and stayed at various castles on the way—with friends of my father, of course. He and the men always shut themselves away and talked with great seriousness.

In due course we crossed the Channel, which to our relief was less turbulent than it might have been, and we arrived—not too battered—at Calais. I had been there before, when I was very young, and what I remembered most from those days was the lighthouse, Tour de Guet, which I saw as we approached the land.

There was a welcome for us at Calais. My father, as captain of the place, was no stranger to the people, for although it was well fortified—for it was known as the Gateway to the Continent and was of the utmost importance to England—the people were a little uneasy as to what would happen to them if the French decided to invade. Sieges were some of the most distressing aspects of war, so the fact that the mighty Earl of Warwick had arrived to check the defenses reassured them.

We were lodged in the castle and the first matter to demand everyone's attention was the wedding of Isabel to the Duke of Clarence.

A thread of misgiving ran through all these preparations. Young as I was, I was aware of it. I thought a great deal about Richard during those days and memories of our friendship saddened me. I knew that the difference between the king and my father were growing more serious with the passing of every week.

I would have to be on my father's side and Richard on that of Edward. So we would be enemies. Such situations do arise between friends in the event of civil war.

I tried to share in Isabel's excitement. This was her wedding and she was marrying the man she loved, which was rare for girls in our position—so it was really a matter for rejoicing in many ways. But there were sinister undertones and Isabel, in her exuberance, threw a little light on what was in my father's mind.

She chattered a great deal about her wedding dress and the entertainments that would follow the ceremony.

"As soon as it has been performed," she said, "I shall be the Duchess of Clarence . . . wife of the king's brother!"

"I do hope it will be all right, Isabel," I said.

"Of course it will be all right."

"You had to come a long way to get married."

She laughed. "It was a great adventure, was it not? I'll tell you something. I shall be more than the wife of the king's brother."

"How can you be?"

She smiled at me, then pursed her lips as though she were holding in a secret.

I feigned indifference, which I knew from experience was the quickest way to get her to tell me.

"I could be Queen of England."

"And I could be the Angel Gabriel."

"Don't blaspheme!" she said severely, which amused me, coming from her.

I still pretended not to be particularly interested and she burst out, "It could seem that Edward is not the rightful king after all."

"What do you mean? He is the eldest son of the Duke of York and York's claim to the throne is . . ."

"I know, I know. That's what people think." She came close to me and whispered, "Some are saying that Edward is not the legitimate son of the Duke of York."

"But his mother is . . . the Duchess . . ."

"Women do not always give birth to their husband's children."

"What are you talking about?"

"Well, they are saying that the duke was away fighting and so the duchess had . . . friends. Well, one of these was Edward's father."

I gasped in disbelief. "It cannot be," I stammered.

"What do you mean: it cannot be! What do you know about it? It can be . . . and it is."

"The Duchess of York. She . . . she's quite regal. They call her Proud Cis because her name is Cecily. She is our father's aunt."

"What has that to do with it? I tell you it is so. Edward is not the duke's son. Therefore he has no claim to the throne . . . and George is the real king."

"What does our father say?"

"He thinks George should be king."

I stared at her. I simply did not believe this. It was some story George had invented in the hope of putting himself on the throne.

"How can you be sure?" I demanded.

"Proud Cis herself said so."

"When . . . ?"

"When Edward married the Woodville woman. She was so angry because he had demeaned himself. Then she said, 'It does not surprise me. You are not king. You were not the son of your father.'"

"Why haven't we heard this before?"

"Because it was hushed up."

"Then why bring it up now?"

"Well, these things come out. You cannot be sure when."

"It's absolute nonsense. No one will believe that of the Duchess of York."

"Of course they'll believe it. The duke was often away fighting somewhere. You don't understand these things. Older people will."

"I do not think anyone will believe it except those who want to."

I felt very shaken. I knew it was a conspiracy and my father was involved in it.

A few days later my Uncle George, Archbishop of York, performed the ceremony of marriage and my sister Isabel became the Duchess of Clarence.

My mother was growing increasingly alarmed. I wished she would talk to me. Isabel was a blissful bride; and as for Clarence, he gave himself such airs that he might have been already the king. I began to dislike him more and more. He was handsome, it was true, and had a certain ease of manner. He had charm like his brother Edward, but there was something good about Edward. He might be self-indulgent, sexually insatiable as they said, but there was an innate kindness of which I detected no trace in Clarence. Richard was entirely different from either of them. But then he was unique. There was no one like Richard.

The situation was growing dangerous. An attempt to depose a king and set another up in his place would surely mean civil war. There was already one in progress between the Houses of York and Lancaster, and although there were intermittent periods of peace, the conflict rose from time to time and was always hovering over the country. But this would be a new situation. My father was hesitating. He was too wily to plunge headlong into that which I was sure Clarence was longing for. He was obsessed by the notion of snatching his brother's crown and placing it on his own jaunty head. Did my father think that he would be able to guide Clarence? The king's marriage had shown him that he could no longer control Edward. But would Clarence prove any easier?

I tried to talk to my mother about it. I felt so much in the dark.

I said to her one day, "Does the king know that his brother has married Isabel?"

"I believe he must know by now."

"My lady, what will he do . . . what will he say?"

"I wish I knew."

"Shall we go back?"

"We must wait and see."

"And will the king be very angry with my father?"

"Your father has been very angry with the king for some time."

"Will they . . . go to war against each other?"

"I hope not . . . I pray not." She set aside her dignity then and drew me against her, holding me tightly. "I do not know what will become of us, my child," she said.

There was disquieting news from England where there was trouble in the north. It was known that there was increasing discord between the king and the Earl of Warwick. The north was for Warwick and there were always people spoiling for a fight.

I have often wondered why men are so eager to go to war, which frequently results in hardship and misery to so many. Can it be because their lives are so dull and war provided excitement? And for the rough soldiery there is, of course, the prospect of looting and gain.

However, there were some men in the north who could not wait and, no doubt believing that they would have the support of the Earl of Warwick, decided to start without him. First there was Robin of Holderness. That was not his real name but leaders of risings were apt to call themselves Robin. It was derived from Robin Hood and there was the implication that the object was to take from the rich to help the poor. So as this rebel came from Holderness, he was called Robin of that place.

Ironically enough, the revolt was suppressed by my uncle John, Earl of Northumberland who had from the beginning been firm in his support of the king. Poor Robin of Holderness paid for his impatience and folly by being deprived of his head.

But no sooner was this Robin dispatched than another and more important one arose. This was Robin of Redesdale. At first we were unsure of his identity. His object in rising was said to be a protest against heavy taxation and the power of the Woodvilles, who were intent on gaining wealth and power for themselves rather than doing good for the country.

It seemed from what we heard that Edward was not very concerned about these risings. The country had had only short periods of peace during his reign and he had always shown himself capable of dealing with these disturbances.

He had set out for the north in a rather leisurely manner and was convinced that Robin of Redesdale would soon go the way of that other Robin.

Then came a piece of disconcerting news. The identity of Robin of Redesdale was revealed and it was none other than Sir John Conyers, and the Conyers family were a branch—though only a minor one—of the House of Neville.

This was a revelation that must have sent a shock through the country. My father was unprepared for it; but he made a quick decision.

He must return to England.

With my mother and Isabel I went to Warwick Castle while my father with his followers rode to London, accompanied by the Duke of Clarence.

We were bewildered. We did not know what was happening. Isabel was most distressed: she complained that she had been torn from her husband so soon after they were married and she could not understand why this had been necessary.

None of us knew what it meant, but we did hear that the people had given our father and the Duke of Clarence a warm welcome. They believed that they had returned to England because there was trouble in the north, and between the Earl of Warwick and the king, the trouble would soon be dealt with. It was quite clear that they had no notion at this stage that there was such deep-rooted trouble between Edward and my father.

However, we were concerned with settling in and it was not very long after we returned when Isabel announced that she was pregnant.

She was delighted though somewhat apprehensive.

"George wants a son," she said. "I am sure we shall have lots. Why look! We have not been married long and already one is on the way."

My mother was delighted and there was little talk of anything else but the coming baby.

Isabel settled down to enjoy the fuss, which I think helped to compensate her for the loss of George.

Sometimes during those days I wondered what was happening and whether the king had made friends with my father and Clarence and whether they had put down the rising in the north. Occasionally there were visitors and they would bring a little news.

We allowed ourselves to believe that the relationship between the king and our family had returned to normal. True, the king could not have liked to hear of Clarence's marriage, since he had forbidden it, but it was done and the king was not one to hold grudges; he must be the most easy-going man in the kingdom, so therefore it was reasonable to suppose that all was now well. After all, that was what we wanted to believe.

Meanwhile Isabel had passed out of the first stages of pregnancy and her condition was becoming obvious. My mother was constantly supervising the ladies and we were all making clothes for the baby. We heard how Isabel and I had come into the world and what a blessing we had been; and the greatest joy a woman could have was to bear a child.

It was all very cozy and comforting and Isabel, being at the center of it, revelled in it.

Then certain items of news filtered through to us and they caused a shiver of alarm. Robin of Redesdale was proving to be no insignificant leader. He was surrounded by determined men and it was startling to learn that all the leaders of the expedition were connected with the House of Neville. There was my father's nephew, Sir Henry Fitzhugh, his cousin Henry Neville, and Robin himself, Sir John Conyers, who had married one of the Neville girls. Their main grievance was that the king had estranged the great lords of the land for the sake of the lowborn, insignificant Woodvilles, who had sought to rule to the country's detriment.

Isabel had lapsed into contentment and did not want to consider anything that might disrupt it. She was sure the king would accept her marriage. Considering the fortune she was bringing to her husband, how could the king complain about the daughter of Warwick not being a worthy match for his brother when he himself had married most unwisely a woman of no standing and fortune?

Each day she looked for Clarence's return. She wanted to talk to him about the baby.

So the weeks passed and after a while we were lulled into a sense of security, and then one day a company of men came riding to the castle. They had been with the army and they were Warwick men, for the badges of the Ragged Staff were prominently displayed.

It transpired that they were on the way to join my father's army and it was during supper when we sat at the big table with our mother that Isabel and I heard what was happening.

It was a terrible shock, for we realized that our father was at war against the king.

"It was at the Battle of Edgecot that the Earl of Pembroke was captured, my lady," said the captain. "My lord Warwick was not present, but we met the victors at Northampton later. It was on the earl's orders that he lost his head."

"Who lost his head?" asked my mother faintly.

"The Earl of Pembroke, my lady, and the Earl of Devon was killed."

My mother was aghast. She knew that my father hated those men. They were his enemies and blatant adherents of the Woodvilles; they were of that clique that had surrounded the king and lured him away from the influence of Warwick.

There were greater shocks to come.

"So that was the end of Pembroke and his brother," went on the captain. "But the real prize was Lord Rivers and his son, Sir John Woodville, and they were taken in Wales and beheaded at Kenilworth."

"The queen's father and her brother!" cried my mother in dismay. "And on the earl's orders!"

"It is the Woodvilles this war is all about, my lady. What a prize that was!"

I had rarely seen my mother so distressed, although she made an effort to hide it from the guests.

I kept thinking about her and when she had retired for the night I went along to her chamber. She was on her knees in prayer and I stood for a moment in silence watching her.

She was aware of me but she did not turn around immediately. Then she said, "Anne, my daughter, what are you doing here?"

"Oh, my lady mother, you are very unhappy. I wanted to be with you."

She stood up and I ran to her. She put her arms about me and held me close.

"I am afraid, Anne. What does this mean!"

I said slowly, "It means that my father is at war with the king."

"They were killed on his orders. The queen is a hard woman. She loves her family. Everything she has done has been to promote them. She would destroy those who stand in her way . . . but to her own she gives everything. And they have killed her father . . . her brother . . ."

"I think, my lady, that she will want revenge."

"What will become of us? My dearest daughter, what will become of everything?"

"My father is very strong, my lady. He will overcome all our enemies."

"You are right, my child. Stay with me. Let us pray together."

Events were taking a dramatic turn and I was no longer outside them looking on.

The change came one day when I was in one of the turrets and saw in the distance a large party of riders. They were, of course, coming to the castle. I ran down calling to my mother.

She was already aware of the arrival.

"Your father has come," she said.

We were in the courtyard when my father rode up and there was someone riding with him, a tall regal figure. I stared. I could not be mistaken. No one else was as tall and commanding in appearance. It could only be the king.

He had dismounted, my father with him. My mother was about to kneel but the king put his hand on her shoulder and kissed her cheek.

"My lord . . ." began my mother.

"The king has come to visit us for a while," said my father.

The king smiled and said what a pleasure it was to see the beautiful countess and her charming daughter. "I do not see my dear sister-in-law."

"She is resting, my lord. Her condition."

The king raised his eyebrows and said, "What good news! My brother is indeed a fortunate man."

Preparations for the arrivals were already in progress. The servants always went into action at the first appearance of visitors.

My father led the king into the hall. That something strange was going on was apparent. There was about my father a certain triumphant air. And where were the king's attendants? But the king was smiling and affable, as though there was nothing unusual in arriving thus.

There was one chamber in the castle that was kept for royal visitors and here the king was installed. Through the castle there was that excitement that a royal visit always generated, but this was something different. Why had we not been warned?

It was some days before I realized that the king was my father's prisoner.

It was all so bewildering. We were in the dark, groping through it for understanding, and it was not until much later that I learned from Richard what had really happened. Richard spoke of it even then with great resentment.

The king had been marching northwards to quell the rebellion when news of the defeat at Edgecot reached him; and when the army knew what had happened they deserted in large numbers, with the result that the king found himself alone apart from a few friends—Richard among them.

They were at Olney when George Neville arrived.

"He did not come as an archbishop," said Richard when he told me of this, "but in armor. I was with my brother and I feared what this meant, for I knew that my brother was conspiring with your father and had done so ever since he married your sister Isabel. I had a feeling that George meant Edward no good, for he had always been jealous of him and resentful because Edward was more gifted, and the elder. George Neville was very respectful to the king and asked him if he would join him and his brother in Coventry for the Earl of Warwick was anxious about the king's safety.

"My brother said, 'Why is the earl so concerned for my safety when a short time ago he was fighting against me?' 'Never against *you,* my lord,' said George Neville, 'but against those who seek to destroy the realm.' I was so angry that I called out to my brother not to listen to the man. But you know how forgiving Edward is. If he has a fault, it is being too ready to forgive his enemies and to believe the best of them. Edward put his hand on my arm and said lovingly to me, 'We are in their hands, brother. Just for this while.' And then he turned to the archbishop and said, 'I see I am your prisoner. What do you ask of me?' 'That you come with me to my brother,' answered the archbishop. And so we went to the Earl of Warwick."

I told Richard how sad I had been when I had heard a garbled version of this. It was heartbreaking for me to think the friendship between our two families was over.

"I was with him," went on Richard, "at the meeting with Warwick. I think your father was more embarrassed than my brother. The earl impressed on Edward that he wished him no harm and talked of his holding him for his own protection. That was not true. The earl had never forgiven him for marrying the queen. There were many of us who thought that was a mistake. But my brother is impulsive in his affections. He gives love without thought of gain. I suppose the marriage was good for him if not for others. It was her rapacious family that caused all the trouble. Oh, Anne, what mistakes have been made! It is true that your father helped to put Edward on the throne, but Edward is a king who will govern; he will not be led. And your father is a man who wants to rule through the king he has set up. It was doomed to fail."

How right he was!

The king was the most agreeable guest and none would have believed he was with us against his will. The servants vied with each other to receive his attention. I never saw a man so lacking in arrogance and self-importance and yet who could convey such a kingly air.

My father was in a state of elation at this point. He believed he had won the battle. He had shown the king that he could not reign without him. But after a while the euphoria began to fade. Edward might be pleasure-loving, seeking the easy way of life by refusing to look at unpleasant facts, but that exuberant personality, those kingly smiles, were what charmed the people. They did not want to lose their genial king. This was Edward's strength. It was nearly ten years since my father had set him on the throne and during that time he had made the people love him. They wanted Edward, and there was unrest throughout the kingdom.

It was known that the king was somewhere in the north, a captive of the Earl of Warwick, which was a signal to some to defy the law. Rioting broke out. This was a situation that could not be allowed to continue and my father realized that the king must be moved to a stronger fortress.

It was a sad day when Edward left Warwick Castle for Middleham. How we missed him! There were doleful faces in the castle. Apprehension returned.

Our father had left with the king and there was further trouble. Rumor reached us that my father's supporters, assuming that the war was over since the king was the earl's prisoner, had returned to their homes, so his army was disbanded.

"Where is the king?" the people were asking. "Who is ruling the country?"

As the violence increased and many were defying the law, my father thought that the people should be shown that Edward was still the king, and he allowed him to make a ceremonial visit to York where he was given a tumultuous welcome.

Richard told me that when he heard this, with Lord Hastings, a trusted friend, he gathered together an army and marched to York; but before they reached that town they heard that the king had taken matters into his own hands and announced his intention of going to London.

My father then realized that he had gone wrong somewhere, and if he attempted to stop the king there would be many to rise against him.

The welcome Edward received in his capital city was enough to convince my father that he had failed. He had won in the field but his victory had been turned to defeat.

He must have realized then that he was never going to gain control over Edward and there was one project left to him.

That was to set Clarence up in his place.

Isabel was now heavily pregnant. In a little more than a month her baby would be due.

It was a bright April day. My mother was making the last arrangements for the birth.

"Children have a habit of arriving before the appointed time," she remarked to me. "I am so glad that Isabel is with me. I am not completely ignorant of these matters, you know."

"I have realized that, my lady," I said. "And I rejoice, too. I suppose everything is all right?"

"What do you mean?"

"Isabel seems a little listless."

"My dear, she is tired. Can you imagine what it is like carrying a baby around with you?"

"But Isabel seems rather frail."

I saw the look of fear cross my mother's face, and I wished I had not said that. I knew she worried a great deal about our health. She herself was a strong woman; she should have had big healthy sons instead of two rather delicate girls. Indeed, it was because I had fancied she was a little worried about Isabel now that had made me so. But I must not talk of my fears to my mother, so I talked of them to one of Isabel's maids.

I had liked Ankarette Twynyho from the moment she had joined the household. She was a young widow who had lived in Somerset before joining us. As she had recently lost her husband she was glad to move away from her village—the scene of her tragedy.

She had been, briefly, in the queen's service and I think she found life at Warwick Castle preferable to serving under the imperious Elizabeth Woodville.

She was entertaining and used to tell us anecdotes about the queen, which amused us, and we came to learn a little about that strange cold woman who, when she had married the king, had set in motion those events that had been so disastrous to us all.

Ankarette reassured me now.

She said, "The duchess is not a robust lady, but she will be all right. Everything is prepared and she will have the utmost care. I can see that the countess is a lady who knows something of these matters, and with everyone in attendance, all will be well."

"You comfort me, Ankarette," I said.

"That's what I am here for, my dear," she said. I liked her Somerset accent and her easy manner with us all; and I could assure myself that, with my mother, Ankarette, and all the others in attendance, Isabel would be safe.

Isabel took comfort from her, too. It was Ankarette who would slip a pillow behind her back when she was looking uncomfortable and who came up with the drink Isabel was just about to ask for.

We were sitting in Isabel's chamber, for often she liked to lie down, and when she did she wanted us with her, and we were talking idly when we heard the commotion below.

I went to the window and what I saw made me gasp with amazement.

I turned and said, "It is my father, and with him the Duke of Clarence."

"Did you say . . . George?" asked Isabel, rising.

And there they were—just a small company of men. I went to the door and I heard my mother say, "Something is wrong."

I started down the stairs. Isabel was following me. My father was already in the hall. He embraced my mother, then me. Isabel ran into her husband's arms.

"There is not a moment to lose," my father said. "You must prepare to leave. We should be on our way to the coast in an hour."

"It's impossible," cried my mother. "Isabel . . ."

My father was silent but only for a second. He looked at Isabel. Then he said, "It must be. Come quickly. Bring only what is necessary. We must get to the coast without delay."

We had always been brought up to obey my father's commands instantly and without question; and my mother had set us an example in this. But this was different. There was Isabel to consider.

Isabel and George were clinging to each other, speaking words of love, and my father was impatient.

"Listen to me," he said. "I cannot explain now except to say that my enemies are pursuing me. If I am captured it will be the end . . . the end of everything. It is imperative that we leave without delay. Everyone . . . the whole family."

"We cannot move Isabel and I shall not go without her," said my mother stubbornly.

"You will go," insisted my father. "And Isabel will go with us. You are wasting time. Believe me, I would not do this now if it were not necessary."

"Is it . . . the king?" began my mother.

"Anne, I am telling you. For God's sake, do not hinder me. It is necessary that we get away . . . all of us. We must get to the coast with all speed. Do not argue. Isabel must come with us. Do you understand?"

"Yes," said my mother. "I understand. But the baby is almost due."

My father sighed. "I know that well. It will not be easy for her, but it must be. My enemies are marching to take me. It will be my head and the end of the family as we know it. So please do as I say. Get ready. We leave in an hour."

That was enough. Isabel was crying in Clarence's arms. She was terrified. She knew we were leaving the country and she hated the sea at the best of times. But now my mother had taken charge.

"Come along. You have heard what your father has said. Isabel, go to your chamber. Anne, get Ankarette to look after Isabel and to prepare at the same time. You have heard your father say we must be ready to leave in an hour."

Our thoughts were in turmoil as we got a few things together. There would have to be a litter for Isabel and that would impede our progress considerably. But the situation was dangerous. I heard my mother murmur, "Why does there have to be all this trouble? Why cannot men be content to remain where God put them? Why all this striving for power?" But the situation was desperate and if my father said he was in danger of losing his head, we knew those words were not idly spoken. We had heard of too many lost heads not to believe such a statement.

By the time the hour had elapsed we were on our way to the coast.

That journey is one I shall never forget. It was brought home to me then how quickly triumph can change to disaster. Only a short time ago the king was my father's prisoner and it seemed that all his plans were succeeding; then suddenly there was a complete change. It was incomprehensible that my father should now be fleeing for his life from the avenging armies of the king.

We were in imminent danger. We had brought the minimum

of goods and servants with us—on our father's orders. Ankarette came, as she was in attendance on Isabel and my mother thought she would be useful. We had to think how we should deal with Isabel as we should no longer have the comfort of the lying-in chamber.

Poor Isabel! I hoped the fact that Clarence was with us would compensate for her discomfort.

My mother and I rode with my father who looked very grim. He seemed to have aged since I last saw him. This was a bitter blow to his pride and I guessed he was blaming himself bitterly because he had let victory slip through his fingers.

But there was no time for brooding on the past. We were making for the shores of Dorset and messengers had been sent on to order that as many ships as possible were ready for us, so that we might embark as soon as we reached the coast. It was imperative that we leave the country at the earliest possible moment.

I wondered why we were going as far west as Dorset, as my father kept some of his best ships at Southampton.

So we rode on during that day, unsure whether at any moment we might be intercepted by my father's enemies and he be taken to London . . . to the Tower, possibly to await his death. And what would happen to us? I was sure the king would not allow us to be treated harshly, but the idea of a life without my father was difficult to contemplate. It must not be, I kept saying to myself. It cannot be. My father was invincible. I had been brought up to believe that, and it was not difficult to convince myself now that it was true.

What a relief it was when at last we were in sight of the sea.

Those who had gone ahead had been successful in commandeering a ship. It was enough. My father and Clarence directed us all on board. Isabel had the best cabin and could be fairly comfortable there, I hoped. I prayed that we might reach Calais before her pains started.

My father's being Captain of Calais meant that we should be sure of care and attention there and in the castle would be all that we needed.

I said to Isabel, "It is fitting that your first child should arrive in the very town where you were married."

However, it was not to be so, and we encountered further misfortunes, for when we joined my father's fleet at Southampton a further shock awaited us.

The new Lord Rivers, who had succeeded to the title when his father was executed, was waiting there for us. He had a score to settle. A battle ensued, during which several of my father's ships were lost. He decided that he would take what were left and get away before Rivers could bring in reinforcements.

The sound of gunfire was terrifying and my mother and I were with Isabel in her cabin where we tried to talk lightly, although we all knew that any moment might be our last.

"Your father always wins in the end," said my mother firmly. "Once we are safe in Calais all will be well. How are you feeling, Isabel?"

Isabel was not sure. She thought the pains might begin at any moment.

"Let us pray that we reach Calais before they do. It is not a long trip really and if the sea is kind . . ."

We were away. The battle was over. I learned later that my father had feared that there might be trouble at Southampton, which was the reason why he had arranged for us to embark in Dorset. He had lost one or two ships in the battle, but we should rejoice because we were on our way to Calais.

How relieved we were to sight land! Our father sent out signals. The Captain of Calais had arrived. He was waiting to be welcomed.

To our dismay we heard gunfire. This was amazing as Lord Wenlock, in charge of the castle, was one of my father's agents. A small boat was sent in to find out the meaning of this apparently hostile reception.

A message came back from Lord Wenlock informing my father that the king had sent orders, which had arrived only a short time before the earl and his party, and these orders forbade him to allow the earl to enter Calais. Lord Wenlock greatly regretted this but he must obey the king's orders.

My father was nonplussed. He had come so far, only to be refused entry. This meant that he was no longer considered to be Captain of Calais.

He was in despair, and just at that time Isabel began to give birth to her child.

This took our thoughts from all other matters. The danger to Isabel was acute as the birth showed signs of being difficult, and we had none of the usual comforts to ease the delivery.

"If only we had some wine," cried my mother. "That might help to soothe her and deaden the pain."

That was one of the most terrifying times of my life. I shall never forget the agonized cries of my sister. I felt sure she was going to die. I kept thinking of her as she had been—so happy, so merry, so contented with her marriage, so gratified that she had so quickly proved that she could bear children; and now, here she was, on a none-too-calm sea without adequate provisions, in acute agony and in danger of losing not only her baby but her life.

At such times one realizes how much one loves people and how heartbreaking it is to see those whom we love suffering, particularly when we are helpless to do anything to alleviate that suffering. Isabel and I had bickered often enough, it was true, but she was my sister, a part of my life, and I could not imagine being without her.

My father was at the door of the cabin. His eyes were anxious and I felt a sudden tenderness toward him. He does love us, I thought. He truly does. It is only that he is so busy fighting to keep his power that there is little time to show it.

"How is she?" he asked.

"Poorly," replied my mother. "If we had a little wine . . . even . . ."

"You think that would help?"

"She could sip it and it has a soothing effect. It might even dull the pain."

My father sent one of the small boats in with a message to Wenlock asking him for wine for his daughter who was in child-birth. He said the man should be his friend but at times like these how could one know who was a friend? But he understood Wenlock must obey the king's orders. Warwick was no longer the Kingmaker; he was an outcast from England fighting for survival.

However, Wenlock did comply with the request and to my mother's delight he sent the man back with two casks of wine. There was something else that Wenlock did. With the wine came a secret message to my father telling him that it would be folly for him to attempt a landing. It was what they were hoping he would do. He had authorized the gunfire to prevent such a landing. The earl should make his way to a French port for it was certain that Louis would be hospitable to his old friend.

It was sound advice.

Meanwhile, Isabel's condition was becoming desperate. The wine helped a little but she was very ill, and I guessed from Ankarette's pursed lips and unhappy expression that something was wrong.

My mother came to tell me.

"She is sleeping now. Poor child. It was a difficult birth."

"And the child? Is it a boy?"

"The child was a boy," she said.

Understanding flashed into my mind.

I said, "The child . . . is dead?"

My mother nodded.

Our great concern was Isabel. My mother and Ankarette were with her. There was no room for anyone else in the small cabin. If I could have been with her I should have felt easier in my mind, but to be shut away from my sister whom I had known all my life and might never know again filled me with numbed misery.

I thought of her trying on her wedding dress, so contented with herself and life. She was to marry Clarence; she would be

Queen of England; the child she would have would one day be king; she would start a dynasty . . . the dynasty of York and Warwick. What dreams to come to nothing!

I prayed for her to live. Perhaps that prayer would be granted. Then I prayed for the impossible—that we could go back to Middleham and be girls together . . . back in the happy days with Richard of Gloucester among the boys who came to my father's castle to learn the arts of war.

At last I was allowed to go and see her, but only for a short time.

My mother had said, "The worst is over. With care she will recover."

She lay back exhausted . . . free of pain . . . the useless, futile, purposeless pain. I felt a sense of relief that she was not yet aware that the child that had cost her so dearly was dead.

My mother came to me and said, "She is breathing more easily. She will recover, I hope and pray. I rejoice that we have not lost our Isabel."

The ship was pitching and tossing. In the extremity of our anxiety we had not noticed the discomfort. Now, as I stood up, I had to cling to my mother for support.

"There is the burial," she said.

I was glad Isabel was spared that.

They had sewn the little body into a sheet. I could not bear to look at it. It was so depressing—small and helpless. All those months it had been growing, waiting for that moment when it would come into the world . . . and it had come only to leave it.

The captain of the vessel was saying a prayer. We stood in silence as the sheet encasing the little body slipped into the water.

THE ROAD TO BARNET

How peaceful it was within those convent walls! I was dazed by all that had happened and although in my heart I knew this was only a respite, there was an overwhelming comfort to be on dry land, away from violent conflict, able to listen to the low soft voices of the nuns and the sound of the bells calling them to prayer.

They had cared for us tenderly since our arrival on the orders of the King of France that they should succor us and give us all we needed to restore us after our ordeal. But I like to think they would have been good to us without that command.

For the first days I just gave myself up to the luxury of that peaceful ambiance; it was only later that I began to ask myself, for how long?

After the burial of the child, we had continued at sea. My father was very angry that he had been denied entry into Calais, and for this he blamed the Duke of Burgundy; he had to appease that anger, and he made a point of sailing along the coast and taking any Burgundian vessel in sight.

We had grown accustomed to the sound of gunfire . . . of the rejoicing when another prize had been captured as we sailed along the Channel, flying the emblem of the Ragged Staff. Warwick, fleeing from his country, denied entrance to Calais, throwing himself on the mercy of the King of France, must show Burgundy and Edward—and Louis—that he was a force to be reckoned with.

There we were—three helpless women, my mother, my sister, and I—only half realizing what was happening to us. It seemed we had lost our home . . . lost everything . . . and were doomed to sail forever on an unpredictable sea.

But it could not last. Of that we were certain. And it was a great relief to us when we sailed into Honfleur harbor, honored guests of the King of France.

What I did not know then was that my father had needed that time he spent on plundering to make up his mind. While he ranged the seas like a pirate, he was coming to a conclusion. He was too ambitious to be easily defeated. He had gambled with Edward first and misjudged him; then in desperation he had turned to Clarence. He was a kingmaker by nature. He himself wanted to rule, but the rights of kings came through inheritance and for that reason he could not be king—but he could make a king who should rule through him.

Now there was only one way he could turn. It must be a complete contradiction of all that had gone before. It needed a great deal of consideration before he embarked on this road. He hated the Lancastrians. Henry was mad and there was his difficult and domineering wife to deal with. Could he do it? That was what he had to decide while he roamed the seas.

And when he went to Honfleur, he had made that decision.

Perhaps it was fortunate for me that I did not know of it, but if I had I should never have guessed what effect it was going to have on me.

But when we came ashore at Honfleur, nothing seemed of any importance but the blessed relief of escaping from the sea; but before we could land we had to have the permission of the King of France to do so and the prizes our father had taken were a stumbling block. The relationship between Louis and Burgundy was considerably strained and the King of France could scarcely receive with honor one who had perpetrated such acts of war upon the duke. So the fleet was sent off while we remained in harbor awaiting Louis's pleasure.

Louis heard of Isabel's condition and declared that ladies should not be subjected to more hardship. He would arrange for us to be housed in a convent while the earl came to his court for discussion between them, which he was sure would be advantageous to them both.

Thus—for us—to the convent and temporary relief.

Under the care of the nuns, Isabel grew a little better. She was more frail and needed to rest often. Deeply she mourned the loss of the child and talked of him often. The fact that he had been a boy made it even harder to endure. He would have been everything that she had hoped for.

"All those months of discomfort and then . . . nothing," she mourned.

"You can have more children. People often lose one," I comforted her.

"I don't want to go through all that again. But I suppose one has to do it. It's one's duty . . . especially when . . ."

I knew she was thinking of Clarence as King of England. She seemed to have forgotten that we were in flight from England, that Edward was king and unlikely to lose his throne to Clarence. Had she not realized yet that her husband was weak and vain, that my father was getting impatient with him and was regretting he had ever thought of putting him on the throne? She would not accept that, of course, and it was perhaps better to let her have her dreams, particularly when the reality was too bleak to contemplate.

My father was in constant touch with our mother. I always felt uneasy when letters arrived at the convent; and I think she did, too. I was always afraid that they would contain orders for us to pack and depart—perhaps go to sea again.

I wanted to stay here. I loved the quiet life, but I knew it was asking too much that it should last.

One day my mother received a communication from my father and she sent for me. As soon as I saw her face I was filled with misgivings.

"There is something I have to say to you, Anne."

"My father . . ."

"I have heard news from him. He mentions you."

"Me? But why?"

"Because it is something that concerns you."

I stared at her in amazement.

"Your father has spent some time with the King of France. Louis is a strange man but he and your father have always been good friends. Part of the trouble was Edward's friendship with Burgundy, and for a long time there has been discord between the kings of France and the dukes of Burgundy."

I knew her well enough to realize she was putting off telling me this news that concerned me, and that was because it was something that I was not going to like. I was beginning to feel more and more uneasy.

"As you know," she went on, "your father was badly deceived by Edward."

"You mean his marriage?"

"It was most unsuitable. Not so much because he married so much beneath him, which he did, of course, but because of those greedy Woodvilles."

"I know all this," I said. "I have heard it many times. Please tell me what it is that concerns you."

"You are of a marriageable age."

I felt terror grip me. They had found a husband for me. A French husband. I should be torn from my home . . . from my mother, from Isabel . . . from Middleham. I had always dreaded it and here it was.

"Many girls in your position would be betrothed by now. It has been a great joy for me to be able to keep you with me."

"Tell me . . . tell me who it is . . ."

"You will be surprised. Your father has always been such an ardent Yorkist. But things have changed. There has been too much perfidy. Your father has decided to support King Henry. After all, as the son of the late King Henry the Fifth, he is the rightful inheritor of the throne. He comes before Edward of York. Now Henry has a son . . ."

"Henry's son! Prince Edward!"

"That is so. I heard he is a handsome boy, perhaps a year older than you . . . which will be just right. You are really very fortunate."

I could not believe this. I had always heard that Henry was mad: Queen Margaret was a virago; their son Edward, a vapid youth of no importance. My father had changed sides . . . so blatantly. How could he? We had been brought up to believe that the Lancastrians were our enemies . . . and now they were planning to make me one of them.

"It cannot be true," I gasped.

"My dear child, it is true. Your father is going to put Henry back on the throne and he wants you to be the wife of the Prince of Wales."

"Oh no . . . please . . ."

She took me into her arms and I saw the tears on her cheeks.

She said, "We have to accept our fate, my dearest. It is what we are born for. It happens to all of us."

I said, "Isabel was happy in her marriage."

"Poor Isabel! That should never have been. You will be happy, my dearest child. It is just at first that it is a little shock, that is why your father wanted you to be prepared."

A little shock! I felt as though the world I had known was falling about me.

There was only Isabel to whom I could talk. She was resting on her bed. She looked beautiful with her long fair hair loose on the pillow, but she was pale and still very frail.

"What has happened?" she asked in alarm.

"I have just been told I am to marry."

"To marry! I expect our father has made some arrangement with the King of France. Who is it?"

"The Prince of Wales."

"The Prince of Wales? He must be a baby."

"Not a son of Edward but King Henry's."

She looked at me in blank amazement.

I went on: "Our father is arranging it with the King of France."

"Why should it concern the King of France?"

"I think it must be that he is going to help our father put Henry on the throne."

"How can he?"

"With arms and money supplied by Louis, I suppose."

"He . . . he can't!"

"Then why should he want his daughter to marry Prince Edward?"

She lifted her head and, resting it on her elbow, stared at me. "What of George?" she asked.

"The plans have evidently changed."

"How can they change?"

"Easily. If our father and the King of France decide to change them."

"I can't believe this. Our father has always been for York. How could he change like that?"

"Because he has quarreled with York. He can no longer make York kings, so he will make a Lancastrian one. After all, as my mother says, Henry is the true king."

"It's nonsense."

I shook my head. "How I wish it were."

"George is to be king."

I did not say so but I thought, that was never a wise plan and could not have succeeded. I could not imagine how my father had ever thought it could. How could he have controlled the volatile George whose only concern would be for his own glory?

I could see the reasoning behind all this. My father must make kings through whom he could rule, and Edward had shown that he would not allow that. But if he could succeed, proud Margaret and Henry could be malleable in his hands.

It made sense; and I had become a necessary part of my father's schemes.

Why had I been unhappy on those violent seas? I should have been more at peace there than I now was in this quiet convent.

My one hope was that it would not be yet. My mother had thought it best to warn me and I could not make up my mind whether it would have been better not to know, so that I could have enjoyed peace a little longer, or to be prepared for the blow that was to come.

Isabel tried to comfort me, but I think she was more concerned as to what it would mean to George. I myself wondered that, too, for if my father were supporting the House of Lancaster, where would George come into this? He would be our enemy. How could there be such conflict within the family, for his marriage to Isabel had made George one of us?

My hopes that the project must fail were short-lived. Once the bargain had been struck my father would be eager to proceed with it. I learned later that I owed the delay to the fact that there was difficulty in persuading Queen Margaret to accept my father as her friend. But I suppose his reputation and power, and the men he could command to serve him, made it difficult for her to refuse him as an ally; and eventually she gave way to what must have been very distasteful to her: accepting me, Warwick's daughter, as her daughter-in-law.

My mother, my sister, and I were all in a very melancholy mood while we waited for developments.

Within a few days of my mother's telling me of the plans for my future, my father arrived at the convent. He had come to take his family to Angers, where I was to be betrothed formally to the Prince of Wales.

My mother must have told him how worried I was at the prospect, for he sent for me.

I went apprehensively, expecting to be peremptorily told to hide my repugnance to the match, but it was not quite like that.

My father was not an unkind man and I believe that, as he studied me, he was thinking of the ordeal he was about to thrust on me. Ambition was the great force in his life and nothing could deter his following it wherever it led, but, at the same time, he could spare a thought for those whom he used to further his ends—particularly if they were members of his family.

"I hear, daughter," he said, "that your mother has told you of the glorious future that awaits you."

"She has told me that I am to be betrothed to King Henry's son."

"That is so. Henry is to be returned to the throne and in due course his son will inherit it. It is a great opportunity for you."

"It is difficult for me to think of him as a husband."

"I'll swear it would be difficult for you to think of anyone as a husband, as one has never been proposed for you before."

"But we were always brought up to hate the Lancastrians."

He waved his hand impatiently. "This will be a great match for you. The best you could possibly hope for. You will see your son on the throne of England. Is that not enough?" I looked at him blankly and he smiled at me. "Your betrothal will take place very soon," he went on. "You should prepare to leave this place."

I wanted to plead with him. I wanted to explain what this prospect was like for a young girl who had not seen very much of the world until lately (when I had witnessed some of the less pleasant aspects of it), who had lived most of her life at Middleham and who had—on those rare occasions when she had thought of marriage—had one in mind who had always been her friend and who, she was sure, had some affection for her.

But how could I explain to this man? He was my father; he was fond of me in a way; but to him I was just an object to be moved around to whatever position could bring most gain to him.

It was an unfair world. It terrified me. I did not want to marry . . . yet. I wanted to go on being a child. I had seen what marriage had done to Isabel and she loved her husband.

I wanted to go back to Middleham, to live quietly there; and vaguely, in my dreams, I had thoughts of Richard's coming there and saying, "Marry me, Anne. I love you and you love me and we both love Middleham. Let us live there happily ever after."

What foolish dreams! How could I ever have thought I could make my father understand them? How could I expect him to abandon a plan that was important to him, for the sake of making me happy and allaying my fears?

I left him and made my preparations to leave.

My mother came to me just before we left. She looked as though she had good news to impart, and she had.

"The wedding cannot take place until there has been a dispensation from the Pope, and that, as you know, takes a little time to come by."

"Then why do I have to leave here now?"

"Because there must be a betrothal before plans go ahead. You see, the marriage is very important to your father, and Queen

Margaret is not very eager for it. She has to be persuaded that it is her only chance of getting the throne."

"She does not want me," I said. "And I suppose Edward does not either."

"They will want you when they realize what this marriage means."

"It is hateful. I am not like a real person. I am just tolerated because of a treaty."

"Marriages of people in high places are often like that, my child."

"I hate it. I hate it."

She put her arms around me.

"It will take a long time for the dispensation," she said, "and you cannot be married without it. Perhaps it will never come."

I looked at her wonderingly, and she tried to brush aside that last remark. But at length she said, "Well, King Edward would naturally try to stop it if he could, wouldn't he? And you know what popes are. They fear to offend people in high places. I am just saying that it may not be easy to get the dispensation."

"But I shall have to go through with this betrothal."

"Yes, you must do that."

"Does that mean I am married to him?"

"In a way, but the marriage is not consummated until the ceremony takes place. That means that you will continue to live under my care until you are actually married."

I must say I felt a little better after that. The marriage was not imminent. Fervently I hoped the pope would refuse to give the dispensation.

We were an unhappy party that left the convent on that June day. Isabel was bewildered, still weak from mental and physical exhaustion, still mourning the loss of her child. I think she was not ambitious for power; but she wanted grandeur and excitement; she had dreamed of herself as a queen and now it seemed that role might well pass to me. That I was reluctant to receive it was of no importance.

I wondered what Clarence was doing. He did not come with the party to collect us. I was shocked by the manner in which my father could coolly cast him aside. I knew that he had been assured that he would be well treated in the new reign. He was to have vast lands that would bring him wealth and a certain amount of power; and if the Prince of Wales and I died without heirs, he was to have the throne. Poor consolation for a man who had so recently been promised it unconditionally.

Poor Clarence! Poor Isabel! But I was far more sorry for myself.

We were going first to Blois, where I was to be presented to my formidable mother-in-law-to-be and my future husband.

Blois is one of the most impressive *châteaux* in France, but I was overcome with dread as we approached those magnificent gray stone walls emblazoned with the swan and arrow, the emblem of the counts of Blois. I felt as though I were going into a dark prison.

Aware of my fears, my mother tried to reassure me and I noticed that even my father watched me with some concern in his eyes. That was because, I told myself with some bitterness, I was important to his schemes. If only King Edward had not married Elizabeth Woodville, this would not have happened.

The dreaded moment arrived, and I was face to face with Margaret of Anjou. She was seated in a chair that looked like a throne, but perhaps that was because she was in it and made it seem so. She was intimidatingly regal—a tall, stately woman with remains of beauty still visible in her ravaged face. There was a hardness of expression that could have been induced by suffering. I felt a twinge of pity for her. What bitterness must have been hers, proud woman that she was! She had married a poor weak man and tried to maintain him in his place. I believe she must have given the whole of her married life to fighting for his crown and my father had been the one who had taken it from him and put it on Edward's head. Now that was changed, which was, of course, the reason why I was here.

Even as she looked at me, I could see why she hated me, as she must have hated everyone connected with the House of Warwick.

Coldly she extended her hand. I knelt and took it. Her eyes assessed me, summing up every little detail of my appearance. I could feel those cold eyes attempting to pry into my mind.

"You may rise," she said at length.

I heard that when my father had first seen her she had been so determined to refuse his offer that she had kept him waiting for hours before she would receive him, and when she did she made him kneel for fifteen minutes before bidding him to rise. I could imagine how my proud father relished that. But he was a man to whom the project of the moment was of paramount importance and he would endure a great deal to succeed in his plans. How I wished they did not include me!

"Sit beside me," she commanded. "I would speak with you."

I obeyed in silence.

"Your father has told you of the great honor that awaits you."

"He has told me I am to be married, your grace."

"To the Prince of Wales," she said. "You will be presented to him shortly. Your father and I have agreed to this marriage. You are indeed fortunate. I trust that we shall soon be back in England, in our rightful place. In the meantime you are to be betrothed. I have told your father that there will be no marriage until the kingdom is in King Henry's hands."

That was the best news I could have, and I hoped it took a long time, and my hopes that it would were high. Edward was not going to relinquish it easily. Richard would be beside him to hold it with him. Indeed, even with all my father's power, it was going to be a hard task to wrest the crown from Edward. And I was not to enter into this odious marriage until they did!

She clapped her hands suddenly and imperiously. "Tell the prince that I wish to see him," she said to the woman who came hurrying to her.

My heart was beating fast. She did not like me. She hated this marriage. She was accepting it under duress because it was the price my father demanded for helping her husband to regain his crown and she would suppress her dislike of anything connected with Warwick to realize her greatest ambition. As for my father, he wanted revenge on Edward; he wanted to set up his own puppet. But how would he fare with such a woman as this? And, of course, he wanted to see his daughter on the throne, so I was to be used to bring about his desires. I must marry this prince whom I had never seen. I must provide heirs to the throne that my father might be satisfied and the future kings of England would have Warwick blood in their veins.

I had never felt so humiliated. I was just a creature to be used to satisfy their ambitions. It was a sordid bargain, and I was at the center of it.

He stood before me—my future husband. He was of medium height and tolerably good-looking; his chin was weak and there was a slackness about his lips and a glint in his eyes as he studied me. I did not like his manner.

I suddenly realized that I was comparing him with Richard; and I faced the truth then that, up to this time, I had cherished the thought that marriage with Richard was feasible. The brother of the king and Warwick's daughter. Yes, it could have been a possibility. Was I not—as Isabel had reminded me—one of the richest heiresses in the country?

I was afraid of this man. I tried to remember what I had heard of him and could not recall. Few people had talked of him; they had believed that his mother had left the country forever. Edward of York appeared to be firmly on the throne and had heirs to follow him—so why should people be interested in Henry's son?

"The Lady Anne Neville," said Queen Margaret. "Lady Anne, the Prince of Wales."

He took my hand and I wondered if he were aware that I cringed. Perhaps he was, for he looked faintly amused.

I wanted to shout, I cannot marry you. I will not. There was a hint of derision, even of cruelty in his smile. I knew that I had been a fool to show my fear.

Angers is a beautiful city situated on the left bank of the River Maine just before it joins the Loire, but to me it will always be one of the places I most wish to forget.

My mother might try to soothe me with assurances that the ceremony that was about to be performed was not in itself a marriage. Queen Margaret herself had insisted that that should not be performed until her husband was firmly on the throne of England. I kept reminding myself of that. On the other hand, betrothal was binding and was in some respects tantamount to a marriage.

The massive moated castle, with its seventeen towers, was like a prison to me. How often I thought of Middleham during those dark days! Oh, to be there . . . to be young again . . . getting to know Richard . . . forming that friendship which, as far as I was concerned, would last through life!

But what was the use of dreaming of Middleham? I was at Angers where I was to be the sacrificial lamb offered to my father's ambitions.

And there I was at the altar. All present were required to swear on the relic of the True Cross to be faithful forever to King Henry the Sixth. The betrothal ceremony followed and all the time I was thinking, I shall never be happy again.

When it was over, I was to be in the care of my future mother-in-law until that time when I should be truly married. I was glad there were those two events that must take place before that could

be: my father must win the crown for King Henry and there must
be a dispensation from the pope. I prayed fervently for the delay
of both of them.

There were festivities to celebrate the occasion. Let others celebrate! I could not do so.

This was not exactly marriage, I kept telling myself, though it
was as binding as marriage. The difference was that there had to
be a marriage service before we could live together as husband
and wife.

How I rejoiced in that! Perhaps, I thought, it will never come
to pass. I had to tell myself that. It was my only consolation.

I was now to live with Queen Margaret. Under her protection,
they said; but in truth I was a hostage. I was there to remind my
father that it was his duty to restore Henry the Sixth to the throne
and remove Edward whom he had put there.

Isabel had gone to my mother. How I longed to be with them!
Here I was among strangers.

My father, meanwhile, with the Duke of Clarence, had set out
for England to keep his promise.

By the grace of the King of France, Queen Margaret was
allowed to keep her little court at Amboise where I should be
until the marriage. I had said good-bye to my mother and Isabel,
which was a terrible wrench for us all, but everything had been
arranged and agreed by my father who was now with Clarence
making his way to the coast in preparation for the onslaught on
England.

I had never felt so lost and alone. Everything familiar was

gone and in place of my gentle mother who loved me was this fierce woman who, in spite of her truce with my father, hated everything connected with him.

Amboise is beautiful—perhaps one of the most beautiful small towns of France—and the *château* is one of the country's most impressive. I shuddered as we approached. To me it looked like a fortress standing on its rocky eminence. It must have held many prisoners and I wondered how many of them had lain forgotten forever in its gloomy *oubliettes*. The feelings of those prisoners as they entered that place must have been similar to my own. It was an ancient place. I remembered hearing that Julius Caesar had been here and had made the caves famous because he had used them to store grain, and ever after they were called Caesar's granaries. When one is on the brink of disaster such inconsequential thoughts will come into the mind.

The gray walls, green with moss, looked impregnable, and as we went under the arch toward the castellated walls, a terrible feeling of dread came over me.

The days that followed were some of the most unhappy in my life. More were to come as I grew older, but then I was prepared for evil and had grown a protective shell of stoicism. At that stage I suppose life had been too easy for me . . . until that terrible day when we had taken ship to France. Always my mother and Isabel had been with me. Now I was parted from them, to be in hostile company—a hostage while my father redeemed his promise.

When I heard that the Prince of Wales was not leaving for England I was dismayed, but relieved when I discovered that he was not living with his mother. He was going on a mission, with

Louis's blessing, to raise men for the armies that would be needed to defeat Edward. I had thought at first that I would have to endure his presence and that had alarmed me. It was amazing what pleasure even the smallest relief could give me.

I tried to find out all I could about this man who was to be my husband. It was not easy, for the queen's attendants regarded me with the same suspicion as Margaret did. They were very much in awe of her, which did not surprise me.

There was one thing I heard about him that filled me with apprehension, and made me feel that I had summed up his character correctly.

"The prince is a real warrior," I was told by one of the women who could not resist the opportunity to tell me. "It was after the battle of St. Albans. Two of the enemy were captured . . . both men of high rank. They were brought before the queen because the king was too feeble at that time to take his place. So there were these two . . . proud gentlemen . . . Yorkists who had been fighting against the king and queen. It was his mother's wish that the prince should be with her—in place of the king—at such times, and she turned to him and said, 'What shall be their sentence?' The prince was only eight years old, but his mother thought he would have to grow up quickly and he did not disappoint her. 'They must be sentenced to death,' he said. 'By what means?' the queen asked him. And what do you think the prince said?"

"I do not know. Tell me."

"He cried, 'Cut off their heads!' There! And him only eight.

His mother said that, as he had passed the sentence, he must watch it carried out."

"And . . . did he?"

"That he did, my lady. He sat there clasping his hands and smiling as the blood spurted out."

I shuddered. And this was the man they had chosen to be my husband!

Looking back, I do not know how I managed to live through those days. I dreamed of the wildest means of escape—running away, joining gypsies, casting aside everything I had ever known . . . anything to be free. I was terrified of this marriage. I waited in trepidation each day for the return of the Prince of Wales and for news of what was happening in England. My father would land; he had been well supported by the King of France; he had men and money. Could he overcome Edward? And when he did? I should be married then in very truth to this young man who, in my mind, was fast becoming a monster.

I could not bear it. I felt frustrated and so vulnerable. If only I could have talked to Isabel . . . explained to my mother . . . pleaded with my father.

But in my heart I knew that none of these could avail me in any way . . . except give a grain of comfort to share my fears and sorrow.

I was doomed.

I found a secluded corner in the grounds where no one went very much. A seat was cut into the thick stone of the castle. Overgrown shrubs surrounded it. I could be almost sure of a little solitude there and went there often to brood and ask myself if there was anything I could possibly do to avoid my fate.

I was sitting there one afternoon, and the hopelessness of my position swept over me afresh. My father could not fail to succeed. Very soon would come the news of his victory; then this sad frustrated life would change . . . to something worse.

I could not bear it. The desperation of my plight swept over me and I began to weep silently. I sat very still and allowed the tears to trickle down my cheeks.

Then suddenly I heard a rustle in the bushes and, to my horror, I saw the queen approaching.

She stood for a moment glaring at me.

"Why do you weep?" she asked.

I could not answer. I could only cover my face with my hands while the sobs shook my body.

There was silence. I guessed how she would despise me. She would be asking herself, what is this bride we have to take for my son? What sort of queen will she be? What sort of mother for the heirs of England?

In that moment I did not care what she thought. I just sat there, holding my hands to my face, finding some small comfort in giving vent to my grief.

After a while I let my hands drop. She was still standing there. She said in a voice I had never heard her use before, "What grieves you?"

Before I could stop myself, I blurted out, "I want to be with my mother and my sister. It is so strange here . . . so far from home."

Immediately I had spoken I was ashamed of myself. My words

sounded so ridiculously childish, and doubly so in the presence of this woman who had been my enemy before she knew me. She would deride me, despise me. Perhaps she would think me so unworthy that her son must not marry me at any price, I thought, with a ray of hope. But a crown to her would be worth any price.

"How old are you?" she asked.

"I am fourteen."

Did I imagine it, or was there a slight softening of her features?

"I was about your age when I first went to England . . . to a foreign country . . . to a husband whom I had never seen," she said slowly. "It is a fate that overtakes most of us."

"I know."

She spread her hands and lifted her shoulders. "So why must you be so sorry for yourself?"

"I suppose because it has happened to others, that does not make it easier to bear."

"Tears never help," she said, and left me.

Oddly enough, that was a turning point in our relationship and later I began to learn a little about Margaret of Anjou.

It was only a few days after the incident that I found myself alone with her. She had dismissed her attendants so that she might talk to me.

She was a strange woman—dominating and single-minded. She would have been a good ruler, but she lacked the power to attract people to her, which Edward had in such abundance. She was strong; she chafed against defeat. It had been an ironical turn of fate to give her Henry the Sixth as a husband. There could not have been two people less alike. Yet it emerged that in a way they had been fond of each other.

That first occasion after the scene in the gardens was a little awkward, but during it she managed to convey to me that she was not devoid of feeling and not entirely unsympathetic toward me. She could understand the terrors of a child. After all, I was only fourteen years old and she saw that it was an ordeal to be taken from my mother and sister, the companions of my childhood, to be put with those who had been the sworn enemies of my family for as long as I could remember.

I cannot recall much of that conversation, except that in a brusque sort of way she tried to cheer me, chiefly, I think, by letting me know that it had happened to her, and although she deplored my attitude toward what was an ordinary fate, she did understand my fears, for she had suffered them herself.

After that I often found myself alone with her. We were anxiously awaiting news from England and, as had been the case at Middleham, we were constantly alert for messengers coming to the *château*. What Margaret wanted more than anything was news that Warwick's armies were succeeding; and this would be the signal for her to return to England with her son.

During the days that followed, I began to get a glimpse into what had gone before this terrible conflict that was called the War of the Roses and that had thrust our country into the worst of all calamities which can befall a country: civil war.

Like myself, Margaret had had a comparatively happy childhood, although her father, René of Anjou, had lived in acute insecurity during most of Margaret's early youth.

She spoke of him with an amazing tenderness; in fact she surprised me as I grew to know her. Her imperious manner, her fierce and passionate nature, her capacity for hatred, which she bestowed on her enemies, covered softer traits; she could love as fiercely as she could hate, and as I caught glimpses of this softer side I began to change my opinion of her.

"When I was born," she once told me, "my father had only the country of Guise. He was of small importance. Then he inherited Lorraine, but there was another claimant who was victorious over him and as a result he was taken prisoner, and for a long period of my childhood he remained so. He was still a prisoner when he inherited Provence and Anjou. My mother was a woman of great spirit. My dear father was too gentle. All he wanted was to live in peace with the world. He loved poetry and such things." She spoke with an exasperated tenderness.

"How different he must have been from my father," I said.

"Ah, Warwick!" There was a hardness in her face. "That man, your father, ruined our lives."

I was foolish to have mentioned him, for she told me no more on that occasion, and seemed to forget that there had been a little friendship between us. Foolishly I had reminded her that I was Warwick's daughter.

I remembered not to do that again.

Later it transpired that she had been brought up by her strong-minded mother, but with René a prisoner, her mother must go to Lorraine to take charge there, and Margaret was sent to Anjou to be with her grandmother, Yolande of Aragon, who governed that land.

"We lived mainly in Angers," she said. "You remember Angers?"

I shivered. How could I forget Angers?

"My grandmother was a wonderful woman. My mother was a wonderful woman. There are times when I believe it should be left to women to govern."

I looked alarmed and she gave me a somewhat pitying glance that betrayed her judgment that I was not going to be one of those.

"I was fortunate in my mother and my grandmother," she said. "It was a sad blow to me when my grandmother died. But my father was free then. He came with my mother to Angers and we were all together for a while . . ."

"It must have been wonderful to be united with your family."

"Such pleasures do not last. I was your age when I was betrothed to the King of England. But I had been on the verge of betrothals many times, so I was not sure whether this one would ever come to pass. It might have been like all the others."

"Why were you betrothed so many times?"

"Because my father's fortunes were ever rising and falling. In the beginning I should have had a very poor match but when he inherited Lorraine and Anjou, well, it was a different matter."

"There are always such reasons why we are betrothed," I said sadly.

"But of course. My child, marriages are the strongest of alliances. Never forget that. It is the duty we are called on to accept . . . whatever is best for our countries at the time."

"I know."

"I thought I was so fortunate," she said. "I was married to a man with a very gentle nature . . . a good man—a saint perhaps. But good men do not necessarily make good kings and saints were never meant to wear a king's crown. The outcome usually is that they have no will to keep it and do not hold it long."

"Perhaps it is good when they marry strong wives."

A wry smile touched her lips.

"My mother and my grandmother taught me self-reliance," she said. "That is the best lesson any woman can learn."

She looked at me a little severely, thinking, I was sure, that women who had learned that lesson did not give way to tears.

But there was a hint of kindliness in her stern manner now and I began to look forward to these sessions with her. Oddly enough, I began to realize that she did also.

And so I grew to know my mother-in-law-to-be and, in place of the fear and revulsion that she had at first aroused in me, there was an admiration that was tinged with affection.

I liked to hear her talk of the past and she seemed to take a certain pleasure in doing so. Perhaps she thought it was good for me to know what had happened to others so that I might become less concerned with my own fate. I think she also wanted to stop herself starting at every sound . . . to forget, even for half an hour, the desperate need to hear good news from England.

She made me see and feel her departure for England. I could picture her as a beautiful child, for she must have been beautiful. There were still remains of beauty to be seen and sometimes when she talked of the past and her eyes would soften in reminiscence and her lips would curl into a smile of remembering happiness, I would be struck by it.

Through her eyes I saw the brilliant cavalcade. It was a match desired by the French as well as the English.

She said, "The King of France took me into his arms and kissed me. That was when I was formally handed over to the Duke of Suffolk who had come to collect me. My parents were there and they rode with us to Bar where I had to say good-bye to them."

"How very sad you must have been. How frightened."

"I was sad," she said. "I loved my parents dearly, but I knew it must be. We went to Paris. The people expressed their pleasure with enthusiasm. They love these marriages. They are a chance for revelry and they always think they will bring peace to the country. They called me the little Daisy." She gave a short, ironic laugh. "Daisy! They do not call me that in England. Little Daisy! In England, I am the hated Jezebel. And then I met the man who . . . next to your father . . . was to be my greatest enemy."

"Do you mean the Duke of York?"

"I do indeed, and as I talk to you now I can see his head in its paper crown on the walls of the city of York." She had changed. She was the vindictive, hating woman when she talked of the Duke of York, father of Edward who soon, she hoped, would be replaced by her husband.

"He was a rogue, though I did not know it then. And his wife . . . she was worse. She gave herself airs even then."

"They called her Proud Cis," I said.

"Cecily, Duchess of York, would be mother of kings," she said bitterly.

I might have reminded her that she was indeed the mother of a king, for Edward had reigned for nearly ten years.

"I had no notion then what to expect from that family," she said. "Nor from your father. That cursed war . . . the War of the Roses. Roses should be beautiful ornaments. And they betrayed their king and went to war. They are going to regret it. Edward will go the way of his father."

"Please tell me how you felt when you first saw England."

Her eyes went hazy and a smile touched her lips, softening her face miraculously.

"The crossing! I thought I should die! And I was not the only one. I thought, I shall never see England. I forgot all my fears for the future. I thought, this is the end. This is death. They told me that as soon as my feet touched dry land the sickness would pass. It did . . . for some of them. But not for me. It was horrific. My face and body were covered in spots. They thought I was suffering from the small pox. I pictured myself disfigured forever. I thought, this is how my husband will see me for the first time. I was vain about my appearance. I knew that I had some beauty. Beauty is one of God's gifts. It is so useful. It wins special privileges. It is admired and treated with gentleness wherever it is. And I thought I should lose that. Beautiful people learn what a precious gift they have and once a woman has possessed it she will cling to it and cannot easily let it go. Imagine my feeling—a young girl about to lose her beauty!"

"But you did not."

"It was not the small pox. I began to recover. My spots went as quickly as they had come, and I was myself again. I cannot explain to you the relief, not only to me but to everyone. We disembarked at Southampton and there I was told that the king's squire had brought a letter of welcome from the king. Would I receive him, they asked? How could I not receive the king's squire? He came in so respectfully. He knelt before me. I was still feeling very weak, I remember. I was seated in a chair with rugs about me.

"He was a very gentle young man with a soft, sweet expression; he was most humble. He handed me the letter and I told him that when I read it I would write to the king. They said to me afterward, 'Did you like the squire?' and I said, 'He seemed a most modest and worthy young man.' Then they laughed. The squire, they told me, was the king."

"Why did he come to you thus?"

"He told me afterward that he had feared I might be scarred by the small pox and he wanted to see me first to realize how badly I was marked. He wanted to be prepared in case he was going to be very shocked, and he did not want to betray his feeling on first sight of me. Oh, he is a very gentle, kindly man, but . . ."

She was silent and for a long time sat staring into space, reliving it all, I supposed.

At length she said, "Alas, he was not of the nature to be a king when there were others fighting for the crown."

The softness vanished. She was thinking of those hated men: the Duke of York, his son Edward, and most of all my father.

Suddenly she seemed to remember who I was. She peered at me, frowning. "Why do I talk to you, Warwick's daughter? I hate Warwick. I hate him more than I hate the Duke of York. York is dead now. Never shall I forget the head. Have you ever seen a head without a body?"

I shuddered and shrank from her.

"It is a good sight when it is the head of one you hate. And the paper crown . . . that was amusing. He had so longed for our crown . . . Henry's crown . . . and it was meet and fitting that he should die ignobly wearing a crown made of paper. I see you turn from me. I am in truth a hard, cruel, wicked woman. What did they tell you of me?"

I was silent, amazed by this sudden change in her. She was a wild and passionate woman and I did not always understand her.

There was another time when she said to me, "Why do I talk to you as I do, Lady Anne? I do talk to you, do I not? Let me tell you this. You do not understand. To talk to a child is like talking to oneself. Perhaps that is it. Warwick's daughter! Daughter of the man who ruined my life. Oh, I had forgotten. He is my friend now." Then she fell to laughing. "Oh, if only Henry were strong! I should have married a strong man . . . a man like Edward who calls himself King of England. A man like Warwick. What a pair we should have made! But they married me to Henry. He knows nothing of the evil ways of men. He is a stranger to evil. For him it does not exist because he does not possess it himself. He would be every man's friend, so he believes every man to be his friend. He shrinks from punishing his enemies. Oh, why am I talking to this child of matters she cannot understand?"

"I am understanding now," I said. "You have told me so much."

She was looking at me, but I was sure she did not see me. Her thoughts were far away.

A little later she told me about the scene in the Temple among the roses. "There was a meeting in the Temple," she said. "It was all about the losses in France. Henry's father was the great victor. He strode through France, subduing the French. Harfleur, Agincourt, Orleans, Paris. It was all his. He would have been crowned King of France if he had not died. My Henry was in fact crowned there. And all that has been lost. They blamed it on Somerset. There will always be scapegoats. But the English were beaten because of divine intervention. It was Joan of Arc, with God's guidance, who turned the English out of France and made the poor weak dauphin a wise king. But Warwick, your father, wanted to turn my Henry from the throne and put his own king there. He wanted to show the world that he was the Kingmaker. It is your father I speak of. Do you hear me, child!"

"Yes, I know," I said.

She looked at me and smiled suddenly, her mood changing. "And you are his daughter, a meek, fragile child. Life plays tricks. King René, my father, was a lover of peace and poetry, and he sired me. I should be more fitting to be Warwick's daughter. Is that not odd of fate, child?"

"Yes," I said. "It is very odd."

"I was telling you. They were at the Temple. The whole company was aware of the enmity between Somerset and your father.

Warwick was blaming Somerset for the losses in France, which was nonsense. Warwick was blaming him because he knew he was my man; and Warwick was laying his plans then. I do believe that your father longed above all things to be king. He could not be, so he had to be content by making them. Somerset was a Beaufort . . . grandson of John of Gaunt, who was a son of Edward the Third. 'Tis true that he was born out of wedlock to Katherine Swynford, but she afterward married John of Gaunt and the children were legitimized. So you see why the Beauforts are a proud race."

"Yes," I said. "I have heard that."

"They make their presence felt. Somerset despised Warwick. Where would he have been but for his marriage to Anne Beauchamp and through her getting the Warwick title and estates? To come to wealth and power in such a way does something to a man. He must forever be putting himself forward so that none may doubt that he came to greatness through his own endeavors. You may have heard the story how they walked in the gardens after the meeting, to cool their tempers perhaps, and then Warwick picked the famous quarrel with Somerset, accusing him of ambitions that I believe Somerset had never dreamed of. I knew Somerset well. They said he was my man. That was why Warwick hated him. His hatred was really directed at me."

"Why should he have hated you, my lady?"

"Because he wanted to guide the king and I had shown that it was my place to do that. He hated me because I was strong and saw through his schemes. So he struck at Somerset . . . my best friend . . . but he meant the blow for me. There in the gardens he accused Somerset of bringing defeat and humiliation to the country. He talked of the great victories of the king's father, which had been brought to nothing."

I shivered. I had heard so many times of the encounter in the rose gardens. But always from the other side. It was Somerset who was the enemy: Somerset who had lost the territories in France, who was the tool of that virago, the queen—who was now our friend.

"It is clear why Warwick was for York. There are blood ties between them. He wanted to set a king of his choosing on the throne because he knew I would never allow him to govern Henry.

"It became clear in the gardens that day that Warwick was planning the destruction of the House of Lancaster, and wanted to set up York in its place. Somerset, on sudden impulse, plucked one of the red roses and held it high. The red rose is the symbol of our House of Lancaster, just as the white is that of York. Somerset said, 'I pluck this red rose, the symbol of the House of Lancaster, which I serve with my life.'"

"I know," I said. "And then my father picked a white rose and said, 'This is the white rose of York. Let every man take the rose of his choice. Then we shall know who is with us and who against us.'"

"Ah. You have heard the story. Who in this kingdom has not? And that was it. The stage was set. The War of the Roses had begun."

"Madam," I said. "Are you well?"

I thought she looked as though she were going to faint. She was lying back in her chair, exhausted. I knelt beside her and she

put out a hand and touched my hair. That was unusual, for she
was not given to affectionate gestures.

"Warwick's girl," she murmured. "Why do I talk thus to Warwick's girl?"

We sat in silence for some minutes and then I knew that,
although I was Warwick's daughter, she no longer hated me.

Although I could not cast off my terrible fears of the future, my
strange relationship with Queen Margaret did help to make the
days more tolerable. We were all wondering what was happening.
How was my father faring? Where, I asked myself, were Isabel
and my mother?

I often thought about Richard. What was he doing now?
What was he thinking? He would be a staunch supporter of his
brother and therefore my father's bitter enemy. It was all so unexpected. My father had been one of the heroes of his youth. He
had often betrayed his admiration for him and I think he had
ranked only second, after his brother of course, in his estimation.
And did he ever spare a thought for me?

It seemed incredible that everything should have changed so
suddenly and in such a manner.

Queen Margaret was growing more and more impatient for
news.

"So many things have gone wrong in my life," she said.
"Sometimes I fear that nothing will ever come right."

I did not know what to think. I must be loyal to my father,
but if he were victorious Richard must be defeated; and the outcome of my father's victory must be the marriage I dreaded.

As the days passed I thought more and more of the ordeal before me. I could not like what I had seen of the prince. Moreover, I could not forget that I had heard of his asking for those executions and his sitting watching with apparent satisfaction while heads were severed. It was terrifying.

He had been only young. Eight, they said. And he would have been brought up to hate his enemies. But at the same time I was deeply disturbed.

I wanted to find out more about him and it was not difficult to lure the queen into talking of him, for he was her favorite topic of conversation. I was realizing more and more what a sad and frustrating life she had led. She cared more deeply for her son than she ever had for anyone else. All her hopes were in him. She was prepared to make any sacrifice for him, and while she hated her enemies so fiercely, even more intensely did she love him.

I was developing a fondness for the queen. True, I was greatly in awe of her and at times the fierceness in her eyes repelled me, but now that she was talking to me with a certain frankness and making me see the sadness of her life, I realized how events had affected her, and I began to make excuses for her.

I looked forward more and more to our encounters, and I believed she did also.

And so I led her to talk of her son.

"My son!" She said the words with something like adoration. "Anne Neville, there is nothing so wonderful in the world as holding one's own child in one's arms. One passes through a painful ordeal, and then one hears the cry of a child . . . your own child . . . a child that has grown within you and is part of you."

"Yes," I said. "I understand that."

"I had thought it was a blessing that would be denied me. My son Edward was not born until eight years after my marriage."

"And all that time you longed for a child."

"All kings must have sons. I thank God daily for mine. Ever since he was born I have planned for his future . . . for what would be good for him. Now I am proud of him. He will be Edward the Fifth of England, and when I see the crown placed on his head, that will compensate me for all my sufferings."

"Kings seem to have troublous lives," I commented.

She gave me a scornful look. "A king has his destiny to fulfill; and those who turn him from his throne should be punished with death. How well I remember my joy. I could not believe it. Of course, in the beginning I had hoped, I had longed and prayed . . . but I had thought, Henry being as he was, that I should never have a child. You would not understand my joy."

"I think I do," I said.

"Of course, there were my enemies. York." She laughed with glee. "Imagine York's feelings when he heard. This child would block his way to the throne. So they started rumors. The child could not be Henry's, they said. How could Henry beget a child? But you are too young to understand. What did I care? I laughed at them. I was exalted. I was the mother of a king-to-be. Oh, that was a wonderful time."

"I can imagine how you felt when he arrived."

"There was great trouble before that. It must have been two months before the birth when Henry showed signs of his first illness. It was a great sadness, a great anxiety. That should have been a time for rejoicing. We did not know what ailed him. It was only later that we learned. He could not move. He lay in his bed . . . remembering nothing. It was the beginning of his strangeness. He was unaware that he had a son."

"Poor King Henry."

"That affliction came through his mother—the daughter of Charles the Mad of France. They say such illness is one that can be passed on. The mother escapes but she gives it to her son."

"How very sad."

"It is at the root of all our troubles. These people would never have dared . . . if Henry had not been . . ."

She could not bring herself to say the word insane. I reached out and touched her hand. She took mine and held it briefly. I was always moved by these outward signs of affection between us. She was beginning to accept me as her daughter-in-law in spite of the fact that I belonged to the hated Neville clan.

It was on that occasion when she told me about the Tudors.

"I should have liked to have known Henry's mother," she said. "She was French so we should have had something in common. She was a lady with a strong will, though outwardly she was very gentle. She had a very unhappy childhood, largely due to her father's madness and her wanton mother. For a time she and her many brothers and sisters lived in abject poverty. That was while her father suffered his periodic bouts of insanity. I believe when he was well and took up his duties of kingship that was changed. But poor children, it went on for much of their early childhood. Then she married Henry, the great conqueror of France, and it seemed that everything was going well for her, until her husband died and she was left with a little baby . . . my Henry. Henry often talks to me about his mother, and always with affection. It is because of her that he has been so good to the Tudors."

"Who are the Tudors?" I asked.

"Oh, they are worthy men. They have always supported the House of Lancaster. Of course they would. Are they not Henry's half-brothers? You see, when King Henry the Fifth died, Katharine, my Henry's mother, was considered to be of little importance and her son had his own household—governesses and nurses and so on—and was taken right out of her hands."

"I always think that is cruel to children."

"Kings and queens have their duties and they are not in the nursery. Katharine made a life for herself with Owen Tudor. That is where the Tudors come in. It is a true story of romantic love lived in secret."

I listened avidly to what she told me of the widowed queen who had fallen in love with the humble Welsh squire and had married him . . . some said; others were sure that she had not; but they were able to live together slightly removed from the court and so enjoyed a happy life with their children until they were discovered by the Duke of Gloucester, brother of King Henry the Fifth, who destroyed their happiness. Owen Tudor was arrested on a charge of treason and the queen separated from the children and sent to Bermondsey Abbey where she died.

"What a sad end to their story," I said.

"Life is often like that, as doubtless you will learn."

"And what happened to Owen Tudor?"

"He escaped from prison. Henry was good to his half-brothers and they have been loyal to him. They have served the House of Lancaster well. Owen was taken prisoner at Mortimer Cross and beheaded in the marketplace at Hereford on the orders of that man who calls himself King Edward the Fourth."

"Why do there have to be these wars? Why cannot everyone be happy!"

"Because there are rights to be fought for." She was fierce and angry again, and her anger was for the loyal Tudor who had lost his head, and I could not help remembering her glee when she had talked of the Duke of York's head with the paper crown. I recoiled from her. That was typical of our relationship. I felt repelled one moment and drawn to her the next. I suppose her feelings for me were somewhat similar. There were times when she remembered I was a member of that hated family, and at others she saw me as a poor helpless girl, buffeted by fate—just as she herself must have been at my age.

War was a futile and terrible operation. Richard would not agree with me; nor would my father. Wars brought wealth and power to some, and it seemed that was what most men wanted.

One day when I was with the Queen we heard the sound of approaching riders. We rose and went to the window. Two men were galloping up to the castle. They had clearly ridden far.

I saw the queen catch her breath and without a word she hurried to the door and went down the staircase. I followed her.

The men leaped from the horses and came toward us. They

were dishevelled and travel-stained but I knew before they spoke that they were the bearers of good news.

"Madam . . . my lady." They knelt to the queen. "The day is won."

There was ecstasy in the queen's face. It was clear that my father had succeeded.

The messengers were brought in. They must be refreshed, but first we must hear just a little more . . . enough to reassure the queen that the victory was secure.

"Your Grace . . . my lady . . . when the earl landed the south fell into his hands with ease. Edward, who called himself king, was in the north subduing a rebellion there."

"And what of Edward now?" asked Margaret.

"He is in flight, my lady. They say he has left the country."

"He would not come here, I trow," said Margaret grimly.

"It is believed he is on his way to Holland."

"And the Duke of Gloucester?" I heard myself saying.

"The Duke of Gloucester, my lady?" said the messenger puzzled. "He would be with his brother, I doubt not."

"The imposter has been truly routed?" asked the queen. "There is no doubt of this?"

"No doubt, my lady. No doubt at all. The earl has ridden through the streets of London, King Henry with him."

She clasped her hands and smiled at the messengers.

"You have ridden far, my good men. You shall rest a while. You shall be refreshed with food. Then you shall talk more to us."

She summoned one of the guards and instructed him to look

after the men who had ridden so far with the good news and were now clearly exhausted.

Then she turned to me. "The waiting is over. Your father has fulfilled his promise to me. And now, my child, you shall be the future Queen of England."

I could not share her exultation, but she was too happy to notice.

I think that must have been one of the happiest moments of her life.

Later I heard more of what had happened. Edward had been betrayed by the man who had been his most ardent supporter— my uncle John Neville. My father had often referred to John as one of the few Nevilles who had been a traitor to the family.

When my father had turned against Edward, John had maintained his loyalty to the king. He said he had sworn to serve Edward and would not break his vows and so could not follow his brother—mighty as he was—in this campaign to replace Edward with Henry.

Such loyalty from a Neville should have been well rewarded, but Edward had made a great mistake when he had slighted John Neville. One would have thought that the very fact of John's being a Neville would have made Edward appreciate his loyalty. But this Edward had failed to do. John saw himself as Lord of the North, holding it for Edward. Edward's mistake was to take the earldom of Northumberland from John and bestow it on Henry Percy, compensating John with the Marquisate of Montagu. John Neville considered this gross ingratitude after he had turned his back on his family to support the king. It was the deciding factor, the turning point, for, Warwick being in charge of the armies in the south, John only had to turn his army against the king to capture the north. This he did and Edward's army, realizing that he was on the point of total defeat, deserted him. Thus he lost the day and had no recourse but to flee the country.

My father, having unmade Edward, then proceeded to make Henry king.

For so long we had waited. Now was the time for us to return to England. I was deeply disturbed. The one thought dominating my mind was my marriage to the Prince of Wales, which would now be celebrated.

We must leave Amboise for Paris, said the queen. There we should meet Edward and we must make plans without delay.

I wondered if she noticed how depressed I was. She might have expected me to rejoice with her at my father's victory. She was almost reconciled to accepting me as a daughter-in-law. I had managed to please her, perhaps she thought I was quiet and unassuming and would be docile.

There were two thoughts dominating my mind. I should have to marry Edward in England, so there would be a little respite. I tried to put that out my mind, telling myself there would be some time before it could happen. There would have to be a great deal of preparation. The other thought was Richard. What had happened to him? Where was he now and what was he thinking? How long would he and Edward be content to stay in Holland? They would be certain to make an attempt to win back the throne.

I went to find the messengers to see if they had any news about Richard. I could not have asked such questions in the queen's presence.

I found them in the kitchen. There was a plate of bread and meat before each of them.

They rose as I entered and I bade them be seated. I told them that I did not want to interrupt their meal for they must be hungry and weary.

"'Tis less wearying bringing good news, my lady," said one.

"Aye," agreed the other. "There's always a good welcome for good news."

"How are the people taking the change at home?" I asked. "I always heard they were very fond of King Edward."

"Aye, 'twas so, my lady. He is such a bonny man and loved by the ladies, and the men too have a place in their hearts for him. But the battle went against him and he lost . . . and now he's gone."

"Who went with him?"

"A few of his friends."

"His brother, the Duke of Gloucester, of course."

"Oh aye. Certainly the little duke. He's always with his brother. A fine man, Edward. Every inch a king."

"And what about King Henry?"

"Poor King Henry. He has been treated as no king should be. I was there at the time . . . long ago it seems now . . . when they brought him through the Chepe and Cornhill to the Tower. They had bounded his legs to a horse and put straw in his hair, and jeered at him as he passed along. That was no way to treat a king. People remember, but they say Henry bears no grudge. He's a

good man . . . bit of a saint, they say. Should have been a monk
not a king. He might have had some peace then. I doubt he wants
to be king. I reckon he'd be happier with Edward on the
throne . . . if only he was treated right."

"And you really think they have been illtreating him?"

"I saw him before I left . . . riding through the streets, king
again. The bishop and the archbishop, brother of the Earl of Warwick, went down to the Tower to bring him out. Those who were
with him said they found him dirty and neglected . . . like a
shadow, they said, or a sack of wool—and as mute as a crowned
calf. So they dressed him up in fine clothes and set a crown on his
head and they took him to Westminster. They'd made a king of
him. But he did not look like one and the people were all talking
of King Edward."

My feelings were mixed. I had been so sorry for the queen and
now she was in a state of bliss; but I was fearful for myself because
this turn of events had brought me closer to what I dreaded more
than anything in the world.

And at the back of my mind was the thought of Richard. I
could picture his sorrow and anger at seeing his brother driven
from the throne. My heart was with Richard, but it was my own
father who had brought this sorrow in him. I had been brought
up to revere my father. I had been told many times that he was
the greatest man in the kingdom. But I loved Richard: I had been
enchanted by his brother Edward and I could easily understand
why the people loved him and wanted him for their king. How
would they like his going and seeing in his place one who was like
a sack of wool and a crowned calf?

Something told me they would not and this was not the end of the conflict. And I guessed that the same thoughts were in the minds of the messengers.

I left them then, for no more was to be learned. They had been sent to bring the glad tidings and their duty was done. When they had rested for a night they would return to England.

And what of us, I wondered?

The queen sent for me.

"I confess," she said, "that I did not always believe that your father would do this. I did not trust him entirely. But he has proved himself to be a man of honor."

Had he, I wondered? He had turned from the king and supported his rival. Was that honorable? And he had done it because he had wanted power, and if he could not reach it through one king he would try to do so through another. But little as I knew of state affairs, I sensed in that moment that my father had made a mistake. The people would never accept Henry; and was Edward the man to stand aside and let them?

Margaret went on, "First we must give our thanks to God for this victory and when that is done we will make our plans. As soon as we are in England you shall be married. This I have promised your father and I shall keep my word. Now let us plan. We shall be leaving here for Paris. My son will have heard the good news by now. He will be there. Then we shall go to England to claim our crown. You look thoughtful, child. You must rejoice. This is a happy day for us all. The House of Lancaster is back where it belongs."

We did not leave immediately. The next day messengers arrived at the *château* with the news that the King of France was on his way to Amboise to visit Margaret. She must of course be there to receive him.

More than a week passed before the arrival of the king and in the meantime the *château* was given over to preparation for his visit. It was unthinkable that we could leave at such a time.

In due course he arrived with his queen, Charlotte of Savoy.

He received the queen—and me—in a very friendly manner and told us that it was a source of great pleasure to him to know that events were going well in England.

Louis was an extraordinary man. I could not trust him. He was quite unlike a king: he had little dignity, was careless in his dress, and there was a complete lack of formality in his speech and behavoir. He was amiable, but there was a watchfulness about him, a certain slyness that suggested he might be planning something that was quite alien to his utterances.

I could not get out of my mind the stories I had heard of his vengeful nature and how he had made a particularly gruesome prison of his *château* of Loches where he imprisoned his enemies in the *oubliettes* there—those dungeon-like underground prisons into which men were thrown and left to be forgotten as the name implied. What had impressed me so deeply was that Louis was reputed to pay periodic visits to Loches that he might peer down on those men whom he had imprisoned and then watch as they progressed toward their grisly end. There were also rumors that he imprisoned men in iron cages and reduced them to the state of animals.

Some might say that there would always be those to malign kings and people in high places, but I could believe these rumors of Louis, even while he was displaying such friendship toward Margaret and benignity to me.

I liked his wife, Charlotte; she was a placid woman who was now pregnant. I had heard it said that she was either giving birth or preparing to do so; and it was maliciously hinted that Louis far preferred the society of his mistress, Marguerite de Sassenage, and spent only long enough with Charlotte to impregnate her and so keep her busy bearing the children of France.

I could understand how he had earned the sobriquet of the Spider King. However, Charlotte seemed happy enough, so perhaps she was as eager to be rid of him as he was of her.

He certainly seemed to be pleased by what was happening in England, and was eager to celebrate the victory. That seemed reasonable enough as King Henry was related to him; moreover Margaret was French. Naturally France would support the House of Lancaster against that of York. It was Louis who had brought my father and Margaret together and prevailed on Margaret to make up their quarrel. So this was his victory as it was Margaret's.

It was easy to talk to Louis. I had heard someone say of him that if one had met him by chance one would take him for a man of low condition rather than a person of distinction. There was truth in that, for he was a little slovenly in his dress—rare in a king of France—so that one did not feel, when talking to him, that one was with the king. It seemed that he preferred to be with the humble rather than the nobility.

"It pleases me," he said, "to contemplate your good fortune. Your father is a man I esteem as much as any man I know. He will rule England wisely with the help of the queen. The poor king is alas in a sorry state. But with the Earl of Warwick to guide him he will be in good hands. We shall be good neighbors, which is what I have always wanted." He smiled slyly and I wondered how sincere he was in this. "The rightful king will be restored to the throne and one day you, my dear, will be Queen of England. That is what gives me pleasure."

The celebrations were not of long duration, for I had discovered that the king was parsimonious in the extreme, and could not bear to see money wasted.

He spent a good deal of time with Margaret, and I for one could not regret his delaying our preparations to return to England, for I knew what awaited me there.

He was at the *château* for about two weeks, which was a long time for him. He was restless and spent much time wandering about his kingdom.

So far Prince Edward had not come to us and the queen was very eager to make some plans with him. She believed he was in Paris and after the king had departed we set out for that city.

It was now well into November and the weather was not good, which meant that our journey was considerably delayed. We were naturally anxious to know what was happening in England and we were ever on the watch for messengers, but as winter was with us and the sea was so treacherous at that time, it might be difficult for them to reach us.

Edward was not in Paris when we arrived and we must wait there. Fortunately, due to our benefactor, the King of France, there was no lack of hospitality. I was surprised that Margaret did not chafe more against the delays. Then I came to the conclusion that she wished my father to bring the country to a settled state before we returned.

I think Edward was gathering together an army. Perhaps he, too, was hoping that when we returned it would be to a welcome and not to deal with uprisings and such like, which might well occur after the banishing of a popular king and replacing him by one such as Henry.

I was unsure of what was happening. I knew that my mother was still in France. Isabel had returned to England with Clarence, who had followed my father there. They were still allies at this stage, but I fancy uneasy ones. Clarence had been convinced that he was to have the throne. I wondered what his reactions were when the plans were changed and Henry was to be restored.

After a while Prince Edward arrived in Paris and my fears were confirmed. He was in a state of great excitement seeing himself as king. He did not believe that his father could ever reign. It might well be that he would become regent until Henry's death. His formidable mother would expect to reign with him. But she doted on him and he saw a glorious future before him, I was sure. Of course, he had to take me as part of the bargain. I shivered at the thought. It had been like a cloud hanging over me—and now the storm was about to break.

We should be married in England, for it would not be fitting for the heir to the throne to marry in a foreign country. I guessed that as soon as we returned the arrangements would be made. The thought filled me with panic.

How could my father have done this to me? But what did any of these power-seeking men care whom they used as long as advantage to them was the result? How I wished I had not been born Warwick's daughter. I should have been much happier as one of the village girls. I longed more than ever for those childhood days at Middleham.

In truth Edward frightened me. He kissed my hand as though with affection; he spoke to me caressingly; and his eyes studied me. What did I see there? A faint contempt. I would be unlike the women he had known. What sort of women would he like? I had heard of no romances. Perhaps he was the kind who visited low taverns, who indulged his lust with serving maids. I could think that very likely. I was small—too young to be formed as a woman yet. My hair was my real beauty—being long and fair. I supposed I was not ill-favored. Both Isabel and I had been referred to as beauties. But that was a term applied to all princesses or ladies of the nobility—especially when they were being used as bargaining counters in proposed marriages. I had an idea that I should not suit his fancies: he would prefer someone bold, practiced . . . not an inexperienced girl.

Yet there were times when I seemed to detect a sly lust in his eyes and that alarmed me. I wished Isabel were here. If only there was someone I could talk to . . . someone comfortable and homely, someone like Ankarette Twynyho.

But there was no one and I felt very lonely and full of fear.

Every morning I reminded myself: the marriage cannot take place until we are in England. And I prayed for more delays.

Edward spent a good deal of time with his mother. His stay with us must be brief, she told me. He should not delay long before going to England to claim his inheritance. Louis had been

helpful, but getting money from him for supplies was not an easy
task. He was notoriously mean and wanted some reward for his
beneficence.

How glad I was when Edward left us, but now we ourselves
must prepare in earnest for our return to England.

The winter is not the best time to travel but we set out on our
journey. By this time it was the beginning of March and we were
often hindered by the snow. We would be received at some
château on our way and often found ourselves delayed by snow-
blocked roads. It was a long and uncomfortable journey, but with
the coming of April we found ourselves at Honfleur, to be confronted by a truly turbulent sea. We dared not risk the crossing
while such conditions prevailed.

Each morning when I awoke the first thing I did was look out
of my window. I would rejoice in that heaving mass of water. I
would lie in bed at night and listen to the wind that howled and
the waves that pounded against the shore.

We cannot go yet, I would whisper gleefully to myself; and I
would try to shut out the memory of Edward's contemptuous yet
lecherous eyes.

When messengers arrived I guessed they had something of
great importance to tell us since they had braved the sea.

I was with the queen when they reached us. They were
brought in immediately.

This time they did not come with smiles and good news but,
as the bearers of ill tidings will be, they were hesitant to impart it.

"Tell us your news," said Margaret sternly. "I am waiting."

"Your Grace, my lady, Edward of York, with his brother, the Duke of Gloucester, Earl Rivers, and Lord Hastings, have landed at Ravenspur and are marching on to York."

The queen closed her eyes. I went to her and took her by the arm. She shook me off a little impatiently, angry that I had assumed weakness in her.

"Ravenspur," she said. "Where is that?"

"It is at the mouth of the Humber."

"That is the north. He has ill judged his landing. The north was always for Warwick. What other news?"

"He has a force of two thousand with him—English and Burgundians."

"Two thousand! What chance will they have?"

"I have to tell your Grace that he has reached the city of York and York has opened its gates to him."

"The traitors!"

"There are rumors that Edward of York has come back only to claim his dukedom."

"Impertinence," murmured the queen.

But she was very shaken, I could see. She dismissed the messengers and motioned me to sit with her. I did so. She took my hand suddenly and pressed it. And then we sat on in silence.

The days that followed were like a dream. The gigantic waves still defied us to do battle with them. All we could do was look out over that stormy sea to England and wonder what was happening there.

We had always known that Edward of York was not the man to stand aside and let the Earl of Warwick take the crown from him. He would rally men to him; the people loved him. He looked like a king; he acted like a king; and if he made mistakes, they were kingly mistakes. I had always known that the people would not want Henry. They might pity him, but pity should not be for kings. They hated Margaret merely for being a foreigner, if for nothing else, but there was plenty more to turn them against her. They did not want her or her son or her husband. They wanted Edward. There might be mighty kingmakers like my father, but it was almost always the people who kept kings on their thrones.

I learned afterward what was happening in England.

My father had never really succeeded in ruling the country. People wanted a king, a figurehead, someone above them, aloof, because of the aura of royalty, which they regarded as holy. A king must be a minor god who can wear a golden crown and purple velvet and on whom they can bestow their adulation.

There was something else that happened at that time. When Edward had landed, the Duke of Clarence had cast aside his allegiance to the Earl of Warwick and gone to Edward.

I can imagine his appeal. "We are brothers, Edward. Should we be enemies? I was seduced by the earl. I listened to evil council. You are my brother, Edward. I want to serve you. Can you forgive me?" Surely it would have been something like that.

And Edward would forgive. When those who had served him ill came to him and begged for forgiveness, it was usually readily given. And this was his brother.

I wondered if it occurred to Edward that Clarence had come back to him because my father had set Henry on the throne after hinting that it was to be for him, Clarence? Surely that must have occurred to Edward? But, as I heard, readily he embraced his brother. It was like the parable of the prodigal son.

Richard talked of it later to me. He said, "It was always like that with George. He would do something very wrong and then he would beg for forgiveness. He was never denied it—not by my brother nor my sister Margaret, whose favorite he was. Even my mother would relent for him."

So there had been another blow for my father. But it was more than that. The country wanted a king and who had the King-maker given them? Poor pathetic, saintly, half-mad Henry? Certainly not. They had Warwick to rule them. And Warwick, mighty as he was, lacked the aura of royalty.

What was happening in England? I asked myself as we waited there at Honfleur.

The sea was a little calmer.

"We cannot wait forever," said Margaret. "A great deal is happening in England. I should be there. We must delay no longer."

Prince Edward had joined us. He had gathered men and supplies from Louis and we were ready to cross. I heard that my mother was about to return to England and I was relieved also to be told that she was well. I wished that I could see her and could have been comforted by her presence all these months when I had been with the queen. But I should see my mother when I returned to England. I should also see Isabel.

The crossing was all that we had feared it would be and we arrived at Weymouth feeling battered and exhausted.

Somber news awaited us there.

My father was dead. He had been killed at the Battle of Barnet.

AT WARWICK COURT

It had happened just as we had embarked on that stormy sea. I could not believe it. To me he had always seemed indestructible. My poor mother, I thought. What is she feeling now? They had been deeply attached to each other. Although he was rarely with us, I had never heard of any infidelity on his part. She had brought him the means to become the man he was and I believed he was ever grateful to her for that. He had always treated her with the utmost respect. I think he cared for us children in his way. True, he had been about to involve me in a match that was most distasteful to me, but it was the rule for parents in his position to regard their daughters as instruments for bringing glory to the family.

"Warwick is dead!" We heard that everywhere. People talked

of little else. He was no more—the man who had been the most influential in England, the man whose power enabled him to make and unmake kings.

I felt lost in a bewildering world. My father dead! Where should we go now?

The queen took the news calmly. It occurred to me that, although she expressed her sorrow, she was not entirely displeased.

Warwick had set Henry up as king; he had carried out his part of the bargain. If he had lived, he would have wanted to rule. That was at the very root of his ambition. He had made kings that he might guide them and Margaret was not one to be guided.

So now . . . he had served his purpose. He had brought Henry back to the throne. And then . . . he had fought at Barnet.

She was studying me speculatively. I guessed she was thinking: with Warwick no more, of what importance was his daughter?

She did not dislike me anymore. In fact I believe she had a certain fondness for me. Perhaps she despised me a little because I was not ambitious, not fiercely desirous for a crown . . . as she was. But there was some rapport between us and that hatred she had had for me in the beginning, as Warwick's daughter, was no longer there. She had even become reconciled to accepting me as a daughter-in-law.

But now where did I stand when my father was killed in battle? Perhaps she was wondering whether she need honor the pledge she had made to marry me to her son.

I would be wholeheartedly grateful to her if she would not agree to that.

What strange days they were—days of much activity and terrible uncertainty.

Messages came to us from the Duke of Somerset. It would be advisable for us to go to Lancaster to rally troops. The Lancastrian cause had not been lost by the desertion of the Duke of Clarence and the death of the Earl of Warwick.

I wished that I could have seen my mother. I did receive a letter from her and it was heartbreaking to read it.

She was suffering deeply from the death of my father.

"I know not what will become of us," she wrote.

She told me that she was going to Beaulieu Abbey. I was not to worry about her. She hinted that she believed Edward would not be harsh with us.

It was a comfort to hear from her. I, of course, betrothed to the Prince of Wales, was as deeply embroiled as she was. The fact that I was innocently caught up in a matter for which I had no enthusiasm was of no account. I had become one of them now— a Lancastrian. I was allied to my future mother-in-law, and I must needs follow her.

We set out from Weymouth. Margaret was full of energy. She rode at the head of the cavalcade with me beside her, and she rallied men to her cause as she went through the towns and villages. The imposter was back in England; he had murdered the worthy Earl of Warwick. She was caring for his poor fatherless daughter. The earl must be avenged. They must ride with her to drive base Edward out of the country.

By the time we reached Bath we had a small following. There

we were met by riders who came from Wales with the news that Jasper Tudor was gathering together a fine army to fight for Henry.

Knowing of the queen's approach, Jasper Tudor had suggested that she join forces with him, for Edward of York, with his army, was not far away and, having got wind of their arrival, was bearing down on them.

After consultation with her captains, that was what Margaret decided to do. I was full of admiration for her. She would have been an excellent commander if she could have dispensed with that arrogance. How different Edward was! He was friendly with the humblest soldier; he made them all feel they were all men together to work to the best of their ability, he no less than the lowest rank. His popularity was the secret of his success.

There followed the fatal Battle of Tewkesbury.

I was riding with Margaret at the head of the cavalcade when we were met by Prince Edward with the men he had assembled. He told us that Edward of York was in the vicinity and the two armies must soon come face to face.

The prince persuaded his mother to go with me to a small religious house on the road along which we were passing. He said the battle would be short and triumphant but he did not want to suffer the anxiety of knowing that his mother and I might be in danger. It seemed wise that we should remain with the nuns.

"I shall be content knowing you are there," he said. "And I shall soon be with you to tell you of our victory."

I looked anxiously at the queen. She had been known to ride into battle with the army and for a moment I thought she was going to refuse.

"You must do as I say," he said. "I leave my bride in your charge. How could I give myself to battle if I must be in a state of anxiety about your safety?"

I was aware of the thoughts that were passing through her mind. She was no longer young. It was ten years since Henry had lost his crown and she had lived in exile most of that time.

Edward was insistent and finally she gave way.

"We shall be waiting most eagerly," she told him.

"I know, dear lady mother. And you shall be the first to hear of our victory."

I was very relieved when at last she agreed to stay at the religious house to wait for news of the battle.

The nuns received us warmly. I doubted they were partisan. To them we were just two women in need of shelter. True, one of us was a queen and the other destined to become one, but I am sure, whoever we had been, they would have given us shelter.

I was glad to be at peace, if only for a short time. I was exhausted mentally as well as physically. The more I saw of my prospective bridegroom, the more I dreaded the marriage and that now seemed close.

I thought about the armies that would be facing each other. Richard would be beside his brother. I felt desperately sad because we were on opposite sides. I prayed that Richard might come safely through this conflict. As for my future husband . . . I tried not to think of him.

We did not have to wait long for news. We received it from the soldiers who had come straight from the battlefield. They were in sore need of attention. I was not sure on which side they had been fighting. They had simply found their way to the nuns, hoping they could have their wounds attended to. I went with the nuns to help if I could.

One of the men who was lying on a pallet looked at me and said, "My lady, you are . . ."

"Lady Anne Neville," I said.

And at that moment Margaret appeared. She had heard that there were arrivals at the house and she was hoping for news of a Lancastrian victory.

"What news?" she cried. "What news?"

Both of the men were silent. I could feel my heart beating wildly.

"I am the queen," said Margaret with an intimidating manner. "I demand to know."

One of the nuns said, "Your Grace, this man is badly wounded."

"That I perceive," retorted Margaret. "The queen asks him a question and he is holding something back."

"The day has gone against us, my lady," said the man.

"Against the Prince of Wales?"

"King Edward is victorious, my lady."

"I do not believe he could be."

The man closed his eyes and lay back on his pallet. She went to him and would have shaken him but two nuns laid hands on her and forcibly held her back.

Margaret in her fear and anxiety looked as though she were about to strike them.

I said quickly, "When the men have recovered a little perhaps they will be able to tell us more, my lady. Just now they are too exhausted."

She stepped back.

"It cannot be," she said. "Edward would not let it be. We had the men . . . we had everything."

"Let me take you to your room. Rest a while. I will go back, and help with the nuns. As soon as there is news I will come to you."

To my surprise she allowed me to lead her away. I think she was so afraid that everything had gone wrong that she wanted to hold off the truth for a little longer until she had schooled herself to receive it.

I made her lie down on the pallet in her cell. I said, "Rest assured I shall soon be with you."

"Perhaps Edward will come. They are not far away. He will come as soon as he is able."

I left her and went back to the nuns and the wounded men.

One of the men said, "The queen has gone?"

"She is resting now," I told him.

"My lady, the battle has gone against us. The army is routed. King Edward is victorious. My Lord Somerset has been captured. The army is finished. It is the end, my lady. The king is back."

"Are you sure of this?"

"I have seen it with my own eyes."

"I understand," I said.

"I dare not tell the queen, my lady."

"What are you holding back?"

"It is the Prince, my lady. He has been slain. I beg of you, take this news to her. She must know . . . and I dare not tell her."

I stared at him. Could this be true? I tried to imagine what this would do to her. She was a strong woman—I had good reason to know—but if this were true and the Prince of Wales had indeed been killed . . . how could I tell her?

I did not tell her. I must be sure that it was true before I did. I spent a restless night. In the early hours of the morning I awoke to find someone in my cell-like room. It was the queen.

She said, "You are awake, Anne?"

"Yes," I replied. "I cannot sleep."

"Why is there no news? Edward said he would send word when the battle was over. Surely it cannot still be going on."

"It is over," I said.

"You know something. These men . . . there is something they have told you. Tell me. I command you."

I was silent. She had risen. She took me by the shoulders and shook me.

"Speak," she said. "Tell me the worst. I forbid you to withhold it. Tell me."

"The battle is over," I said. "The Lancastrian army is in retreat. The Yorkists have won the battle of Tewkesbury."

"Then why was I not told?"

"The men were afraid. They began to tell . . . and then they were afraid."

"How dared they keep back anything?"

"They feared to hurt you."

"What else?" she demanded.

I was silent.

"Not you, too, Anne Neville," she cried. "You must not with-hold news from me."

Still I was silent.

Her eyes were wild. It was as though she were on the verge of madness. I thought, how can I tell her that her son is dead?

She must have read my thoughts. I had told her the field was lost. She knew that in any case from the men. What worse news could there be, and where was Edward? Why had he not come? I think she knew in that moment.

I had never seen such blank despair. I wanted to comfort her but I did not know how.

She said quietly, "It is Edward."

I nodded.

"What? Captured?" There was hope in her voice.

Still I was silent.

"Tell me, in God's name, tell me."

"The men may be wrong," I said.

"What did they tell you?"

"That they saw him."

"Yes . . . yes."

"He was slain."

"Then he is dead. My son is dead!"

I had gone to her. I put my arms around her. "The men were wrong," I said. "You know how these stories get around."

She sat on the pallet and stared ahead. I saw the tears on her cheeks.

"He was everything to me," she murmured. "When he came . . . he was the best thing that ever happened to me. He was bright and beautiful. I used to watch him when he was a little boy . . . watched him for the madness of his father. But there was no madness. He was bright and beautiful. He would have made a great king. He would have made up for everything. He is not dead. He cannot be dead."

I said, "The men were wrong. It was something they heard. They must have been wrong."

She turned on me angrily. "Then where is he? If he were alive, he would have come here. He knew I was here. He would have come to me. I have lost him. Nothing matters anymore. Oh, God in Heaven, why did You not take me first . . . not my bright and beautiful son?"

"We must not grieve. We shall hear more news later."

She said, "Yes, we shall hear more news. But in my heart I know. Never more shall I see his dear face. This is your loss, too, my daughter. I have begun to think of you as my daughter. You were to have been his bride. You have lost a husband even as I have lost a son."

She gripped my hands and I said again, "It could be untrue. We must remember that."

She shook her head. "I *know*. It is the end. Why did we do this? First Warwick and now Edward . . . my Edward. Nothing was worth it. York could have the crown . . . if they had left me my son."

I could think of no way of comforting her. She had loved him. She was fiercer in love even than in hatred. Sometimes I had wondered whether she had cherished him so fiercely because he would be king and bring the House of Lancaster back to rule, but now I knew that she loved him not only as the one who was to restore her pride and fulfill her ambitions, but as a son.

She said, "Leave me now. I would be alone. Leave me to my grief."

I wanted to remind her that we had only the soldiers' word for this. There could be a mistake. But she was not listening. All I could do was leave her alone with her grief.

The next day there was confirmation. The prince had indeed been killed in battle. The Lancastrians had been defeated. The Duke of Somerset and several important leaders had been captured and executed without delay. The Lancastrians had been completely routed, and King Edward of York had come back to stay.

The advice given to us was that we should stay in the religious house in which we were now sheltering. We had to remember that we were the declared enemies of the triumphant king and our fate would be uncertain. So, for the time being, we should remain where we were.

It was sad to see the grief of the queen and yet even as I did so I was saying to myself: I am free. That which I most dreaded will never come to pass.

My future was indeed uncertain. Perhaps I should be sent to the Tower. I was one of the king's enemies. So was my mother. Isabel, however, was on the winning side because Clarence had changed loyalties just in time.

Anything could happen to me; but all I could think of was that I need no longer dread my marriage.

Another dreary day passed. I knew that something must happen soon. I thought of the gray walls of the Tower of London, which I had passed so many times and which had never failed to fill me with dread. Some prisoners spent years of their lives there without knowing for what reason. That would not be the case with us.

Margaret was so numbed by grief that I believed she did not care what became of her. It was different with me. I was fifteen years old; my life was just beginning and I could not bear to think of its being spent in some damp, dark prison. I had escaped from a fate that terrified me. Could it be to fall into one equally undesirable?

So I lived through those hours, startled at every sound, ears alert for arrivals.

They came at last. The guards surrounded the house and their captain confronted the nuns.

I heard their voices below and went to the queen. She was sitting in a chair, a book of Holy Writ in her hands.

I said, "There are guards here. They have surely come for us."

She nodded. I could see then that she did not care what became of her.

"There is nothing we can do," I said.

She closed the book and stood up for the guards were at the door. Two of them came into the room.

"You are Margaret, one-time Queen of England, and Lady Anne Neville," said one.

Margaret looked at them with haughty disdain and said, "That is so."

"You are to prepare to leave. Be ready please in half an hour."

They had spoken courteously but firmly. Then they left us.

Margaret sat staring before her. I went to her and took her hands.

"We must obey them," I said gently.

She gave a harsh laugh.

"Yes," she said. "We are the prisoners now."

The nuns watched us pityingly as were taken away. I guessed they thought it would be death or imprisonment for us.

As we rode off I thought the countryside looked beautiful; the grass and trees seemed brighter than ever before. That was because I was telling myself that this might be the last time I saw them.

I wondered what it was like to feel the ax on one's neck. One quick blow . . . and then oblivion perhaps.

Fifteen years is not very long to live. It seems a pity to learn a little about life and then to be forced to leave it.

I looked at the queen; she still seemed indifferent to what was happening. Perhaps she truly did not care. All she could think of was that Edward was dead . . . her bright beautiful boy on whom her hopes had been fixed. Now there was only poor sad Henry for her. Did she wonder what would become of her? If so, she gave no sign.

And so we rode with the dismal cavalcade to where we had no idea.

At last in the distance we saw the city of Coventry and when we reached it we came to rest before a gray stone building.

There was a great deal of activity around us and as soon as we were led into this place Margaret was taken away, and I was left in the care of two women. I wondered who they were. They appeared to be ladies of the court.

"I'll dare swear you are tired from your long ride, Lady Anne," one of them said to me.

"It was a little exhausting."

"We are going to bring you some food and perhaps you would like to wash your hands."

"I should be very pleased to do so."

A basin was brought in. They stood with me and one of them gave me a towel. Then they came with bread and meat with a flagon of ale.

I thanked them but could eat very little. I was wondering what was happening to Queen Margaret and what was in store for me.

A long time seemed to pass. The ladies were speaking in whispers together. They had clearly been sent to watch over me. Eventually two guards appeared at the door and I was told to follow them.

With wildly beating heart I did so and was taken to a small chamber. Standing by the window was the tall figure of a man, legs astride, his back to the door.

One of the guards said, "The lady, your Grace."

He swung around and to my amazement I realized I was in the presence of King Edward. I was so astonished that I could only stare. Then, recovering myself as quickly as I could, I advanced and knelt.

I dared not look up at him. I was trembling and my heart felt as though it were trying to leap out of my body.

I felt a hand on my shoulder.

"You could rise," he said. "It is not very comfortable on the knees."

I stood and lifted my eyes to his face. He was smiling and I was struck by his beauty.

"Little Anne Neville," he said. "Why, you are only a child still." He drew me to him and kissed me, first on one cheek and then on the other. I was amazed at the warmth of his greeting.

"You tremble," he said. "You must not be afraid. No harm shall come to you. You are not to blame. They used you, little Anne. I know that well. My brother assures me that you would be our friend. Is that so?"

My eyes filled with tears as I lifted them to his face. I loved him then and I knew why it was that the people would have him as their king. He was a king in very truth for that gentle softness in no way detracted from his strength. Indeed, it added to it. I knew now why Richard admired him so much.

He said, "I sent for you. I wanted to speak to you myself. My brother—my favorite brother Richard—has told me of your friendship at Middleham. How old are you?"

"I am fifteen, your Grace."

"So young . . . so very young. But you will grow up soon. You have suffered too much. You lost your father. That was a sadness for me. I want you to know that when the battle went against him, when I knew that he was in dire straits, I sent one of my men with my orders that his life should be saved. He was too old a friend of

mine to die in conflict against me. It was none of my choosing
that there should be war between us. We were friends for years and
then . . . But it is passed and he has paid a bitter price, and you,
his daughter, are here. I know that you were put into the hands of
the enemy. I know that you were betrothed to the prince. That is
over now, Lady Anne, and you are going to be looked after. What
say you to joining your sister, the Duchess of Clarence?"

"Oh, your Grace, if only I might!"

"You shall. She will be eagerly awaiting your arrival. And then
you will be returned to what you meant to be . . . a good subject
of the king, eh?"

"Oh, yes . . . indeed yes, your Grace. I am so grateful."

"There, my child. You have a pretty face. You need rest
though . . . looking after. It has been a hard time, has it not? But
our troubles are over, little Anne, yours and mine. So, let us
rejoice. Very soon you will be with your sister. So prepare. But
first, there is someone who would like to see you. Wait here and
he will come to you."

I could not believe this. I had heard that the king liked to
abandon formality at times; I had heard that he was generous and
was often criticized for dealing too leniently with his enemies; but
still I was astonished. Of course, he knew that it was through no
desire of mine that I had been placed in the position I was in; but
I was overcome by his air of bonhomie and the manner in which
he had brushed aside the fact that I had been captured with the
enemy and indeed had been made one of them. I was touched,
too, by the way in which he had spoken of my father who had
been killed fighting in an attempt to destroy him.

He was an unusual man and I felt in that moment that I would be loyal to him for the rest of my life.

I was left alone for a few seconds and then the door opened and Richard came in.

"Anne!" he cried and came toward me, his arms outstretched. He held me tightly against him for a few seconds. Then he drew back and looked at me. "You've changed," he said.

"It has been a terrible time, Richard."

"I have thought of you often."

"And I of you . . . so much."

He had changed, too. He had not grown very much and still there was an air of delicacy about him. He must be nineteen now, for he used to say in the old days that he was four years older than I. But he was a man now . . . no longer a boy.

We just stood looking at each other.

I said at length, "The king has been so good."

"He is the most wonderful man on earth."

"I understand how you feel about him. He says I am going to Isabel."

"For a while," he said. "Then we shall see. Is that what you want?"

"I should like it very much. And my mother . . . ?"

"She will be in sanctuary for a while where it is safe for her. My brother George thinks you should go to your sister and, of course, Isabel will be delighted that you do."

"Richard, what of Queen Margaret?"

Richard's face hardened. "I do not know," he said. "It is not decided."

"Poor woman. She mourns the death of her son so deeply."

"Traitors," said Richard. "All of them. And her son . . . you mourn him, too? You were betrothed to him."

I shivered and he put his arm around me.

"I did not like that overmuch," he said.

"I hated it, Richard. It is wrong of me, but I cannot help but be glad that I escaped."

"The whole of England should rejoice that you have escaped," he said. "This will be the end. There will be no more Lancastrian risings. They are well and truly beaten, God willing, forever."

"Do you believe that to be so, Richard?"

"My brother with myself and our faithful friends are going to make sure that it is so. Anne, there is so much to talk of. But this seems hardly the time. When you are with your sister, you will be in my brother's household. I shall see you often. There is so much to catch up. So much time has been wasted."

I nodded. "This has happened so suddenly. Only a few hours ago I was riding to Coventry wondering if my destination was the Tower."

"You were never blamed, Anne. I am sorry about your father. Edward is sorry, too. He tried to save his life. He offered him a pardon . . . before Barnet . . . but the earl would not take it. He had to go on to the end. How did it happen? He had always been our friend. How could he have turned traitor as he did? I looked up to him so much. Next to Edward I admired him more than any man I knew. He was so brave . . . so clever; he knew so much . . . and then suddenly . . . it ends."

"It was a great tragedy," I said.

He took my hands and smiled at me. "We have to forget it, Anne. We have to start afresh."

He looked at me rather shyly and then, drawing me to him, kissed my lips.

I was still bewildered. The contrast had been too sudden. A warm contentment was beginning to creep over me. It was like the old days at Middleham. Richard was back in my life.

There was much to look forward to. We talked for a short while in a leisurely way, recalling the old days.

Coventry will always have a special place in my thoughts, for I had entered that city feeling all was lost and there I found hope for the future.

I did not know what was happening to Queen Margaret. I did not see her so was unable to tell her of my good fortune. Poor Margaret! How different her fate was from mine. She would be the king's prisoner, his deadly enemy. In spite of his generous leniency, I could not believe there would be a very happy fate in store for her.

Isabel was waiting for me at Warwick Court in London. I ran to her and we were in each other's arms, clinging together.

"Isabel!" I cried emotionally. "Is it really you? My sister, I can't believe this is true."

"It is. It is," she cried. "And Anne . . . how thin you are! I must look after you, I see."

"So much has happened. There is so much to tell."

She put her arm through mine and, looking over her shoulder

at the attendants in the background, went on: "I will take the Lady Anne to her chamber."

I had wondered fleetingly why I should be going to Warwick Court, which had been one of my father's residences. It was the custom for property of traitors to be confiscated. But of course Isabel was not a traitor, being the wife of Clarence who had repented in time.

The room to which I was taken was one that I had occupied on other visits to Warwick Court on those rare occasions when the family had been in London.

She shut the door and we were alone. She stood looking at me and I noticed how she had changed. I suppose she had never been the same since she had lost her baby. Memories came back to me of that terrible night at sea when I had watched that little body being consigned to the waves. How tragic everything was!

"I have thought so much about you," said Isabel. "To be with that terrible woman."

"You mean Queen Margaret? She was formidable. But I grew to be quite fond of her, in a way."

She smiled and shook her head at me. "You were always too easily beguiled. And betrothed to that young man! Her son! I have heard such stories about him."

"I never knew him. I only feared that I might have to."

"Well, that is over now and you are back with me. George is going to be your guardian. He will look after you."

"George!"

"Of course. It must be George. Isn't he my husband, and you are my sister. It's natural."

"Perhaps our mother?"

Her face clouded. "What of our mother? I worry about her. What will become of her? Our father is branded traitor and she, his wife, they will say shared his guilt."

"What else could she have done but what she did?"

"That, sister, is not considered. She was with him. She helped him. She was against Edward and therefore I fear for her."

"The king is not unkind. He was good to me."

"George spoke for you . . . begged that you should be brought here."

"I thought it was Richard who spoke for me."

She smiled. "Oh, perhaps Richard, too. But the king has put you in our charge, which is the natural thing to do."

"Yes, I suppose so. But how I do wish we could hear from our mother."

"George will let no harm come to her. He knows that would hurt me. We can trust George."

I felt an uneasy qualm. I had never felt that I could trust George. I could not forget that it was only a little while ago when he was with my father. He had thought he could drive his brother from the throne and take it himself. And when my father's prospects were in doubt, George immediately made peace with Edward. Was that a man whom one could trust?

But he was Isabel's husband and she cared for him. She should, of course, know him better than any.

She was looking at me with concern. "You are so thin," she repeated. "And you look pale. I am going to look after you. I shall keep you quiet for a while, make you rest and go early to bed. My poor little sister, you are too young to be at the center of drama as you have been of late."

"I am so happy to be with you, Isabel. If only our mother could be here I should be content."

"Who knows? She may be joining us. George will see what can be done. Now you will rest. Are you hungry? Come and lie down. I insist. I will sit with you and we will talk . . . and talk."

I obeyed and she did and, although a certain peace crept over me, it was tempered with faint feelings of apprehension.

Perhaps I could not believe that after all the stirring events of the past I could ever live quietly and at peace again.

I was exhausted and slept well. In the morning a woman came to attend to my wants and to my pleasure I saw that she was Ankarette Twynyho whom I remembered from the past.

Ankarette was the jolly, talkative woman who had been widowed when she was quite young and had served Queen Elizabeth Woodville for a few years before coming to us. She had been a favorite with the queen, perhaps because of her avid interest in people and her talent for gathering gossip. I remembered Isabel's telling me that the queen had recommended her. It was a pleasure therefore to see Ankarette.

"The duchess has been so anxious about you, my lady," she said. "She could speak of nothing but her dear sister, the Lady Anne. And when we thought you were going to marry Prince Edward . . . I can tell you we were all dismayed. That would have put you good and truly on the other side, would it not, my lady?"

"Alas, Ankarette, I was not consulted in the matter."

"That's so my lady. I often think how lucky some of us be when it do come to mating. There was I with my Roger. I could have been a contented wife . . . but the Lord saw fit to take him."

"So you have suffered, too, Ankarette."

"Aye. But I've had my good fortunes and one of them has been to serve the duchess and now you, my lady."

"I am pleased to see you again, Ankarette."

She was indeed assiduous in her care for me; and it was from her that I discovered what was happening outside Warwick Court.

It was she who told me how Queen Margaret had ridden, as a prisoner, in the triumphant procession into London when Edward returned to the capital, king once more, with the Lancastrian armies in full retreat, and the man who had called himself Prince of Wales now dead and his mother the queen, whom the people had hated, vanquished while her husband, poor old Henry, was a prisoner in the Tower.

"Poor soul," said Ankarette. "I could almost find it in my heart to be sorry for her. True, she has brought great trouble to this country. Ah, if only poor King Henry had been the man his father was . . . then we should have had none of this War of the Roses. But then we could not have had King Edward . . . and he's the man the people want. He's a king . . . every bit of him. So you see, my lady, that is life. A bit of good . . . a bit of bad . . . both meted out to us all. Let's hope we've had our share of the bad for a while and now let's have a strong dose of the good. But the shame for that poor queen . . . a captive driven there with the victors and her husband a prisoner . . . her armies defeated. No matter what she is, you must spare a thought for her."

"Yes," I said. "She would suffer deeply. I grew to know her. She cared so much for her son. I think perhaps that now he is dead she does not mind so much what happens to her."

"Poor soul," said Ankarette.

It was not long before there was more startling news, and it was Ankarette who imparted it to me.

She made a habit of going into the streets and talking to people whenever she could. It was sure that when she was in the country she must have missed this a great deal, but here at Warwick Court, she had ample opportunities and because it was in London, at the center of events, she could keep us well informed.

Thus I heard of the death of Henry almost as soon as it had happened.

She liked to talk to me because I was particularly interested in what the people thought; and this was an item of such magnitude that everyone would be talking about it. Indeed it was not long before the rumors began to be circulated.

Ankarette said, "They have announced that King Henry died in the night . . . the very night of that very day when King Edward rode in triumph into the city. He died, they said, of displeasure and melancholy." Ankarette raised her eyebrows. "There are some who are asking if people can really die of such maladies."

"He was without a doubt very weak," said Isabel.

"He was weak of mind, my lady, but do people die of that?"

"I suppose," said Isabel, "that if a man is sufficiently afflicted, he can die of anything."

Ankarette shook her head. "They are already whispering . . ."

"Are there not always whispers?"

"To die at such a time, they are saying. He was kept alive, some say, because he was mad and unfit to rule. If he had died before . . . while the prince was alive, that young man would have been ready for the crown . . . a king, some would call him instead of a prince. That would have been dangerous. They are saying that the king had been allowed to live while there was the threat of the prince. But now he is dead, there was no longer any need to keep the king alive."

"You listen to too much gossip, Ankarette," said Isabel.

"It is one way of learning what is going on, my lady."

"One learns a great deal about what people *think* is going on."

"And somewhere in it there might be a grain of truth," insisted Ankarette.

"What will this mean?" I asked.

Isabel said, "There will no longer be a threat from Lancaster. The prince and heir is dead. King Henry is dead. The House of York is next in line. So whatever was thought before, everyone must see now that Edward is the rightful king."

"The House of Lancaster still exists," pointed out Ankarette. "There are the Tudors."

"They descended from Queen Katharine, wife of Henry the Fifth, I believe," I said.

"Through Owen Tudor," said Isabel. "They are bastards."

"Some say there was a marriage," I reminded her.

"Nonsense," she retorted. "The House of York is now firmly on the throne. There is no one to displace them now. I am sorry for poor Henry, but he did not care much for life."

"I wonder what Queen Margaret feels now," I said.

"Oh, you are too kind to her, Anne," said Isabel. "She has caused great trouble. Now that is over. There must be an end to war."

"That is what people are saying," said Ankarette. "But they also say that King Henry was murdered . . . and the people do not like a king to be murdered."

"Well," said Isabel. "He died of displeasure and melancholy. That is what we are told and let us believe it."

"One cannot always believe what one would wish to," I replied.

"Perhaps not. But it is often comfortable if one tries to."

She was right, of course, and poor Henry, I believed, had had no great wish to live in his clouded world. For him it could have been a welcome release, as it was for the House of York and the nation.

His body was exposed at St. Paul's for the people to see and some said there was blood on it, which gave credence to the rumor that he had met a violent death. Afterward they took his body to Blackfriars and there it lay for a while before it was taken by barge to Chertsey and buried in the abbey there.

There was a feeling of relief throughout the nation. The popular King Edward was on the throne, and this was surely an end to the War of the Roses.

The days passed slowly at first and then more rapidly. I was so relieved to be with Isabel and to know that Richard would be coming to see me whenever he was free to do so.

Isabel told me how distressed she had been when George had turned against his brother.

"It was our father who persuaded him," she said. "He adored our father. He looked up to him so much."

I was amazed. Did Isabel not know that George adored only himself and had harbored a grudge because he had not been born the eldest son and above all things he wanted the throne? I suppose our father had promised him that—or hinted at it, more likely. Our father had been too wise a man to have put his trust in Clarence. But Isabel loved him. That surprised me really, although of course he was rather handsome; he had his brother Edward's good looks, but he was not quite as tall, not quite so handsome. It was a case of "not quite" with George. But I supposed he would be considered attractive until he became petulant, bad-tempered, and treacherous, and no doubt love was blind to these faults, which was fortunate for Isabel.

Strangely enough, I think that next to himself he cared most for Isabel. Perhaps he found her devotion to him sweet. However, it was not the disastrous marriage it might have been. I knew that he, as she did, longed for a child, and they mourned the loss of that one who had been born at such an unfortunate time. But for that there would have been a bonny son by now.

I saw Clarence once or twice during that short period. He was extremely affable to me. He told me that the king had granted him the guardianship of my person and he was going to look after me and make sure of a happy future for me.

His words should have been comforting but when he smiled at me I felt a shiver of alarm. I kept remembering that he had been a traitor to his own brother, who had done nothing but good to him and had shown such amazing magnanimity in restoring him to the favor he had enjoyed before his act of blatant treachery. I could never feel safe while he was at Warwick Court.

I did ask Isabel about our father's property.

"He would be called a traitor," I said, "and surely when traitors die their goods pass to the Crown?"

Isabel said, "You and I are the heirs of our father's estate and I am, after all, the Duchess of Clarence."

"And our mother?"

"She, I think, forfeits her share. She is, after all, the wife of a traitor. It is realized that you were forced into your position and are not judged guilty for that reason. I am not sure of these matters. However, this place passed to me and George, of course, and I daresay Middleham as well. I am not sure. It is too complicated for me. But there is nothing for us to worry about as far as our inheritance is concerned."

"But our mother . . ."

"She is in sanctuary still. George thinks it is wise for her to remain there for a while."

"I wish we could see her."

"I am sure we shall one day."

"I should like her to know that we are together."

"I think she does know that."

"Then she will be relieved."

Isabel nodded. "I am sure she will be forgiven soon."

"She must be very sad. She and our father were very fond of each other."

"What a tragedy it all was! Why did the king and our father have to quarrel?"

"I think they both misjudged each other, but it is done now and at least you and I are together."

"Let us be thankful for that. I have been asking George what we should do about arranging a match for you."

I was silent.

She went on, "George thinks you are too young yet. I said, 'But she has already been betrothed and would have been married by now if everything had gone differently.' But George thinks you should wait a while. He says you have been through a terrible ordeal with Margaret and you need rest and care. Later we will think of it."

I was grateful to George and I was thinking of Richard. I wondered whether he was thinking of me.

I could not talk about Richard to Isabel. She would guess my feelings for him because she knew of our friendship in the past, so it was pleasant to be able to speak of him with Ankarette, taking care not to betray the extent of my interest in him.

I said to her one day, "I believe the Duke of Gloucester is often in the company of the king."

"Oh yes, so it is said. Indeed, they do say that Richard of Gloucester be the king's very favorite of all his family. He were mighty fond of his sister, Margaret, that married into Burgundy, which was a very good marriage from all ways you look at it. Think what a help she was to the king when he was in exile."

"The family always stands together. So you think the Duke of Gloucester is his favorite brother."

"That I do. Well, the little duke admires the king and 'tis no hard job to be fond of someone who sets you up like that, I reckon. Duke Richard has stuck by the king through all his trials. The one King Edward can trust most in the whole country is his brother Richard."

That was true, of course. Richard would always be faithful.

I said, "He was with us quite a long time at Middleham. He came to my father's castle to learn what young men have to . . . mostly about going to war."

"Aye, I do know."

"They had a man who was at Agincourt to teach them."

"He must have been getting on in years."

"Yes, but he was more or less a boy when he fought in that great battle, and, as you say, very old when he taught the boys."

"Well, they grow up, don't they? Why, the little duke himself must be nigh on twenty. They'll be finding a wife for him soon, I wouldn't mind wagering."

"Do you think so?"

"You mark my words. Soon someone will come on the scene. You'll see. In the meantime, he's doing what you expect all young men to. There's a little boy, so I've heard."

"A little boy?"

"Yes . . . name of John. John what I don't rightly know he'd be called. There's a girl, too. Katherine, I believe. But the boy's not long arrived."

"I don't understand. What have these children to do with the Duke of Gloucester?"

She looked at me in astonishment. "Why, he be their father, of course. You look really shocked. Why, my Lady Anne, what do you expect of a young man? They say he is good to their mother and makes sure they are well cared for. He's quite fond of them, they say."

"Richard . . . a father!"

"I've heard it's all very respectable . . . well . . . as respectable as such things can be. He's no rake like his brother. He just has his mistress and I've only heard of the one. And now there are little ones. All very natural, of course. I reckon he'd marry her if she were Lady this or that. But what can he do . . . he being the duke and brother to the king? Widow . . . I've heard when she was very young. 'Tis a terrible thing for a woman to be widowed young . . . as I can tell you."

"I see," I said. "These children . . . how old are they?"

"Well, as I've heard . . . can't say more . . . the boy's a bit of a newcomer, not more than a few months. The girl would be older. Two years maybe."

"So it has been going on for a long time."

Ankarette was saying, "He's quite a young man. They say his brother keeps him with him as much as he can."

I was not listening. I was thinking: Richard with a mistress! And all this time I was thinking he was in love with me!

Isabel noticed my preoccupation.

She said, "You have to grow away from the past. You have to be thankful for what you have. We were unlucky enough to be born at this time. There were wars and troubles all through our childhood. We did not hear much about it when we were at Middleham, but there was always conflict of some sort waiting to spring up. Then there was that time at sea when we had nowhere to go and they would not let us land at Calais."

I put my arms about her and we wept together, she for her baby and I for Richard who loved not me but someone else.

I had wondered why he had not come to see me. Now I knew why.

But when we had been together he had talked to me as a lover might. Or had I been mistaken? Had I read into his words what I wanted to read?

This was a bitter blow. I was only realizing now how much he meant to me.

They would, no doubt, find a husband for me sooner or later. What a fool I had been to think of Richard! Just because he had drawn me to him at Middleham, because he had been part of my childhood, one whom I had always looked upon as my special friend . . . and all the time he had been in love with someone else. He was the father of two children.

It was a shock to me when he arrived at Warwick Court. I told myself I could not face him and wondered if I could excuse myself. Could I become suddenly ill? But Isabel would know I was not.

I had to face him. I had to stand beside Isabel and receive him.

He took my hand and kissed it; then he looked eagerly into my face and I could have sworn I saw love there. Images came into my mind of him with this woman . . . this widow who would know of matters that I would not understand. How to please him, how to attract him. I kept thinking of the two children . . . a family.

He wanted to know how I fared. He looked at me anxiously.

"You do not look well, Lady Anne," he said.

"My sister has been somewhat tired of late," said Isabel. "She eats too little and does not take enough interest in what is going on. She broods. I scold her but she takes no notice of me."

"That is a great mistake," said Richard.

"That is what I tell her. What is past is gone."

"One must look at the future," added Richard, smiling at me.

We talked lightly. Richard said he would have come before but the king had to make sure that the country was quiet and only two days after his triumphant entry into London, they had had to be in Kent subduing threats of risings.

"Soon he will have everything under control," he said. "The king grows in stature every day."

"So you think, my lord duke, that all will soon be well?" asked Isabel.

"I am sure of it," he replied. "The people are going to realize how fortunate they are in such a king. Edward is going to be the greatest king England has ever had."

"Does that mean you will be staying in London?" I asked.

"I cannot believe that will be so. Suffice it that we are here now."

I think Isabel guessed that he had come to see me and she left us together.

As soon as we were alone, Richard turned to me.

"Anne," he said. "I have wanted to speak to you for so long. I know you are very young still, but you have had so many experiences. I was heartbroken when I heard of your betrothal to Edward. Thank God that marriage was averted. I do not know what I should have done if it had not been."

"Why?" I said, a little harshly.

"Why? But we have always known . . . have we not? Has there not always been this special love between us?"

"Love?" I said, trying to remain cool.

"Anne, I have always loved you. I thought you cared for me."

I was silent and he said rather pathetically, "Is it because I am small? I am not as straight-backed as I should be. I am lacking . . ."

"I would not have you other than you are," I said. "It is . . ."

I could not go on but he insisted: "Please, Anne, tell me what is wrong."

"I . . . I have heard . . . perhaps it is only gossip. Oh, it must be. I don't think I could bear it if it were not . . ."

"Of what do you speak?"

I said, "Of your mistress . . . of your . . . family."

He looked at me in amazement. "Tell me what you have heard," he said.

My spirits were lifted. I was wrong, of course. It was just stupid cruel gossip. I had been foolish to listen to Ankarette.

"I have heard that you have a mistress and there are two children," I blurted out.

"Do you think that because of that I cannot love *you*?"

"I believe you cannot love two people at the same time."

"Listen to me, Anne. It is true. There are these two children. I was going to tell you of them. They live with their mother whom I have seen from time to time. There will be an end of that now. It was just . . . a friendship."

"With two children?"

"They are pleasant children. You would like them."

"How can you tell me this?"

"Because it is true and I would have no secrets from you."

"And you still see this woman?"

"I shall not do so when you promise to marry me."

"What about her?"

"She has always understood. I shall see that she is well provided for. She will probably marry."

"And your children?"

"They shall be cared for. I hope one day . . ."

"Yes? What do you hope?"

"That you will receive them. Katherine, the little girl, is an enchanting creature. I believe John will be, too, but he is young yet."

I said, "This has been a shock to me."

"I understand and I am sorry."

"I feel bewildered. I had never thought . . ."

"My dear Anne, you have been sheltered from the world. There is nothing extraordinary about this . . . except that I have had only one mistress. Most men have had scores. The king . . ."

"I could not have been in love with you if you had been like the king in that respect."

"I am not like him. All I wanted was to live . . . naturally. I am a man. I have waited so long for you. That is all. I love you as my wife and you only. Anne, I want you to promise that you will marry me."

"I have looked forward to this for so long and now it has come . . ."

"I understand that you are shocked. I should have explained to you myself. How did you hear?"

I did not want to betray Ankarette, so I said, "It was the women talking."

"Gossip," he said.

"But true."

"Please understand. You will understand. It is not unusual for a man to take a mistress when he has so long to wait for his true love."

I put my hand in his. "Richard," I said. "I know one thing and that is that if you go away from me now and we have not plighted our troth, I shall be desperately unhappy."

"If only you will understand."

"I will try to understand. Then I shall be happy. It is hard at first."

He put his arms about me and kissed me tenderly.

"Anne, you are so young. You will grow up . . . with me beside you. It is what I have always wanted. Even in those days at Middleham I loved you . . . I looked for you. I wanted your admiration. I always wanted to do the things that were hard for me, to make you proud of me."

"I am proud of you and I do love you. The past does not count really. We can be together. That is all that matters."

"I shall speak with my brother. I know he will want my happiness and he will give his consent to our marriage now that he knows you want it, too. We have come through our troubles, Anne. We are going to be happy from now on."

"Yes," I said slowly.

"You still look sad. Why? You are not still thinking of . . . ?"

"No. I was thinking of Queen Margaret."

Richard looked puzzled. "Our enemy! Why should you think of her and at this moment?"

"Because I am happy and she is so sad. I am free and she is a prisoner. I was with her so much, I grew to know her . . . admire her in a way. I know she was rash and impulsive and arrogant . . . but she is courageous and I shall never forget her misery when she heard of the death of her son."

"The man who would be king!"

"He had a right, Richard. He was the king's son."

"There are some who doubt Henry was able to beget a son."

"There will always be rumors."

"You must not think of her. She is being taken care of."

"Is she? In some dark dungeon in the Tower?"

"I doubt my brother would be overharsh with her."

"I wish I could see her once more."

"Do you really mean that?"

"I should like to let her know that I cared for her. I think she must be feeling very much alone. She liked me . . . in a way. I think I could bring her a little comfort."

"Do you want that very much?"

"Yes, I do."

"Perhaps it could be arranged. I could ask the king. I think he might grant such a request."

"It would ease my mind a little. I am sure she will be stoical. I think she lost heart for battle when her son died."

"I will see what can be done. And Anne . . . will you promise me that you will forget everything that puts doubts into your mind now that you and I have found each other at last, and all obstacles are being swept away, leaving it clear for us to be together for the rest of our lives?"

"I will," I said.

I felt elated. The past did not matter. He loved me more deeply than he had ever loved another woman.

I was happy, happier than I had ever been before.

A COOKSHOP IN THE CHEPE

I could not keep the news to myself. As soon as I saw Isabel I burst out, "I am going to marry Richard! He has asked me and we have the king's consent."

She embraced me with affection.

"I always knew it," she said. "You were meant for each other. You are both quiet and serious . . . different from George, and me. Is it not strange that we should be sisters and they brothers . . . and so different? Richard was always fond of you and you of him. You could never hide your feelings. Two sisters marrying two brothers. What could be closer than that? We shall be having a wedding soon."

"He was only waiting for my consent and now that I have said I will marry him there should be no delay."

Later that day a messenger came with the news that if I would make myself ready a guard would come to escort me to the Tower where I might see the prisoner, Margaret of Anjou.

Isabel was amazed.

I said, "I told Richard that I was unhappy about the queen and should like to see her, so he has arranged this for me."

"To prove he will do anything for you!"

My spirits were high. I said blithely, "It would seem that that is so."

"He must have asked the king himself. No one else would have dared given permission for you to visit such an enemy."

"She is a poor, tired, lonely, unhappy woman."

"She is a lioness, momentarily caged. Such a woman would be capable of anything. I am indeed surprised that this visit is allowed. As I said, it clearly shows what Richard will do for you."

She kissed me. It was wonderful to see her pleasure in my happiness.

I shall never forget my meeting with Margaret.

She was there in her dark cell—a strongly guarded prisoner, a proud woman in defeat; but somehow she managed to create an aura of majesty.

"They told me I was to have a visitor," she said. "I did not expect it to be you."

She was pleased to see me and I was so glad that I had come. She knew it would not have been easy to get permission.

"I have thought of you so much," I said.

"You, too, have been in my thoughts. Are they treating you well?"

"I am with my sister."

"And your mother?"

"She must remain in sanctuary at Beaulieu."

"So it is only you who has been forgiven."

"It would seem so. I am to marry the Duke of Gloucester."

"The little duke! Ha! My boy was tall and handsome. What we have missed, you and I!"

I said, "I have known the Duke of Gloucester since my childhood. We have always been friends. I am very happy because I am to marry him."

She did not answer. She was staring ahead of her and I wondered whether my coming had reminded her of her son. But I immediately told myself that he would always be in her thoughts.

"I hope they are treating you well," I said.

"They let me know I am their prisoner."

"You would like to return to France?"

She nodded. "My father will be anxious for me. The King of France is my friend. They may do something . . . but does it matter now?"

"Indeed it matters. When you are free from this place you will be yourself again."

"I have lost my son. I have lost everything that meant anything to me. They have murdered my husband."

"They say he died of melancholy."

Her laugh was bitter, without mirth. "What will they say I died of? Frustration? Humiliation?"

"You are not dead, my lady. Spirits such as yours do not die easily."

"Why should I want to live? Tell me that."

"Who can say what the future holds?"

"I have lost everything. I sit here and wonder, could I have changed anything? Could I have acted differently?"

"Wars are terrible. They destroy people and countries. We should all be better without them."

"What is right must be fought for. The tragedy is when evil prevails."

I looked at her sadly. I could see that her downfall had been because she had never been able to see another point of view than her own and she had an innate belief that she must be right. Poor Margaret!

"And you, child," she said. "You were thrust into this melee to serve your father's ends. I know your heart is with York . . . because of this boy . . . this little duke. And now, strangely enough, you are to get your heart's desire. You are young and I am old. But I was your age once. Do you know I was fifteen exactly a month before I married Henry? I came to England. I was beautiful, full of health and good spirits. They cheered me in the streets of London then. The daisy was my emblem. It was displayed everywhere. Henry was so proud of me and I was pleased with him. Oh, how alarming it is for a young girl to be presented to a husband she has never seen! Even the fact that her husband is the king of a great country does not subdue the fear. Henry was so kind, so gentle. I thought I was going to be the luckiest girl in the world."

"I understand," I said.

"The Cardinal Beaufort . . . he was my friend . . . and then there was the Duke of Suffolk who brought me over and who won my confidence from the beginning. I felt I had the kindest of husbands and friends already in my new country. Where did it go wrong?"

I might have hazarded a guess. It went wrong because Henry was weak and had inherited insanity from his grandfather Charles the Mad; it went wrong because she herself attempted to dominate those about her, because she was arrogant, inexperienced and a foreigner; and because the rival House of York was reaching for the throne.

"The people did not like me," she went on. "They hate people to be in command if they are not of their blood. They said Henry could not beget a child and that I was too friendly with Suffolk. They implied that Suffolk was the father of my child. The cruel lies! They would say anything to discredit me. I hated them."

"There was too much hatred," I said.

"Life is cruel. When I was with child I was so happy . . . so certain that everything would be all right. They did not hate Henry as they hated me. He was so benign, so gentle, so patient, but, of course, he loved learning more than power. He wanted to be a scholar. How happy he would have been in a monastery . . . or a church—although many men of the Church seem to be as ambitious as all others. But Henry was doomed from birth. And then, when we might have had a chance . . . the madness overtook him. Do you know he was not aware that he had a son? For months after the birth he was unaware of it."

I said, "I know of this. You have told me. Put it out of your mind. Do not speak of it. Do not brood on it if it makes you unhappy."

"It is engraved on my mind. I could not forget it. I cannot believe that I shall never see my son again. I brought him up to be strong . . ."

I shuddered, thinking of his asking that men should be beheaded, and sitting beside his mother, watching the executions. Poor child! Poor Margaret! She had made him what he was and what that was I was not sure. I only knew that I had glimpsed cruelty in him and the thought of being married to him had terrified me. I could only rejoice at my escape, though my escape meant her torment.

"I shall never forget Hexham," she said, for it was no use my trying to stop her thoughts going to the past, and with me beside her she must speak of those terrifying events in her life. "That was a bitter defeat for us. The enemy were in command of the field. Henry had escaped. He never had a taste for battle and was always eager to get away from it as soon as he could. I was there with my son . . . a little lad then. I knew they would kill him if they caught him. He was only a child, but he represented a threat to them. He was heir to the throne and while he lived there would always be a rival to York. He was more important to them than Henry. Henry would never be a true ruler, but if Henry died the rightful king would be my boy. They would take the first opportunity of killing him. What could we do? We were without men, even without horses. I took the boy's hand and fled with him into the forest."

"Where were you going?"

"I did not know. All I wanted was to put a distance between us and the Yorkist army. So into the forest we went. I told myself we would meet someone who would be loyal to us . . . who would help us. But we had not gone far when we ran into a gang of thieves. They surrounded us. I shall never forget how their eyes glinted when they saw the jewels on our clothes. They proceeded to rob us. We had stepped from one danger to another."

I reached out and took her hand. "Please do not speak of it. It distresses you."

She smiled sadly. "It is over. I have suffered far worse than that encounter. I would rather be in that forest surrounded by robbers than here in this doleful prison. We had good fortune there, for while the robbers were quarreling among themselves over our jewels, I saw the opportunity to escape. I took Edward's hand and we plunged into the forest. The trees were thick and close together and we were soon out of their view."

"You will escape from this place," I said. "I know it. Your spirit is too strong to be suppressed. Was it not always so?"

"But now I am old I have no one to care for."

"You have your home . . . your father. You love him. You would rejoice to see him again."

She nodded. "Yes . . . yes, that is true. And in the forest there was some good luck: We had not gone far when we came face to face with another robber. He was different from the others—a tall man of rather noble countenance and somewhat courtly manners. He was an outlaw. I presented my son to him. I said, 'This is the son of your king. Save him.' I had taken a chance, and

it was strange, for a change came over his countenance. He was
touched, perhaps by my pleading, perhaps by Edward's beauty
and dignity. He said, 'Follow me,' and he took us to a hut that he
inhabited with his wife. They fed us and led us to safety."

"Who was he?"

"A Lancastrian gentleman who had lost his home and fortune
in the wars and taken to the life of an outlaw in the forest."

"It is an inspiring story," I said. "I am glad you told me. Does
it not put new hope into you?"

"You comfort me," she said. "Tell me. Why do they let you
come to see a dangerous prisoner such as I?"

"Perhaps they do not think you are dangerous."

"As long as I live they will regard me as such."

"I think the Duke of Gloucester pleaded with his brother the
king, because he knew how much I wanted to see you."

"I shall remember that," she said. "It will help me through the
days of darkness."

"Then I am doubly glad I came."

Still gripping my hand, she said, "Life is strange. Here are
you, the daughter of the man whom for so long I regarded as my
greatest enemy, and out of your compassion you are the only one
who comes to cheer me."

"You were friendly with my father at one time."

"That was not friendship. For him it was vengeance on the
man he had set up and who had defied him. He used me for that
purpose. As for myself, I knew this. I merely wanted to use his
revenge for my purpose. That is not friendship."

"How I wish it had never been."

"The tragedy is that that is the wish of most of us at some time in our lives."

"I must go," I said. "My visit was to be only brief."

"I shall never forget that you came."

She took me into her arms. "The pity of it," she said. "You and I have known true friendship. In spite of ourselves, love sprang between us."

"I shall pray for you," I told her.

"And I for you. All happiness to you, my child . . . who should have been my daughter."

"I always loved Richard of Gloucester," I said.

She smiled at me sadly and the guard came to take me away.

When I returned to Warwick Court, Isabel was waiting for me. She listened, not very attentively, to my account of my visit to the Tower and then suddenly burst out: "George is displeased!"

I looked at her in astonishment. "Why?" I asked.

"It is really about you and Richard. He does not think it is right."

"I do not understand."

"He says you are too young and inexperienced for marriage."

"What does he mean? Most people of my age would be married by now. I should have been married already if Edward had lived."

"George is against it, Anne."

"It is not his affair."

"It is, because the king made him your guardian. I believe you cannot marry without his consent."

"This is nonsense. Richard had actually talked of our marriage with the king who has given his consent."

"George insists that the king has made him your guardian and your betrothal therefore is his responsibility."

"It is all a misunderstanding, I am sure."

"George is truly angry."

"If George is displeased by the match I am sorry, but that is not going to stop Richard and me doing what we want to."

"I think it could, Anne."

"I never heard anything like this."

"George says that Richard only wants to marry you because you are an heiress."

"I am sure Richard thought of no such thing."

"Don't be simple, Anne. Of course he thought of it. You know our father was the richest man in England. Our mother has a great deal, too. You and I have a large inheritance."

"I thought our father's estates would be confiscated, for according to the king, he died a traitor."

"I do not know about that. Many of his estates were brought to him by our mother and George says that because I am his wife they now belong to him and me."

"Shouldn't they belong to our mother?"

"We are not sure whether she is judged a traitor or not. She is really under restraint and cannot leave Beaulieu, so she is in a way a prisoner. I had not thought of these things, but George knows, of course."

"Is that why George married you?"

She flushed hotly. "George and I were in love when we were at Middleham."

"So were Richard and I!"

"Well, George is against it. He is going to the king to protest."

"Richard will also go to the king, I am sure."

"Then it will depend on which one wins with the king."

"It will be Richard, of course."

"Why?"

"Need you ask? Not so long ago, George was fighting with our father against the king. He wanted the throne for himself, and he married you because you were our father's daughter . . . a great heiress. All that time Richard was faithful to his brother, the king. So I am sure that he will choose to be on Richard's side in a conflict like this."

"I do not believe that. He gave his word to George that he was to be your guardian."

"The guardian of my fortune, do you mean?"

I thought Isabel was going to strike me.

She turned and walked deliberately away.

Later George made a point of seeing me. He was suave and his anger had evidently calmed a little: I just saw a gleam in his eyes that betrayed it.

"My dear Anne," he said. "I wanted a word with you. I believe Isabel has spoken to you?"

"She told me that you do not approve of my proposed marriage."

"The king has appointed me as your guardian, and your happiness is a matter of concern to me."

"It would not seem so my lord, for my happiness lies with Richard."

He smiled at me with a show of patient indulgence.

"My dear little Anne, you are young. You know nothing of the world. Why, but a short time ago you were betrothed to Henry's son."

"I was considered to be old enough by my father."

"A marriage of expediency that would have been."

"It would seem that many marriages are, and if one can make one for love, how fortunate that is!"

"Romantic dreams are very pleasant, but they are often out of touch with reality. Do you think your marriage to my brother would be one of love on his side?"

"I know it. You forget, Richard and I know each other well. We were together at Middleham."

"Do you know what Richard wants?"

"He wants to marry me, for he has told me this."

"He wants to marry your fortune, child."

"As you did Isabel's? No. Richard does not want that."

"You speak foolishly. I married Isabel because I loved her as she did me."

"Then, as you were not greatly concerned about her fortune, you will understand our feelings . . . Richard's and mine."

"I was never concerned about such matters, but I cannot say the same for my brother."

"You are indifferent then to money . . . to power? You lack his ambition?"

He knew it was a reference to his traitorous act when he had believed he had a chance of gaining the crown.

"I am as ambitious as most men, but I know what is more important."

He was lying, and he was aware that I knew it. I guessed that soon his anger would break out.

"I should tell you," I said firmly, "that I intend to marry Richard."

"Remember that I am your guardian and I am determined that you shall not be forced into marriage with the first fortune hunter who comes along."

"You speak of Richard thus?"

"Richard wants your fortune, and therefore he can be so termed. But I shall protect you from him . . . and from yourself. It is my duty."

I said, "I believe Richard will not submit to *your* wishes."

"I repeat: he seeks marriage with you because of your fortune. The Earl of Warwick's estates are large. He wants a share. It is as simple as that. He would marry you and then make sport with his mistress. Did you know he had a son not very long ago?"

He was watching me closely, expecting to see the horror on my face.

I said coolly, "I did know of this. Richard told me."

"And you said, 'Very well, fair sir, I am content. Marry me and

enjoy your mistress to your heart's content!' Is the title of the
Duchess of Gloucester worth such humiliation, Anne?"

"I believe you yourself, my lord, were not entirely chaste
before your marriage. Most young men are not. Marriage is
sacred according to Holy Church. When we are married Richard
and I will be faithful to each other."

"When he had his hands on your fortune, you would see."

I understood perfectly. Isabel and I were joint heiresses. If I
married we should have to share. He did not want that. He
wanted me to remain unmarried. Then the whole would be
Isabel's . . . which meant his.

He sat there smiling, watching me. But it was an evil smile.

I was trembling a little, and I was afraid he would notice.

I stood up as firmly as I could. "I will leave you now," I said.
"And I assure you that both Richard and I intend to marry each
other."

He gave me a look of assumed sadness and said, "I am your
guardian. I must do all I can to protect you."

I turned and left him.

Ankarette talked to me when I was retiring for the night.

"The Duke of Gloucester came to Warwick Court today," she
said. "But the guards would not permit him to enter."

"What?" I cried. "How could that be?"

Ankarette paused, the gown that she was about to hang up
still in her hands. "There is a quarrel between him and the Duke
of Clarence. The guards were uneasy. I should think so! They will

have offended the Duke of Gloucester mightily. To call on his brother and be refused admittance!"

"What . . . is this quarrel?"

She lifted her shoulders. "They say the king is involved . . . and he does not know which one to favor. The king loves his brothers well and when they are fighting together over some matters he wants to please them both."

I did not say any more. Clearly Ankarette did not know the cause of their quarrel, but I did.

I was afraid. I woke in the night, trembling. I had been haunted by vague nightmares. Clarence was in those hideous fantasies . . . smiling . . . but the smiles were a mask. I knew that evil lurked behind them. And I was in his power. He was my brother-in-law. It was he who had command over me. Richard was trying to rescue me. There was conflict between the two brothers, and the king stood between them. He could save me, but where his family was concerned he was weak. He wanted to please both his brothers. He wanted to give me to Richard and at the same time please Clarence by preventing the marriage.

It was not surprising that I was afraid.

I had always been wary of Clarence. I had never understood Isabel's infatuation with him. I always thought that in the first place she had wanted a husband and an ideal choice seemed the powerful brother of the king who would have been in line for the throne if Edward did not have a son; he had been a very acceptable *parti;* and it had gone on from there. Indeed I believe he cared for her. I should have thought him incapable of real affection, but there are many facets to people's characters and I suppose a man could love one sister and be ready to destroy the happiness of the other.

I lay shivering in my bed. He was determined not to share my father's fortune. To what lengths would he go to keep it to himself?

I thought I had escaped from all my troubles. I had contemplated a happy life with Richard—but I could see that I should have to fight my way to it.

But Richard was close by. He would help me. He had tried to see me and had been held off by his brother's guards. He would not allow that to pass. He would come again, possibly with his own guards.

Meanwhile I tried to fight off these alarming thoughts and, as the night closed in on me, I lay listening for footsteps outside my chamber. I did not know what action he would take but I was fearful.

People died of strange maladies that were never explained. King Henry had died of melancholy, they said. There could be many causes, I supposed, for sudden and convenient deaths.

When daylight came, my spirits revived a little.

Richard was not far off, I kept telling myself. He would save me.

It was during the morning. I could not bear to be within those walls and went into the courtyard and sat on a wooden seat there. I did not want to talk to Isabel. I could find no comfort from her. She would support her husband; she would say I was young and inexperienced, that George was my guardian and he had my good at heart.

I gazed at the cobbles, thinking of Richard's coming to Warwick Court and being barred by the guards. I could imagine his anger. He would not let it rest there. He would come again. I knew it.

A serving maid slipped unobtrusively into the courtyard. I had not seen her before. There were so many serving maids at Warwick Court that I could not be familiar with them all.

She came and stood before me, looking cautiously about her, and said in a low voice, "My lady, I must speak to you. I have a message from . . . the Duke of Gloucester."

My heart began to beat very fast. "Give it to me," I said.

"I have to speak to you, my lady. I dare not here. People may be watching. Could I perhaps . . . come to your chamber?"

"Yes . . . yes. Come now."

"My lady . . . if you will go to your chamber, I will come to you when I can. I will bring you something . . . I can say you sent for it . . . if I am asked."

"I will go to my chamber now."

"Please, my lady . . . sit a while . . . then go. I will join you as soon as I am able. It is important to take care."

She bobbed a curtsy and walked away.

I forced myself to sit for a few more moments, then I walked around the courtyard and after that went up to my chamber. I did not have to wait long, which was fortunate, for my impatience was unendurable.

She came in almost furtively.

"My lady," she said. "I have this message from the Duke of Gloucester."

"How did it come to you?"

"I have a friend who is in the duke's service at Crosby's Place."

I nodded. I knew Richard was often at Crosby's Place when he was in London.

"Yes, yes," I said. "Give me the message."

"It is not written. I have to tell you."

"Then do so . . . please . . . quickly."

"The duke has tried to see you and been refused admittance."

"I know this to be."

"There is a quarrel between the brothers and the king wishes to please them both. The duke, my lady, wants you to go to him."

"Where?"

"That is what I have to tell you. If you will be ready to leave after the household has retired for the night, a carriage will be waiting to take you into sanctuary. There the duke will be waiting for you. I will conduct you to the carriage when you are ready. The duke is very anxious to get you out of Warwick Court. There must not be battle between the two brothers. If there were the king could come down on any side. The Duke of Clarence now has you in his possession. The Duke of Gloucester would have you in his."

"I shall be ready," I said.

"Oh . . . er . . . my lady, if aught should go wrong . . . I beg of you not to mention my part in this."

"I promise. I would not."

"It would be the end of Jack and of me . . . if my lord of Clarence . . ."

"I understand. I would never betray you for helping me."

"There will be feasting in the great hall tonight, as the duke is here. As soon as you can retire to your room, do so, and be ready. I will come to your door. Come out at once and follow me. I will take you to the carriage and there leave you. You will go straight to sanctuary and tomorrow the Duke of Gloucester will come to you."

"Thank you a thousand times. I shall never forget what you have done for me."

She kissed my hand and left me.

I do not know how I managed to suppress my excitement during that day.

I was with Isabel in the afternoon. We sat over our needlework as we often did. I must have seemed preoccupied, but that was not unnatural.

Isabel did say, "Anne, I think you are beginning to realize that George is right."

I nodded and hung my head.

"He is, when all is said, only trying to do what is best for you. He has your welfare at heart."

Still I did not answer. I was amazed at my duplicity, but I did have to keep reminding myself that I must not betray by the slightest word or gesture that I was contemplating flight.

There was a great deal of revelry in the hall that night, as was the custom when the Duke of Clarence was present. The long tables were filled with retainers—and there were all the squires and pages who were considered necessary to the comfort of the diners.

The minstrels were playing in the gallery as the scullions and serving men and women hurried back and forth to the kitchens.

The duke was seated at the center of the table on the dais and Isabel was on his right hand, I on his left.

He was very merry and I noticed that now and then he put out a hand to caress Isabel. She was smiling and happy. My heart was pounding. I longed to be free to go to my chamber and be conducted to the waiting carriage.

Clarence was particularly affable to me. I think Isabel must have told him that I had come to my senses and that I understood I should be wise to obey my guardian and be a docile ward in the future.

He was drinking heavily, I noticed, but he frequently did. He called for a song. It was about love and he listened with a sentimental gleam in his eyes.

He patted my hand. "Anne," he said. "My dear little sister. I am going to see that all is well for you. Your welfare is one of my greatest concerns. You know that, do you not?"

He put his face close to mine and I said, "I know that you think of my future, my lord."

"You are my dear wife's sister, and everything concerning her is dear to my heart. Come. Drink with me . . . to our happy future. Wine . . . wine . . . good Malmsey wine for the Lady Anne."

One of the men filled my goblet.

"To the future," said Clarence. "Our friendship, Anne, yours and mine. It is as steady as a rock and always will be. Come, you are not drinking. I want to see the contents of that goblet go down. Otherwise I shall think you are not sincere with me."

I forced myself to drink.

"There. Now we are friends. Did you see that, Isabel? Anne and I understand each other. So no more anxiety, my dear, on our account."

"Anne knows that you are concerned for her good," said Isabel, "do you not, Anne?"

"I know that my lord duke is concerned for my future," I said ambiguously.

"Well," said Clarence, "let us have another song. Tell those minstrels. This time a merry roundalay."

So they sang and some danced and it seemed a long time before I could escape to my chamber.

Once I was there, I put on a cloak and waited, but not for long. There was a gentle rap on the door.

"Are you ready, my lady?" She spoke in a whisper. "Bring nothing. Those are my lord's orders."

"I am ready."

"Then come."

I followed her down the spiral staircase. Quietly we went. I was praying that we should meet no one on the way.

We were fortunate and reached the courtyard unseen. We sped across it . . . out through the gate . . . and there was the carriage waiting.

She opened the door and I stepped in.

"God's speed, my lady," she said, and ran back through the courtyard. And I was jolting along, away from captivity . . . away from the Duke of Clarence.

A drowsiness began to creep over me. I could scarcely keep my eyes open. So listless did I feel that I did not even begin to wonder why, when at a time like this I should expect to be particularly alert.

The carriage had stopped. The driver descended and looked in.

"Are you comfortable, my lady?" he asked.

"Yes. Have we arrived?"

"Not yet. We've a little way to go."

"Where are we going?"

"Can't say. Waiting for instructions. All's well. Take a little nap. You'll soon be there . . . where they will be waiting to welcome you.

I closed my eyes. It was so easy to slip into sleep.

I awoke suddenly. I could not remember for the moment what had happened. Then my mind cleared. I was in the carriage going to the sanctuary where I should meet Richard.

I sat up. I was not in the carriage. I was in a small room . . . an attic room. There were rushes on the floor and I was lying on a pallet. There was an unusual smell. Later I recognized it as rancid grease and other unpleasant ingredients.

I put my hand to my throat and touched the coarse material of my gown. But when I had left I had been wearing a velvet dress and cloak. I was supposed to be meeting Richard. I must be dreaming. I tried to shake off the dream but it was becoming like a nightmare.

The unfamiliar room . . . the unfamiliar dress . . . I could hear the sound of voices below . . . shouting, raucous voices . . . and horses' hoofs. I was in a street.

I called out, "Who's there? Where am I?"

A woman who had been sitting in the shadows stood up and came over to me.

"You all right, Nan?" she asked.

"Nan?" I asked.

"You had one of your turns."

"I'm not Nan."

"No," she said. "Not that again. We're getting tired of your fancies, Nan. Let's stop it, eh?"

"I cannot understand what you are talking about. What am I doing here? I was in the carriage going to sanctuary."

She laughed.

"Anything to get away from the pots and pans, I see. And don't give yourself such airs. Talk proper like the rest of us. We've just about had enough of you showing off, just because you was once a lady's maid to some grand lady . . . and ever since you've been aping her. We don't swallow that, Nan. We never did. You're just Nan. Now get up and down to that kitchen. If you're quick, you might be in time for a crust of bread and a sup of ale."

A terrible fear was creeping over me. I said, "Do you know that I'm the Lady Anne Neville?"

"Yes," she said. "And I'm His Grace of Canterbury. Come on, up with you."

I rose unsteadily to my feet. I noticed that one side of the room sloped down to the floor.

I said, "Please tell me what has happened. I left Warwick Court in the carriage. What happened? I must have gone to sleep."

"Asleep and dreaming, that's what you've been doing . . .

when you ought to have been washing them pans. There's work to be done in the kitchen, my girl. The place don't run itself."

"Oh, God help me," I prayed. "I am going mad."

I was given a push that sent me reeling against the wall. I turned to the woman appealingly. "Will you please tell me what this means? Who brought me here? Where are my clothes? Will you tell me where I am?"

"You're out off your mind, Nan, that's what you are. You know where you are and where you've been this last month. Sometimes I think you're truly addle-pated. We don't believe your stories about you being this and that great lady. Stop it, Nan, or people 'ull say you're really off your head. You won't know the difference twixt what is and what ain't."

She pushed me toward the door. It opened onto a flight of stairs and, seizing my arm, she made me descend them with her.

We went along a dark corridor and another door was opened. I was dazzled by the light that came from a window through which I glimpsed a yard containing several tall bins.

I blinked and saw that I was in a kitchen. A man was standing against a bench. His shirt was open at the front, disclosing a hairy chest, and there was a black fuzz of hair on his arms. He was tall, commanding-looking and he surveyed me with some interest.

"Oversleeping again," said the woman.

"I demand to know where I am and who brought me here," I cried.

There were two girls, one plump with a saucy, laughing face, the other small, pale and insignificant.

The saucy one pranced into the center of the room and said,

"I demand to know where I am and who brought me here," in an attempt to imitate my voice.

"Who are you today, sweeting?" said the man.

"What do you mean?"

"Lady Muck or Madam Slosh?" asked the saucy one.

I was staring at them aghast. I had been the victim of a conspiracy. It was becoming obvious to me that there had been some diabolic plot and these people were involved in it.

I said, "I am the Lady Anne Neville. I left Warwick Court, as I thought, for sanctuary. Will you take me there immediately?"

The tall man bowed. "My lady, your carriage awaits," he said.

"Where is it?" I asked, and they burst into laughter.

"Here," said the saucy girl. "We've had enough of this. Don't stand there. Will your ladyship get on with washing them pans? They'll be wanted for the midday trade."

I had never washed pans. I did not know how to begin. The thin girl was at my side. She said, " 'Ere, I'll give you a 'and."

I heard someone say, "She is going to faint or something."

I was pushed into a chair. The kitchen was swimming around me. Thoughts chased each other through my mind. The girl who had told me that she had a message from Richard . . . the attentions of Clarence as he had sat beside me . . . his favorite Malmsey wine, which he had insisted on my drinking. Yes, it was a plot . . . a dastardly plot. It had nothing to do with Richard.

There had been something in the wine to make me drowsy, to dull my senses; the driver of the carriage had waited until it had had its effect so that I should not know where I was being taken.

And they had brought me here to this dreadful place. Richard would not know where I was.

As the horror of my situation dawned upon me, I felt numb with terror. All these dreadful people around me were involved. They were trying to tell me I was not myself, that I belonged here. I was someone called Nan.

I felt my whole life slipping away from me. I was a prisoner in this frightening place. I was caught, trapped in a conspiracy devised by the Duke of Clarence.

Even now when I look back at that time, I find it hard to believe it ever happened to me. It was so wildly melodramatic and there were times during that terrible period when I found it difficult to cling to sanity, and they almost convinced me that I was mad.

I would whisper to myself: I am Lady Anne Neville. I am the daughter of the Earl of Warwick. I am betrothed to Richard, Duke of Gloucester. These people are liars, all of them. They are playing parts that have been written for them as in a play. Why? And who is the playwright?

I knew, of course. It was Clarence. He was my enemy, our enemy: mine and Richard's. He was going to prevent our marriage at all costs. That was why he had put me here. To be rid of me? But why send me here? Why could he not simply have killed me? Because he dared not? Richard was my protector. Clarence was the king's brother—but so was Richard.

What if Clarence ordered these people to kill me? They could bury my body somewhere here, or throw it into the river, and no one would hear of me again.

I was in a state of numbness for two days; after that, growing a little accustomed to my dismal background, my mind roused itself from its hopeless lethargy and I began to consider what I might do.

I was forced to work by threats of physical violence from the woman whom I had first seen when I had awakened in these sordid surroundings. I had to try to play the part assigned to me—that of kitchen maid.

I discovered that I was in a cookshop that sold meat pies. I was carefully watched and never allowed out of the kitchen when the shop was open. The two girls served the customers.

I had to watch the meat on the spits and wash the pots and pans. I was no good at it. I would be forced to stand at a tub with hands thrust in greasy water up to my elbows, scouring the utensils used for cooking. The big woman would call to me to fetch this and that, and as I did not know what she was talking about in those first days I was clumsy and inadequate. I was constantly being called a dolt, a fool. Addle-pate was the favorite epithet; and even if I had realized what was expected of me, it was difficult to understand their speech, which was very different from that to which I was accustomed.

I began to know something of these people. The man spent his time between the kitchen and the shop. His name was Tom. He, with his wife Meg, were the owners of the shop. She was the woman whom I had first seen on awakening. Then there were the two girls—Gilly, the bold one, and Jane, the other.

I was aware that all of them watched me with a certain furtiveness, which raised my spirits a little. I felt it implied that they all knew I was not this Nan and had been brought here against my will, and that they had been instructed to obey the orders they had received. They had to pretend that I had been with them for some time and that I was addle-pated Nan who dreamed of grandeur because I had once been a lady's maid to a rich woman.

At first I had insisted that I was Lady Anne Neville and that a message should be sent to the Duke of Gloucester telling him where I was.

They had jeered at that.

"The Duke of Gloucester? Did you hear that?"

"Aye, I heard. 'Tis a wonder she stoops so low. Why not to her friend, the king?"

I said, "Yes . . . yes. Send to the king. Tell the king. Then you will see."

"Perhaps he'll send his crown for you to wear," suggested Gilly.

That was not the way. I must find out what this meant. I must delude them. I must be quiet and watchful. I must try to find a way of getting out of this place.

The two girls, Gilly and Jane, slept in a room similar to mine. I slept alone, which was significant, and every night my door was locked, I knew, because I had thought to steal out of the place when they were asleep. I could only be locked in at night because they wanted to prevent my escape. I guessed they dared not let me escape.

In those first days I had eaten little. I could not bear the food that was offered. I was not prepared to eat with them. Their manners sickened me.

Two days and nights had passed. How had I endured it? Whichever way I turned, I met with the same treatment. They were all insisting that I was Nan, the half-mad serving girl suffering delusions that I was a fine lady.

At the end of those two days I was in such deep distress that I had to do something. Despair sharpened my wits. I had to pretend to accept this . . . for only then might they drop their guard a little, only then might I discover what their intentions were, only then might I find a way to escape.

I had detected a hint of kindliness in Jane. She was rather inclined to be put upon—more so than Gilly, who could stand up for herself.

Jane and I often did the menial tasks together. I watched her when she helped with the pots and pans. She would show me where to find those implements that I had to take to Tom or Meg.

I said to her one day when we were alone in the kitchen, "Where are we? Where is this place?"

"It's in the Chepe," she said.

I had heard of the Chepe. It was a street in London.

"Who comes here to buy the pies?"

"All sorts."

"Why am I not allowed in the shop?"

"Dunno."

"You are."

"Sometimes."

"You see people then?"

She nodded.

"How long have you been here?"

"Since Lammas last."

"You had never seen me before that day Meg brought me down to the kitchen and I fainted, had you?"

She did not answer and turned away.

I must be careful. I must not alarm her, for alarmed she undoubtedly was when I tried to extract information from her. She knew, as they all did, that I was not Nan who had been working with them for some time and who suffered from delusions.

"Does anyone else work here?" I asked at another time.

"Only us."

"Do any of the people from the court ever come here?"

"I dunno."

"People from Crosby's Place . . . the serving men and women there? There must be hundreds of them."

"I dunno."

"People from Warwick Court?"

She shrugged her shoulders.

I thought, some might come here. I knew that when my father had been in Warwick Court his men were all over London. I had heard it said that the emblem of the Ragged Staff was seen in taverns all over the city. And if the taverns, why not the cookshops?

They were watchful of me, very wary. I think the quietness that had come over me made them wonder. I had ceased to insist that I was Lady Anne Neville. To them it could seem now and then that I had accepted my role of addle-pated Nan, but they were a little suspicious still.

Tom alarmed me. I would be aware of his eyes on me as I worked in the kitchen. Sometimes he would shout at me, declare that I was a fool, an idiot. At others he would say, "That's good. Coming on, eh?" and he would touch my shoulder. I recoiled when he did that. I could not bear him to be near me. Both Meg and Gilly watched him closely, I noticed.

Whenever I found myself alone with Jane I tried to talk to her. I said to her one day, "Meg seems very anxious to please Tom."

Jane looked at me in astonishment.

"They are very happily married, are they?" I went on.

She reverted to her usual reply. "Dunno."

"Do you think she is a little jealous?"

This was dangerous talk. Jane looked furtive. Then a rather sly smile curved her lips. She said, "Master . . . he be terrible fond of women."

The weather was hot. The smells of the kitchen permeated the entire place and they nauseated me. I wondered how much longer I could endure this. I tried to tell myself that something must happen soon. Richard would discover I was not at Warwick Court. He would want to know where I was. He would search for me.

I noticed that Tom's eyes strayed toward me often. I thought he was going to find fault with me, but he did not. He asked me to bring one of the pans to him and when I did so, his hand touched mine. I hurried away as quickly as I could. I kept thinking of Jane's words: "Master . . . he be terrible fond of women." Poor thin, dirty, dishevelled creature that I must appear to be, I was yet a woman and I trembled.

That night I lay in bed telling myself that I must get away. I must run into the shop, tell someone who I was. I must endeavor to get into the streets. I would run and run. I must find someone who could guide me to Crosby's Place.

I dozed fitfully, for I was always exhausted at the end of the day. I ate scarcely anything. I was growing thinner. It was only my firm belief that this could not last forever that gave me the strength to go on.

I awoke startled. It was as though I had had a premonition of hovering evil. I sat up. I could hear the hammering of my heart.

Then the key was turning in the lock. The door opened quietly and I saw the tall figure of Tom, his eyes glittering, his mouth slightly open, showing his yellow teeth. He was coming toward me, leering, and I could not fail to be aware of his intentions.

With all the strength that I could muster I leaped up. I shrieked loudly. As he came forward, horror and disgust gave me some impetus and I managed to slip past him. He reached out to take hold of me but I evaded him. I was on the stairs that led down to the kitchen. I screamed as he came after me.

Blindly I ran. He was close behind me. I heard him cursing me under his breath.

I was shouting, "Go away. How dare you! Leave me alone! Do you know who I am? If you dare touch me!"

I felt sick with fear and horror. I reached the kitchen, I was pulling at the door that led to the shop. My one idea was to try to get out of this place.

And then I was aware of Meg.

She was standing, her arms akimbo, her eyes blazing. I ran toward her. "Save me," I cried. "Don't let him . . ."

She seized me and pushed me behind her.

She started to shout, "You fool! You goat! You'll be having us all on the gallows. You mad or something! And all because you can't see a girl without you've got to be at her. What do you think they'd do to you if they found out, eh? It wouldn't be a nice cozy rope for you . . . and all of us in it with you. Did you fancy the lady, eh, you idiot?"

I was cowering against the wall. Meg was magnificent in her rage. I was amazed by the effect she had on him. He was staring at her with fear in his eyes. She had changed him from a man determined to satisfy his lust to a cringing object of fear. Her words had struck home. They knew who I was. They had been paid to keep me prisoner, to make me believe that I was a deluded kitchen maid. And for the first time since I had entered this place they had betrayed that. They could not have been more explicit. No longer could they tell me I was demented Nan, the fanciful dreamer. I was myself, the one I knew myself to be. Further attempts at subterfuge would be useless.

Meg said, "Get back to your room, Nan. You're safe enough from this idiot. I'll see to that. And I'll see to you, too, me lad, before you get us all into trouble that'll be the end of us."

She pushed me toward the door.

I said, "You had better let me go before it is too late. If you let me go now I will do all I can to save you from the consequences of your actions."

"Shut your mouth," she said.

She pushed me before her and we mounted the stairs. Another push sent me into the attic. The keys were still on the outside of the door.

"You'll have no more visits tonight . . . nor any other," she said.

She locked me in and I heard her go down the stairs.

I leaned against the attic wall, feeling dizzy but in a way triumphant.

I had had a miraculous escape from a fate that would have been intolerable to me. I felt sick when I remembered that loathsome, panting, lecherous creature and what he was contemplating doing. Meg had saved me. I was grateful to her. But she had done more than that. She had wiped away any vague doubt that might have been springing up in my mind. I was myself; I was sane, and I must get away.

They would realize of course that they had betrayed themselves this night, and that Meg was afraid of what danger they might be in. This would certainly be brought home to Meg when she recovered a little from the rage against her husband.

So, horrified as I was by the incident, I knew I should rejoice in it. Meg would be watchful over her husband's attitude toward me in the future and that was the best safeguard against him that I could have.

Sleep was impossible. I lay on my pallet and tried to make plans for escape.

Two more days passed. Tom did not look at me. He was clearly ashamed to have been humiliated and defeated by his wife . . . before my eyes.

Meg avoided me, too. I was glad of that. Her attitude had changed toward me. She was less abusive. I tried to talk to Jane about the streets outside. I said I wished I could go out with her when she went out.

She was silent.

"Could you take me with you?"

She shook her head.

"Jane," I persisted. "Had you ever seen me before that night when I came?"

She was silent.

"Tell the truth, Jane," I pleaded. "You were told I was mad Nan and you must pretend I worked here with you but I thought I was someone else. That's right, is it not, Jane?"

She shook her head. "You're Nan," she said, as though repeating a lesson. "You worked in a grand house once and thought you was the lady there . . . Lady Anne something. You wasn't right in the 'ead."

"Jane, you know the truth."

"Don't you get at me."

"Jane, if when you go into the streets, you could tell someone . . ."

She moved away from me. I could see that she was frightened. I wondered about Gilly. She was brighter than Jane. Suppose I tried to bribe Gilly to get me out somehow? How far could I go with her? I felt those two girls were my only hope. Clarence . . . and it must have been Clarence . . . would have made the contract with the cookshop owners to keep me a prisoner. I could expect no help from them.

Then it happened. Lust was Tom's downfall, as I supposed it had been of many before him.

After that terrible night, I had become aware of things that had escaped me before. I had seen Tom with Gilly and I guessed that there was some relationship between them. Danger of discovery by Meg would no doubt add an excitement for the guilty pair.

Gilly was a lusty girl and I imagined there would not have been a shortage of lovers in her life, and, like Tom, she would not be the sort to deny herself. For two such people to find themselves in close proximity must have inevitable consequences.

It was the opportunity that I had been waiting for.

It happened in the afternoon, which was a slack time for business. Jane was in the shop in case any customers came in, which was rare between the hours of three and five o'clock. I was in the kitchen, finishing the pans, when suddenly there was a commotion.

Through the window I saw Gilly running into the yard. Her blouse was half off her shoulders. Tom was with her, red-faced and dishevelled, his shirt open—and behind them, the avenging Meg.

Jane came into the kitchen. She was giggling. "Caught," she whispered. "And no wonder—the way they was carrying on. Anytime . . . anywhere . . ."

Meg was angry. She was shouting. "You find your own men, you slut. Get out of this place. I've a mind to send you both off. As for you . . . you rake . . . you can't leave 'em alone, can you? Can't have her ladyship, so you'll take the slut."

Gilly approached Meg. They were both big women.

Gilly's hands shot up and caught Meg by the hair. Meg kicked out and in a moment they were both rolling on the ground, fighting each other.

I had never seen two women fighting before. It was a shocking sight. Tom stood by, looking bewildered and ineffectual. And Jane and I remained at the window, looking out on the scene.

I do not know who was the victor. They seemed to come to a sudden decision. They both stood up and glared at each other. There was blood on both of their faces; their hair hung loose about their shoulders and they looked sub-human.

Then I heard Meg's voice, strident and authoritative: "There's no place for you here. You get out, and sharp. This is my shop." She turned to Tom. "And I'd have you remember that, too. I want you out of this place, Miss. I'll not have your sort here and it's out, I say."

I could see the dismay in Gilly's face. It was one thing to fight with Meg in the backyard, but another to be out on the streets. For all her bravado, Gilly depended on her place in the cookshop.

She turned to Tom. "You going to stand for that?"

He did not answer. I saw the power now of Meg. It was her cookshop, and she was not going to let anyone forget it. I wondered briefly how two such women could have fought over Tom. Had I been Meg I should have been glad to turn him out, along with Gilly.

But evidently she did not feel the same. Tom was hers and she was going to keep him, even though it did mean fighting a constant battle against his straying desires.

Gilly hurled a stream of abuse at Meg first, then at Tom.

Then she came inside and left Tom and Meg in the yard. She went up to the room she shared with Jane and, as I heard her heavy footsteps on the stairs, an idea came to me.

I ran up the stairs after her and went into her room. She was sitting on her pallet, glaring before her.

"What do *you* want?" she demanded.

"To talk to you."

"Get out."

"No," I said. "I won't. Where will you go?"

"None of your business."

"Yes it is. You have nowhere to go. Your face is cut. Can I help you?"

"I said get out."

"I know how you could do well. You could have a cookshop of your own . . . if you did what I said."

"Addle-pate," she said, but a little more gently.

"Why should you stay here and work for them . . . even if you could? Why should you be on such terms with a man like that? You could have a shop like this one and choose your own husband."

"Get away with you."

"Be sensible . . . before it is too late."

She wavered. "How?" she said.

"You know I am not Nan, do you not? You know I was brought here one night and you were told to play your parts . . . to pretend that I was the simple kitchen maid who thought she was a grand lady. You know I *am* Lady Anne Neville. I was brought here because there is a dispute over money. If you will go to Crosby's Place and ask to see the Duke of Gloucester . . . if you will tell him you have news of the Lady Anne Neville . . . he will see you and listen to you. Tell him where I am and when he comes to take me away from here I shall see . . . we both shall see . . . that you are well rewarded."

"You're mad."

"I'm not . . . and you know I am not. Give it a chance. You'll never have another like it. Where will you go when you leave here? This is a chance for you . . . take it."

"Who'd listen to me?"

"The Duke of Gloucester would. He wants to find me. He will listen to anyone who tells him where I am. Believe me. I am speaking the truth. These people will be punished for what they have done. You should not be a party to their crime. This is a chance for you. I beg you, take it, not only for my sake, but for your own. Do as I say. What harm can it do?"

"Go to Crosby's Place?" she murmured.

"Yes, to Crosby's Place. You could do it. You know how to make people listen to you. Ask someone to take you to the Duke of Gloucester."

"They'd laugh at me."

"Tell them they'd be sorry if they did because you come from Lady Anne Neville, daughter of the Earl and Countess of Warwick."

There was a gleam of interest in her eyes.

"Do it, Gilly," I pleaded. "You have nothing to lose and everything to gain."

"You really believe it, don't you? You really believe you are this high and mighty lady."

"I am Lady Anne Neville, Gilly. Prove it by doing what I tell you. I promise you, you will not be forgotten. Both the duke and I will be forever grateful to you if you bring about my release from this place."

"Get away from me," she said, and started tying up her things in a bundle.

I left her. I was half hopeful, half despairing.

I was not sure what she would do. Shortly afterward she left the shop.

I was lying on my pallet. Meg had locked me in. She kept the keys now, and I was glad. It gave me a certain sense of security.

I was thinking of Gilly, wondering what she was doing. Had she gone to Crosby's Place? And what would the guards say when a woman with a bruised face and ragged, none-too-clean garments asked to be taken to the Duke of Gloucester? She would be driven away.

Yes, but Gilly was not one to be easily thrust aside. Everything depended on whether she believed me. If she did, then she would persist.

After all, as I had pointed out to her, she had little to lose and much to gain.

Would she ever get to Richard? If she mentioned my name . . . Yes, he would surely receive her if he heard that. But how would she ever get near him?

Then . . . I heard the shouts from below.

"Open up! Open up!"

Meg was calling. I heard Tom's voice. Through the windows I

could see the torches. Then the door was burst open and I could hear people. They must be crowding into the shop. There were footsteps on the stairs.

A voice called, "Anne! Anne! Are you there!" It was Richard.

I was almost faint with joy. I beat on my door.

"Here, here . . . Richard!" I called. "I am locked in here."

Then I heard him shouting, "Where is the lady? Take me to her! At once, at once, I say!"

Footsteps. The key in the door. And there he was.

For a few seconds he did not recognize me, and instantly I was conscious of how I must look.

Then I cried, "Richard! You've come! Gilly found you. Oh, thank God."

I ran to him and he caught me in his arms. The joy of that moment, after so much degradation and humiliation, was almost too much to bear. I felt the tears on my cheeks. I was free. The nightmare was over.

SANCTUARY

What followed was like a dream and I remember only snatches of it. The ecstasy of riding those night-quiet streets on Richard's horse; the bliss of being close to him; the horror of realizing what I must look like in my greasy gown, my hair unkempt, my person redolent of the nauseating smells of the cookshop that had sickened me on my arrival and to which I had grown a little accustomed.

I was not the Anne whom he had known all his life; I was an unwashed, ill-smelling, dirty kitchen slut.

Yet he held me close to him. He was very tender but angry. I knew he was seething with rage. We did not speak of that then but we should later.

As we rode through those streets I was thanking God and Gilly. She had done it. I would tell Richard that I had promised to reward her and I must be sure that she received that reward. She had made this possible; she had succeeded in getting through to Richard and it was due to her that he had found me.

He said, "I am taking you to St. Martin's. There you will be safe . . . in sanctuary. No one can harm you there. The nuns will look after you. Later in the day I shall come to see you, then we will talk."

How well he understood! I did not want to talk yet. All I could do was say to myself: I'm free. It is over. I shall never be in that dirty kitchen again, never shiver on my pallet, listening for footsteps on the stairs. I meant to wash the stains from that place off my body and the memory from my mind.

I was taken into St. Martin's. I bathed and the clothes I was wearing were taken away and burned. My hair was washed. It was wonderful to feel it fresh and sweet-smelling about my shoulders.

I was given a gray habit to wear until I could have some of my own clothes.

I slept in a small cell with a crucifix hanging on the wall. It was luxury to me.

And later Richard came to see me.

"Anne!" he cried. "You look like my Anne again—though very demure. Like a nun. Never mind, you are back with me. I cannot bear to think of it. It fills me with fury."

"But you came. I knew you would come if only I could get a message to you. Gilly . . . that woman . . . I want her to be rewarded."

"She shall be. She has already been given food, clothing, and money. Have no fear on that score. I am as eager to reward her as you are. Now tell me . . . if you wish to talk of it. Or would you rather later? There is so much we have to say and we have some time now."

I told him briefly what had happened: how I had been driven away through the night because one of the maids had told me she had a message from him and that I was being taken to sanctuary on his orders.

"I must have been drugged," I said, "for I slept through most of the ride and when I awoke I was in that place."

He held me tightly against him.

"This is George's doing," he said. "He is determined to prevent our marriage, because while you are unmarried he is your guardian, and has control of the Warwick fortune in its entirety. If you married half of it would come to you. That is the reason."

"If that is so, why did he not kill me?"

Richard was tense with emotion. "He dared not go so far as that. Our brother has been lenient with him . . . too lenient. George relies on his charm and the family affection . . . but he could go too far and he knows that. George is a schemer but his schemes are often wild. He acts first and thinks afterward. We have seen that before. His one thought would have been to get you away from me so that our marriage was not possible. In due course he would have come up with another scheme and then tried to put that into action in his clumsy fashion."

I shivered.

"Don't be afraid," he said. "Nothing like this shall ever happen to you again. We are going to be married. There are only two obstacles to overcome. We must have Edward's consent and I know he will want my happiness. Then there is the dispensation from the Pope. We are akin, Anne, you and I. Well, there should be no delay about that."

"Your brother will try to prevent it. I'm afraid of him. Looking back, I think I always have been."

"I will take care of George."

"It is not good that there should be this trouble between you."

"It is not good but it exists. I could kill him. I am not sure I will not. When I think of how I was turned away when I came to see you . . ."

"Tell me."

"I was told you were ill . . . too ill to be seen. You can imagine how I felt. I said, 'However ill she is, she will see me.' He said he could not allow it. It would endanger your life. Oh, what a hypocrite he is! Oh yes, I shall certainly kill him one day."

"And you went away and came back again?"

"I did. I said I *would* see you. I did not believe you were too ill to see me. I tried to force my way in but his guards surrounded me. I could see that one of us would come to some harm if this persisted. Edward would be angry. He had impressed on us both to remember we are one family and we must stand together.

"I came back again. This time I saw your sister Isabel. She was very distressed. She said you had run away and she did not know where you were. Then I knew the situation was really serious. I suspected my brother of some nefarious plotting but I could not think what. I insisted on searching Warwick Court. In fact I have been searching all over London. He always had his hangers-on . . . people in his service. It has ever been like that. He likes to do things in secrecy, but he is quite without common sense. I was frantic with anxiety."

"And when Gilly came to you?"

"Ah . . . that woman. She had some trouble getting to me. Thank God she was not one to give up! She kept screeching your name. She cried out that they would be in trouble if they did not take notice of her and bring her to me, because she had news of you. At last she managed to reach me. I could scarcely believe her story, but I was determined not to pass over any possibility. So I came . . . and here you are now . . . safe in sanctuary, thank God."

"And what of your brother?"

"He will not be able to reach you here. You are in sanctuary. This day I shall see Edward. I shall tell him what has happened. He will help me, I know. Once he gives his consent, George will be powerless."

I closed my eyes and was silent for a moment.

He said, "What are you thinking, Anne?"

"This time yesterday I was there . . . hopeless . . . helpless . . . wondering if I would be there forever. And now, here I am, safe with you. It has come about so quickly. I cannot believe it to be true."

"It is true and soon I shall take you away from here."

"I believe I shall never feel safe . . . from George."

"Once you are married to me, he can do nothing, and you will remain in sanctuary until that day."

"You understand. It is like a nightmare. It is over, I know, and yet I cannot believe it. If I close my eyes I think I am lying on the dirty pallet . . . dreaming."

He kissed me tenderly. "It is over, Anne," he said. "You will forget. When we are together it will pass from your mind."

I was not sure that it ever would. I felt I would always remember that hot kitchen, Tom's lecherous eyes, two women fighting in the yard. They had been written indelibly on my mind and would stay there forever.

I said, "What of those people in the cookshop?"

"They have all been arrested."

"Tom, Meg, and the girl Jane?"

"They will be questioned."

"And punished?"

"Surely they deserve it?"

"The real culprit is your brother. What will happen to him? I hope they will not be punished unless he is."

Richard was silent. Then he said, "This day I shall speak to Edward. The main thing is that you and I shall marry. I shall not feel really at ease until I am taking full care of you. At the moment my mind is at rest because you are here in sanctuary and I know you are safe. We have to be content with that for a while, Anne . . . but only for a little while."

"It is contentment enough for me to know that I am free of that place and with you."

He held my rough hands and looked at the broken nails. Then he kissed them.

"These will heal," he said. "You will grow away from it, Anne.

I assure you of that. My first and most important mission in life will be to care for you."

Then he left me and I sat for a long time, marveling at the chance that had been brought to me out of that nightmare.

I saw Richard next day. He had seen the king and told him the whole story of my adventure. Edward was deeply shocked, not only by what had happened to me but that Clarence should be suspected of having arranged it.

He sent for Clarence.

Knowing the three brothers as I did, I could well imagine the scene between them when Richard described it to me. I could feel Richard's smoldering anger, hear Clarence's lies, the implausibility of which he would try to hide with a persuasive charm; and I could picture Edward, hating above all things trouble in the family, seeking first to placate Richard and then George.

"I accused him of doing this dreadful thing to you," said Richard, "and he promptly denied it. He had the effrontery to say that you had attempted to run away because you were afraid of *me.* You did not want to marry me and thought you might be forced into it. He was so absurd that even he began to realize it. He said he knew nothing of the cookshop. He was your guardian. Edward had given him that right and duty and he intended to keep it."

"But what did the king say?"

"He could not believe George, of course, but you know how they have always been with George. When caught in some wrongdoing he would flash that innocent smile on Edward or our sister Margaret and come up with some wild excuse, and he would be forgiven. That was how it was with Edward. He said, 'Anne is safe now. She had a frightening experience, poor child. We must be kind and gentle with her.' And he was ready to dismiss George's part in it. It was not that he believed George was innocent, but he did not want to know about it."

"But surely some action should be taken against him? And what of the people in the cookshop?"

Richard lifted his shoulders. He said, "They were too frightened to talk coherently. Edward said, 'Anne is safe. Let that be an end to the matter.' And they were released."

"At least they were not the real culprits."

"No. But you suffered at their hands."

I shivered. Indeed I had. I said, "And George . . . for his part in it?"

"My dearest Anne, George joined your father and fought against the king and for a while it cost Edward his throne, and yet when George came back and said he was sorry, it had all been a mistake . . . well, it was like the parable of the prodigal son. We killed the fatted calf. That is my brother Edward, and do not forget he is king and his word is law."

"So this matter is waved aside, is it?"

He nodded. "But the important thing is, Anne, that you and I want to marry and George is going to raise obstacles to that."

"And Edward will let him?"

"Edward wants to remain on the best of terms with both of us."

"Is it not a little difficult in these circumstances?"

"It is very difficult, but Edward is a master in such diplomacy. It is why he is the king he is. Conflict is something he abhors. It is ironical that he should have been at the center of the War of the Roses."

"Do you think he will give his support to George and there will be no marriage for us?"

"I think he will prevaricate and that the speedy marriage we hoped for may be delayed."

"If George's misdeeds are going to be passed over as though they never happened he will try again."

"I think he has had a shock. I shall not allow his crime to be forgotten. He insists that you ran away and were kidnapped by the cookshop people and forced to work for them. That would not seem wildly impossible, except, as I pointed out, I had learned from you what had happened and that made nonsense of his tale."

"And the outcome is . . . ?"

" . . . that he refuses to relinquish his guardianship of you, and he will not give his consent to our marriage."

"But surely, if the king will give his consent . . . ?"

"George insists that Edward made him your guardian and as such his consent is necessary."

"Then that means . . ."

"It means that I shall not allow George to prevent our marriage, but instead of the ceremony's taking place immediately, there will be some delay while I deal with George and try to make the king see the truth about him."

"What of the cookshop people?"

"They have been allowed to go. George declares it is a

monstrous charge and they did what they thought was best. They saw a homeless and what they thought demented girl on the streets; they needed a kitchen maid so they took her in. That is their story. A gently nurtured young lady was naturally devastated to find herself in such a position and when she tried to explain, they did not believe her and thought she was deranged."

"I am surprised that this can be acceptable and allowed to pass as though it were a normal happening."

"If George were not the brother of the king it would have turned out very differently, I assure you. George is powerful because the king does not want to offend him. He has affairs of state on his mind. He told me that he cannot have a quarrel between his two brothers. He needs our support—George's as well as mine."

"How can he trust George who has already shown that he can be a traitor?"

"He doesn't really trust him, but he deludes himself into thinking that he does. Edward is the finest man in the world but he has a very soft part . . . and that is his heart. He is devoted to his family. I know he loves me . . ."

"And he should. Have you not always stood by him?"

"Yes, and he remembers that. But he loves George, too. He still thinks of him as his little brother. George would have to do something really terrible for him to turn against him."

"I should have thought he did that when he was leading an army against him."

"As your father did. But he, too, was forgiven in the end. That is Edward. And I love him dearly for it. He is the best brother a man could have."

"I know how you feel for him, Richard, but he should return your devotion in some way. How can he placate George at your expense after all he has done, not only to me but to you and to the king himself?"

But Richard could only say, "That is Edward," and he went on to tell me that George accused him of wanting to marry me for my fortune. "He has gained a great deal through Isabel and he does not want to share it. He wants it all."

"What of my mother?"

"She is virtually a prisoner."

"Richard, I want something done about her. I cannot be happy while she is shut away."

"She is in sanctuary. No harm can come to her."

"But she is accustomed to being with her family. She will be pining for us."

"Something will be done. I know Edward will help us."

"Providing it is not against George's wishes?"

Richard was thoughtful. "It might be that he will try to hinder your mother's release. After all, her fortune is involved in this."

"He is monstrous. This is all because of George's love of money and power. I wonder Isabel is so fond of him."

"George knows how to charm . . . just as Edward does. But Edward's affability comes from the heart. George puts on a mask whenever he thinks the need arises."

"Only when we are married and freed of George shall I be at peace," I said.

Richard understood and I think agreed with me.

Isabel came to see me at St. Martin's. I was shocked by her pallor and I could not help noticing how thin she had become.

"Oh, my dear Anne," she cried. "I have been hearing about that terrible thing that happened to you. How could you have run away like that without telling me?"

"I was promised that I was being taken to Richard."

"How could you go to him then? To leave us when we were looking after you!"

"Isabel, you don't understand. George was keeping me from Richard."

"Of course he was not. Or if he were, it was only because Richard is after your money."

"Richard was not after my money. That is George."

"My dear sister, this has upset you. Let us not talk about it."

I said with some exasperation, "Isabel, we must talk about it. It is at the heart of the matter. I want to marry Richard. I am going to marry Richard and no one—not even George—is going to stop us."

"Anne, you are very young."

"Oh no, please. Not that old theme. I was not too young to be betrothed to Prince Edward. Most girls in our state are married by the time they are my age. Why this sudden concern for my youth? I have been through a great deal. I am not a child and I want to marry Richard. I always wanted to marry Richard."

"There are those terrible stories about him. Those children . . . and he is their father. What do you think of that?"

"That is over."

"That is what he tells you."

"Most young men have a mistress before they marry."

"And what about the children?"

"Isabel, you know very well that there is nothing unusual in this. Richard will be faithful to me from now on."

"What if he is like his brother the king? They say no woman is safe from him."

"Simply because these women do not want to be safe from him. You know very well they go to him most eagerly. Richard is not like the king. George is more like he is."

"Are you suggesting that George . . . ?"

"I am not suggesting anything. But it is silly of you to talk thus of Richard. Richard is a normal young man and I know he will be a good husband. This thing that George did to me . . ."

"George did nothing to you except care for your future. He was very worried when you ran away."

"It was his doing. He arranged it. He deluded me into thinking I was going to Richard. He made one of his servants trick me; he sent me to that horrible cookshop. Isabel, you can have no idea what it was like there . . . that kitchen . . . and I had to wash the horrible, horrible pots. It was the most menial of all the tasks. Imagine that."

"It was horrible, but you should not have run away. You should have trusted us."

"I trust you, Isabel, but I do not trust George. I know he is behind this and I know why. It is unfortunate that you and I are heiresses, Isabel."

"When George married me he did not think of that."

I did not say what was in my mind but merely marveled that she had lived with him so long and did not know this. I think he was fond of her because she saw him as the George she wanted him to be rather than the one he was, and that suited him very well. And I knew that whatever evidence was brought against him she would never believe it.

I talked then of our mother.

I said, "Richard wants her release. Would it not be wonderful if she could come and live either with you or with me?"

"George thinks it is better for her to remain at Beaulieu."

"She is more or less a prisoner there."

"Oh no. She lives in comfort. She is very happy there."

"Isabel, you know our mother. She will never be happy while she is parted from us. She always wanted to be with us in the old days."

"Well, we are grown up now."

"Richard will ask the king if she could be released and be with one of us."

"Why don't *you* come back here with me?"

I looked at her hopelessly. What was the use of telling her that, having once savored something of George's "protection," I was of no mind to try more of it. But she was his wife and theirs was what would be called a happy marriage. She would never look closely into George's motives. I wondered whether she was afraid she might see something that she would rather not.

How I wished that I could have talked to my mother!

Perhaps I should soon. Richard was a determined man. His

methods were not impulsive like those of George, and I felt sure
he would get his way in the end.

I talked to Isabel of the old days; we laughed a little. I could
see that that was the best way and I was pleased to be with my
sister again.

Time began to pass. The king would not give a decision. Richard
explained to me that he felt he could not offend George. George
was so hot-headed. One never knew what steps he would take.
He had too much power and he had a following in the country.

"Bear with me for a while," he said. "I promise you all will be
well in the end, but we must proceed slowly in the matter."

Going slowly was the last thing we wanted.

"There is, of course, the dispensation from the Pope," Edward
had said to Richard. "You should have that, you know."

I wondered about George then. Would he have some plan to
bribe the pope, to persuade him in some way to withhold the dispensation?

But in spite of all these obstacles that had to be overcome, I
could not help feeling an immense relief every day to be in such
comfortable surroundings. Always the memory of the cookshop
must come back to me, no matter what happened, and I must say
to myself, at least I have escaped from that.

It may be that such experiences bring some good to us since
they make us less likely to complain about minor irritations.

Christmas came. I must spend it in sanctuary. Richard said he
would not have a moment's peace if I were to emerge.

He told me that it had been a miserable festival at court. Edward was not pleased because of the strife between him and George, and whenever he and George were in each other's company they came dangerously near to conflict.

Edward was getting angry. "He is so lenient most of the time," said Richard. "But he does hate trouble in the family. So you can imagine, Christmas was not what it should have been."

Then came the day when Richard arrived at St. Martin's. I could see at once that he was very excited.

"Edward has a solution," he cried. "I wonder if you will think it a good one."

"If it means that I can leave here and we shall be together, I certainly shall."

"The heart of the matter is, as you know, the Warwick inheritance. Edward feels that if George had the larger share of it he might be prepared to give his consent—as your guardian—to our marriage."

"I do not care for the estates."

"Nor I. It will make my brother very powerful, of course, and that is not good. He has enough already to make him a menace. Nothing will satisfy him but to have the bulk. He wants Warwick . . . the castle and the earldom . . . and Salisbury as well, which are the important ones, of course. And you and I are to have Middleham."

I clasped my hands in pleasure. "Oh, that will be wonderful, Richard. How often have I dreamed of Middleham!"

"Yes. Middleham will be ours. The place we love best, and with it all your father's northern estates. And there is something else, Anne. Edward wants me to hold the north for him. He says there is none other whom he can trust to do it. Our home would be in the north."

"In Middleham!" I said ecstatically.

"We should be back there in the place that has so many memories for us."

"That makes me very happy. And George has agreed to this?"

"Not yet. It remains for him to do so."

"Do you think he will?"

"He wanted everything, of course, and that is what he was planning to get."

"But he failed to do so. Perhaps . . ."

"We must wait and see. But I have a feeling that he will take what he is offered. The earldom of Warwick will surely tempt him."

"I long to hear that he agrees, but I cannot help thinking that he has come out of this far too well. When you think of what he did to me . . . I believe he intended to be rid of me altogether."

"He would not have dared. Anne, what do you say to this chance? Are you sorry that I have told you Edward will agree to it?"

I shook my head. "I only hope George will."

When the proposition was put to him George was a little hesitant, I heard. He had schemed to have the entire inheritance and no doubt felt he had been cheated of it. But, thanks to circumstances and Gilly, that plot had been foiled; and here I was, safe in sanctuary. And while his villainy had not brought its just deserts, he was still able to bargain; but at length he realized that he must settle for the larger share of the Warwick fortune.

Richard told me how Edward had sent for him.

"There were tears in his eyes," he said, "and he turned to me and cried, 'The Lady Anne is yours, and I wish you great happiness in your marriage. And now all you need is this dispensation from the Pope.' And when he said that there was a hint of mischief in his smile."

"Why? What did he mean?"

"That he would not expect a man in love to give too much thought to such a matter."

"You mean . . . ?"

"That nothing should be put in the way of our marrying and since the dispensation from the Pope was so long in coming, we might do without it."

He put his arms around me and held me tightly to him.

"There shall be no delay," he said. "We have waited long enough. It will not be a grand ceremony, of course. We do not want to call the Pope's attention to our disobedience. But do you care? Do I care?"

"We do not," I said.

"Then let there be a wedding, and then . . . to Middleham!"

THE DUCHESS OF GLOUCESTER

Richard and I were married and there followed two of the happiest years of my life. We were young: when the ceremony was performed I was sixteen years old and Richard was twenty— but only in years. We had both suffered experiences that had inevitably matured us. We were both deeply aware of our good fortune in being together and were determined to enjoy this happy state to the full.

How fresh seemed the northern air! And what a happy journey that was, riding side by side on the way to the home that we both loved.

The north was for Richard. The people liked his quiet ways, preferring them, I imagined, to the ostentatious splendor of his brother the king. They came out of their cottages to cheer for the

Duke of Gloucester and to give him a "God bless you, your Grace," to which he responded with a dignified greeting.

How different he was from Edward and George, that pale shadow of his magnificent brother! These people knew that they could trust Richard and it was to him that they gave their loyalty. Edward had shown his wisdom when he had selected Richard to guard the northern territories.

And there was the familiar castle. My heart bounded with emotion when I saw it. It would always be home to me. Of course, there were sad memories. I felt a longing for my mother and a sadness for my father. I could not help recalling those days when he had come to the castle, his followers about him, to the shouts of "A Warwick," and I could see the banners of the Ragged Staff waving in the breeze.

We had been so proud of him, Isabel and I, as we watched from the turret. Our father—the king of the north—the king of the whole country, in fact if not in name, for we knew it was he who made the king and decided how he should rule. Then I thought of his body lying on the battlefield at Barnet . . . stripped of power . . . stripped of life. A kingmaker but in death no different from the commonest soldier.

But these were morbid thoughts. I was home with my husband. At last we were together; and the past must be forgotten because it had led us to this.

How happy we were! How we laughed and remembered! There was the field where the boys had tilted; there had the hero of Agincourt taught them the arts of battle; there was the seat near the well where Richard had sat, tired from the exercises, with me beside him, the only one who was allowed to see him at such a time because no one must know that he was not as strong as the others, and I could be trusted to keep the secret.

There was much to occupy us. Nobles from the surrounding country came to Middleham to consult Richard, and each night there was entertainment in the great hall. Then Richard must make his pilgrimages through the neighborhood, and I accompanied him. How proud I was to see how the people respected him. I liked their frank manners. I was one of them, born and bred among them. It seemed fitting to them that the lord of the north should be allied with Warwick's daughter.

It was comforting to be free of court intrigue . . . far away from Clarence and his schemes . . . though I should have loved to see Isabel and my mother.

I could sleep beside Richard and there were no more dreams of the cookshop. With each passing week it became more and more like a hazy fantasy.

We were far away from London, far from the court. And that in itself was wonderful.

I told Richard that George was welcome to have the rest of the Warwick estates because he had left us Middleham.

So passed those idyllic days, and then came the discovery that I was to have a child.

I had never thought such happiness possible. There was only one thing now to make me sad, I told Richard.

He was eager to know what it was.

"It is my mother. They say she is in sanctuary, but it is prison to her. How she would love to be with me and particularly to be with her grandchild."

"Edward has half-promised that she shall be free," he said. "I expect George is persuading him that it is better to keep her at Beaulieu. When I see him I shall talk to him."

"To talk to him you would have to go away," I said, "and that is the last thing I want."

He looked at me rather sadly then. I knew that this cozy happiness of ours could not go on forever. One day there would come a summons for him and he would have to leave me.

I did not want to think of that. I just wanted the joy of being here with my husband where we could both look forward to the coming of our child.

Isabel wrote to me. She was exceedingly happy.

"I am going to have a child," she said. "Oh, Anne, you cannot understand how I have longed for this! Do you remember how we set out for Calais? Oh, how I suffered! That fearsome journey . . . with the ship pitching over the sea . . . and there was I . . . in agony. And all to no avail! Do you remember, Anne?"

I did remember. It was one of those memories I should never forget. I could recall it as clearly as though it had happened yesterday . . . the solemn prayers and the little body being swallowed up on that turbulent sea.

"I am at Castle Farley, which is near Bath. Here I shall stay until the child is born. I am a little frightened, but this will be different from that other. If only our mother were here! She should be with me at such a time, but George says it is better for her to be where she is."

George, I thought! It is George again who is attempting to guide our fates. Why will he not let my mother go? And why does the king think that he should be placated at such cost to us all?

"George is sure the baby is going to be a boy. I hope so, too, but I am sure I should love a little girl. Oh, Anne, I do so wish that I could see you! The north is so far away. Richard will surely be coming south some time. You must come with him, I shall want to show off my child.

"Do you remember Ankarette Twynyho? She has gone back to the queen. The queen wrote to me most graciously and said that she had lost one of her women who is traveling with her husband for a year or so and Ankarette was so good with the children. She does not know of my condition, of course. So would I "lend" her Ankarette?

"So Ankarette has gone back to her. She is quite pleased to do so, I think. She will get the best of the gossip at court. So I must needs manage without her. And at such a time!

"However, I am surrounded by good friends, and think of all Ankarette will have to tell me when she comes back!"

It was with great pleasure that I wrote and told her that I, too, was about to become a mother.

I was a little sad, thinking of her. She was such a part of my life. We had bickered, as sisters will, but there was a strong bond between us. How I wished that she had not married George. But to our father it had seemed desirable that his daughter should marry the brother of the king he had made, but Isabel's marriage had come out of the attempt to unmake that king. Well, Isabel and I were there to go the way our father decided and our future had been planned by him to augment that power which had all come to nothing on the field of Barnet.

I thought of the marriage he had arranged for me and that brought back memories of Queen Margaret. I believed she had left the Tower and was in some mansion under the care of her hosts—which meant that she was a prisoner still. I wondered if she would ever be allowed to go home to her family. I knew that she would be a sad and lonely woman, for never would she recover from the loss of her beloved son.

Life was cruel. Life was hard. One must rejoice when happiness came, even when one's instinct warned that it can only be transient.

Then came the day when my child was born—a beautiful boy to gladden our hearts and fill us with pride. This was the culmination of happiness.

It was Richard's wish that we call him Edward after the man he most admired, and I had no objection to this.

I heard from Isabel and was overjoyed that she, too, had come safely through her ordeal. She had not been blessed with the longed-for boy, but she was very pleased with her daughter who was to be called Margaret.

I wanted my life to be always as it was at that time. If I could only know that my mother had her freedom I would have been completely happy.

Richard shared my contentment with our life at Middleham,

but he had certain anxieties. There was always the danger of the Scots making trouble on the border; moreover he was a little unsure of some of the nobles. The lords of the north had been the Nevilles and the Percys, and since the power of the Nevilles had declined with the death of my father, the Percys were in the ascendant. Richard, as the king's brother, was in command over all, of course, but this rankled with the Percys. Conflict with this powerful family had to be avoided, and this was a continual concern to Richard. If we were to keep peace in the north, he needed to have the Percys working not against him but with him and he had to be constantly on the alert.

I knew that he had sent a message to Edward explaining the situation, so I supposed I should not have been surprised when an emissary from the king arrived at Middleham.

He was closeted with Richard for some time and I was fearful of what news he brought. Richard was soon able to tell me and he was very grave.

"There is trouble brewing," he said.

"Is it Clarence again?"

"I fear he may be involved in it."

"Oh, Richard, what is it all about . . . and what does it mean?"

"The king is riding north."

"Coming here?"

"No. I am to meet him at Nottingham."

He smiled at my woebegone expression. "It is just a meeting, but I like this not. George will always make trouble. My brother does not seem to realize how dangerous this is. The plain fact is that George resents not being born the eldest of us all. It is something that has been with him all his life."

"What is he doing now?"

"Nothing openly. But I believe he is in league with John de Vere, who is out to make trouble. Edward has wind of it."

"John de Vere. Is he not the Earl of Oxford?"

"He is and a firm Lancastrian. The de Veres always were. He was with your father when he restored Henry to the throne and fought against us at Barnet. Then he escaped to France. From there he has worked consistently against us. Now he is reported— with Louis's help—to have gathered together a squadron of men to make a landing. He cannot do much so there is little fear on that score, but what is alarming is George's subversive connection with him."

"Why does Edward not see the danger George is to him?"

"He will not take it seriously. George is still to him the naughty, charming little brother. You have to admit he has a persuasive way."

"Not to me. I shall never forget. But what of you, Richard? What does this mean?"

"I am to meet the king at Nottingham. He is inviting Henry Percy to be there. He is most eager to secure a pact between Percy and myself. We cannot afford trouble in the north at this time. Do not be sad. I shall be back ere long. Edward will not want the north to remain unprotected."

There was truth in that and I felt a little happier.

Richard was ready to leave early next morning. I was at the gates to see the last of him before he left.

"Take care of our son in my absence," he said. "And of yourself. I promise I shall soon be back."

"I hope so, because I cannot be happy without you."

Then he rode south to Nottingham.

How I missed him! But how grateful I was to have my son to care for!

I promised myself that we should not follow the usual practice of sending him away to be brought up in the house of some nobleman. He should be brought up at Middleham and learn all he needed to learn here. I would not have him taken away from me.

The days seemed long. Always I was on the alert for the sound of horses' hoofs, which would herald Richard's return or some messenger from him.

I sat with my women at our needlework and we took it in turns to read aloud. Perhaps one of us would play the lute as we worked or we would talk.

I was never far from little Edward. There was great alarm when he developed a chill. I sat by his cot all through the night, unnecessarily, said his nurse, but I insisted. Children had ailments and quickly recovered from them, she assured me; but as I listened to his breathing disturbed by an occasional cough I suffered agonies. I lived through his death, the funeral obsequies, and I could see the little coffin, and Richard's homecoming to hear the dreadful news. I passed one of the most miserable nights of my life. And in the morning he was better.

If Richard had been here he would have shown me how foolish

I was, or would he? Where our child was concerned he was as vulnerable as I was.

I prayed for my child. I had come through a great deal to reach this happiness. I could not lose it now.

I knew I should always be uneasy while Richard was away. I would always fear evil. I had been immature when I had been thrust into an unkindly world. It had left its mark on me. I should always be watching for disaster, even in the midst of my happiness.

Richard knew of it. He said I should grow away from it. But should I ever do that?

However, my child was well again, and I prayed that there would be no more alarms from little Edward.

He charmed my days. He made Richard's absence bearable. But at every moment I watched for Richard's return.

At last he came. He was in good spirits. I was in the solarium when he arrived and I ran down to meet him as he leaped from his horse.

"All's well," he cried, catching me in his arms. "Come, I must tell you."

It was wonderful to sit beside him, his arm encircling me, while now and then he would hold me fast to him as though to imply he would never let me go.

He must first hear of little Edward. He was sleeping now, I told him, and his nurse never allowed him to be awakened, even for such an important event as the return of his father. I told of his chill and my agony. Richard laughed and said the nurse was right. I must not be foolishly anxious. I should rejoice that we had a healthy son.

"Now for the news," he said. "The great Earl of Northumberland, Henry Percy no less, was at Nottingham, there summoned by the king. My brother exerted all his charm. He flattered Northumberland, knew of his love for the north, realized his loyalty and so on. But I was Lord of the North. I was keeping it loyal to the crown, and, as Percy knew, that was to the advantage of us all and should remain so. He had summoned Percy so that he and I should make a pact. Percy should be treated with all the respect due to him. He should maintain all the rights that had belonged to his family. The king was asking for his cooperation, for his help in keeping peace in the north. He was certain that, for Percy's own good and the good of us all, Percy would want to be part of that pact. I was, however, holding the north for the crown and I was in charge. If there were any differences of opinion, I would consult Percy. But I should be in charge. Percy agreed. He does really care about the north. He wants no trouble, and I believe he trusts me. We swore to stand together. I would respect his wishes; he would accept me as the higher authority. It was all very satisfactory."

"Then it was a successful meeting, and I am glad that the king realizes your presence is needed here—not only by Percy and the rest, but by your wife and son."

"I think he understands that, too. He would not call on me to leave here unless there was something serious afoot."

As he looked a little grave I said, "Do you think that is likely to be?"

"De Vere is ineffectual. What gives me cause to worry is that George might be involved in his schemes."

"Against the king?"

"It would not be the first time he has been against the king. It saddens me. It saddens Edward that we have to be suspicious of our own brother."

"Perhaps the king will realize the folly of giving way to him. He does act so impulsively. It is all so obvious."

"I know. So we must be watchful. I have another piece of news for you, and I think you will like this better."

I waited expectantly as he paused, smiling at me.

"Sir James Tyrell is going to Beaulieu."

"To my mother?"

"My brother George is not in the highest favor with the king. Although Edward has tried to tell himself that the rumors about George's connections with de Vere are false, in his heart he can't help knowing that there is some truth in them. You know George has been putting obstacles in the way of your mother's release? Well, I thought this was a good time to put my point of view, as Edward is not inclined to favor George at this moment. Edward said, 'Where would the Countess go if she left Beaulieu?' I replied, 'Where, but to her daughter at Middleham? Anne longs to have her with her.' Then the king said to me, 'Richard, you have ever been loyal to me and I love you dearly. If it would please you to take the countess to Middleham, then do so . . . and to hell with George.' I wasted no time and I think it will not be long ere your mother is with us."

I could not contain my delight.

I said, "Surely this is the happiest day of my life! How delighted she will be. How she will love little Edward! I cannot wait for her arrival. And you, Richard . . . my dearest Richard . . . have done this for me. All my happiness comes through you, and everything that went before . . . yes, everything . . . is worthwhile since it has brought me to this."

I was eager to give my mother a wonderful welcome when she came to Middleham. For days I set the household preparing. I was glad that Richard would be able to join me in letting her know how happy we were to have her with us.

She arrived at length with Sir James Tyrell, who had been sent by Richard to bring her. He trusted Tyrell, he told me. He was a stalwart Yorkist and had received his knighthood for his services at Tewkesbury.

She had changed. It was, after all, a long time since I had seen her and I could imagine what parting with her family had meant to her.

We clung together, looked at each other and then clung again.

"My dearest, dearest child," she kept saying, over and over again.

Arms entwined, we went into the castle. It was as dear to her as it was to me.

"This," she said, "is coming home."

Happy days followed. We were together most of the time. We talked constantly of the old times, the days of my early childhood. There was sadness, of course. There were so many memories of my father, that ambitious man whose desire for power had been the very pivot around which our lives revolved.

Now he was gone; I was happily married; so was Isabel, and although she was not with us, at least we both knew that she was happy and that her new daughter was a delight to her.

At first my mother did not want to talk of my father, but later she did and she told me how terribly disturbed she had been when the rift with Edward had occurred. She had understood his anger when the king had married Elizabeth Woodville, but had realized that he had miscalculated when he refused to accept the marriage.

"Your father was right, of course," she said. "That is, about the marriage. Trouble would certainly be the result—not so much because of the marriage itself, but because of her ambitious relations. Who would have thought that a marriage could have had such an effect on us all?"

"Dear Mother," I said, "marriages are important. If my father had not married you, he would not have wielded the power he did. His wealth and titles came from you and therein lay his ability to make and unmake kings. Who can say what is the greatest cause of the troubles that have beset our country? We have to accept what is and when we are happy rejoice in it, for it may not endure."

"How wise you have become, little daughter," she said.

"I have seen something of the world now. I have seen how people live in the lowest places—something most people born as I was never see. I think it may have taught me a little."

"Then let us not repine for what has happened. Let us be glad that we are together. But how I wish Isabel could be with us! I should love to see her with my little granddaughter."

"At least we are together, Mother."

"I shall be forever grateful to Richard," said my mother.

"And I, too," I assured her.

We had news from Isabel. To her delight she was once more pregnant. My mother fervently wished that she could go to her, but I pointed out that even if that were possible, she would come into the clutches of the Duke of Clarence, who had done all in his power to keep her confined at Beaulieu. I could see that she did not entirely believe this. She, too, had been a victim of George's charm. It amazed me how that man could perpetrate the most atrocious crimes and with a smile shrug them aside with an air of "let us be friends" and all seemed to be forgiven.

Richard had once said he hoped that would not always be so, and there would come a time when his brother the king would see George for what he was.

However, though my mother could not go to Isabel, we could talk about her, which we did at great length. I was secretly envious that I was not in like state, and I hoped that this time Isabel would be blessed with the boy for which she so fervently longed.

There was a further summons for Richard. The king wanted his presence in London. It was sad saying farewell to him, but he hoped he would not be long, and he assured me that he would be back at Middleham at the earliest possible moment.

The days passed pleasantly with my mother, and we had little Edward with us whenever possible. He was now beginning to take notice; he could crawl around and was learning to stand up.

He smiled to show his pleasure to see us and I was gratified that the pleasure was clearly the greater for me. He was adorable.

Richard returned and with him, my son, and my mother safely at Middleham, I was deeply content.

There was good news from Isabel. She had a boy—another Edward. A compliment to the king, of course. Isabel wrote that the boy was strong and handsome and that Margaret was a beautiful child.

I rejoiced for Isabel and the talk at that time was almost always of babies, for my mother took great pleasure in recalling incidents from my and Isabel's childhood.

But it was inevitable that there should be another call for Richard. He was too important to be left entirely in the north when he had succeeded in bringing order there so that it was the least troublesome zone in the kingdom.

This time it was to London he must go. We said a reluctant good-bye and he went with the usual promise to return as soon as possible.

After he had ridden away, life went on as before and every day I watched for Richard's return.

It seemed long before he came and when he did I realized he had some weighty matter on his mind, and I could not restrain my impatience to hear what it was. He was a little secretive at first, but he soon realized that I should have to know.

"The king is contemplating going to war with France," he told me. "He suspects Louis of offering help to de Vere and, as you know, George may have been concerned in this."

"If he goes to war that will mean . . ."

". . . that I go with him. And, of course, George also."

"Surely he cannot trust George!"

"He cannot do anything else. George would hardly fight on the side of the French."

"He would if he were offered a big enough bribe."

"Suffice it that both George and I have promised to take one hundred and twenty men at arms and a thousand archers into the field with him. Edward has made Parliament give him large sums of money: he is going around the country getting what he calls benevolences from the people. He is doing very well. You know how popular he is. People can't resist him. With his good looks and graces, he is charming the money out of their pockets, and he will soon be able to equip himself in the necessary manner."

"And so . . . ," I said mournfully, "you will go to France with him."

"I must," said Richard. "He is my brother and it is at the king's command."

"But why should he want to go to war? I thought he was eager for peace."

"He thinks this is the best way to get it. Louis is interfering and you know he is Edward's enemy because of his connections with Burgundy."

"I do not see why we should be concerned with the quarrels between Frenchmen. Why cannot France and Burgundy settle their own problems?"

"They are our problems, too."

"I hate the thought of war."

"It may not come."

"But you say you promised to go and the king is collecting this money."

"Let us wait and see. But . . . I had to tell you."

"Yes. I would rather be prepared."

"Anne, there is something else I must tell you."

"Yes?"

"I love you, Anne. I have always loved you. You were always in my thoughts . . . always."

"And you in mine, Richard," I replied.

"Those other things . . . they were not important in the way you were. You must understand . . . and it is for you now to say yes or no and, of course, I shall understand."

"What is it, Richard? It is unlike you not to come straight out with what you want to say."

"While I was in London I had news . . ."

"News? What news?"

"You know of the children . . . John and Katharine?"

"Yes," I said slowly. "You did tell me."

"It is their mother. She is dead. And the children . . . they are in the care of a family. They could, of course, stay there, but . . ."

I was aghast. I said, "You want them to come here?"

He looked at me almost pleadingly. "It is for you to say."

I was silent. I felt a slight tinge of anger. I wanted to shout: No! I will not have them here. I know it happened. It was before we were betrothed, and I was to marry the Prince of Wales. You had this mistress. She was dear to you. She must have been. There are two children and now she is dead you want them to come here . . . to be brought up with Edward. I will not have it.

He said, "I see that I have shocked you."

Still I did not speak. I was afraid of the words that I might say. I was on the point of shouting, no, I will not have them here . . . a constant reminder. I will not have those children here with Edward.

He turned away very sadly. "I do understand, of course," he said. "I should not have thought of it. You must forget I suggested it."

Forget? How could I forget? He had spoiled his homecoming.

There was a rift between us. He had brought no good tidings with him. First he might be snatched away from me to go to war and secondly he wanted me to have his bastard children in my home.

My mother knew that something was wrong. I told her first about the possibility of war and then about the children.

She was very thoughtful. She said, "I can see how he feels. They are, after all, his children."

"But how could they come here?"

"They could, of course. But it depends on you."

"They would expect to be brought up with Edward."

"They are his half-brother and -sister."

"My lady Mother, they are bastards."

"'Tis no fault of theirs."

"You think they should come here?"

"It is for you to decide. Richard has suggested it, has he not? It would depend on how much you love him, of course."

"You know I love him."

"Not enough to give him this."

"It is because I love him so much that I cannot bear the thought of his having children who are not mine."

"It is a selfish love," said my mother. "And the essence of love is not selfishness."

She left me then.

Why had this to happen? Why did that woman die and leave her children to be looked after? How old were they? The boy must be about two years older than Edward; the girl could be several years older. Richard's children!

He looked so melancholy that he reminded me of the young boy who was ashamed because he tired more easily than the others. I had been sorry for him then and that was when I began to love him.

Soon he would go to war. He would fight valiantly for his brother's cause. Who knew what would happen to him in the heat of the battle? My father had died at Barnet, the Prince of Wales at Tewkesbury, Richard's father at Wakefield. War was death and destruction. And Richard was going to war with a heavy heart because he was anxious about the future of his children.

Perhaps I had known from the beginning what I must do. I wished I had not been asked to do it, but my mother was right. Love was selfless and I did love Richard, and I could not bear to see him unhappy as he was now.

I had made up my mind and as soon as I did so I was happier.

"Richard," I said, "when would John and Katharine be coming to Middleham?"

He stared at me and I saw the joy dawn in his face.

He caught me in his arms. "You will have them here?"

"But, of course," I said.

"I thought . . ."

"It was a shock. I am a silly jealous creature. I could not bear the thought of there being anyone but myself."

"There will never be anyone else, and there has never been anyone quite like you."

I said, "I think it will be good for Edward to have other children in the nursery."

I awaited the arrival of the children with a great deal of apprehension. Richard was nervous, too. Any day the summons might come for him to go to the king; he had already gathered together the company of men he would take with him. I knew how he hated leaving Middleham at any time; but now, with his children coming here, he felt that his presence was needed more than ever.

So it was an uneasy time. And at length the children arrived. I was glad they had come before he had left.

They were handsome children, both of them—fair-headed, with what I thought of as the Plantagenet look—tall, strong, vital. The boy was two years older than Edward and perhaps a few months more, and the girl, I guessed to be about seven years old. They were not in the least overawed, although Middleham must have seemed grand to them after their mother's dwelling and that of the family with whom they had been staying prior to their arrival here. I noticed they were very respectful to Richard. I guessed he had visited them only on rare occasions of late and they would have been told that he was of great importance, being the brother of the king.

They eyed me shrewdly.

I said, "Welcome to Middleham. You are Katharine, and I believe you are John."

"I am John Plantagenet," said the boy. And the girl added, "And I am Katharine Plantagenet."

"Well, this is going to be your home now."

"Yes," said Katharine, "I know. Our mother is dead. They came and took her away in a box."

She looked pathetic, so young and vulnerable. I put my hands on her shoulders and kissed her. "I hope you will be happy here," I said.

Then the boy came and stood before me, holding up his face to be kissed.

Richard looked outwardly calm but I well understood his emotions and I was gratified that I had agreed to have the children, for I was recalling what a mistake it would have been to refuse to do so.

I felt that the first encounter had gone off very well.

Little Edward was interested in the newcomers. They were merry and inclined to be boisterous and clearly they found the castle of great interest. John shrieked with pleasure at the armor in the hall because he had at first thought it was a man standing there. Katharine was a little more restrained.

On their first night I went to see them after they were in their beds. They were both crying quietly.

I said to them, "Tell me what is wrong."

"John wants our mother," said Katharine. "And so do I."

I was moved. They were so young, so vulnerable. I wondered briefly what would have become of them if I had refused to take them in. They would have stayed with the family they were with, I supposed. Instinct told me that they were the kind of children who would have come through whatever troubles overtook them. But I was glad I had not turned them away.

I was going to forget that they were the result of Richard's love for another woman. I was the one who now had his love and trust and I wanted him to know how grateful I was for this, and I was going to do my best to be a mother to his children.

I said, "I shall be your mother now."

Katharine's sobs ceased and so did John's. I bent over Katharine and kissed her and suddenly she put her arms around my neck. John was waiting for me to do the same with him.

"You are going to like it at Middleham," I said. "You will have your own horses and you can ride on the moors."

They were both sitting up in bed listening to me. And I told them that when I was a little girl I had lived here with my sister. I explained how we did our lessons in the schoolrooms, which they would now have, how we learned to ride and in time were able to go wherever we wanted to on our horses.

They listened intently and I saw the sadness fade from their faces.

I said, "I am glad you two came here."

And I was.

My mother was delighted. She said, "It is good to have children in the house. Houses that have stood for many years need the young to bring them to life."

Edward was very interested in his new sister and brother. Sometimes I was afraid they would be too boisterous for him. He had taken after Richard in looks and physique. I worried about him. He seemed so small. I had always been a little anxious about him but I think I became more so after the other children came.

Richard was delighted by my reception of them. He was not able to show them how much he cared about them. He was a little aloof and while they regarded him with awe and the utmost respect, it was to my mother and me that they turned.

"It is easy to see," I said, "that I am taking the place of their mother in their minds, which is how I would have it."

A few weeks passed while we waited for that summons that would call Richard to the king's side. I was dreading it for I knew it meant war. Why did there have to be these conflicts? Of what use were they? What good did they bring to anyone? We heard from occasional visitors to the castle that the king was raising a great deal of money from his benevolences. It seemed that when he appeared, handsome, splendid, and extremely agreeable, with a smile for the women and a word for the humblest, he won all hearts. It seemed inevitable that soon he must raise enough money to set out on his mission of conquest. Men were flocking to the banner of the white rose of York set in the blazing sun. War excited men. It was an escape from their humdrum lives, a chance to win booty. It was saddening. Many of them would die; others would be badly wounded. How could they want their peaceful lives disrupted just for temporary excitement?

So the days passed. My mother was so happy to be at Middleham away from Beaulieu.

"Freedom is one of the most precious gifts a man or woman can have," she said. "I had certain comforts at Beaulieu, but there was always the knowledge that I was a prisoner. Here, I feel free and I am so happy to see you with Richard. He is a good man and he loves you truly. I am so glad he is only brother to the king and the king has sons. And in any case Clarence comes before Richard."

"You are thinking of the throne."

"It is not good to be too close to it. If your father had not wanted to rule . . . if he had been content to live without power, what a different life we should all have had! He would be with us now. It is a blessing that you should be here at Middleham, away from all the intrigues and power-struggles of the court."

"I know that well. But soon Richard will have to go to war."

"It is the curse men bring upon themselves," said my mother. "Why does Edward want to go to war? He is now safe on the throne. He must be one of the most popular kings England has ever had. Why? Why?"

"The people want wars. Look how they are flocking to his banner."

She shook her head sadly.

We were at the window. The children were in the garden with one of the nurses. John and Katharine were running and leaping, Edward toddling after them.

"They are so happy together," said my mother, dismissing the gloomy subject of war. "How right you were not to refuse to take them in, Anne."

"Yes. Richard is very content to see them settled. I think he worried a great deal about them."

"Naturally he would. He is a good father."

"He will see that they are brought up as befits their birth," I said, "and that they are well provided for."

She nodded.

"Yes, I am glad they are here. I thought I should resent them, but I find I do not. I see them as what they are . . . little children . . . Richard's children and responsibility, and that makes them mine. But there is one thing . . ." I said and she looked at me expectantly.

"Tell me, Anne," she said.

"When I look at them, I think that Edward looks a little frail."

"He is young yet."

"I think those two were lusty from birth. They have so much energy. John jumps all the time as though he finds it difficult to stand still, and Katharine seems to be constantly repressing her high spirits. They make Edward seem delicate."

"He is young. He will grow out of it."

"Oh yes, of course," I said, allowing fears to be set aside. "He will."

The expected summons had come and Richard, with his men at arms and archers, set forth on the march south. I stood with the children, watching him go, feeling sad and full of fear.

There is a great drawback about being happy and contented with life, for a person like myself lives in constant fear of losing that blissful state. But so must every loving wife feel when she sees her husband leaving for the wars.

I felt a burning anger. It was unnecessary. It was not as though we were being attacked. I thought of all those men going into battle to bring suffering and misery to people who had done them no harm—whom they did not even know.

Those were long and anxious days that followed. We were waiting all the time for news, both longing for and dreading it. Those hot days of June were hard to live through. "What is happening in France?" was the often unspoken question on everyone's lips.

The months passed. June. July. August.

I remember that September well. We had heard only fragments of news. We had one or two visitors at the castle and though they had not been able to tell us much news, we did gather that there had been no fighting in France, that King Edward and Louis had been in conference together and we should soon have news of the Treaty of Picquigny.

I was immensely relieved. But what did it mean? Edward had sailed with his magnificent army, accompanied by his brothers and their followers to join forces with the Duke of Burgundy against Louis. And there had been no fighting!

The tension was lifted a little. I felt I could wait for Richard to return.

It was September when he came. He was quiet, brooding . . . and I knew that he was disturbed.

He told me about it, how the king had acted in an unprecedented manner. It was the first time I had known him critical of his brother. Of course, he had disapproved of Edward's way of living, his insatiable sexual appetite, his marriage, which had caused such disasters, but previously he had always hastened to his defense. Now he was indeed dismayed and disillusioned.

"We went to France," he said. "We had the finest English army ever taken to those shores. Henry the Fifth would have been proud of it."

"Yet there was no fighting?"

"My sister Margaret of Burgundy met us. She gave us a welcome. Alas, if only we could have relied on her husband. He is not called Charles the Rash for nothing. He was not prepared. He had marched off some time before to besiege a city against which he had a grievance, and so lost most of the forces he had on this senseless exercise. Not that that need have deterred us completely. We had this magnificent army."

"So it was decided not to fight the French?"

"Louis is sly and very clever. He knew full well that he could not stand against us. His real enemy, of course, is Burgundy. What he did suggest was a meeting between himself and Edward; and when this took place he offered Edward terms for peace that my brother could not refuse."

"But that is wonderful! It has stopped the war!"

"Anne, those men were brought out to fight. They had been promised the spoils of war. They had left their homes, their work, their families, to fight for the king, to bring glory to England.

This contrived peace, these bribes from Louis would bring them no benefits. They would go home empty-handed."

"But sound and well in body."

"They were looking for adventure and gain. Don't you see? That had been promised them. They had been taken from their homes merely to give a show of might to Louis."

"But there is peace!"

"Burgundy is incensed."

"Well, he was not ready for war, was he?"

"But don't you see? Edward has become friendly with his old enemy, the King of France."

"And stopped a war."

"I believe this was what Edward had in mind all the time. He did not tell me."

"Would you expect him to?"

Richard looked at me steadily and said, "Yes." And then I saw the pain in his eyes, the humiliation, and what was hurting him most was to be at odds with his brother.

"Tell me about the treaty," I said.

"It is to be a truce between the kings for seven years."

"Seven years!" I cried. "Without a war!"

"Trade comes into it. There is to be an abolition of tolls and tariffs charged on goods passing from either country, and that is to be for twelve years. And there are two clauses that mean most to Edward. His eldest daughter, Elizabeth, is to marry Charles the Dauphin; and if Elizabeth should die before the marriage, her sister Mary will take her place. But what delights my brother most is that Louis is to pay him a pension of 50,000 gold crowns each year. The first instalment has already been received by him."

"Then surely," I said, "he has achieved much with his magnificent army?"

"The army went over to fight and the men are disgruntled. They are murmuring among themselves. What gain is it to them if the king gets his pensions and his daughter is to marry the Dauphin of France?"

"It is peace," I insisted.

"Many of the nobles were against it. Louis invited those whom he considered important enough to his *château*. He entertained them lavishly and gave them bribes until he had most of them on his side. Louis is shrewd. He is wily. He knew that he could offer a great deal and still it would not amount to what he would have lost by fighting against an army such as Edward had managed to put in the field." He laughed bitterly. "He was concerned about me. He knew that I deplored the whole matter. He asked me to dine with him. His flattery was sickening. What do you think he offered me? Not money. That would be too blatant . . . too undignified to one in my position. He offered me some fine plate and horses. I declined them. I said to him quite frankly that no amount of plate or fine horses would make me a party to this treaty."

"And what said Louis to that?"

"Louis is all suave politeness. He looked a little sad, but put on an air of understanding and implied that our differences of opinion made no difference to our friendship."

"Which is true, of course."

"He will hate me forever."

"Oh, Richard, I am so sorry about this, but I cannot but rejoice to have you with me."

He said he, too, was glad to be home, but he wished it had been from a more honorable venture.

He stayed at Middleham for some time after that. I wondered whether Edward would do something to bring their relationship back to the old footing. But there was no summons and I wondered how deep was the rift between the two brothers.

While he was with Louis, Edward must have made a bargain with him regarding Queen Margaret, for shortly afterward she was allowed to return to France. I heard later that her father gave the Château de Reculée as her home. It was near Angers, that place where I had been betrothed to her son. Poor Margaret! I was sure she would pass her days in utter melancholy.

The king, his magnificent army intact, returned to England. He must have been feeling very pleased with himself. As far as I was concerned, I thought he had managed a very clever stroke of statesmanship, to have brought about peace without fighting, as well as making arrangements for trading and having acquired a pension.

But there were many who did not see it as I did—Richard for one.

But during the next months he seemed to forget his disappointment.

The northern marches claimed his attention and that was where his heart was. He was happy to be away from the court; he loved to ride with the children and to watch our little one grow. There were times when he was called away to various part of the northern territories, but he was never away for long and when he returned there were always happy reunions.

I was glad of my mother's company. We often spoke of our regret that Isabel was so far away. She wrote to us from time to time, as we did to her, and we would anxiously await news of little Margaret and Edward.

We heard that she was once more pregnant. I felt envious. I yearned to have another child. I continued to worry about my Edward's health, particularly as his half-brother and -sister seemed to grow every day. Edward was so small and thin; he tired far more easily than John who with his sister made such a healthy pair that they continually drew my attention to Edward's frailty.

Isabel wrote that she had not been well. That irritating cough had come back, as it did periodically. Perhaps she would be better when the baby was born. George was eager to have another boy, but to her it was of little importance: all she wanted was a healthy child.

"The queen has been most gracious," she wrote. "She seems determined to be friendly. She has sent Ankarette Twynyho back to me. She said that Ankarette was so good with children and for ladies in my condition, so she would thank me for lending her and would send her back to be with me at such a time. I am pleased to have Ankarette with me. She is full of gossip and regales me with talk of the court and Madam Elizabeth herself who, it seems, is more regal than the king ever was. Ankarette says the Woodvilles run the court and the queen is always seeking higher and higher places even for the most insignificant members of her clan."

My mother said, "The queen is very clever. Any woman who has managed to keep Edward all these years must be. I know how she does it, of course. It is by closing her eyes to his many *amours*. I do not think I could have done that if I had been in her place and I thank God I was never called upon to do it in mine. I was lucky in my marriage."

"My father was lucky, too. Where would he have been without you?"

"Your father would have been a great man. It just happened that the wealth and titles I brought to him helped him to get what he wanted a little earlier."

"And brought him to his end," I said sadly.

"Yes, that is true. But most men of influence end up either on the battlefield or the block."

"Would it not be better to have no influence and die peacefully in bed after having lived a long life?"

"I feel sure they would not agree with you, Anne. And what a morbid subject! Do you think we should make some garments for Isabel's baby? I should like to try that new embroidery stitch I learned the other day."

So we stitched and we talked and we often spoke of Isabel.

We were stunned when the news came. I helped my mother to her bed. I had never seen her so stricken.

Isabel was dead. She had died after her little boy was born and he soon followed his mother to the grave.

I could not believe it. Isabel . . . dead! There were so many memories of her. She had been so much a part of my childhood. She was too young to die.

My mother wept in silence at night. By day she was withdrawn. I had never seen a face so sad as hers.

As for myself, I was equally desolate. It was inconceivable. Never to see Isabel again! Never to receive a letter from her.

I thought of those little ones: Margaret and Edward. Poor motherless children. And George? He had loved her, I believe, in his way, although I could not believe he would ever love anyone but himself. I had never heard that he was unfaithful. At least he was not like the king in that respect.

How hard it was to believe that Isabel was dead, and for a long time afterward I would find myself thinking, I will write and tell Isabel that.

Death was in the air. Isabel had died in December just before Christmas—a sad time to die—and in January there was another death.

Isabel's was of little importance in court circles, but that of Charles the Rash was another matter.

The Duke of Burgundy dead meant that the heiress to his vast estates was a woman—his daughter Mary. So Mary of Burgundy had become the most desirable *parti* in Europe.

Richard was thoughtful. He talked to me of it.

He said, "I wonder what Edward is thinking now. Louis paid him to keep away because Burgundy was Edward's ally and Louis feared Burgundy more than he feared England. But what will happen now that Burgundy is no more?"

"There is, of course, Mary."

"A woman!" said Richard. "Whom will she take for her husband? That is what everyone will be watching. She will need a strong man to stand beside and hold what she has inherited. You will see now, there will be a rush to marry her from all the most ambitious men in Europe."

"Poor Mary," I said. "She will be married for her estates."

"I believe her to be a strong-minded young woman," said Richard. "She might insist on making up her own mind as to which man she will marry. It will be interesting. Her stepmother—our sister Margaret, as you know—may have some influence with her. If she had an English husband, that would do us no harm. Margaret will surely think of that."

It soon became clear that the demise of the Duke of Burgundy was going to have a big effect on a number of people.

In the first place, Edward called a council and Richard was summoned to London. As always he was loth to leave Middleham and the family life that he loved.

"Why should you not come with me, Anne?" he said.

I was pleased, although I hated the thought of leaving Middleham and the children. Yet I felt that on this occasion Richard particularly wanted to have me with him. Always at the back of his mind was the question of what George might do next. Isabel was dead and George would be free to marry. I believe some premonition of what would happen was in Richard's mind. It might have been that he needed someone with him to whom he could talk freely, someone in whom he could have complete trust. I was that one.

"The journey will be hard going," he said, "for we shall have to travel with all speed if we are to get there in time for the first day of the council meeting."

I knew I could leave the children in the care of their nurses and attendants, and Richard and I left for the south.

I felt uneasy to be at court. Clarence was there. He met me with an absolute nonchalance, as though the cookshop incident had never happened. He talked sentimentally of Isabel and said he was heartbroken; but his expressions of pleasure at seeing me and his recollections of his dear Isabel struck me as somewhat false. As with his brother Edward, when one saw them after an absence, one was always aware of their outstanding good looks—the height, the splendid physique, the clean-cut features, the almost perfectly masculine beauty. But I fancied Clarence looked a little bloated: his complexion was more florid. I knew of his fondness for good malmsey. Isabel used to say she often chided him for drinking too much, and when he drank he went into realms of fancy, seeing himself as the all-powerful one—the king, no less.

When we arrived in London the council was already sitting. Edward, I knew, would be delighted to have Richard's support. He would be very wary of Clarence. I wondered that he allowed him to come to the council after his past record. Edward seemed to wave all that aside simply because he would not let himself believe that he had a brother who would betray him if he had a chance to do so.

After that first council meeting, Richard told me that the discussion had centered on trade. The great concern was what the effect would be on our English markets, and of course whether

the death of Burgundy—England's ally and Louis's enemy—
would give Louis an opportunity of refusing to honor his treaty.

However, Edward had a secret meeting with Richard and this
I believe was at the root of his concern as much as any other.

In our apartments, as we lay in bed, Richard unburdened
himself to me. After all, I was with him that he might talk openly
to someone whom he could trust. He had once said that talking
to me was like talking to himself and as he listened to himself he
saw a subject from a different angle. Moreover he knew that
everything he said to me would go no farther.

"Edward's real concern is not so much with trade and the pension, for he believes he can keep trade going and still have a hold
on Louis. But our sister of Burgundy is trying to arrange a match
between Mary and George."

"But Isabel . . ."

"Isabel is conveniently dead. If I know our brother, he will be
on the look-out for a convenient match . . . and what could be
more so than this? Burgundy is one of the greatest estates in Europe.
Clarence is avid for power. He wants the throne of England, of
course. In his heart Edward knows that. But there is another matter. Burgundy has always believed it has a claim to the English
throne. What do you think would happen if Clarence married
Mary of Burgundy?"

"I think in the first place that Edward would never allow it."

"You are right. I know he seems easy-going, but when it is
necessary, he can be strong. He likes peace. He is affable almost to
a fault and it will need a good deal to provoke him. But in a matter like this he will stand firm."

"Margaret, your sister, wants it."

"Margaret always loved George dearly. I was so jealous of him when we were young. As I have told you, to Margaret he was always her dear little brother, so handsome and charming. Edward was the same as far as George was concerned. But Edward will certainly not allow this Burgundian marriage."

"And Clarence?"

"I am afraid he will be vengeful."

"Against the king? Will he dare?"

"When he is in one of his impulsive moods, he will dare anything. He does not look beyond the immediate present. He sees his wild dreams come true. I'll swear that now he is seeing himself Lord of Burgundy and doubtless . . . in due course . . . conqueror of England."

"He frightens me, Richard."

"He frightens us all. If he were not the king's brother—and Edward were not the man he is—Clarence would have lost his head long ere this. Margaret stresses the point that Mary should marry an Englishman to ensure that the ties between us are kept intact. We all agree. But what Englishman? Not Clarence. Not Rivers."

"Rivers?"

"The queen's brother. Edward had allowed his name to go forward as a possible husband. It is only because the queen has pleaded for it. Everyone knows how she constantly puts forward members of her family. That has been one of the main troubles since Edward married her. Edward placates her, particularly when he knows there is not a chance of her attaining her ambitions."

"You mean that Edward has actually allowed Rivers to seek Mary's hand in competition with George?"

"He will not allow Clarence to be in the running."

"Yet Rivers is there?"

"Rivers has not a chance. Mary would laugh at the suggestion. So would everyone else . . . except the queen, who is robbed of her good sense where the promotion of her family is concerned. She thinks that because she, a woman of no standing, succeeded in marrying a king, she can pair off members of her family with all the great houses, not only in England but in Europe."

"And your sister Margaret favors Clarence! Does she have much influence with Mary?"

"She may have, but Mary is a strong-minded young woman. She will have her own views, I doubt not. What she needs is a strong man beside her and neither Clarence nor Rivers would fit the role. She would, of course, reject them both. But, in view of Margaret's preference for George, Edward says he cannot allow his name to go forward."

"I can see why he is worried. But what will Clarence say when he, the king's brother, is rejected by the king while Rivers is offered?"

"He will be furious. There is no doubt of that."

"And say that the king favored his wife's brother and rejected his own."

"He will say a great many things, then lose his senses in his favorite malmsey and think up some ambitious project."

How I wished we could leave court and all the intrigues. My heart was in Middleham. I think Richard's was, too.

I was with Richard when Clarence stormed in. Richard dismissed everyone else and I was alone with him and his brother.

"I will endure this no more," burst out Clarence. "There is a conspiracy against me."

"That is not so, George," began Richard. "And if you are referring to this Burgundy matter . . ."

"My brother would not allow me to accept the offer. Yet that nobody . . . that upstart, prancing Rivers . . ."

"George, Edward knew from the beginning that Rivers would be unacceptable."

"He has insulted me. I am not good enough. I, the king's brother, the Duke of Clarence of the House of York . . . yet that ninny . . . just because he is the brother of that . . . witch! God give me patience. How much longer shall I endure these insults? I . . . who have every right to the crown of this land . . ."

"George, be careful," said Richard.

"You, brother. You are a toady. Edward is the king, you say. You dance to his tune. You are his favorite brother because you have no spirit. We should stand against him . . . both of us."

"This is treason," said Richard.

George laughed at him. "The good little brother. Was it not always so? Edward is right. Edward is wonderful. We must obey Edward, even when he marries a witch. Edward could never leave women alone . . . and he learns nothing. He is duped by that witch who would set her family up against us. This is the end."

"Have a care, George, lest it should be the end of Edward's leniency toward you."

"I shall endure no more."

"You have endured nothing. Mary herself will choose her husband. If she wants you, the offer will be made, and rest assured she will laugh the idea of Rivers to scorn."

"Our brother must be mad to allow his name to be suggested."

"Only because it will not be received with any seriousness."

"Our sister Margaret wants me. She has said so."

"George, if Mary wants you, rest assured there will be a match for you with Burgundy."

"Edward will try to stop it."

"Wait and see."

"You and I should stand against this tyranny. Oh, I know you, little Gloucester. You would never stand against Edward . . . treat you how he would."

"I have never had anything but love and kindness from him."

"That's because you toady all the time."

"Would it not be better if you were a little more loyal to the king?"

George stalked impatiently from the chamber.

When he had gone, Richard said, "You see how indiscreet he is? I only hope he does not destroy himself."

"If he is destroyed, he will have none but himself to blame."

"He is inflamed by wine. He will calm down in time."

"I hope it will be soon. He seems very eager to marry again although it is only a short time since Isabel died. I thought he cared for her. I know she cared for him."

"A lot of people have cared for George. We all did. I have told you often how Margaret and Edward doted on him. George cares

only for himself. He is a dreamer of wild dreams. He sees a con-
summation of these dreams but he refuses to accept what is necessary to reach it. That is his trouble. He has already had a try for
the throne with your father. He refuses to see that Edward has
been amazingly kind to him, to take him back . . . to treat him
like a brother. Anyone but George would have learned his lesson.
But George never learns. I fear for him and for us."

"Richard, you have so many cares," I said. "I wish we could go
home and live quietly."

Richard sighed and I knew he shared my wish.

Clarence was certainly in a wild mood. His anger was directed
mainly against the Woodvilles, and he decided to take the law
into his own hands.

At first there were rumors that shocked me deeply.

I heard two of the women who had accompanied me from
Middleham discussing Isabel and I wanted to know what they
were saying about my sister. They were loth to tell me at first, but
I insisted.

"They are saying that she was poisoned, my lady," said one.

"Poisoned! My sister! That is not true."

"My lady, it is what is said."

"I want to know more of this."

"The duke, my lady, is prostrate with grief."

Prostrate with grief, I thought! It did not seem so since he was
proposing to marry Mary of Burgundy.

"They say he is determined to find the culprits."

They could tell me no more. I asked Richard about it.

"There will often be such rumors," he said. "One should not

take a great deal of notice of them. It may be that someone was saying Isabel was young to die and the rumor starts. People are always ready to suspect poison when someone dies."

"Isabel was never strong."

Richard looked at me anxiously. I guessed what he was thinking. Why should Warwick, the strong man, and his healthy wife, produce only two delicate daughters? I guessed that thought had often been in his mind. With Isabel's death, his anxiety about my health had been increased.

I went to him and laid my hand on his arm.

"I am going to live for a long time," I said. "I must . . . for you and Edward. As for Isabel . . . that last child, little Richard, was too much for her. She was not well before. She had already had three children . . . the last two too soon together. This rumor of poison is nonsense."

On Isabel's death Ankarette Twynyho had returned to her native village in Somerset and decided that she would settle there among members of her family. I am sure Ankarette would have been very contented and would have become quite a figure in the village with her anecdotes about the court and people in high places.

She had served the queen as well as my sister and therefore Clarence turned his attention to her.

He must have been the one who set in circulation the rumors that his wife has been poisoned, and as his hatred against the Woodville family had been intensified by this recent rivalry for the hand of Mary of Burgundy, he decided he would find a way of calling attention to their villainy.

With a company of guards he rode down to Somerset and there found Ankarette. His men seized her and took her off to Warwick to be tried for the murder of my sister and her baby son.

Clarence implied that she was a servant of the queen and that the queen had sent her to my sister with instructions to poison her and her child.

He set up his own judge and jury who, on his orders, found her guilty of the crime and condemned her to death by hanging.

The sentence was carried out without delay.

When I heard the news I was overcome with horror. I had known Ankarette well. She was quite incapable of such a deed. She had been very fond of Isabel and had loved all children.

Clarence was crazy. Why should she want to poison Isabel? Clarence hinted that the woman was obeying the orders of her mistress, the queen.

Richard was both bewildered and shocked.

"What a fool my brother is!" he cried. "He acts without thinking. He just wants to strike a blow at the Woodvilles and he does this terrible thing to an innocent woman. After this, they will work against him more than they ever did before. He has proclaimed himself not only their enemy but as a reckless, foolish man, a creature of no judgment. He will destroy himself."

I thought perhaps that would be the best thing . . . for him and for us all.

"You see what he has done?" went on Richard. "He has not only murdered this innocent woman, but he has behaved in a manner that would only be permissible if he were king. He has taken the law into his own hands, which no subject must do. He must stop this rash behavior or he will certainly find himself in such danger from which even the king will not be able to save him."

As for myself, I was shocked beyond measure. I could only think of poor Ankarette, that chatty, lovable woman, hanging lifeless from a rope.

MYSTERY IN THE
BOWYER TOWER

I t was a great relief to return to the sanity of
Middleham. How thankful I was that Richard was
lord of the northern marches, so that we could live
there in the free fresh air.

There was a great welcome for us. The children were waiting to greet us. My anxious eyes went immediately to Edward.
His cheeks were pink because he was excited and that gave him
a healthier look. I was eager to discover how he had been while
I was away. As for the other two, they were clearly in good
health and spirits. I saw the pride in Richard's eyes as they rested
on them, and also the faint anxiety when his eyes turned to
our son.

Isabel's death and that of Ankarette had upset me a great deal.
Isabel had never been robust but her daughter, Margaret,

appeared to be a fine healthy child. I had heard that Edward, the Earl of Warwick—for the title had gone to Clarence—was quite healthy but lacking, so it was said; slow to speak, slow to walk. My Edward was bright enough; it was just that he was a little frail compared with his half-brother and -sister.

I must stop worrying about his health, I chided myself. I must stop thinking about Ankarette. I must stop that dread I was beginning to feel concerning my brother-in-law. But having once been the victim of one of his mad schemes made that difficult. He was ruthless in his quest for power.

I wondered how long the king would allow him to go on wreaking havoc on the lives of those about him; and once more I rejoiced that we were removed from court and such intrigues.

Those were uneasy months. We had the occasional visitor from court and when we learned what was happening there my relief was intensified.

We heard that there appeared to be open hostility between the king and the Duke of Clarence, and that Clarence made a point of staying away from court as much as possible. On the rare occasions when he was at the royal table he ostentatiously inspected each dish that was put before him and refused all drinks. It was a studied manner of implying that he suspected poison. He talked openly about the manner in which his wife had been poisoned and the wicked woman who had been sent by the queen to perform the dastardly deed. She had been rightly punished, but it was those who paid her to commit the crime who were the true culprits.

Such talk was very dangerous.

"It is said," our visitor told us, "that the king is fast losing patience with the duke. As for the queen and her family, they are determined to be rid of him. I am sure some charge will be brought against him ere long. They do not take the accusation of being involved in his wife's death lightly."

Richard said little to our guest, but afterward he confided in me that Edward must be realizing at last that he would have to take some action against George. Who could guess what mad scheme was on his mind?

Even in the north we heard of the trial of Dr. John Stacey. In fact the whole country was soon talking about it.

Stacey was an astronomer at Oxford who was accused of witchcraft. He was arrested and under torture admitted that he dabbled in the evil arts and implicated a certain Thomas Burdett who was employed in Clarence's household.

That was when interest in the case became so widespread, because under torture Burdett admitted that they were studying the stars for the purpose of reading the fate of the king.

Even Edward must take note of this. He had set up judges to discover the nature of these investigations and the verdict was that these people had been concerned in prophesying the death of the king and, moreover, using their arts to bring this about. This was treason and sentence was passed on all the men involved. They were taken to Tyburn and hanged.

This should have been a warning to Clarence, as one of the accused was a member of his household.

Clarence never learned lessons. He railed against the injustice done to innocent men. He blamed the Woodvilles. They controlled the king. The king had no power over his wife and her rapacious relatives were running—and ruining—the country.

Every day we waited to hear of some outrageous act. Edward's patience was at an end.

It was a June day when a messenger came to Middleham from the king. Clarence had been committed to the Tower and Richard was commanded to come to court without delay.

The king's younger son, Richard, Duke of York, was to marry Anne Mowbray, heiress of Norfolk, and Richard must play his part in the ceremony.

"Marry!" I cried, when Richard told me. "He is only a child."

"I believe all of four years old and his bride is six. But she is one of the richest heiresses in the country. This will be the queen's contriving."

I was horrified to contemplate such a marriage. Why, the boy was much the same age as my own son Edward.

However, for such an occasion, the Duke and Duchess of Gloucester must be present.

It was a long and tiresome journey and I knew Richard's heart was heavy. Clarence was a menace and there would be no peace while he was allowed to pursue his rebellious ways—but for a brother to be a prisoner in the Tower was something Richard found hard to accept. I was sure the king felt the same.

When we arrived in London, Richard went at once to the king. He was with him for a long time and when he came back he was very sorrowful.

"I think Edward is probably going to forgive him," he said. "He cannot bear to think of the little boy whom he used to love so dearly as an enemy. He said to me, 'He wants my crown, Richard. I believe nothing else will satisfy him. He is so wild . . . so foolish. How long does he think he would last as king? He never thinks beyond the moment. There is more to being a king than wearing a crown and smiling at the loyal shouts of the people. George will never understand this.' I said, 'You have done the only thing possible by sending him to the Tower. He will come to his senses there. It seems the only way to make him realize the dangerous position he has put himself in.' I think he agreed with me but he is wavering."

It was shortly after that when Cecily, Duchess of York came to visit us. The duchess, Richard's mother and my father's aunt, was a lady of great presence. She was indeed one of the most regal persons I have ever met; and I believe that since her son Edward came to the throne she behaved as though she were a queen, demanding homage from all those who came into contact with her.

In her presence one felt impelled to show the respect due to royalty.

She was a very handsome woman. In her youth she had been noted for her beauty and known as The Rose of Raby; but now her face was ravaged by sorrow. I had heard that she had never recovered from the death of her husband, for they had been a devoted couple and she had accompanied him on many of his campaigns even when she was pregnant, which she invariably was at that time.

Seeing her now in her old age, but still a commanding figure, I could imagine how angry and humiliated she had felt when her husband's head, adorned with a paper crown, had been set on the walls of York. It must be a consolation for such a woman that her son, Edward, was now King of England.

I went to her and knelt, which seemed the natural thing to do in her presence. She bade me rise.

She said, "I am in great distress. I would speak with Richard."

"My lady," said Richard. "Anne and I have no secrets from each other. You need have no fear to speak before her."

She looked at me intently. Then she said, "Very well. Stay here. It is of George I wish to speak."

"George is the king's prisoner," said Richard in dismay.

"His own brother!" cried the duchess. "There should not be quarrels within the family."

"George has been behaving very foolishly," said Richard. "He has done so many reckless things damaging to the king. And now he has allowed himself to be involved in this witchcraft plot against the king's life."

"George is a little careless. He means no harm, I am sure."

Richard looked faintly exasperated. I guessed he had heard that said so often in his childhood.

"My lady mother," he said, "you must know that George has committed many acts for which other men would have lost their heads."

She looked at him disbelievingly. "I know he has a streak of mischief."

"Mischief indeed! Do you know he shut Anne up in a cook-shop and left her there to work in the kitchens? Do you call that a streak of mischief? He should have lost his head for that alone."

"Richard! You are speaking of your brother."

"I know it and I wish he were any man's brother but mine."

"You must not talk thus of George. Anne, you must persuade him. You must understand that this is his brother . . . my son!"

"Could *you* not speak to the king, my lady? George's fate is in his hands."

"I have spoken to the king. Naturally I spoke to him first."

"And did he not listen?" asked Richard.

"He listened. He was all charm and sympathy, but there was a hardness in his face. It was that woman. *She* is against George. Edward should never have married her."

"I believe that at this time it is not the queen but Edward himself who is beginning to realize what a danger George is to him."

"Listen to me, Richard. Edward is fond of you. You are his favorite. You always adored him so blatantly. Edward is a fine man . . . a great king . . . but he grows hard. And we are speaking of his brother."

"Edward is the most forgiving man I know. He has forgiven George over and over again. But this time George has gone too far."

"But you will speak to him, Richard. I, your mother, beg you to. No . . . I command you to. George is mischievous. Edward knows this. It is not to be taken too seriously. If you will talk to Edward . . . explain he means no harm . . . he will listen to you."

"I think he will make up his own mind in this matter. George has been judged a traitor and you know the penalty for that, my lady."

"Edward cannot allow his own brother to be put to death!"

"I am sure he will not allow that. He will soften toward him as he has done so many times before."

"Richard, you must speak to your brother. I beg you to."

"Then I will speak to him."

"Remind him that George is his brother."

"He is not likely to forget that, my lady."

"I rely on you."

"I will tell him of your feelings, but it may be that this time George has gone too far."

He would promise nothing more.

She was displeased. She was one of those women who expect immediate obedience from everyone around them, and that includes their own children.

The wedding of the Duke of York to the little Norfolk heiress was a grand affair. The bridegroom was very handsome—as all the king's children were—with his sturdy young body and fair looks. The king was clearly proud of his family and he had good reason to be, and so had the queen. She was very contented. There was no question about her beauty; she was dazzlingly so, even now. But there was something very cold about her; she was statuesque and her perfect features might have been cut out of marble. She was clearly proud of her achievements—widow of a humble knight to become Queen of England and moreover hold her place in the heart of the philandering king all these years. Of course, she was clever. Many still said she relied on witchcraft and her mother had undoubtedly been a witch. A strong woman, the queen's mother. She had been married to the mighty Duke of

Bedford and had become a widow when she was only seventeen years old; and then she had fallen passionately in love with Sir Richard Woodville, had married this comparatively humble man and had remained in love with him, it was said, all through their married life. She was an exceptional woman and belonged to the royal house of Luxembourg. She was the one, it was said, who had bewitched the king into marrying her daughter.

And now here was Elizabeth Woodville, proud of all she had achieved. Her eldest son Edward was now Prince of Wales and his brother, the little bridegroom, Duke of York. There was one of her children whom I noticed particularly. This was Elizabeth, the eldest of her daughters, for whom she demanded great homage because of the proposed union with the Dauphin of France, which had been one of the results of the Treaty of Picquigny. Elizabeth was addressed as Madame la Dauphine, which I thought a little premature, remembering what often happened to these proposed alliances.

The marriage of the two children was taking place in St. Stephen's Chapel from the walls of which hung blue velvet decorated with the golden fleur-de-lys. Lord Rivers led in little Anne Mowbray.

Both children did as they had been told, although I am sure neither of them had a notion of what it was all about. And when the ceremony was over, it was Richard's duty to scatter gold coins among the crowd waiting outside. And then Anne Mowbray, with Richard on one side and the Duke of Buckingham on the other, was escorted to the banqueting hall.

There were shouts of loyalty from the people. Weddings were

always a source of interest and enjoyment and the wedding of such a young pair was particularly delightful to them.

It was on this occasion that I exchanged a few words with the queen. She said how grieved she had been to hear of Isabel's death.

"She was delicate, of course," she said. "There are some of us who should not bear too many children." She was a little complacent, implying she, who had borne several children and still retained her youthful looks and beauty, was most certainly not one of them.

"I sent Ankarette to her to help her." Her face hardened. "That was a terrible case. Ankarette was a good woman. She served us both well."

"I know, your Grace," I said.

She touched my hand lightly. "There are some wicked people among us," she whispered. "It is best that they are under restraint. I must go to Madame la Dauphine. I am pleased to see you here, duchess."

It was gracious of her to speak to me. I think she wanted to stress to me that the Duke of Clarence was unworthy to live.

The next days were given over to jousting. Knights came into London from all over the country to take part. The Woodvilles, of course, were very much in evidence and the occasions were graced by the presence of the queen and Madame la Dauphine. The absence of the Duke of Clarence was very noticeable.

Richard told me that he had spoken to Edward about their mother's plea for leniency.

"I should add mine, Anne," he said. "But I am so unsure. He is our brother. He has been near me all my life. We were brought up together."

"Edward, too."

"No, Edward was not with us. There were just the three, Margaret, George, and myself. We were the only ones in the Fotheringay nursery—the young ones. I am glad no decision rests with me. Poor Edward. I know what he must be feeling now. His thoughts will be in the Bowyer Tower with George."

He told me later that Edward had sent for him and had talked of Clarence. In fact Edward could think of nothing else. He said that if he were wise he would let George suffer the penalty of treason. "For," he went on, "there have been so many of his acts that are treasonable.

"I had to admit that that was so. But I asked him how he would feel if he gave the order for his brother's execution. That order would have to come from him. 'It would lie heavy on my conscience,' he answered. And it would. Poor Edward, I pity him."

I said, "He should not reproach himself. He has been a good brother to George and George has scarcely been the same to him."

"I have suggested that he go to George and talk to him. Give him one last chance . . . and if he should err again . . . then make his decision."

"And what said he to this?"

"I believe he is going to do it. I feel sure he will forgive George."

Then I said, "The trouble will start again. It is inevitable."

"You think the king would be justified in signing the death warrant of his brother?"

"Justified, yes. But I do understand what you mean about its lying heavily on his conscience."

"We shall have to see. Edward is going to the Tower. He will go without ceremony. We shall soon know the outcome."

We did. When the king returned from the Bowyer Tower, the first thing he did was send for Richard.

I waited in trepidation to hear the news, for I guessed something of significance must have happened. Richard was absent for a long time and when he came back to our apartment he shut himself in. I went to him and he allowed me to enter his chamber, where I found him looking very distressed.

"Richard!" I cried. "What is it?"

"I . . . cannot believe it," he said. "This is the end. It must be."

"The king has forgiven him?"

He said nothing. He just stared ahead.

I sat on the arm of his chair and stroked the hair back from his face.

"Tell me, Richard," I said. "I feel I should know, because of what I have suffered at his hands."

"It is a most astonishing turn of events," murmured Richard. "He is mad . . . completely mad. He has thrown away his chance. This must be the end. He himself made the decision."

"Richard, I beg of you to tell me what has happened."

"Edward went to him . . . ready to forgive him once more.

But no sooner did George see him than he began to abuse him, shouting that he had brought a breed of reptiles into the family, that he had married a witch and not only had he married her but it seemed he had married her blood-sucking relations also."

"The king would have been in no mood for such talk, I should have thought."

"You would have thought correctly. He ordered George to be silent. He accused him of acts of treason. He told him he had come to help him, but was growing less and less inclined to do so. George was reckless. He had clearly been drinking. A great butt of malmsey had been delivered to his cell on George's orders. Edward went on trying to reason with him. George is shrewd at times and he knew that the king was trying to find reasons for releasing him. Oh, what a fool George is! He could have been a free man today, but he was never very good at reasoning. He was always caught up in the passion of the moment. He went on ranting against the queen and the Woodvilles. Then he said a terrible thing. He said that when our father was away in battle our mother took a lover and the result was Edward, which meant that Clarence was the rightful heir to the throne."

"What a monstrous story!"

"An insult not only to Edward but to my mother."

"I wonder what she would say if she knew?"

"She would be incensed—as Edward is. He said to me, 'You see how he is? What can I do? He is my brother. If I let him go free, how can I know from one day to the next what he will do?' I said to him, 'You shall be confronted by our mother. Perhaps then she would not plead for you so earnestly.'"

"I cannot imagine what she would do if she heard such a rumor," I said.

"Edward does not want her to know what Clarence has said of her. He said it would shock and depress her too deeply. She was always a devoted wife to our father. She was even with him in campaigns whenever she could be. This is a terrible slight on her good name, and so unjustified. But it shows that George will say anything that occurs to him."

"Do you think this will be the end of him?"

Richard was thoughtful. "There is one other matter," he said slowly. "I think Edward was on the verge of telling me, but changed his mind. I am of the opinion that it shocked him so much that he could not speak of it even to me."

"So you have no idea what it was?"

"None at all. As I remember, Edward spoke somewhat incoherently. He said, 'There is something else . . . disastrous if he succeeded.' Then he paused for a long time. I asked him what it was and he said, 'Oh, 'twas nothing in truth . . . just slanderous nonsense. The sort of thing George would think up.' I again asked him to tell me, because I could see that, in spite of the manner in which he was trying to brush aside this thing, it had affected him deeply. 'Nothing . . . nothing,' he said, and he made it clear to me that the matter was closed."

"Do you think that Clarence has offended him beyond forgiveness?"

"I do."

"I suppose the slur on his legitimacy is enough."

"I think it is such nonsense that it could easily be disproved."

"But it shows he is his brother's enemy."

"That is no new discovery. I have a notion that it is this other matter that has made up the king's mind. But knowing Edward, I am unsure. Our mother begged for Clarence's life, and Edward hates there to be rifts in the family. There is Margaret, whom he has offended by refusing to consider Clarence's marriage to Mary and allowing Lord Rivers's name to go forward. He wants harmony all around him . . . so . . . I do not know what George's fate will be."

We were not long kept in doubt.

Next day we heard that the Duke of Clarence, the worse for drink, had fallen into a huge butt of malmsey and been drowned.

The court was stunned by the news. It was well known that the Duke of Clarence was a heavy drinker, and it seemed plausible that, in a drunken stupor, he had reached to fill his goblet, toppled into the butt, and, being intoxicated, was unable to get out. It was ironical that he had been killed by his favorite drink and in a butt that he himself had ordered to be brought into his cell.

I had other suspicions. After what Richard had told me, it seemed certain that he had been killed on Edward's orders.

Duchess Cecily was stricken with grief. She seemed like a different person from Proud Cis, as they called her. She was very sad when she spoke to me.

"Edward is a great king," she said, "and state affairs are safe in his hands. His father would have been a great king, too. How I wish there had not been this quarrel in the family! We should all stand together. There is strength in union and danger in discord."

As I tried to comfort her I could not help wondering what she would have said had she known of the slander that her son would have brought against her. Perhaps then she would have understood why Clarence had to die and that he was indeed a menace to his brother, and the peace of the realm.

Richard was very distressed by the whole matter. We talked about it a little. I knew he thought that Edward had arranged for the death of George . . . in which case it was murder.

"If Clarence had lived," said Richard, "there would have been trouble sooner or later . . . risings all over the country . . . men dying in a foolish and hopeless cause. And just suppose Clarence had triumphed over Edward . . . imagine what harm would have been done to the country. In such a case murder would be justified."

We discussed this for a while and I think we both felt that if the death of one foolish and reckless man had been brought about in order to save the lives and suffering of thousands, the deed was not to be judged as murder but justice.

"Edward was never a vindictive man," insisted Richard. "Whatever happened on that night was justified."

I knew Richard felt better after he had come to that conclusion, and we did not refer to his brother's death again.

Mary of Burgundy had now married the Archduke Maximilian, son of the Hapsburg Emperor Frederick the Third, so the matter that had aroused such fury in Clarence and led to his death was now concluded.

There was another arrest that puzzled Richard. It had taken place on the very night of Clarence's death. This was that of

Robert Stillington, the Bishop of Bath and Wells. He was a good Yorkist, but he was accused of uttering treasonable words that could be prejudicial to the state. It was a small matter and Still-ington was soon released, but I was to remember this some time after, although it seemed of very little importance at the time.

There was nothing now to detain us. Richard assured Edward that it would be unwise for him to stay too long away from the north. Edward embraced Richard warmly, calling him his "loyal brother." Richard was deeply touched. He told me that Edward had said, "Never have I had any cause to doubt your loyalty to me. I should thank Heaven for giving me the blessings of my brother Richard."

I guessed then that the death of his brother weighed heavily upon him. After taking a tender farewell, during which the king commanded us both to take care of ourselves and each other, for he loved us both dearly, we returned to Middleham and our family.

THE LORD PROTECTOR'S WIFE

What joy to be away from the intrigues and troubles of the court! And there was our family eagerly awaiting us. What a pleasure to slip into the lives of a country nobleman and his wife, to be chatelaine of the castle, to immerse myself in domestic matters! We must, perforce, frequently entertain, but what enjoyable occasions they were! There would be dancing and singing; and often, to the delight of the children, the mummers came to perform.

I would accompany Richard on his various progresses through the northern towns. I enjoyed these visits, especially those to York, which city was the very bastion of the House of York. It was always thrilling to approach those white walls with their battlements and barbican gates.

York was the important town of the north. Some said it was as important as London. The minster, which had only recently been completed, was the glory of the city. The wealth of York was due to its merchants, who carried on a thriving trade, not only throughout the country but on the continent.

The people of the north appreciated Richard's steadying influence. There was always a great welcome for us and I was always thrilled to hear the shouts for Gloucester as we rode along. Richard received this homage with a restrained dignity, but I knew he was proud of what he had been able to achieve in keeping the north peaceful and content for Edward.

We endeavored to be there during the week after Trinity, so that we could witness the miracle plays that were often performed in York at that time, when the actors were the traders of the town and they enacted scenes from the Bible.

This state of utter contentment could not be expected to last forever. There was trouble with the Scots.

Messages came from Edward. He believed that Louis was contemplating the situation in Burgundy and was getting restive. Maximilian was an energetic young man but he lacked the money that he would need if he were to hold out against Louis, and once the French king had brought Burgundy under his control, he would set himself free from the treaty with England. Paying the pension to Edward must rankle, and Edward was sure he was persuading—perhaps bribing—the King of Scotland to harry the English on the border.

James the Third of Scotland was something of a weakling, a man of little judgment, but he might believe that with the backing of the French king he could achieve victory over his old enemy.

The trouble began with border raids, which went on from time to time. However, Edward had information that this was just a preliminary exercise, and he wanted Richard to get an army together and march.

This was a bitter blow. War had come to our beloved north. It continued sporadically over some months, which kept Richard away from home; and at length came the summer and he was ordered to come to Edward because their sister Margaret was paying a visit to England. Richard must be there to greet her, and plans for a Scottish invasion could be discussed at the same time.

So even at Middleham it was impossible to find absolute peace.

I accompanied Richard to London where lavish celebrations were in progress to welcome the important lady, Margaret of Burgundy. However, Richard reported to me that there was a certain coolness between her and Edward. She asked a great many questions about her favorite, George. Edward had allowed him to become a prisoner. She found that hard to understand. She knew well her brother. George was just a charming, mischievous boy. It was difficult to make her see that mischief that can be charming in the young can take on an alarming quality in the mature. But so blinded was Margaret by her love for George that she was determined to defend him without reason.

Richard said it was not a happy meeting. Margaret, of course, had had a purpose in coming, and she was disappointed in the outcome.

"She fears that Burgundy is weak," said Richard. "Maximilian desperately needs help and she has come to ask Edward for it. 'Help against the King of France!' Edward cried. 'He is my bene-factor.' It's true, of course, and Margaret must have known that the enmity between France and Burgundy was England's strength as it had ever been. And yet she was asking him to take up arms against the King of France!

"'What of my pension?' demanded Edward. 'Are you pre-pared to replace it?' Well, he did not expect an answer to that question, I am sure. So, Margaret, who has come to England to ask for aid for Burgundy, will be disappointed."

She returned to Burgundy, hurt and disillusioned; and we went back to Scotland and the war.

Two years passed. Richard and I had been married for ten years and there was no sign of another child. That was a source of great sorrow to me. Moreover, my fears regarding my son's health were growing. He was a dear boy—quiet, gentle, and loving—but it was very clear that he lacked the strength and vitality of his half-brother and -sister.

As for myself, I was often overtaken by lassitude, which tired me, and I would have to retire to my chamber to rest, though I tried to keep this a secret from Richard.

How thankful I was when he brought the war with the Scots to a satisfactory conclusion. It was a great joy to see more of him, but there was a constant nagging fear for my son's health . . . and now my own.

Richard would not have our boy forced to take part in military exercises. He remembered the days of his own youth when he had striven to keep up with the boys of his age. Our son was more inclined to study and Richard said he must follow his own inclinations.

Little Anne Mowbray, the child bride of the Duke of York, died. I heard it said that the queen genuinely mourned her, for she had taken her little daughter-in-law into her household after the marriage; but she was heard to comment that, in spite of the child's early death, her fortune had passed to the Duke of York and that clearly gratified her.

There was another death, and that was to have a startling effect on us all.

It happened at the end of March of that year '82, but we did not hear the news until some weeks afterward, and even then I did not realize the importance to us.

Mary of Burgundy, out riding, was thrown from her horse and died from her injuries. She had left two children, a girl and a boy. Now Maximilian must bear the burdens of state alone. Margaret wrote to Edward begging for help, and Maximilian added his pleas to hers; but there was nothing Edward could do while he had his treaty with the King of France to consider.

We were expected to travel to the court at Westminster to celebrate Christmas. Edward sent for us with an affectionate message. He wanted to thank his beloved brother in person for the splendid victories over the Scots.

Richard and I—with our son—set out for the south.

That was to be a memorable Christmas. It was the beginning of change—a sad and unhappy change for me, in spite of the worldly glory it brought. I had no wish for it; all through it I yearned to be back at Middleham, but alas we cannot order our lives and must accept what comes to us.

The king greeted us effusively. He was as magnificent as ever. True, he had grown fat, which was not surprising if what one heard of his self-indulgence was accurate. His complexion was florid and his magnificent eyes faintly bloodshot. Yet he still looked like the model of a king, in spite of the pouches under his eyes. He was distinguished among all those surrounding him: he was smiling, benign, friendly, jocular, and approachable. I have often thought that no monarch could have been more loved by his people. They would always smile on him no matter what they heard of his countless mistresses, and his unpopular marriage. Yet there was the queen, as beautiful as ever, the years seemingly unable to touch that ice-cold perfection; and all her children—two sons and five daughters—were as beautiful as their parents.

The king embraced Richard. "My brother," he said. "My dear, dear brother. God strike me if I ever forget what I owe to you! Welcome. We see too little of each other. And Anne, Anne, my dear sister. We are going to put some color into those cheeks; we are going to make you dance the night away; we are going to put some flesh on those beautiful bones of yours. You don't look after this dear girl enough, Richard. I must have a word with you on that score."

"I am well, my lord," I insisted.

He kissed me. "We are going to make you even more so. And my nephew . . . welcome, fair sir. We are delighted to have you with us. Your cousins are waiting to greet you."

He exuded bonhomie and goodwill and I believe it was genuine. He loved people and he wanted them to love him. It was impossible not to fall under his charm.

Little did we know then that the blow was about to fall.

Richard was with him when the news came. He was glad of that. He told me about it afterward.

"Messengers arrived from Burgundy," he said. "I could see that my brother was not very eager to receive them. He was ever so. He hated bad news and always wanted to hold it off, even for a little while. He had been thinking of Christmas and the festivities. You know how he always enjoys revelry and such. Perhaps he had an inkling of what was to come. 'What think you this news from Burgundy may be?' he said to me. 'It is doubtless Maximilian begging again.' I replied, 'What will happen to him now? He is not strong enough to stand against Louis.' 'He's energetic enough,' said Edward. 'What he needs is arms and men. A war cannot be fought without them.'

"He was thoughtful and, I could see, a little worried. I said to him, 'Why not send for the messengers? Why not see what they have to report?'

"He looked at me steadily. 'You speak sense as always, Dickon,' he said, calling me by my childhood name. 'We'll send for the men.'"

"And when they came?" I asked.

"I had never seen him so affected. The men had letters from Margaret. My brother read them and I saw the blood rush into his face; his eyes seemed as though they would burst from his head. I said to him, 'What is it, Edward? You can trust me.' He put out a hand and I took it. I had to steady him. I thought he was going to fall. His face was suffused with rage. I led him to a chair and forced him to sit down. He did so. He continued to shake. He thrust the letter into my hand. 'Read that,' he said.

"I read the letter he gave me. I could not believe those words. Maximilian, unable to go on without help, had given up and made peace terms with Louis. There was to be a marriage between the dauphin and Mary's young daughter, Margaret; and the little girl's dowry would be Burgundy and Artois.

"The letter fell from my hand," went on Richard. "I was as stunned as Edward. My first thoughts were of my niece Elizabeth, known throughout the court as Madame la Dauphine. Another would have that title now. I was not surprised at my brother's wrath. This alliance between Louis and Burgundy would mean that there was no longer any need for Louis to keep the peace with England."

"Will this be the end of the king's pension from France?" I asked.

"I could see that that was what was hurting Edward most. I was very alarmed for him, Anne. I have never seen him as he was then. It was always his way to shake off trouble. He had always been optimistic . . . even at the worst of times. Then . . . he leaned forward in his chair, and suddenly I saw his face suffused with purple blood. I loosened the shirt at his throat as he gasped for breath. Then I shouted for help. When they came in he had slipped to the floor. He looked so big, so helpless, so different from himself."

Richard put his hand over his eyes. "I love him, Anne," he murmured. "He was always my wonderful brother. So big, so strong . . . so powerful. It was heartbreaking to see him thus."

I tried to comfort him. "Richard," I said. "This cannot be . . . the end."

"The physicians are with him. They say it is a seizure. He clings to life. He knows he must not leave us."

I prayed with him and we waited for news.

The king had recovered. He sent for Richard, and I waited in trepidation for his return. I was very relieved when I saw him for I knew that the news was good.

Richard was smiling. "He is magnificent," he said. "He looks almost his old self. He says that the Christmas festivities are to go on as usual and he wants them to be more splendid than ever."

"He has completely recovered then?"

"It seems so. I wonder if he feels as well as he implies, for he did speak to me very seriously. He said, 'My little Edward is but a child. He is twelve years old. He is young to have responsibility thrust upon him.' I said, 'But that will not be for many years.' 'Oh yes, yes,' he replied. But I saw the clouds in his eyes and he went on slowly and thoughtfully, 'I have had a seizure, Dickon. When this sort of thing happens, it can be called a warning. Oh, I don't mean I am going to die tomorrow. I have years yet. I must have . . . because Edward is so young.'

"I said, of course he would fully recover. He is as strong as an ox. We could not do without him. Little Edward could not. I could not. England could not. He took my hand and pressed it. He told me he had known all through his life, which had been a somewhat turbulent one, that he could rely on me. I had never failed him. Some had and he was sorry indeed for what happened to them. 'My good friends at one time,' he mused. 'Warwick, George, they betrayed me. But never you, Dickon, never you.' I was deeply touched, and I told him how I had always loved and admired him. He had been the hero of my childhood, I said, and he continued to be.

"We sat in silence for a long time. Then he said, 'I want you to promise me this. If I were to have another seizure, and if that time . . .' I shook my head and said, 'No, it will not be so.' He ignored that and went on, 'I want you to be the one to look after Edward. Guide him . . . you shall be Protector of England until he is of an age to govern. Then I want you beside him.' I assured him that I would follow his wishes. Whatever he asked, I would do for his sake. He seemed contented then. I said, 'But you are going to live for a good many years yet, Edward.' 'At least twenty,' he said with his old jocularity. He seemed happier then."

"He must be worried about his health."

"Yes . . . he began to talk about his achievements, as though he wanted to justify himself."

"Perhaps," I said, "he felt a twinge of conscience about taking the throne from Henry who was the rightful king."

"I guessed it was on his mind. It was right that Edward should take the crown for England's sake . . . but as you say, Henry was in the direct line. He did not speak of Henry. He went on to stress the improvements he had brought to the country. Trade had increased. 'I always had sympathy with the merchants,' he said. 'And some of their wives,' he added, trying to introduce a lighter note. I said in the same mood, 'I believe Jane Shore is still in favor.'"

"Perhaps that was not wise, since he was stressing his virtues."

"Oh, he never looked on his amorous adventures as sins. They were natural, he would say, and gave not only pleasure to himself but to his partners in the exercise. 'It is a king's duty to please his subjects,' he always said. No, he did not mind the reference to Jane; he is always happy to speak of her. I believe he cares very deeply for that woman.

"He went on to say that he understood business, which most kings did not. 'There is more to governing a kingdom than going to war and giving pageants,' he said. I replied, 'Well, trade certainly has improved and you have brought law and order to the land.' 'And,' he added, 'I have started to build St. George's Chapel at Windsor, which will be a splendid asset to the nation. I have built libraries. And who was it who brought Caxton with his printing to these shores? Did I not do that?' 'You have done a great deal for the nation,' I assured him.

"Then he went on to talk of that which had always been a matter of contention between us: the French pension. He said, 'I know you disapprove most heartily of that. I understood your feelings. But it was the right thing to do at the time. I had the money for my country, Dickon: Louis's money. True, it is over now. Louis won't pay another crown. Why should he? He is no longer in fear of Burgundy, and it was Burgundy he was thinking of all the time. It made him my enemy and Warwick's friend . . . for a while. But Louis's friendship swayed this way and that. Well, after all, he is a king. But let me tell you this: I had Louis's money, which meant that I did not have to tax my own people . . . merchants and such like. That is another reason why trade prospered. So who shall say it was wrong? The money was better spent that way than in profitless war.'"

I said, "It is significant that he should talk to you thus. Do you not think it implies that he is in fear of sudden death?"

"He always opened his heart to me."

"He is anxious. The queen will be deeply hurt and humiliated about the Princess Elizabeth. It is a pity she was so insistent on her being known throughout the court as Madame la Dauphine."

"The queen allowed her avarice and pride to overcome her sense of propriety. She ought to know that royal alliances can never be counted on until they are completed. However, the anxiety over the king's health has overshadowed that other disappointment."

"The queen must be relieved that he is still alive."

"It will make her realize how much she depends on him."

"I think she has always been aware of that," I commented.

During Christmas the king was as merry as ever and the anxiety about his health began to wane. What could be wrong with a man who danced as he did, ate as heartily and indulged in the usual flirtations with the ladies of the court? It had been a temporary indisposition and the king's strong body could shake off such an inconvenience with ease.

He was determined to promote that theory; and to see him dancing in the great hall with his beautiful eldest daughter—now shorn of her grand title and merely Princess Elizabeth—implied that it was the right one.

Richard's fears were allayed.

"It is true," he said. "He has the strength of ten men. He will be all right."

After Christmas we left court for Middleham, and once more I experienced the joy that never failed to come to me when I returned to my home.

It was the middle of April and two months since we had left Westminster. We had settled down once more to the peaceful life—my greatest concern being for my son's health.

He was coughing now and then and I did not like that. It was a continual anxiety. How I wished that I could have other children, but that seemed one of the blessings fate had denied me. Isabel had had four, only two of whom had survived, it was true, but Margaret was by all accounts a bonny child and Edward was in good physical health. Why could I not conceive? Sometimes I wondered if my infertility disappointed Richard as much as it did me. But of course it must; it was only because he was so good and kind that he did not show it.

I was in the solarium when I heard the sound of horses' hoofs. I looked down and saw a messenger. He had apparently ridden far and at great speed.

I ran down. Richard was already with him.

The man gasped out, "The king is dead."

We were stunned. Richard went pale and shook his head. I could see he was clinging to disbelief. He could not speak for a few seconds, then he cried, "When?"

"On the ninth of April, my lord."

The ninth of April, and we were now halfway through the month.

"You come from the queen?" asked Richard.

"No, my lord, on the command of my Lord Hastings."

He produced a letter, which he handed to Richard. I stood beside him and read it with him.

"The king has left all to your protection . . . the heir, the realm. Secure the person of the new sovereign, King Edward the Fifth, and come to London with him at all speed."

When the messenger had been sent to the kitchens to refresh himself, I said to Richard, "What now?"

Richard was thoughtful. Then he said slowly, "The young king is at Ludlow with Lord Rivers. I think my best plan is to send to him there. I will tell him that, as Lord Protector and his uncle, I should be the one to conduct him to London and to decide by what route we shall go. I could meet him on the way. In the meantime I must prepare."

"Oh, what bad news this is, Richard. I know what you felt for him."

Richard was too full of emotion to speak. He went back into the castle and set about making plans to collect his men together so that they might be ready to start as soon as possible for Ludlow.

For several days nothing happened. Richard was growing restive when there was a further message from Hastings warning him that the Woodvilles were bent on getting young Edward to London and there crowning him that it might be said he needed no guidance from his uncle.

Richard was uncertain. He could not understand why there had been no news from Westminster. He had thought his brother's council would have informed him immediately of Edward's death and the fact that they had not done so, together with the communication from Hastings, meant that the situation was beginning to look alarming.

He decided to write to the queen and the council and no sooner had these letters been dispatched than messengers came riding into the courtyard. This time they came from the Duke of Buckingham.

It was clear that Buckingham expected trouble, but Richard was wary of him. He was very different in character from Richard. Buckingham was adventurous, taking a delight in being at the center of some daring enterprise. It was understandable that Richard was a little suspicious of him. He knew he bore a grudge against the Woodvilles and would seize any opportunity to strike at them, because he had never forgiven the queen for forcing him to marry her sister Catherine. Buckingham had been only twelve years old at the time and had bitterly resented being used. He belonged to one of the most noble families of the realm and had been married merely to further Woodville ambitions.

Buckingham's message was that he was ready to serve Richard and he believed it was imperative for him to come to London without delay.

Richard now realized that it was time he left. He sent Buckingham's courier back with a message that he was leaving

Yorkshire for London at once and would meet Buckingham on the way.

I was uneasy. I did not like the manner in which things were working out. It seemed more and more strange that no word had been sent to Richard from London; also, in the messages from both Hastings and Buckingham, there appeared to be a warning.

Richard knew of my fear.

I said, "I am glad you have friends in Buckingham and Hastings."

"I am going to need all the friends I can find, Anne," he said gravely.

"I would I could come with you."

"I, too, wish that could be so. But not this time. It would not be wise."

"What will you do?"

"As Hastings suggests. Secure the king and ride with all speed to London. I am coming to the conclusion that if I do not do this the kingdom will soon be in the hands of the Woodvilles."

He was ready to leave. I felt sick with anxiety as I watched the White Boar banner fluttering in the breeze. Then he rode away at the head of three hundred men. He would take no more. He did not want it to appear that he came with an army.

Edward was holding my hand firmly. John and Katharine stood beside him; and we watched until they were out of sight.

I knew this was the end of the cozy life at Middleham.

After Richard had left I grew increasingly concerned. Our king was a boy in his thirteenth year, King Edward the Fifth. I had often heard how disastrous it was for a country when a king was a minor. There were always too many powerful men trying to manipulate the boy king. Poor Henry the Sixth had been a baby when he came to the throne. How different the history of our country might have been if his father had lived longer! There would have been no War of the Roses, no kingmaker. Perhaps my father would have lived the life of an ordinary nobleman, spending more time with his family on his own estates. We could have been a happy family. Perhaps Isabel would not have died. Certainly she would not have lost her first child at sea. My mother would never have been a prisoner at Beaulieu. I should never have been affianced to the Prince of Wales and put in a cookshop from which, without good luck, I might never have escaped.

It was all conjecture, but what else was there at such a time? I was in ignorance of what was happening. I feared for Richard. The king had appointed him Protector of the Realm and guardian of the king, but I knew full well that there would be opposition to this, and the Woodvilles, headed by the queen, would do everything in their power to get the king in their control.

The children asked questions. "Where is our father? What is happening?" Katharine was getting too old to be put off with easy answers. She talked to the women. She knew something of what was going on; and she would tell John and Edward.

I said, "Your father has gone to London because there is a new king."

Edward asked, "What has happened to the old one?"

"He died," I told him, "and when a king dies, if he has a son, that son becomes the new king . . . even if he is only a boy."

"How old is the new king?" asked Edward.

"Twelve years old."

"I'm ten," he said proudly.

"It is young to be a king," I went on. "Your father has gone to help him."

"Then everything will be all right," said Edward.

I wished I could have shared his confidence. I was convinced that the situation was fraught with danger. What a tragedy that Edward had died! He was not old. He had lived just over forty years and had seemed so strong, indestructible, until he had had the seizure at the end of the previous year. But of course he had never denied himself anything that his deeply sensuous nature demanded, and hearty eating and insatiable sexuality had taken their toll. Now he had left us with a twelve-year-old boy to rule us, and powerful families attempting to take power.

These were days of deep anxiety and my cough was always worse at times of stress.

I yearned for news. Visitors to the castle were very welcome for they all talked of the death of the king and there were various versions of what was happening or about to.

There were some who came from London, and they were only too eager to tell us all they knew. We learned that there had been much speculation as to how the king had died. The general view was that he had caught a chill during a fishing trip he had taken with a few of his closest friends. The rain had been torrential and they had been in wet clothes for several hours. In view of his recent illness, they said, the king should have been more careful of his health. There were some who said he had never recovered from the tertian fever, which he had caught when campaigning in the French marshes; others said he had lived too well; and, of course, there was the inevitable murmur of poison. But the prevailing verdict was that the king had died through an excess of living.

I learned that he had been ill for ten days, during which he had busied himself with setting his affairs in order.

"They laid out his body on a board in Westminster," said one informant. "He was naked, all but for a loin cloth—a splendid figure of a king, even in death. The Lords Temporal and Spiritual came to gaze at him, and after that the corpse was embalmed and lay in state in St. Stephen's Chapel for ten days before it was taken to Westminster Abbey. A life-sized model of him was placed beside the bier. The figure was dressed in royal robes holding the orb and sceptre . . . so lifelike that it might have been great Edward himself. Then he was taken to Sion House where the cortège stayed overnight, and then on to Windsor to be placed in the king's own chapel of St. George."

I said, "It was what he would have chosen. He would have wanted to go in splendor."

"I have it on authority, my lady, that the cost was one thousand, four hundred and ninety-six pounds, seventeen shillings and two pence."

"He would have liked that, too."

My thoughts were all for Richard and some time later I was to hear the truth of all this from his lips. Then I learned how near he had come to failure; and had things gone against him at this time our lives might have turned out to be entirely different.

What was happening was that when Richard was approaching Northampton, he received a message from Lord Rivers saying that he had left Ludlow with the king in the hope of reaching Northampton on the twenty-ninth of April. He asked Richard, if he reached that town first, to wait there for him, Rivers, to arrive with the king. If Rivers arrived there first, he would wait for Richard. That seemed a very desirable arrangement, for Richard could then take the king to London.

But when Richard reached Northampton, there was no sign of Rivers, and, having settled his followers in the outlying district, Richard went to an inn where he proposed to spend the night. While this was happening, Rivers arrived. He was very respectful to Richard, hailing him as the Lord Protector and explaining that, as he had been unable to get accommodation for himself and his party in Northampton, he had gone on to Stony Stratford. He himself had ridden back to Northampton to explain to Richard what had happened.

Richard was immediately suspicious of this story, but gave no sign of it. The account of lack of accommodation was false. Richard had been able to find room for his men. However, he invited Rivers to sup with him.

While they were talking, the Duke of Buckingham arrived and the three of them supped together.

It was quite a merry party and after they had retired Buckingham came to Richard's room, and they discussed the situation. It was clear that Rivers had been deceiving them, said Buckingham. He had obviously planned to get the king to London before they arrived there, and to crown him so that he, being the anointed sovereign, would decide whether to accept the guardianship of his uncle. And, of course, he would be primed by his mother not to do so. "You can depend upon it," said Buckingham. "Rivers has already sent a message to Stony Stratford telling them to leave at once."

Richard was too astute to have allowed that to happen, and immediately Rivers had arrived at Northampton, he had ordered that no messages were to be sent from the town until he gave permission. So, he assured Buckingham, the king would stay at Stony Stratford until he arrived to conduct him to London.

Buckingham was impressed by such sagacity and again pledged his support to Richard.

Richard's next step was to arrest Rivers and to ride to Stony Stratford with Buckingham where the king, with Lord Richard Grey and the aged Sir Thomas Vaughan, whom Edward had appointed to be young Edward's chamberlain and counselor, was eagerly awaiting the return of Lord Rivers.

I was sorry for that young boy when I heard this. He must have been bewildered to have kingship thrust upon his young shoulders. What had he thought, expecting to see his genial uncle, to find the Duke of Gloucester in his place? He would have been dismayed, I knew.

Richard acted promptly. Richard Grey and Thomas Vaughan were arrested, and Richard took charge of the king. The next move was for Edward to enter his capital in the company of the man whom his father had appointed Lord Protector of England and the guardian of his son.

It was others who told me of that ride into London. The king won the hearts of the people, as children do. He must have looked charming, dressed in blue velvet, riding between Richard and Buckingham, both clad in somber black. It was a colorful occasion for the City fathers were present in their scarlet trimmed robes, with several hundred leading citizens in purple gowns—all come to greet the new king. There were cheers for the king and the Protector and murmurings against the hated Woodvilles. The queen had already fled to sanctuary with her younger children.

The new reign had begun.

A message came from Richard. I was to prepare to leave for London without delay. The coronation of the little king was to take place on the twenty-second of June, and naturally I must be present with our son. Richard was living in Crosby's Place and was occasionally at his mother's residence of Baynard's Castle. When I was approaching London I should send a message to him and he would meet me.

It was news I had been longing to hear. The first thing I did was go to my son's apartments to tell him we were going to join his father. I heard him coughing as I approached. He smiled at me, almost apologetically, as he did when I found him coughing. My love would overwhelm me at such moments. I was deeply affected that he should have thought he must feel ashamed of his weakness.

I embraced him and said, "How are you today, my son?"

He said, gasping a little, but brightly, "I am very well, my lady."

I knew this was not the case.

I asked John how his brother was when they were together.

"Oh, he gets tired quickly, my lady," he said. "He only has to do a little and he must rest."

I sent for one of the physicians and asked him to tell me truthfully what he thought of Edward's condition.

"He is not strong, my lady," was the answer. "He needs great care."

"I know that. I am proposing to take him to London to join the duke."

The physician looked grave. "In my opinion, my lady," he said, "that journey might tax his strength too far."

"Too far . . ." I echoed in dismay.

"It is just that he needs much rest and when his cough is bad it is not good for him to be sleeping in strange places and facing all kinds of weather that he might encounter on the roads."

I was in a quandary. I must join Richard but I dared not risk my son's health by taking him with me.

Edward wanted to come and I did not know what to say. If his health suffered through the journey I should never forgive myself for putting him at risk. Richard would be bitterly disappointed. As I did, he tried to convince himself that Edward would grow out of his weakness. Richard himself had done so. He had been delicate as a child, yet he had grown healthy, even though he lacked the strong looks of his brothers. And what had happened to them? Excesses had killed one, folly the other. Richard, happily, was given to neither of these weaknesses.

I knew in my heart that I must not submit my son to the rigors of the journey, and when the time came, I set out, leaving injunctions that Edward was not to tire himself and that I must be sent news of him regularly.

So I rode south to join Richard.

He met me on the outskirts of London. I thought immediately that the last months had aged him. He looked drawn and there was a new wariness about him.

He was bitterly disappointed, as I had known he would be, that Edward was not with me, but he thought I had been right not to bring him.

We rode together through the city to Crosby's Place. Much as I missed my son, I was glad to be with my husband, though I was not sure at that time who had the greater need of me.

When we were alone together Richard told me how glad he was that I was with him.

We did not speak a great deal of Edward. I think we were both afraid to face our fears and were trying to convince ourselves that he was merely suffering from an illness common to many children.

Richard then told me about the manner in which he had brought the king to London and added that the relationship between them was not a comfortable one.

"I see nothing of my brother in him," he said. "He is all Woodville. I fancy he resents me. He blames me for the fact that his mother is in sanctuary and Rivers, Vaughan, and Grey are imprisoned. It was necessary, Anne. There would have been war.

They will have to lose their heads . . . and soon, I think. I wish the king would trust me."

"Poor child, this is too much for him. He ought to be spending his time in childish pastimes, rather than finding himself the center of intrigue."

"I would Edward were here. None of this would have happened if he had lived."

"How I wish that, too!"

"Anne, what am I to do? It is my duty to my late brother who suspected something of this might happen. He has left me a sacred duty. It is England that is important. There must not be a civil war again."

"I am sure you will prevent it, Richard. You are wise and calm. You do not seek revenge on these enemies . . . only that what is done to them shall be to the benefit of the country."

"That is so. But I do not know whom I can trust, Anne. What joy it is to have you with me! To you I can open my heart and speak as though I were communing with myself. Every man about me could be a potential traitor."

"You have good friends. Buckingham, Hastings . . . and what of Francis Lovell, who was with us in the old days at Middleham?"

"Francis is a good friend, yes. Oh, there are a few, but I think of those powerful men in high places who could do me much harm. I never trusted Lord Stanley. He is shifty. This side one day . . . the other the next. You know he was connected with our family at one time?"

"He married my father's sister."

"And now he is married to Margaret Beaufort. She is a strong-minded woman and Stanley is easily swayed. Moreover, she is the mother of that young man now skulking in Brittany, but methinks with an eye on the throne."

"Not Henry Tudor!"

Richard nodded. "I suppose he considers himself the Lancastrian heir now."

"How could he? He is of such dubious birth."

"Men such as he is brush aside such matters. King Henry allowed Margaret Beaufort's marriage to Edmund Tudor, whom he called his half-brother, and Edmund Tudor may—or may not—have been the legitimate son of Queen Katharine, Henry's father's widow, by Owen Tudor."

"But it is very dubious indeed. Oh, Richard, I should not concern yourself with such a man."

"You are right. My enemies are closer at hand. There is another who gives me cause for uneasiness, and that is John Morton."

"You mean the bishop?"

"Of Ely, yes."

"Did he not work with your brother?"

"Yes, but only when the Lancastrian cause was lost. He is ambitious, as so many of these churchmen are. They disguise their lust for power under a cloak of piety. They are the ones I do not trust, the ones to fear most."

"Dear Richard, you are overwrought. The death of your brother has affected you more deeply than you realize. I know how you cared for him, how he was always in your thoughts."

"That is so."

"Once the little king is crowned and on the throne you will have about you a council whom you can trust and your cares will be lifted."

"You may be right. How pleased I am that you are here!"

I was greatly cheered, but I wished I could dismiss any anxieties about my son.

Trouble came from an unexpected quarter.

Richard said to me, "Jane Shore is now Hastings' mistress."

"I have heard that she is very beautiful," I replied. "And I remember her having been wooed by Hastings in the first place. Then your brother saw her and forced Hastings to give up the pursuit."

"That may be true. Hastings and my brother revelled together. They had similar tastes for women and fast living. I think that was at the root of the friendship between them."

"So now Jane has gone to her original wooer."

"She will no doubt pass from one to another. She is that sort of woman."

"I have heard that she is kindly and that her lovers are men whom she esteems. She was obviously devoted to the king and completely faithful while he was her lover."

"She would not have dared be anything else."

"I think we should not judge her too harshly, Richard, if we are going to exonerate your brother for his part in the liaison. Rumor says she was faithful to him and he was hardly that to her, even at the height of his passion."

"That was his way. It was different."

"Different laws for the sexes. Well, that seems to be an accepted idea. In any case, why worry about Jane Shore and Hastings? Your brother is past caring."

"It seems . . . disrespectful . . . in some way."

"Oh Richard!" I laughed at him and he laughed with me.

But the affair of Jane Shore and Hastings did not rest there.

Jane Shore was the sort of woman whose actions would be widely noticed and talked of. Her close relationship with the king had made of her a prominent figure. It was such women who often received confidences—sometimes indiscreet—from their lovers and through them could become involved in intrigue.

I had thought, from what I had heard of Jane, that she would be the last to be caught up in such a situation, but it seemed I was wrong.

After the king's death it was revealed that she had briefly become the mistress of the Marquis of Dorset, the queen's son by her first marriage to Sir John Grey. Dorset had received the promotion meted out to all the Woodville family. He had become a great friend of the king, which was not surprising. He was extremely good-looking, like most of the Woodvilles, adventurous, profligate, amusing, the sort of man Edward liked to have about him. It was well known that they indulged in adventures together and, knowing the two men, it was easy to guess the nature of these adventures.

Dorset had apparently admired Jane for a long time and, if it had been left to him, he would have tried to wean her from Edward, but Jane was too faithful, and perhaps wise, to let that happen. But on the king's death, there was no reason why she should not go to Dorset.

Richard shrugged his shoulders when he heard of that liaison. He found such gossip tasteless: he did not want to be reminded of that flaw in the character of his dead brother.

But this relationship between Dorset and Jane could not be lightly dismissed when it was learned that he had vessels in the Channel that he was equipping. This could only be for one purpose: war.

Lord Rivers and Lord Richard Grey were prisoners. Elizabeth and her family—with the exception of the king—were in sanctuary. Dorset would have his reasons. He knew he was in danger and escaped to the continent. It was just before this that Jane Shore became Hastings' mistress.

With a woman like Jane this seemed natural enough, but what was surprising was that she was found to be visiting Elizabeth Woodville in sanctuary, and these visits had begun before Dorset left the country. And now she was living with Hastings.

"The wife and the mistress, what can that mean?" said Richard.

"The queen never interfered with the king's mistresses," I said.

"No. We all know that. She is a wise woman. We must be watchful of this. We must find out why Jane Shore is visiting the queen."

At the time I thought it was perhaps not so strange that Jane should go to see the queen. Jane was a refined woman. She had been the wife of a goldsmith—a rich man—and she had been well brought up by her own family. She had not been accustomed, of course, to living in royal circles until she met the king, but she had been with him for a long time and would have become conversant with the manners of the court. She could well become on friendly terms with the queen.

The matter flared into significance one day when William Catesby came to see Richard.

I had heard of Catesby. He was well versed in the law and was a protegé of Lord Hastings, through whom he had acquired a high position in Nottingham and Leicester.

I knew that Richard thought highly of his abilities.

Richard spent a long time with him, and after he had left remained shut in his apartments, seeing no one for about an hour.

I was getting anxious about him. I guessed that Catesby had brought bad news. So I went to Richard's private chamber and scratched lightly on the door. There was no answer so I opened it and went in.

Richard was sitting staring before him.

"Richard!" I cried. "What ails you?"

He looked at me blankly and said, "I cannot believe this, Anne. And yet . . ."

"Tell me," I begged.

Then it came out. That arch plotter, Dorset, with whom it seemed Jane had become obsessed, had prevailed on her to win Hastings to the side of the Woodvilles. It had not, apparently, been a difficult task, as Hastings was already wavering. Dorset had insisted that Jane become Hastings's mistress, so that she could discover whether it might be possible to break his allegiance to Richard and get young Edward crowned and rule through him with the Woodvilles.

I said, "I cannot believe this."

"There is evidence," Richard told me. "Undeniable evidence.

Catesby was aware of the plot. Hastings has betrayed me, Anne. Dorset has escaped to France and Hastings is plotting with Elizabeth Woodville. Jane Shore has been carrying messages from Dorset first and then Hastings . . . to the queen."

"But Hastings is your friend, Richard. He was the one who came to tell you of the king's death and warned you against the Woodvilles. He was one of Edward's best friends."

"In depravity," said Richard bitterly.

"It was more than that. They trusted each other. Hastings knows that you are the king's choice. You are the one he chose to look after the young king and the state."

"Anne, I have evidence that he is a traitor. I know he is plotting to thrust me aside . . . to crown the king and then he, I presume, with his dear friends the Woodvilles, will set about ruling the country."

"Are you sure?"

"I have proof. Catesby has shown me a letter that Hastings would have sent to the queen. There can be no mistake. Hastings sought to embroil Catesby in the conspiracy, but he would have none of it."

"What are you going to do, Richard?"

"Act promptly."

So many people have heard of that dramatic meeting in the Tower. The date was the thirteenth of June and two meetings of the councilors had been called for that day. It was announced that arrangements were to be made for the coronation of the king and this was to be dealt with. There was one other matter that the Protector was eager to settle without delay.

At the meeting, over which Richard presided, were Hastings, Stanley, Morton, Chancellor Rotherham, Buckingham, and a few others.

They assembled as arranged in the White Tower. Richard sat at the head of the table and the meeting began.

Later Richard told me about it in detail—how they had come unsuspecting to the table. Hastings was as affable as ever; Morton talked about the strawberries in the garden of his palace in Ely Place and begged Richard to allow him to send some to Crosby's Place because he was sure they would please me.

Richard said, "I accepted his offer graciously and wondered how long I should allow this meaningless chatter to continue. I stood confronting them all . . . Hastings, Morton, Stanley . . . there was not one I trusted. I asked them if they were aware that before my brother died he had named me as guardian of his son and Protector of the Realm? They all looked astonished. Indeed, what I had said was true, they declared. All were aware of it.

"Then I said, 'You know it well, but there are those among you who would seek to deprive me of these rights given to me by my brother.' They all continued to look astounded. I looked straight at Hastings and said, 'And you, my lord Hastings, what think you of these plots of treason?' Even then he did not realize what was behind this. He looked bland enough, sleek and contented, plotting with the Woodvilles by day and indulging in night sports with Jane Shore, I thought. 'What say you?' I insisted; and he had the temerity to reply, 'But if they had done this that your lordship suggests, they should be punished.' 'With death, my lord Hastings?' I asked. 'With death,' he repeated."

"He must have realized then that you knew of his perfidy."

"I am not sure that he had till then, but in the next moment he must have, for I cried, 'There are some among us who stand against me. Jane Shore, who was my brother's mistress, is involved. She visits the sanctuary and is in league with the queen . . . and there are others.' I was looking straight at Hastings and he knew then that I had uncovered the plot and that I was aware that Jane Shore was his messenger and the nature of her mission. I said, 'Lord Hastings, tell us again what the fate of those who scheme against the government should be.' 'If they have done such things,' said Hastings slowly, 'and if such things can be proved against them . . .' I could contain my anger no longer. Smooth-voiced traitor that he was, he enraged me, the more so because he had feigned to be my loyal friend.

"I shouted at him, 'Enough of your ifs and ands, Hastings. *You* are the traitor. You have done these things and you are guilty of treason.' He was stricken. I saw the shame on his face. I thought of the worthlessness of his assumed friendship, and I wanted revenge. I said to him, 'I swear I will not dine while your head is on your shoulders.' Then I rapped on the table and shouted, 'Treason!' The guards, warned what to expect, came in.

"I pointed to Rotherham and Morton, for they were involved in the plotting, though not as deeply as Hastings. I said, 'Arrest these men and take them to the Tower.' I was not sure of Stanley. When could one ever be sure of Stanley? I did not want to be unjust. Nothing had actually been proved against him. Yet I suspected him. 'Put him under house arrest,' I said. Then it was Hastings's turn. He was a proved traitor and I ordered that he should be taken out to the Green at once and his head severed from his shoulders."

I could not believe this. I stared at Richard in dismay. Knowing him, I was well aware of the depth of his feelings. He had liked Hastings: Hastings was the kind of man whom people did like.

"It had to be," said Richard. "They took him to the Green. They found a priest and he was shriven; they could find no block, so they used a piece of wood that was lying around, intended for repairs that were due to be done to the chapel. And there Hastings lost his head."

I covered my face with my hands and Richard put his arms about my shoulders.

"It had to be, Anne," he said. "You do not understand how ruthless these people can be."

"Oh, Richard," I said. "I understand too well."

I learned what happened after that dramatic scene; how the cry of "treason!" had been heard coming from the Tower and was carried through the streets of London; how the people crowded into the streets; how they brought out their weapons to protect themselves and their homes because they feared there might be riots.

Richard had sent for the Lord Mayor of London, Sir Edmund Shaa, a goldsmith, highly respected in the city. "There must be no trouble," he said, and a proclamation was prepared at the instigation of Sir Edmund, who read it aloud in the streets of London.

"Lord Hastings has been executed," ran this statement. "He

was a traitor to the Lord Protector and the Government. He was planning to rule all England through the new King. He had enticed the last King into evil living and he had spent the last night of his life in the bed of Jane Shore, the whore, who was herself involved in plots against the Government."

The trouble was subdued, but Richard's conscience continued to trouble him. He knew how fond Edward had been of Hastings; he himself had liked the man. But he had acted in the only way possible, and by doing so he had killed a man he had thought to be his friend. He took Hastings's widow Katharine under his protection. She should have her husband's property; he would always make sure that the child of the marriage—a boy not yet of age—should be cared for.

I was glad of that; and I think Richard felt a little better after it was arranged; but I doubted he would ever be able to banish from his mind the memory of Hastings's perfidy and his tragic end on Tower Green.

Richard had no wish to punish Jane Shore but her share in the conspiracy could not be ignored. His brother had really loved that woman. She had not been one of his light loves. She and Elizabeth Woodville stood apart from the myriads of women in Edward's life, and Richard felt he would be haunted by his brother's reproachful ghost if he harmed her.

He was in a quandary. Her name had been mentioned in connection with treason. She had carried messages, knowing full well what she was doing, and it must be made clear that those who indulged in such practices could not go unpunished.

She was a harlot and there was a recognized treatment for harlots. Richard did what others had done before him; he decided that he would not judge her himself. He would pass her over to the Church.

She was brought before the Bishop of London's court, which sentenced her to suffer the penance demanded by the Church for such as herself. She should be deprived of her possessions, those which had been bestowed on her by her lovers and were therefore tainted with sin; and she must walk through the streets in procession to Paul's Cross, barefoot and wrapped in worsted, a lighted taper in her hand.

I heard from my women, some of whom had seen the spectacle, that crowds had gathered to see this notorious woman. She looked very sad, but her beauty impressed all those who saw her. Though her feet were bleeding from the rough cobbles that she had to tread, she held her head high and walked with dignity.

Poor Jane Shore, the beloved of Edward, Dorset, and Hastings, too. I thought a great deal about her and wondered if she mourned the death of Hastings, and what her fate would be. I supposed there would always be men to care for her. She was that sort of woman.

There were rumors all over London. The king's coronation had been postponed until November. Hastings had been executed without trial; the queen was in sanctuary. Why did she think it necessary to seek such protection? The king was living in the state apartments in the Tower of London. And there was tension on the streets. People were waiting for something to happen.

Richard was worried. Morton and Rotherham were in the Tower, having been arrested at the time of Hastings's execution. Buckingham consulted with Richard and they decided that Rotherham was an old fool who could not do much harm, and it would be wise to release him. As for Morton, he was of a different caliber. He was a man to be watched. Suppose he, Buckingham, took charge of Morton, who was a very cultured man? If he were separated from fellow schemers and shut away somewhere in the heart of the country, he might settle down to study and enjoy it. Suppose Buckingham sent him to his castle at Brecknock? There he would live a secluded life of culture, which would keep him out of mischief. From time to time Buckingham would visit him and make sure that there was always a watch kept on him. That seemed an excellent solution.

As for Stanley, they knew where they were with him. He was a man who would be where his best interests were. It was not so difficult to keep an eye on such men.

It was then agreed that the great problem was the queen. If she would come out of sanctuary and live in the manner of a queen dowager, the people would be satisfied and cease to wonder about her. She was the Protector's sister-in-law, the beloved widow of his brother who had been very dear to him, therefore he and the queen should be good friends.

When the suggestion was put to Elizabeth, she would not consider leaving sanctuary, thus proclaiming as clearly as if she had made an announcement from Paul's Cross that she did not trust her brother-in-law, nor the government.

"Then if she will not come out," said Richard, "the Duke of

York must join his brother in the Tower. The king is lonely. He wants his brother with him."

Elizabeth refused to let her son go and Richard was growing angry with her.

"She has been a trouble since my brother set eyes on her in Whittlebury Forest," he said to me. "How I wish he had never seen her! Think of it! There would never have been a quarrel between Edward and your father. Was that not all about her? And her family. They have been responsible for war and bloodshed and now here she is . . . telling the world she is afraid of me, afraid of the government, seeking sanctuary, refusing to let her son go. I tell you, the Duke of York is going to join his brother in the Tower."

There was conflict between the churchmen. Richard said that Elizabeth was using young Richard of York as a hostage and that was why she would not let him go. That could not be countenanced any longer. The Archbishop of Canterbury thought that to take the child would be going against the sacred law of St. Peter. However, the general opinion was that the situation was too dangerous to allow the queen to hold her son a hostage and he must be brought out to join his brother in the Tower.

It was unfortunate that the plan had to be carried out in the only way possible, for Elizabeth would never have let her son go unless forced to do so. Armed men were sent to the queen. The Archbishop of Canterbury, Thomas Bourchier, was extremely dismayed, as he believed that it was not right to remove any person from sanctuary against that person's will. But, having been overruled, he was obliged to allow the deed to be done.

He begged the queen to let her son go. She said she would not do so. She wished to keep her children with her. They needed their mother at such a time. The king was in the Tower awaiting his coronation, which should have taken place by now, but some people had seen fit to postpone it. For what reason she had not been told.

The archbishop explained to her that the king needed his brother and asked for him to join him. The two boys should be together, and he feared that if she did not allow him to go willingly, he would be taken by force, which would not be good for him.

Elizabeth wanted the archbishop's assurance that her son would be respected according to his rank, well cared for, and protected. He gave her this assurance and at length the archbishop took the nine-year-old Richard of York by the hand and led him out of sanctuary.

Richard told me that when he was brought to Westminster Hall he had a brief interview with him.

"He was sad at leaving his mother and sisters but was looking forward to being with his brother," he told me.

"Poor child," I replied. "It is tragic when he is so young to be taken from his family."

"Well, he will be with his brother," said Richard.

However, that rather delicate incident was over, very much to Richard's relief.

There was no doubt that the treachery of Hastings had hurt Richard deeply and made him more aware of the dangers that surrounded him. More than ever I longed for Middleham and the everyday affairs of family life.

Between them, Richard and Buckingham had decided that they must be rid of the Woodvilles. At that time Earl Rivers, Richard Grey, and Sir Thomas Vaughan, who had been arrested at Stony Stratford, were awaiting sentence. These men were all a potential danger to the realm. The Woodvilles must be stopped from making trouble, if there was going to be a chance of governing the country without continual conflict.

Sir Richard Ratcliffe, a man whom Richard trusted, was sent to see the execution of these men carried out.

Richard had known Ratcliffe when his grandfather was comptroller of Edward's household; and later when he had fought with Richard in the north and they were besieged at Berwick, Richard had awarded him a knighthood. Richard said he was a man on whom he could depend.

Ratcliffe went to Pontefract, where the executions were speedily carried out.

I wondered what the feelings of Elizabeth Woodville were at that time. So many of her family had perished. Her two sons were in the Tower and no longer under her care. She had been a very ambitious woman and she must have known when she married the king and there was so much opposition to the match that her life would be fraught with dangerous difficulties. We had all had ample proof of her ambitions but she did indeed love her family. She had made that clear enough.

Now the death of the king had brought far-reaching changes to her life. She must have wondered with trepidation what the future held.

Meanwhile rumor was rife. The young king was not crowned.

Was it not time this ceremony was performed? The government announced that in due course preparations would be made for the coronation. It was unfortunate that, in view of the troubles, it had been necessary to postpone it.

There were even rumors as to what was happening to the king and the Duke of York until they were seen on the Green before the Tower practising shooting arrows. Then the rumors died. There would soon be a coronation. The Woodvilles had always been unpopular so not too much sympathy was wasted on them.

The general opinion was that the Protector was a serious man—not attractive and lovable like his brother, but serious-minded, and men seemed to respect him. Moreover, the late king had found him so reliable that he had left the government of the country in his hands.

The death of a king that left a boy on the throne was an uneasy situation. It had risen before when Henry the Fifth had left a baby to follow him. And what trouble that had caused! Now they had a wise protector. He might not be charming and handsome like his brother, but if he were a wise ruler, what did that matter?

That was the mood of the people when Robert Stillington, Bishop of Bath and Wells, made his extraordinary announcement.

He came to see Richard at Crosby's Place and was with him for a long time. Then Richard sent for the Duke of Buckingham and the three of them were together all the morning.

I knew that something of great importance was happening.

It was much later in the day when I was alone with Richard and I begged him to tell me what was happening.

He hesitated for a moment or two and then, seeing my hurt expression at being shut out of his confidence, he said, "It is so extraordinary . . . so . . . so wild. I cannot believe it, and yet Stillington knows. Do you remember, he was in the Tower for a while after George had made those statements against my mother's virtue?"

I cast my mind back. It had happened at the time the Duke of Clarence had been found dead in a butt of malmsey. We had wondered why Stillington had been arrested in the first place, and then released so suddenly.

"I remember," I said.

"I know now what that was all about, and it is disturbing, Anne. It is alarming in a way. The amazing possibilities . . ."

"Please tell me calmly, Richard," I said.

"The bishop says that Edward was not indeed married to Elizabeth Woodville and that those boys in the Tower are bastards."

"But that is impossible!" I cried.

"No . . . very plausible in truth, knowing Edward. And when you hear how it happened you will agree. Edward was very young at the time. You know how reckless and impulsive he could be where women were concerned. It would not be the first time he had been so overcome by passion that he threw away all caution. Apparently what he did was marry a woman named Eleanor Butler, and although she went into a convent later, she was alive when he went through a form of marriage with Elizabeth Woodville . . . which means that there was no true marriage to Elizabeth and her children are illegitimate."

"I cannot believe that, Richard."

"Stillington says he performed the ceremony with Eleanor Butler."

"Can this be proved?"

"Stillington swears it."

"And this Eleanor Butler . . . who was she?"

"She was no goldsmith's wife. She was the daughter of the great John Talbot, Earl of Salisbury, and widow of Sir Thomas Butler. She must have been older than Edward and apparently a lady of virtue because she would not submit to him without marriage. Hence he took this reckless step."

"If this is true . . ."

"If this is true," he repeated, turning to me, his eyes gleaming, "you know what it means."

"It means that you are the king."

He nodded.

"Oh, Richard," I cried in dismay, "it cannot be."

"If it is true, it must be."

A terrible feeling of foreboding swept over me. I tried to lose it in disbelief.

"The king would never have done such a thing."

"He would, Anne. You know he would. He chose to forget his marriage to Eleanor Butler. The affair was long over; she had retired to a convent; she was as good as dead. He became besotted by Elizabeth Woodville. She insisted on marriage, so he went through a form of marriage with her."

"And all those children . . ."

"Let us face it. They are illegitimate. They must be, if the marriage to Elizabeth Woodville was no true marriage."

"What will Elizabeth Woodville *do*?"

"Shed some of that arrogance, that insufferable pride mayhap. The upstart is reduced to what she was before the king raised her up."

"Will the people accept this?"

"Everyone must accept what is true. Anne, I see you are full of disbelief."

"Why did not Stillington say this before?"

"I believe he did."

"When?"

"He must have let it out to Clarence. Oh, don't you see, Anne? That is why Clarence died in the Tower. It comes back to me now. Think back to the time of George's death."

"I remember he said that Edward himself was a bastard."

"Yes, that calumny against our mother. George said Edward was the result of a liaison between our mother and a man of low birth. You know my mother. Do you believe that?"

"I should find it very hard to."

"Exactly. That was one of George's fabrications. This is different. Casting my mind back, I remember how Edward went to visit him in the Tower. It was the night of his death. Edward came back. He was stunned. I had never seen him like that before. Now I know what happened. Stillington must have spoken to Clarence of the king's marriage to Eleanor Butler, and when Edward went to see Clarence in the Tower, Clarence told Edward that he knew this. The next morning Clarence was found dead in a butt of malmsey."

"You mean Edward ordered him to be killed!"

"It was a good enough reason, surely?"

"Edward . . . to murder his own brother?"

"I know Edward well; he would reason that the death of one worthless man, obsessed by delusions of his own grandeur, was necessary in order to avert a civil war and the death of thousands. Edward was right in what he did, Anne. It is perhaps wrong to condone murder, but the life of one against those of thousands must be considered."

"And Stillington was sent to the Tower."

"Yes, because Clarence betrayed that the information came from him. Indeed, he was the only one from whom it could have come. You can imagine what happened. He was immediately imprisoned in the Tower, lest he should do more damage. Then Edward relented. I imagine he would go to see Stillington who would have been very contrite and swore he would never let the information pass his lips again, and possibly to deny it if it ever came to light through any other source. Edward was never vindictive. That has been shown again and again. He was always ready to forgive his enemies and live in peace with them. It may well be that he trusted Stillington so he was released and kept his silence."

"Until now."

"Yes, till now, when it cannot harm Edward."

"But it can harm Edward's family . . . his son . . . who is now king."

"I shall have to do my duty, Anne."

"You think the people will want that?"

"I must do what is right."

"You mean . . . take the throne?"

"I think it is the only way. The king is but a boy. It is not good for a country to have a child king. A strong man on the throne gives stability to a country."

"You will be King Richard."

"And you will be my queen."

I closed my eyes. I was overwhelmed by foreboding.

Richard's first step was to call a meeting of the council and to lay the disclosures to them.

I waited at Crosby's Place to hear the result of that meeting. I soon heard that there was unanimous agreement that Richard must take the throne.

There was tension throughout the city. One could not help but be aware of it. The citizens knew that some great event was about to happen, though they were as yet unsure as to what it was.

There was much coming and going to and from Crosby's Place and Baynard's Castle. I hoped the Duchess of York was unaware of the slander that had been uttered against her, for I was sure that proud lady would have been incensed. Richard insisted that it was a slander and, in any case, what need was there to prove Edward's legitimacy now that he was dead? Suffice it that the young king and his brother were bastards. That was enough to displace them.

It was arranged that the news should be brought to the people on the following Sunday. The mayor, Sir Edmund Shaa, had a brother Ralph, who was a friar and well known to the people of London because he often preached at Paul's Cross in a most eloquent manner, and crowds flocked to hear him. It was suggested by the mayor that Friar Ralph should make the announcement.

Richard, with Buckingham beside him, and with all the noblemen and dignitaries of the city, rode in procession to Paul's Cross. Abandoning his customary robes of black, Richard wore purple velvet, for it was not fitting for a king to be attired in somber black.

Crowds thronged the streets and there at Paul's Cross, Friar Ralph spoke. He based his words on the text: "Bastard slips shall not take root." Then he told the crowds that Edward the Fourth's marriage to Elizabeth Woodville had been no true marriage because he had pre-contracted himself to another lady, Dame Eleanor Butler, daughter of the Earl of Shrewsbury. That lady had been living—albeit in a convent—when Edward had gone through the ceremony of marriage with the Lady Elizabeth Woodville. Therefore that was no true marriage, and the children of the union were illegitimate. This meant that the boy whom they called king, and his brother, known as Richard, Duke of York, had no claim to the crown.

On the other hand, there was Richard, Duke of Gloucester, who, since his brother was dead and had left no legitimate offspring, was the next in line to the throne.

They had all witnessed the fine qualities of Richard. He had proved himself to be a serious man, a great ruler, and he was truly English. Of the sons of the late Duke of York now living, he was the only one who had been born in England. Did the people want an English king? Well, they had one in Richard the Third.

How I wished that I had been there then! Richard needed me. I could guess his feelings, for the people were deeply shocked by these revelations. They had loved their handsome Edward and were deeply touched by the little king, and ready to love him, too.

They went quietly away, no doubt to discuss their thoughts on the new reign in the security of their own homes.

The people's reception of the news was disconcerting, and it caused Richard a good deal of anxiety.

"They said nothing," he told me. "There was no sign of approval, or disapproval for that matter. They just seemed shocked. It was a most unusual reaction."

"The news must have astounded them as it has us all."

"Perhaps it was that. But I wonder what it means."

"Richard, if this is true . . . you must be the king."

"If only there were proof . . . documents . . ."

"Edward would certainly have made sure that they were destroyed."

"Edward was notoriously careless about some things. He believed that people were sufficiently fond of him not to betray him. You see, it did not occur to him that Stillington would be a danger until he betrayed the secret to Clarence; and he was amazed when your father turned against him."

"Oh, Richard, if only Edward had never married Elizabeth Woodville!"

"Oh, it was the same pattern. Eleanor Butler would not submit without a contract and nor would Elizabeth Woodville. And when Edward desired a woman he forgot all else. It was that trait in him that brought so much trouble."

"What are you going to do, Richard?"

"Buckingham wants immediate action. He thinks that now Friar Ralph's announcement has been made there should be no delay."

Buckingham was firmly beside Richard. He was wildly enthusiastic, which was typical of Buckingham. He reminded me of Clarence, and I had learned to beware of such men.

He took immediate action. First he came to see Richard, who shortly afterward told me what happened.

"Buckingham is going to the Guildhall with some of his followers, and he has primed them as to how they should act."

Heralds went through the streets, announcing that Buckingham would be at the Guildhall and had something of importance to tell them. The people crowded into the Guildhall where Buckingham's men were assembled in some force . . . ranging themselves among the people.

There Buckingham spoke of Stillington's disclosure and made it clear who the real king was. He said they could not have a better. He was the man who had been chosen by his brother Edward to govern the kingdom and care for Edward's son. But we now knew that the young boy had no claim to the throne and he was not the legitimate heir of the House of York. But they had a king, a mature man, a man who had proved himself worthy to take the crown . . . a man who had a right to it . . . a man who was entirely English: King Richard.

Then he cried in a loud voice, "Will you accept Richard of Gloucester as your King Richard the Third?"

I was glad I was not there. I was glad Richard was not there. The silence in that hall would have been unbearable.

One could say that the people had been taken by surprise, and their response was not immediate. They hankered for big golden Edward, and if they could not have him, they wanted their pretty little king.

Then Buckingham's men began to shout, "Long live King Richard the Third, the rightful English king!"

The next day Parliament met and Richard's claim to the throne was raised before both Lords and Commons, who were together for this special occasion. The illegality of Edward's marriage to Elizabeth Woodville was referred to and the conduct of the Woodvilles and the havoc they had wrought to the country was stressed. It was God's answer to a union that was repugnant to Him, for that union had been no true marriage and consequently Richard of Gloucester, the undoubted son of the Duke of York, was the true king.

"We shall humbly beg and beseech his noble Grace to accept and take the crown and royal dignity."

Thus ran the proclamation and it was unanimously approved.

The result of this meeting and the agreement reached there was that a great company arrived at Baynard's Castle. It was composed of nobles and leading churchmen; and there the Duke of Buckingham read out the proclamation that had been approved by Parliament.

It must have been an impressive scene, with Richard standing at one of the battlements of the castle, looking down on the assembly below.

When Buckingham had finished reading the proclamation,

Richard said he would accept the crown. He descended from the battlements and rode at the head of the cavalcade to Westminster Hall. There he sat in the marble chair assigned to the king and swore to dispense justice without fear or favor and to do all within his power to serve them well as their king and ruler.

A new reign had begun. Edward the Fifth was no longer the accepted king. The people had accepted Richard the Third.

QUEEN OF ENGLAND

So I found myself Queen of England, and I think I must have been one of the most reluctant to wear the crown. There was nothing I wanted so much as to return to Middleham, for Edward to have come miraculously alive so that we were no longer in the center of the stage. I wanted to be with my son, to nurse him back to health. I worried continually about him; as for myself, I was both physically and mentally exhausted.

There was to be a speedy coronation for a king was not recognized to be a true monarch until he had been anointed and crowned.

My gown had to be produced at the utmost speed and my seamstresses worked unceasingly through the days and nights to complete it. It was made of purple velvet and cloth of gold, and it was quite magnificent, but I felt no great interest in it, so full was my heart of foreboding.

I was undoubtedly in a nervous state, likely to be easily upset and see portents of evil in the most ordinary happenings.

We were to leave Baynard's Castle for the Tower, where we would spend the night in accordance with the custom, and the two young princes who were still there occupying the state apartments had to be hastily moved out so that we could occupy them. It seemed symbolic.

The two boys were lodged in a tower near the Water Gate. I wondered what they thought, particularly little Edward who had been brought up to regard himself as the heir to the throne. He had been treated with special homage since the death of his father and a boy would surely relish such treatment. I wondered how he was treated now. From king to bastard must be rather shocking in his young mind.

I should not be thinking such thoughts. I should remember I was the queen now. All eyes would be on me. That made me worry about my appearance. Did I look pale and wan? I was far too thin and getting more so. How I wished I were strong and healthy like Elizabeth Woodville, the mother of many children. How she had enjoyed her role!

Richard was constantly enquiring about my health. Sometimes I thought he was asking himself if I would ever be pregnant again. Then my thoughts switched to that other subject that was of greater concern to me than anything: my son's health.

I doubt we could have been ready for the magnificent display that our coronation turned out to be if preparations had not already been made for another—that of young Edward the Fifth.

London was in a merry mood. Coronations are always welcome. They provide a holiday and interesting sights, free wine, dancing, singing, carousing in the streets—an excuse to make a colorful occasion in their drab lives.

Because Richard had been lord of the north and his most faithful followers came from that part of the country, several thousands of them came south to share in his triumph. They created quite a stir in their rusty armor and their shabby uniforms; their rough manners were regarded with contemptuous amusement by the southerners. They camped in Moor Fields and were quite a side attraction.

Richard was glad to see them and went out to greet them, and tell them how pleased he was that they had come to his coronation. He brought them into the city, riding at the head of them and they settled around Baynard's Castle.

"They are my friends," Richard said. "I could trust them to serve me to the end. They may lack elegant uniforms and graceful manners, but their honesty and fidelity is unquestionable."

I believe he was enthralled by what was happening to him. He was as ambitious as his brothers. Though he would never have attempted to take the throne as Clarence had, but since it came to him as his right, he rejoiced in it. He was born to govern and he could now use his talents to their full. I could see the rising excitement in him. I told myself I must suppress my fears and try to be a worthy consort. I would pray every night that I might have a family of strong boys. "Soon, oh Lord," I begged. "It is time I had children and I have great fear for Edward."

The day before the coronation, when we came to the Tower, Richard looked magnificent. In the past I had been used to seeing him in somber black; now he was in blue cloth of gold with a cloak of purple velvet trimmed with ermine. Alas, I was forced to ride in a litter drawn by horses.

I stood with Richard at the High Altar. Our gowns were removed so that we were both naked from the waist while we were anointed with the sacred Chrism. It was a solemn moment. Scenes from the past kept flashing through my mind. Isabel, so excited because she was hoping to marry Clarence and she believed she might be queen; that haunting burial of a baby at sea; myself in the cookshop kitchen; the news of my father's death; the death of the Prince of Wales . . . the grief of his mother. There was so much tragedy to be thinking of while they were proclaiming me queen.

Then we were arrayed in cloth of gold and crowns were put on our heads; the trumpets sounded, and as I listened to the loyal shouts, I was brought out of the past to the dazzling present.

Richard and I had a short respite alone in the privacy of our chamber before the banquet began.

I saw that Richard was exultant.

"This seems unreal to me," I said.

"'Tis real," he said. "Sometimes I think it was always meant to be."

"You . . . the king!"

"Edward would understand," he said. "He knew his son had no right. Who could know that better than he did?"

"But he hoped no one would ever question that right."

"That is true. But right is right and truth will come out."

"You should not be thinking of your brother on a day like this," I told him.

"I think of him every day."

"You will be a good king, Richard."

"I shall do my best. Are you feeling well, Anne? You look very tired."

How those words depressed me! I strove so hard not to look tired, and when they were so solicitously said they hurt the more.

I talked of Buckingham, who had been much in evidence.

"One would have thought it was his coronation," I said.

"How he would have liked that!"

"He was certainly the most brilliantly attired person present."

"That is Buckingham."

"That blue velvet, blazing with gold decorations!"

"Well, he is a handsome man and likes to call attention to the fact."

"He certainly did."

"He has been a good friend."

"So," I said, "a little flamboyance can be forgiven him."

"A thousand times," said Richard.

Then we went to Westminster Hall, where tables had been set out to accommodate the guests. Richard and I took our places at that one which had been placed on the dais, there to be served by the greatest nobles in the land.

It was a nice touch that Richard ate from dishes of gold and silver offered to him by two men whom I knew well but had not seen for many years. One was Francis Lovell and the other Robert Percy, those boys who had learned the arts of war and gracious living at Middleham when Richard was there.

It was a thrilling moment when Sir Robert Dymmock rode in as King's Champion. He looked splendid in white armor and his horse was decorated in red and white. When he made the challenge, I saw the look that passed across Richard's face and I knew of the turmoil within him. I guessed he was still thinking of his brother Edward, wondering if he were looking down and seeing him in what he would think of as his son's place.

But it had been proved. Edward had not been married in truth to the boy's mother and Richard was the rightful king of England.

I longed more deeply than ever for the peace of Middleham.

No one challenged the King's Champion, and there was a cry of "King Richard!" which echoed through the hall. I sank back in relief listening to the loyal shouts.

And I saw the pleasure steal across Richard's face. He was the accepted King of England.

A newly appointed king must show himself to his subjects all over the kingdom, and as soon as London settled down after the coronation, we set out on a royal progress.

The highlight of this was our arrival in Yorkshire, the stronghold of the House of York and where Richard knew the most loyal of all greetings could be expected.

I was happier than I had been for some time, because my son Edward was to come to us there that he might join in the welcome that was given. The people would want to see their Prince of Wales with the king and queen, said Richard.

I could scarcely wait to see him.

We reached Pontefract where Edward was to join us.

He had not yet arrived but messengers were waiting to tell us that he was close by.

What joy it was to see him when he came to the city! But that joy was tinged with fear, for he had not come on horseback as I should have expected, but in a chariot. The doctor had said the ride would be too great a tax on his strength.

To my tortured imagination, it seemed that he looked more pale, more frail than when I had last seen him.

After the formal greeting, I was alone with him in the chamber that had been prepared for him. He was a little breathless.

"It is exciting, my lady," he said. "My father king and my mother queen, and I the Prince of Wales!"

"I think you should be resting, Edward. It has been a tiring day."

"I am well, my lady mother," he replied, apologetically, trying to suppress his breathlessness.

I put my arms around him and said, "Edward, my darling son, tell me just how you feel. Is there any pain? You may tell me, you know."

He hesitated, then he said, "Oh no, my lady. It is nothing. I am well . . . really well. Just a little tired."

"Dearest Edward," I said. "There is nothing to be ashamed of. Good health is given to us by God. It is His will and we should not seek to excuse our weakness."

I held him against me and he put his arms around me.

"I want to be big and strong," he said. "That is what my father wants me to be."

"When your father was about your age he used to get tired . . . even as you do. And see now, he is big and strong . . . a king."

He nodded and gave me a tender, pathetic smile that touched me deeply and made me sad.

"Tomorrow," I told him, "we shall ride into York. That is your father's favorite city."

"It is because we are of the House of York."

"That is true. How is Middleham, Edward?"

"It is as ever, my lady."

"Do you think of me when you are there?"

"All the time. When I hear horses approaching, I always hope that it is you . . . or a message to say that you are coming."

"I would I could be with you more . . . or you with us."

He smiled at me a little sadly, and I guessed he was thinking of the strain of the journey and the demands that would be made on a Prince of Wales at court.

He is too serious for his age, I thought, and I longed for him to be carefree as other boys of his age.

"In York, we shall be meeting many old friends. Your cousin is going to join us."

"Which cousin is that, my lady?"

"Your cousin Edward. Oh, how many Edwards there are! They are all named after Edward the king. He was such a well-loved person in the family. Your cousin, Warwick, perhaps I should say."

"He is twice my cousin," said Edward.

I nodded. "That is so—the son of my sister and your father's brother. We must welcome him warmly for he has neither father nor mother now."

"Is he coming back to Middleham?"

"That has not yet been decided, but he will be under your father's care. Edward, why do you not lie down for an hour or so? I shall see that you are ready in good time before you are expected to join us."

He looked grateful, and I went out and left him. I was uneasy and above all things I should have liked to take him back to Middleham. If there was one person who should be looking after him now surely that was his mother.

Later young Edward, now Earl of Warwick, joined us. I was very interested to see Isabel's son. He was eight years old—two years younger than my Edward. He brought back memories of Isabel; he did not remember his mother, so I could not speak to him of her. He had been barely three when his father had died. Poor little orphan!

I thought he might be a companion for my son, but Richard was unsure whether it would be wise to have him at Middleham. He could not forget that he was Clarence's son. The children should not be held responsible for their father's sins, I said.

Richard thought he would rather wait a while and test the boy before he made him a close associate of our son. In the meantime young Warwick could have his own household at Sheriff Hutton. Richard's nephew John, the Earl of Lincoln, was in residence there; and it seemed to Richard that that would be a good home for Warwick, at least temporarily.

When we entered York we were given a tumultuous welcome. We had been accepted in London but not with the rapturous delight shown to us here.

Richard, of course, had brought peace to the north; it was up here that his worth was recognized. He belonged to the north and the northerners showed that they realized this.

The people of the town had long awaited his arrival and had been making lavish preparations for weeks. The streets were hung with banners, there were pageants at every corner, and the mayor and the aldermen with noted citizens of the town, all in their colorful costumes, were waiting to proclaim their loyalty.

Richard was overcome by emotion. This greeting came from the hearts of these people and was not given in exchange for a holiday and free wine. On behalf of the citizens the mayor presented Richard with a gold cup filled with gold coins, and for me, there was a gold plate similarly filled.

I had rarely seen Richard so pleased. "These people do not pretend," he said. "One senses their loyalty. Their feelings come from the heart. We will stay here for a while and there is no reason why Edward's investiture should not take place in this city."

I was relieved. This meant that Edward would not have to travel another long distance for a while.

I said I thought it an excellent idea.

"We shall have to send to London for the necessary garments and whatever will be needed," I said.

"That shall be done," replied Richard.

The citizens of York were delighted at the prospect. There were more days of pageants and entertainments. A banquet was given by the mayor, and players were engaged to amuse us.

The investiture itself was a grand ceremony, but for me it was fraught with anxiety. I knew how exhausting these ceremonies could be, and I was watchful of Edward throughout. He had a wonderful spirit. I wished that I could make him see that he must not feel guilty because of his weakness. I wanted to tell him that his father loved him as dearly as I did, but he did not find it easy to show his love. It was not easy to explain that to a ten-year-old boy.

I was relieved when the ceremony was over and Edward had come through without any signs of great exhaustion. We walked from the minster, our crowns on our heads, with our son, now Prince of Wales, beside us, and the shouts of the crowd were deafening.

I wished that we could have lingered at York, but dispatches were coming from London. There was a certain restiveness in the capital. What was the king doing in the north, was being asked. He was not merely lord of the north now; he was King of England. Rumors started that he was so enamored of Yorkshire that he had had a second coronation there.

"One should always take heed of the people," said Richard. "I shall have to leave for the south. Our son should go with us."

"Richard," I said. "Have you noticed how these ceremonies are tiring him?"

Richard nodded sadly. "I am deeply aware of it, Anne," he said. "Will he ever grow out of this weakness?"

"You were not very strong as a boy," I reminded him. "And yet now you are as strong as any man."

"Is his some internal weakness?" He looked at me and, for the first time, I felt there was a hint of . . . well . . . not exactly blame . . . but was it criticism? Edward's weakness came through me. Was he implying that? Perhaps I was too sensitive. Perhaps I imagined what was not there. But I did fancy I read thoughts flashing through his mind. How could the great Warwick have produced such a weakling? Isabel had died. No one believed she had been poisoned by Ankarette Twynyho. She had died of her weakness, but although two of her children had also died, she had still been able to produce two healthy ones. I had been unable to do even that. My only child, the Prince of Wales, was a weakling. And over all these years I had shown no sign of further fertility. I was no use to him . . . as a queen . . . as a wife.

This was unfair, of course. Richard had always been tender and understanding . . . a faithful husband. But the seed was sown and the terrible doubt would live on in my mind. The fault was in me. I could bear only one weak child, and I was therefore unfitted to be the wife of a king. Passionately Richard longed for children . . . sons. For all the venom she had aroused, Elizabeth Woodville had fulfilled her duties as a queen and had produced a healthy brood for Edward.

I was very unhappy.

Richard, sensitive to my sadness, put an arm around me.

"We will take care of him, Anne. We will restore him to health. 'Tis true, I was a poor thing in my youth. I did not have the right frame for all that heavy armor. I used to hide my weakness just as

Edward does. He has no need to do that from us. We understand. We must make life easier for him. Yes . . . when he is older, he will grow out of his weakness, even as I did."

I shook off my foreboding. I would pray as never before that I might be fertile.

"Richard," I said. "He cannot make the journey to London."

"We should all be together. It is what the people expect."

"But after this exhaustion, he needs a long rest. He needs care. He needs freedom from strain. He needs tender nursing."

"So he must go back to Middleham?"

"Yes, Richard, and I must go with him."

"But . . . you should be with me. You have just been crowned queen."

"I want to go with you, Richard."

"I think you, too, find the ceremonies exhausting."

"No . . . no. I get a little tired. I think everyone does. But I am thinking of that special care that only his mother can give him."

Richard stared blankly ahead of him.

I cannot do this, I was thinking. And then: but I must. I should be with Richard, but my son needs me more.

"You think you must go with Edward then?" said Richard slowly.

"I do."

"And you could not leave him to the care of others?"

"I know I should be with you. The people will expect it. There will be rumors."

"Rumors? I shall know how to deal with rumors."

"It is hard for me. I want to be with you. I want to be all that you would wish me to be. I love you, Richard. I have since those days at Middleham, but this is our son."

"I understand," he said. "He needs you more than I do. If you come with me you will be unhappy thinking of him."

"And if I am with him, I shall be thinking of you . . . wanting to be with you."

"It is a situation in which there is no true satisfaction. Life is often like that, Anne."

"I want you to understand, Richard. My heart will be with you."

"And if you were with me it would be with Edward. I see how you feel and I think you are right. Edward has the greater need."

I went to him and put my arms about him. He kissed my hair.

"Very soon," he said, "the day after tomorrow mayhap, I must leave for London and you will go back to Middleham with our son."

Edward and I left York and I insisted that he ride in a chariot. I rode with him, for, as I said to him, I was glad to be carried. I had found the ceremonies very tiring. He looked pleased and I thought what a common trait in the human character it was to find pleasure in the fact that other people suffer from the same weaknesses as we do ourselves.

From then I would get my son to rest by complaining of my own tiredness.

With us rode Edward's cousin, young Warwick. As I watched him I wished that my Edward had his strength. Not that Warwick was all I should have looked for in a son. I was sure that my Edward had the better mind.

I think Isabel's son would have liked to come with us to Middleham, for he and I became good friends and he liked to listen to accounts of my childhood, which I had spent with his mother.

How sad it was, I thought, for a child not to remember his mother and very little of his father.

So I told him how beautiful Isabel had been, how merry, how excited when she had known he was coming into the world, and his sister Margaret also. I was not sure where Margaret was at this time. I supposed she was being brought up in some noble household and I thought what a pity it was that brother and sister had to be parted, and could not enjoy their childhood together as Isabel and I had.

I was sad when I had to leave young Warwick behind at Sheriff Hutton. His cousin John, Earl of Lincoln, who was the son of Richard's sister Elizabeth, Duchess of Suffolk, was in residence there and Warwick was put in his care. We had an enjoyable stay and I was relieved to feel that Warwick would be happy there. We should be able to visit each other, I told him; and that seemed to please him.

Then my son and I traveled the short distance to Middleham.

In spite of leaving Richard, I could not help a feeling of pleasure at being in the home I loved. As soon as we arrived, I took my son to his bedchamber and insisted on his retiring at once.

He was very glad to do so.

I lay on his bed with him; we were contented with our arms about each other. I had made it clear that there was to be no ceremony between us. We were going to forget that I was the queen and he Prince of Wales. I was just his mother and he was my little boy.

For the next weeks I gave myself up to him entirely. I was with him all the day. I watched over his meals, and if I thought he was a little weary, I insisted on his taking them in his bedchamber. There we would eat together.

I have the greatest satisfaction in remembering that my son was happier during that time than at any other.

And what was so heartening was that his health began to improve.

If Richard could have been with us, I think I should have been completely happy. I was the best remedy Edward could have. My loving care was better than any physician.

On some days we rode together, but I would not allow him to be too long in the saddle, although sometimes he wanted to be.

All through the long golden days of September this way of life continued and at the end of each day I would thank God for the improvement in my son. I was able to assure myself that he was going to grow into a strong man.

Perhaps it was folly to believe good can last. The blow came from an unexpected quarter.

Trouble must have been fermenting for a long time before I had a hint of it. Perhaps I should have known there would be some discord. Richard had come to the throne in an unusual manner. Edward's son was still in the Tower with his brother, and the young always touch the hearts of the people. Richard was surrounded by enemies. He, more than any, knew he lacked the charismatic charm of his brother. The people forgave Edward his sins because he was so handsome and charming. Not so Richard. Richard was sober, hard working, trying to do his duty, to lead the country into what would be best for it. But he was not handsome and he rarely smiled.

The people could not love him as they had Edward—only those in the north would be faithful to him because they felt he belonged to them.

It was to be expected that the Marquis of Dorset would make trouble if he could. He was, after all, Elizabeth Woodville's son. He had tried to scheme with Hastings and Jane Shore. Hastings had lost his head and Jane Shore her possessions; but the wily marquis had lived to fight another day.

Naturally he would seize his chance. But what was so shocking, so outrageous, was that his accomplice should be the Duke of Buckingham.

I could understand Richard's dismay and when I heard what had happened—which was not until some time after this had taken place—I reproached myself because I had not been with him.

Yet in my heart I knew I had been right to come back to Middleham to nurse my son.

What had happened seemed unbelievable when I remembered Buckingham's enthusiasm for Richard's claim to the throne. He had been the one to make the announcement and to have his men shout for Richard in the Guildhall. I remembered how he had outdone everyone else at the coronation in his magnificence—his badge of the burning cartwheel displayed on the trappings of his horse, his enormous retinue, which had reminded people how my father used to travel—in his case displaying the Ragged Staff instead of Buckingham's Stafford Knot.

It was inexplicable. What could have happened to make him change his allegiance so suddenly?

I could only think it was some private ambition that had brought about the change. He had a flimsy claim to the throne. His mother was Margaret Beaufort, daughter of Edmund, second Duke of Somerset. Henry the Fourth had tried to exclude the descendants of John of Gaunt and Catherine Swynford from the succession, but there was a theory that this would be illegal as they had been legitimized.

But, of course, if Buckingham was indeed in line to the throne, there was one who came before him and that was Henry Tudor, Earl of Richmond, whose mother was that Margaret Beaufort, daughter of John Beaufort, *first* Duke of Somerset. She had married Edmund Tudor and Henry was her only son. She was now married to Lord Stanley, for Edmund Tudor had died at an early age and Henry Tudor had been brought up by his uncle Jasper Tudor, and he was the son of Henry the Fifth's widow, Katharine, and Owen Tudor.

Lady Stanley was a forceful and formidable lady, harboring high ambitions for her son Henry who was at present in exile in Brittany, no doubt very closely watching events in England.

Buckingham's defection may be traced to an accidental meeting with Lady Stanley when he was traveling between Worcester and Bridgnorth. Buckingham was most impulsive and reckless; the only man I ever knew to rival him in that way was Clarence. They were both feckless and ready to act without giving very much thought as to what the consequence of that action might be. I felt sure this was what had happened to Buckingham.

He was faintly disgruntled because he had not yet received the Bohun estates that Richard had promised should be his, and consequently he was ready to listen to Lady Stanley.

Moreover, he had been on very good terms with Morton, who was his so-called prisoner in his castle. The bishop was a shrewd and clever man who would know how to handle Buckingham. Morton was a Lancastrian who would be delighted to see the red rose flourishing again. Richard had completely misunderstood the characters of both Buckingham and Morton, and it had been a great mistake to put them together. They were schemers, both of them, but whereas Morton was firm in his support of the Lancastrians, Buckingham would sway this way and that according to his feelings at the moment. And at this time he was veering away from Richard; and between them, Buckingham and Morton hatched a plot.

It would be desirable, they decided, to see the Houses of York and Lancaster united. This could be done by the marriage of Henry Tudor to Elizabeth of York, King Edward's eldest daughter. Dorset would be willing to work for such an end because it would bring the Woodvilles back into prominence; and it would rid them of the man who stood in their way: Richard the Third.

They had invited Henry Tudor to come to England with what forces he could muster; and the uprising was planned for the eighteenth of October; and when Buckingham raised his standard at Brecknock, it was inevitable that Richard should get news of the intended attack.

Richard was at his best in such a situation. He quickly marshalled his forces. Luck was with him. There had been heavy rains on the Welsh borders and the Severn and the Wye were in full flood and impassable. Buckingham could not join his allies who were to arrive in a fleet provided by the Duke of Brittany.

Thankfully, the entire mission was ill-fated. A storm dispersed the fifteen ships so that Henry Tudor, with Dorset, was unable to land, and could do nothing but return to Brittany.

Buckingham's attempt to replace Richard had failed.

Richard was incensed. His own motto was *"Loyaulte me Lie"* and he had adhered to it throughout his life. There was nothing he hated more than disloyalty.

He denounced Buckingham as "the most untrue man living" and a price of one thousand pounds was put on his head, and when he fell into Richard's hands there would be no mercy. Richard would remember Hastings—another one-time friend turned traitor—and he had lost his head the very day he was denounced.

I wondered how Buckingham had felt—he, the flamboyant nobleman who regarded himself as of royal descent—a fugitive fleeing for his life.

He went northwards to Shropshire and made his way to one of his old retainers, a certain Ralph Bannister, who helped him and set him up in a hut in the woods surrounding his house at Lacon.

Poor foolish Buckingham! He learned that there were others beside himself ready to betray for the sake of gain. The reward of one thousand pounds was irresistible to Bannister; and one morning Buckingham awoke to find himself surrounded by guards.

They took him to Salisbury on a charge of treason. Buckingham was ever hopeful. He begged for an audience with the king. There was so much he could explain, he declared, if only he had the chance to do so.

Richard was adamant. Buckingham had betrayed him. There was no friendship left between them.

The penalty for treason was death and proud Buckingham who had possessed great wealth, known greater power, who had dreamed wild dreams, lost his head ignobly in the marketplace.

My thoughts during that time were mostly with Richard. I felt that I should be with my son. My son's health was somewhat improved but not sufficiently for him to undertake a long journey. I did not want him to be submitted to the rigors of court life. While he was at Middleham in the keen fresh air, living a comparatively simple life, I believed his health would improve.

Richard wrote urging me to join him.

I tried to explain to Edward. I told him that I would be back soon and if he did everything he was told and did not overtire himself, and took the nourishing food that was prepared for him, he would soon be well enough to join his father and me. In any circumstances we should see each other soon.

And so I joined Richard.

My husband was so pleased to see me that I knew I had been right to come. I guessed that the defection of Buckingham was still very much on his mind.

"There is no one I can talk to as I do to you, Anne," he said. "I know not whom else I can trust."

"I would not have believed this of Buckingham," I replied.

"I should have been more watchful of him. He was never stable. Sometimes I wonder . . ."

I looked at him questioningly as he paused.

But he went on, "He was the one who was so insistent that I take the throne. He believed Stillington absolutely . . . then to turn like that! And to Henry Tudor!"

"I have heard but little of this Henry Tudor."

"An upstart who thinks he has a claim to the throne."

"But how could he?"

"You know these Beauforts. They are so ambitious and strong. They are a bastard branch of the family and should never have been recognized as anything else. Their forebears were born before John of Gaunt married Catherine Swynford. But because they were legitimized . . . well, it has given them ideas of their importance. Buckingham had these because his mother was one of them. And now Henry Tudor is another. He thinks he has a claim through Katharine, the French princess who married Henry the Fifth when he conquered so much of France."

"He is in Brittany now?"

"Yes, sheltered and aided by Duke Francis of that place. I have my enemies, Anne."

"And you have those who love you."

"I have you and Edward, that is true. Anne, what of the boy?"

I said, "He is a little better."

"And what thought he when I wanted you to be here with me?"

"He understood. I have promised him that when he grows a little stronger he shall be with us both."

"Ah, if only that could be! The people need to see him. They like to know their future king."

"That is for years and years ahead."

"It is for God to decide. But the people would like to see him."

"I fear his health would not allow him to come this time."

"Then we must pray that it soon will be. How goes Warwick at Sheriff Hutton?"

"Well, I believe. He rides and exercises well. Learning does not come easily to him."

"That is a pity."

"He is a pleasant, good-natured boy. It is just that he does not think quickly and is slow at his lessons. He cannot read yet. Edward is so different."

"Oh yes, our son lacks nothing in the head. If he could but combine the physique of young Warwick and his own learning, what a boy we should have!"

"We have the most wonderful boy in the world, and I am going to nurse him back to health. In years to come you and I are going to laugh at our fears."

"I pray you will be proved right," he said fervently.

I forced myself to believe it and gave my attention to Richard. I learned how deeply wounded he had been by Buckingham's disloyalty. The hurt was far greater than I had at first realized.

"Why, Anne?" he said to me on one occasion. "He has even set in motion evil rumors about me."

"People listen to rumors but do they really believe them?"

"Rumor is pernicious," said Richard. "People absorb the slanderous words and then in time some of them accept them as truth. Buckingham would have made me out a monster . . . a man of no loyalty or principles, with no right to the throne of England."

"But it was he who pressed you to take it!"

"He could not say that I had arranged for Stillington to betray the truth, though I am sure he would have liked to."

"He would have Stillington to contend with."

"No doubt that was what made him refrain. But he has set about one very unpleasant rumor . . . a very disturbing one."

"What is it?"

"I hardly like to mention it. He says I have caused the princes—Edward and Richard—to be murdered in the Tower."

"Edward's sons! Your own nephews! People would never believe that."

"There are some who will believe anything, particularly if it is evil."

"But the princes have been seen shooting at the butts on the Tower Green . . . so how can they be dead? People only have to see them to know that rumor is false."

"Yes, but I think they should not appear too much in public from now on. When a man such as Buckingham turns traitor, it sets an example for others to do the same."

"An example! To have their heads chopped off in the nearest marketplace?"

"I mean to revolt. People always think they will succeed where others have failed. Storms could easily blow up about those boys in the present atmosphere. The last thing I wish for is more trouble on that score. There is already enough. Buckingham's insurrection has been a shock to the nation. The country needs to settle to a sense of security. Buckingham must be forgotten along with scandalous rumors. I have planned to go on a progress through the country. I want to see the people, to talk to them. You must come with me, Anne. I cannot express how much it pleases me to have you with me."

I had to quell my anxieties regarding my son, and I gave myself up entirely to Richard's needs.

The winter was over and March had come. It was time for us to set out. Richard wanted to make sure of loyal support from all over the country in case, with the coming of spring, Henry Tudor should attempt another invasion.

We traveled through towns and villages and finally came to Cambridge, where we intended to stay for a few days.

Richard was very interested in the university and for some time had been bestowing grants on it, with various gifts. We were received with great warmth. Richard was happier in such an atmosphere and so was I. For those few days I found peace in the cloisters, and I enjoyed listening to the discourse between the king and the ecclesiastics.

I was really sad when we left and made our way to Nottingham.

I shall never forget Nottingham Castle. Little did I guess, as we approached it, that I should encounter such tragedy within its walls. Set in an almost perpendicular rock, it looked impregnable. I studied the intricate stone work on the north side with particular interest because it had been started by Kind Edward and finished by Richard, for Edward had died before its completion.

There were a great many ghosts in Nottingham Castle, for so many people in the past had suffered there. Edward the Second's queen had come here with her paramour Mortimer; I had heard that she slept with the keys of the locked fortress under her pillow every night so she must have been in a perpetual state of apprehension. King Henry the Second, King Richard the First . . . they had all been here.

It was the middle of April—a bright sunny day with a promise of spring in the air. There was no spring for us. It was the end of hope.

It was late morning when the messenger arrived from Middleham. Eagerly Richard and I received him, but when we saw his face, a terrible fear took hold of us.

I heard Richard's whisper: "It is . . . the Prince of Wales . . ."

The man did not speak for a moment; he was afraid—as all messengers are when they carry ill tidings.

"Tell me," said Richard harshly.

Why would not the man speak? Why did he hold us in suspense? Half of me was urging him to speak, the other half begging him not to. I knew what he had to tell us before he spoke. It was what I had been dreading for months.

"The prince is dead, your Grace."

I heard the cry of anguish that Richard could not suppress. I went to him and took his hand.

We just stood there, stunned by the news that we had feared so long.

Richard waved his hand to dismiss the messenger. He could not bear the sight of him. Later we would hear how our son had died. We did not need to know now. We could see it clearly, as though we had been present. We had feared so much . . . lived with the fear so long; we had waited with such great anxiety for messengers, terrified of what news they would bring. And now it had come.

Few children can have been mourned so deeply as our little son. It was more than the death of a child; it was the death of hope; it was the end of a way of life; for me it was the beginning of those fears that came to mock me in the night.

Richard and I were very close to each other during the days that followed.

His continual cry was, "Why should this happen to me? Edward had many children and what sort of life did he live? He was never faithful to his wife; he had countless mistresses; he pandered to the flesh . . . and yet, he left two sons and many daughters. Is this a punishment from heaven?" He turned to me in horror. "Was Stillington's story true? Am I robbed of my son because I robbed Edward's of his crown?"

I tried to comfort him. He had never done aught than what he considered to be right, I reminded him. Edward's sons were illegitimate. They had no right to the throne.

"I cannot rid myself of this fearful guilt," said Richard. "Edward was our son. He was more than our son . . . he was our pledge to the people that there would be a ruler to follow me. I should have taught him wisdom, Anne. He was a good boy. He would have been a good man. He was bright. Think of young Warwick. There he is . . . healthy . . . sporting at Sheriff Hutton, while our Edward . . . What does it mean, Anne? You and I are cursed?"

I said, "Perhaps there will be another."

I did not believe it. If I could not conceive when I was younger, and in a better state of health, why should I now?

The sound of his bitter laugh hurt me and the memory of it stayed with me.

No, there would be no more. The only son I had been able to give him was a puny boy who, with a struggle, had lived for eleven years.

I was no use as a king's wife. I was thirty years of age and barren . . . and kings needed sons.

We mourned together, but something had happened. Perhaps it was in my mind. But I could not but be aware of Richard's disappointment.

"Let us leave Nottingham," he said. "I never want to see the place again. Every time I see it I shall remember that messenger who came here on the most dismal of all days, with the most tragic news that could befall us. I hate Nottingham. This I shall call the castle of my care."

Richard seemed withdrawn and I felt we were no longer as close as we had been before.

He was busy all the time. Summer was coming and affairs of state demanded attention. They did not stand still because the king and queen had suffered the greatest tragedy of their lives.

Richard knew he had put the country into a state of defense. The perpetual bickering with the Scots usually began in the summer, but the English lords of the north who had their property to protect would doubtless keep them in order.

The great concern was Henry Tudor. What was he planning in Brittany? He had made one attempt, but by the Grace of God had been prevented from landing by a storm. Could the same good luck be expected if he were to attempt another landing?

There was a great deal to occupy Richard. I did not suggest returning to Middleham. That could only be a place of mourning for me now.

All peace had gone from my life. I could not believe in anything now—not even in Richard's love. A canker had entered my mind and all I looked upon seemed tainted.

I saw myself, no longer young, weak, useless—a barren queen. I fancied Richard had changed toward me. If he had loved me once he now looked at me through different eyes. I was no longer the woman at his side to help him, to comfort him. I was a burden.

He had chosen unwisely. I had been Warwick's daughter and, with my sister Isabel, the richest heiress in the kingdom. We had been fond of each other in childhood, it was true, and our marriage had been acceptable to him for what it brought. I had dreamed of a great love. But did true love drift away when disaster struck?

There were times when I knew I was being foolish. The death of our son could not have changed Richard's feelings toward me.

Was I responsible for it? Could I be blamed because I could not get a healthy child?

I tried to reason with myself. Richard is a king. He needs heirs. He has to think ahead. Above all things he needs a son to train, to lead, to teach how to take over the government by the time he, Richard, grows old or meets his death. Richard desperately needs a son.

I could not talk to him of the fears in my heart. There were many times when I did not believe in them myself. Richard had never been a man to show his emotions. I used to tell myself it was because they went so deep. They were not superficial as his brothers Edward's and George's had been. Both of them had known how to find the words that pleased, but they lacked sincerity.

So there was I, torn by doubts, entertaining all kinds of pernicious suspicions because I had considered myself and found myself wanting.

Richard was making a show of throwing off his grief but I, who knew him so well, could detect the abject misery in his eyes.

He said to me one day, "Katharine is of an age to be married."

Katharine, with her brother John, was still at Middleham, and Katharine must be about sixteen years old.

"I should like to see her settled," went on Richard. "John, too, though perhaps he is a little young yet."

"Whom have you in mind for Katharine?" I asked.

"William Herbert, the Earl of Huntingdon."

"That seems very suitable."

"As for John, I should like Calais for him."

"Captain of Calais! That would be a very important post."

"He is my son," he said, I fancied, coolly.

And I thought, your son indeed—a strong, healthy boy. My state of mind was such that I imagined what he must be thinking. I can get a healthy son by another woman, but not by my queen.

I heard myself say, "He is young for Calais."

"I thought perhaps next year. I need those I can rely on, and I can do that with my own son. But to begin with . . . Katharine's marriage. I think the time is ripe for that."

Katharine joined us. She was a bright and pretty girl, very excited at the prospect of marriage and, of course, the Herberts were delighted by a union with the king—even though there was illegitimacy, it was still a royal marriage; and the king would look after his own daughter.

So Richard's daughter was married and I noticed that when his eyes rested on her they were filled with pride . . . and something else, I wondered? Was it resentment? Why should he be able to get healthy children by another woman when his queen failed him?

It was becoming an obsession with me. I looked for it on every occasion.

One day he said to me, "I have been thinking of naming Warwick as heir to the throne."

"Warwick . . . but . . . ?"

"We must face the truth, Anne. You and I will never have a child now. It is too late and I would fear for you. But there must be an heir."

"Richard, you are young yet. Pray do not talk of such need for an heir."

"A king's life is often a short one."

"As all our lives may be." I was thinking of Hastings and Buckingham, and I believe he was, too.

"Warwick's father was tainted with treason. Would that not exclude him?"

"It could be dealt with. He is the next in line."

"Richard, Warwick is not fit to rule. He is weak-minded. It would be like Henry the Sixth all over again."

Richard was thoughtful. "There is my sister Elizabeth's son, the Earl of Lincoln . . ."

I looked at him with sorrow and he went on gently, "These matters have to be considered. Sometimes they can be painful. One thinks of what might have been . . ."

He turned away and soon after that he left me.

I went to my chamber and shut myself in.

If only I could bear a son! If only I could be strong! Would Richard love me then? There were too many ifs—and if love must depend on such things, is it love?

Had he ever truly loved me?

I tried to pray. I tried to ask God and the Holy Virgin to help me. But how can one pray for something that, in one's heart, one knows one can never have?

There was a certain amount of talk at this time about the possibility of Henry Tudor's making an attempt to depose Richard and to set himself up as king in his place. His supporters had put forth a proposition that could be attractive to the people.

The Wars of the Roses had appeared to come to an end when Henry died—murdered, most likely—and when Margaret of

Anjou had been driven out of the country and Edward had come so triumphantly back to the throne. But there could be a recurrence of the troubles, and the idea of uniting the House of York with that of Lancaster seemed a good one, since it could mean that the rivalry between the houses could be ended forever. If Henry Tudor, a Lancastrian, were married to Elizabeth of York, this could be achieved.

At this time Elizabeth Woodville, with her daughters, was still living in sanctuary, which must have been very different from the grandeur which she had maintained about her in the past.

This suggestion of a marriage for her daughter had changed people's attitudes toward her. Richard was worried. Elizabeth Woodville was notoriously ambitious, and if she thought there was a possibility of her daughter marrying a king, she would soon be scheming.

"She may be helpless at this time," said Richard, "but a woman who could force a king to marry her and holds her position through so many years must be watched."

He discussed the matter with the men whom he trusted. Ratcliffe, Catesby, and Francis Lovell were deep in his confidence. He regarded them as his true friends and he took counsel with them often.

The result of this was that he promised Elizabeth Woodville that if she would leave sanctuary with her daughters, they should all be perfectly safe and nothing held against them; they should be under his protection; he would see that good marriages were arranged for them and they should each receive property to the value of two hundred marks.

When Richard took a solemn oath before the Lords Temporal and Spiritual, as well as the Lord Mayor of London, and the aldermen, that he would honor this promise, Elizabeth could not doubt his good faith.

From Richard's point of view it was a wise move. Elizabeth Woodville had no loyalties except to her own family and for them she would fight with all her strength. She must be asking herself how long her daughters would have to remain in sanctuary; good marriages were necessary for them before they were too old; and if she could ingratiate herself with the reigning king, why bother to put another in his place?

Not since our son's death had I seen Richard look so amused. I understood the reason why.

"My spies tell me that Elizabeth Woodville has shifted her allegiance. She is breaking off her connections with the Tudor and is urging Dorset to return and try to seek favor here. Do you see what a good move it was to bring them out of sanctuary?"

Attention was focussed on the eldest daughter, Elizabeth. This was naturally so, for she was really at the heart of the matter.

She was invited to come to court—an invitation she accepted with alacrity.

Richard said it was an excellent move. I was not sure, for the moment I set eyes on Elizabeth York, my misgivings increased.

She was tall; she had long fair hair, blue eyes, and a dazzlingly fair skin; she was very beautiful, which was to be expected with such a mother and handsome father. Without doubt she was Edward's daughter. She had charm as well as beauty. She moved with grace and glowed with health and vitality. It was to be expected that she should immediately become a popular figure in the court.

She was very solicitous of me, very deferential. I guessed she had been primed by her mother to be gracious to the king, to charm him, as she would know very well how to do.

The situation had changed. The Woodvilles were back and this time as our friends.

As soon as Elizabeth came to court I seemed to grow more tired, more feeble. I was more conscious of my infirmities and my cough troubled me at awkward moments. But perhaps that was due to the comparison between myself and Elizabeth.

I found I was thinking of her constantly. I would watch her in the courtyard, coming in from a ride—flushed and beautiful, surrounded by admirers. In the dance she attracted the attention of all: she dressed with splendor but good taste. She was so clearly delighted to have stepped out of dull seclusion and was deter-mined to enjoy her new surroundings.

People cheered her in the streets. She reminded them of her magnificent father.

When he ruled, said the people, those were merry days. There was no fear of invasion then, no fear of war when we had a good laughing king on the throne and an heir to follow.

Then the whispering started. Was the king thinking of marry-ing Elizabeth of York? The queen surely had not long to live by the look of her. And what chance was there of an heir from her? But Elizabeth was his niece. Was that allowed? A dispensation from the pope perhaps, but even so. His niece! Popes could be very obliging if approached in the right manner. Think of it. An heir! That was what was wanted. Then we should have a king to follow. Richard was not old. He had many years left. But he must get an heir.

Elizabeth would have fine strong children. Think of her mother and who her father was.

Did I imagine the rumors? Perhaps I exaggerated, but they were there.

My senses had become alert. I fancied I heard scraps of gossip. I saw the watchful eyes. I saw Elizabeth smiling at Richard and I knew he must think her charming. Who could help that? Perhaps she reminded him of Edward whom he had loved so dearly— more than anyone, I now believed. And Elizabeth brought out all her charms for him. Was he not the king? And she would have been instructed by her mother.

But would Elizabeth Woodville want her daughter to marry her uncle? I believed she would find anything acceptable for the sake of a crown.

It is strange how an insidious whisper, a hasty glance, a gesture even can plant suspicions in the mind.

Richard was watched. Elizabeth was watched. And so was I. We were the main characters in the drama that was being built up around us. I was the wife who had become a burden—the wife who must die before the happy conclusion could be reached.

Christmas had come. It was eight months since I had heard of my son's death, but the sorrow was still as great as ever. Richard tried to comfort me, but inwardly I shrank from him. He could not hide from me his terrible preoccupation with the succession. I think it was as great a concern for him as the threat from the Tudor.

London was merry because it was Christmas. The shops glittered with their merchandise and people crowded the streets. It was the season of good will.

Richard must hide his anxieties and therefore Christmas should be celebrated with merriment and good cheer. I think he tried to make it as it had been in his brother's day. That was not possible, for all the show of splendor, but I knew the laughter did not go very deep.

On Christmas Day I dressed myself with great care and had a magnificent gown for the occasion. It was made of damask and cloth of gold set with pearls. I was telling myself I must set aside my sense of foreboding. Richard was most tender to me, always so solicitous. I must cast off these terrible suspicions. They had been brought about by the whispering of evil people and had no roots in reality.

I thought I looked a little better. There was a faint color in my cheeks. This night, I promised myself, I would assume merriment; I would try to believe that I might yet recover and give birth to a beautiful baby boy.

So, in moderately high spirits, I went down to the great hall where Richard was waiting for me. I thought he looked pleased because of my improved appearance.

In fact he said, "You look a little better, Anne."

I smiled and he smiled at me; and together we went into the hall.

There was the usual ceremonious greeting for the king and queen. Richard took my hand and led me to the table on the dais.

And then I saw her. I was startled and then deeply shocked. Elizabeth of York was wearing a dress that was an exact replica of my own.

We gazed at each other; she seemed as astonished and embarrassed as I was.

I gave her my hand and she kissed it. Then she raised her eyes to mine.

I said, "You are wearing my dress and I yours."

"Your Grace . . . I do not know how it happened. I had no idea. May I say how well it becomes your Grace?"

I said, "It becomes you, too, my lady Elizabeth."

Then I moved away. In my present state of mind the demons were back to torment me.

It was deliberate. Someone had planned this. It was a cruel joke. There are two queens, it implied. The one who is on the way out and the one who is about to enter.

Later I said to Richard, "Did you notice the dress Elizabeth was wearing?"

He looked blank. "What of her dress?"

"It was exactly the same as mine."

He did not seem to think it was of any great moment. But how did I know what was going on his mind?

After that Christmas my health declined further. The winter was a hard time for me. My cough persisted. Richard was showing signs of strain.

Nothing was going right. There was the continual threat of invasion. People remembered the last reign with regret. There were evil rumors in the air. Someone had pinned a paper on the walls of St. Paul's with the inscription:

The Rat, the Cat, and Lovell our dog
Rule all England under a hog.

It was a reference to Catesby, Ratcliffe, and Francis Lovell— Lovell being a name much used for dogs; those three were Richard's closest advisers. The Hog was, of course, Richard himself, his emblem being the sign of the Boar.

It was not merely a couplet; it was an expression of the people's growing dissatisfaction and dislike.

Soon it was being sung in the streets. I was sighing more than ever for the old days of Middleham. There had been little happiness for either of us since Richard had taken the crown. How I wished the Bishop of Bath and Wells had never made his revelation. How I wished that the young Edward the Fifth were king of the realm.

There was a continual watch for ships about the coasts, for now an invasion seemed inevitable. On the continent, Henry Tudor was preparing to take from Richard that which had brought him not a vestige of happiness.

There was a burning need for an heir. I would have given Richard everything I had. How ironical that I could not give him what he wanted most.

I was living too long. If I were not here, I reminded myself, he could marry again. He could beget a son and then there would be new hope in the country.

I was taking too long to die. There was a new rumor now. There was nothing too evil they would not say against Richard.

I knew it, by the glances at my food, much of which I took in my chamber, feeling too weak to eat in public. I could see that was in the minds of my women. Snatches of a sentence spoken in a sibilant whisper would reach my ears.

The king was tired of his sick, infertile wife. She was a burden to him, and he could not afford to carry burdens. His own safety was too precariously balanced. He was having her food laced with poison, the quicker to remove her.

It was three months since that Christmas when Elizabeth of York had appeared in a dress exactly like the one I was wearing, showing how different we were—dressed alike, to make the contrast more remarkable. She so sparkling, nubile, gleaming with health beside this poor sad creature, thin, pale, and ailing.

Someone had prophesied my death and the people in the streets were saying I was already dead.

I discovered this when one of the serving women came upon me suddenly and almost swooned. She cried out, "I have seen the ghost of the queen! Poor lady, she has come back to haunt us. Small wonder . . ."

It was disconcerting. I felt I had been buried before I was dead. Killed . . . by the poison administered at my husband's command!

I sat in my chair, my hair unbound, a loose robe about me, shocked and bewildered.

Richard found me thus.

I said to him, "Why am I so weak? Do you know why, Richard? What have I done to deserve death?"

He took my face in his hands and kissed me. "Why do you talk thus?" he asked. "Anne . . . my Anne . . . you deserve to live and you shall."

I shook my head. "No," I said. "My time is near. I feel it close. I am sorry I have been so weak."

"Do not talk so, dear Anne," he said. "You have been so dear to me. You have brought me such comfort in all my adversities. Remember how you pitied me when we were at Middleham? I was so tired . . . and you kept my secret."

"That is long ago, Richard."

"Be of good cheer, Anne. You have no cause to be other."

For a moment I believed him and I was ashamed that, even for a short while, I had allowed myself to harbor thoughts against him.

But in the night those doubts came back. He was so kind, so gentle with me. Then why did I have those dark thoughts? Why did I let myself doubt him? He could never marry his niece. He wanted me to stay with him, to comfort him, as I always had.

It was March and with March comes the promise of spring. But I shall not see that spring.

They say it is an eclipse of the sun. It is significant. Darkness descends on the earth but the earth will be bright again. But there will be no brightness for me. There is darkness all about me. There is so much I shall never see, so much I shall never know.

BIBLIOGRAPHY

Ashdown, Dulcie M., *Princess of Wales*

Aubrey, William Hickman Smith, *National & Domestic History of England*

Bagley, J.J., *Margaret of Anjou*

Clive, Mary, *This Sun of York, Biography of Edward IV*

Costain, Thomas, *The Last Plantagenets: Pageant of England 1337–1485*

Gairdner, James, *History of Richard III*

Halstead, Caroline, *Richard III as Duke of Gloucester and King of England*

Jacobs, E.F., *The Fifteenth Century 1399–1485*

Kendall, Paul Murray, *Richard III*

Kendall, Paul Murray, *Warwick, the Kingmaker*

Lamb, V.B., *The Betrayal of Richard III*

MacGibbon, David, *Elizabeth Woodville*

Oman, Charles, *Warwick the Kingmaker*

Ramsay, J.H., *Lancaster and York*

Ross, Charles, *Edward IV*

Rowse, A.L., *Bosworth Field and the Wars of the Roses*

Scofield, Coral L., *The Life and Reign of Edward IV*

Stephen, Sir Leslie & Lee, Sir Sydney, *The Dictionary of National Biography*

Stratford, Laurence, *Edward IV*

Strickland, Agnes, *The Lives of the Queens of England*

Wade, John, *British History*

Williams, C.H., *The Yorkist Kings*

READER'S GROUP GUIDE

This guide is designed to help you direct your reading group's discussion of *The Reluctant Queen*.

1.

As a reader, what do you enjoy about historical novels like *The Reluctant Queen*? Does knowledge of history enhance your enjoyment of the story or detract from it?

2.

Richard is perhaps most famous as the jealous hunchback who would be king in Shakespeare's tragedy *Richard III*. Jean Plaidy depicts Richard as a loyal, loving subject of his brother the king. What impressions of Richard did you bring to your reading of this book?

3.

At the beginning of *The Reluctant Queen*, Anne is on her deathbed thinking back over the course of her short life, realizing it was never really her own to live. Who or what truly controlled Anne's destiny? On page 8, Anne says that in wealthy, powerful families like her own, where sons are heirs, even girls have their uses. What are they? How does Anne's family use her and her sister, Isabel, to advance?

4.

Anne's father, the Earl of Warwick, is obsessed with power. He will do almost anything—including commit treason—to gain more. How does his attitude affect his daughters? His wife?

5.

King Edward's marriage to the beautiful Elizabeth Woodville is the catalyst for the events that bring about the earl's defeat. What steps does the earl take to seek revenge against the man he put on the throne? Why is he unsuccessful in his attempts to turn the people against Edward?

6.

How does the discord between the king and her father affect Anne and Richard? What does Anne think of her father's actions?

7.

As part of his plans to wrest power from Edward, the earl arranges for Anne's sister, Isabel, to marry the king's brother George, Duke of Clarence, who wants the throne for himself. What was your first impression of George? Is he a good match for the ambitious but innocent Isabel?

8.

As the rift between her husband and the king teeters on the edge of civil war, Anne's mother shares her worries about the future with her younger daughter. What could a war between these powerful men mean for her and her daughters? Although she can't control her husband's actions, she will be held accountable along with him if he fails. Why? Is that fair?

9.

The women of Warwick pay a high price for the earl's lust for power. What happens to each of them? Do you think the earl ever considers them in his plans? The king offers peace and forgiveness to Warwick several times only to be rebuffed. Why? What does this say about Edward? About Warwick?

10.

Anne is betrothed to the Lancastrian Prince Edward as a means of sealing a bargain between her father and the proud Margaret of Anjou. Arranged marriages for women of her status were common at the time, but Anne reacts badly to the news. Why? Imagine having your marriage arranged in such a manner. What does this practice imply about women?

11.

When Anne is engaged to Edward, her mother-in-law-to-be is the formidable Margaret of Anjou. How did the events of her life shape the woman she is when Anne meets her? What was your first impression of her? How did your impression of her change as the book progressed?

12.

How does Anne's relationship with Margaret of Anjou evolve over time? Is she ultimately a woman to be pitied or admired?

13.

As Warwick fights King Edward to put Margaret's son on the throne, Anne considers her loyalties. Does her father deserve her loyalty? Anne feels she loses no matter how her father fares in the war. Why? What happens to her if he wins? What happens to her if he loses?

14.

After the loss at the Battle of Tewkesbury, Anne doesn't know what will become of her, but it seems likely she will go from being the Princess of Wales to a prisoner in the Tower of London in one day. Do you think King Edward deals fairly with her? With her mother? With Margaret of Anjou?

15.

Isabel seems perfectly willing to believe whatever her husband tells her—even when he insists that her mother stay in sanctuary for her own protection long after it is deemed necessary for her to do so. Is she a likable character? How does she ignore her husband's faults?

16.

When Anne and Richard are reunited upon her return to England, she learns that Richard has fathered two children by a mistress. How does she react? Is her reaction reasonable or naïve considering the standards of the times?

17.

The Duke of Clarence is determined to block Anne's marriage to his brother Richard. Why? What does he have to gain? Why won't the king choose sides between his loyal brother Richard and the treacherous duke?

18.

After being deceived and drugged, Anne wakes to find herself a prisoner in a cook shop in London. Although she demands to be let go, the shopkeepers and staff insist that she is a delusional maid called Nan and won't let her leave. How does Anne remain sure of her true identity? What does she do to escape? How is the lecherous shopkeeper, Tom, the key to her rescue?

19.

Once they are finally married, do Anne and Richard have a happy life together? Is marriage to Richard all she hoped it would be?

20.

Richard asks Anne if he can bring his illegitimate children to be raised at Middleham, after their mother's passing. What do you think of this request? Of her reaction? Is allowing these children into her home really a sign of unselfish love for her husband as her own mother suggests? Is Anne ultimately happy with her decision on this matter?

21.

After the birth of her fourth child, Isabel dies. How does the news affect Anne? Both Anne and her sister were fragile women, but rumors sprout up that Isabel was poisoned. Do you think she was? If so, who is a likely culprit?

22.

How does the sudden death of King Edward change Anne's life? Richard's?

23.

Eventually, Richard discovers a secret in his brother's past that challenges the legitimacy of Edward's eldest son's claim to the throne. What do you think of his actions after his discovery? What does Anne think of the change in her husband?

24.

After little Edward's death, Anne is plagued by feelings of inadequacy about herself. Her only son was sickly and Richard has no heir. Do you think Richard blames her for this? Is the young Elizabeth York a real or imagined rival for Richard's affections?

25.

Which of the powerful men in Anne's life ultimately had the greatest effect on her fate? Considering everything that happened to her, do you think Anne felt content with her life at the time of her death?

An Excerpt From

LADY IN THE TOWER
A QUEENS OF ENGLAND NOVEL

THE PRISONER

HERE I LIE IN MY DARK PRISON. I hear voices in the night—those who were here before me, those who had suffered as I am suffering now, numbed by fear, without hope, the prisoners of the King.

They came for me yesterday, and we glided along the river to the great gray Tower. Many times had I seen it before but never with such fearful clarity. Once I came here in great pomp and glory—and that only three years ago—and never for one moment then would it have seemed possible that one day I should be brought here—a prisoner.

It was May then as now and the people crowded the river banks to see me pass. I was proud, so confident, so sure of my power. At the prow of my state barge was the stem of gold with branches of red and white roses—symbolic of York and Lancaster, which the King displayed on every occasion to remind people that the Tudors had united the warring factions; and among those roses was my very own symbol, the White Falcon, with the motto "Me and Mine."

How had I come to pass from such adulation to bitter rejection in three short years? Was it my fault? I must be in some measure to blame. When did I cease to be the adored one and become the outcast?

The people had not cheered me even in my day of triumph. They did not like me. All their affection was for Queen Katharine. They did not accept me. "We will have none of her," they cried. "Queen Katharine is our true Queen." They would have abused me if they had dared. The people were my enemies, but I had greater and more powerful enemies than they were. Now they would be openly gathering against me; even during the days of my triumph they had sought to destroy me; how much more assiduously would they work against me now! And they had succeeded, for I was the King's prisoner.

As I passed through the gate the clock was striking five, and each stroke was like a funeral knell.

Sir William Kingston, the Lieutenant of the Tower, was waiting for me. I murmured to myself: "Oh, Lord help me, as I am guiltless of that wherefore I am accused."

I turned to William Kingston and said: "Mr. Kingston, do I go into a dungeon?"

And he replied: "No, Madam, to your lodging where you lay at your coronation."

They took me there and I laughed. I could not stop laughing, for I, who had come in such pomp and glory just three years ago, now was here in the same apartment . . . a prisoner.

Had they brought me here purposely to remind me? Was it a

touch of that exquisite torture which so many of my enemies knew so well how to administer?

My women tried to soothe me. They knew the nature of that wild laughter; and in time I was quiet.

I thought: I will write to him, I will move him with my words. I will remind him of how it once was between us.

I wrote and I destroyed what I wrote. Again and again I took up my pen and tried to appeal to him.

"Your Grace's displeasure and my imprisonment are things so strange unto me that what to write or what to excuse, I am altogether ignorant . . ."

That was not true. I did know and I would not make it easy for him. I knew him well—his reasoning, his sanctimonious excuses, his mean, hypocritical nature, his passionate desires all cloaked in piety. No, I would not make it easy for him.

My angry pen flew on. My lack of discretion had often turned people against me, but I was reckless. I was fighting for my life. I would let him know that I was aware of the real reason why he wanted to be rid of me.

". . . that Your Grace may be at liberty, both before God and man, not only to execute worthy punishment on me as an unfaithful wife, but to follow your affections already settled on that party for whose sake I am now as I am . . ."

Angrily I wrote—more vehement perhaps because *I* was now in the position of the discarded wife.

He would be angry. He would try to pretend that it was not because he desired another woman that he wished to be rid of me. He was a past master—not of deceiving others, for those about him saw through his utterings and posturings as clearly as I did—but of deceiving himself.

He was superstitious, fearful of ill luck; he committed his sins with one eye on Heaven, hoping to pull the wool over the eyes of God and His angels as he thought he did over those of his ministers and courtiers.

"But if you have already determined of me that not only my death but an infamous slander must bring you the joying of your desired happiness, then I desire of God that He will pardon your great sin herein and likewise my enemies, the instruments thereof and that He will not call you to a straight account of your unprincely and cruel usage of me . . ."

I was again on the verge of hysterical laughter. I must calm myself. Others had suffered like this before me. This place was full of the ghosts of martyrs. What was so important about one more?

I sealed the letter. I would send it to the King. I wrote on it "From the Lady in the Tower."

It must give him twinges of conscience. His conscience was important to him. He referred to it constantly; and knowing him well, I believed that it did exist.

I could see him in my mind's eye so clearly . . . those days at Hever and at Court . . . his little eyes alight with desire for me, his cruel mouth suddenly soft and tender . . . for me. How he had wanted me! He had fought for me with that tenacity which was a part of his nature; he had been determined to have me. For me he had shaken the foundations of the Church; and however

much he declared he did it to satisfy his conscience, he knew . . .
the whole world knew . . . that he had done it for me.

So where did it change? There must have been some point
where I started to go downhill. When? I could have stopped
myself perhaps.

I remembered early days at Blickling and Hever and later at
Court where I was surrounded by those who loved me. My dearest brother George, my friends, Thomas and Mary Wyatt, Norris,
Weston, Brereton—the wits and poets of the Court. We had
talked of life and death, of ambition and achievement; we had
come to the conclusion that we were all masters of our fate. The
wise knew how to recognize danger before it reached them, to
step aside and let it pass by. We were what we made ourselves.

That was George's theory. Some of the others disputed it; and
in a Court where living was precarious and once-great men could
be brought low in the space of an hour it was a debatable
conclusion.

But in my heart I believed there was some truth in it, for if a
man or woman did not wish to face danger he or she could stay
away from where danger would most likely be—and nowhere in
the country was that more than at Court.

So where did I go wrong? Where was that moment when
I could have averted the danger?

I could have produced a son; but that was not in my power. I
had my sweet daughter Elizabeth and I loved her dearly, though I
did not want to think of her, for I greatly feared what would
become of her. She had her governess, a good friend of mine. I
trusted Lady Bryan for she loved the child well and her husband

was a kinsman of my family. When the power had been mine I had always looked after my own family.

But I must not think of Elizabeth now. It is too distressing and could do no good.

But if I had had a son this would not have happened. Henry would have been unfaithful, but the ambitious Seymour brothers would not have been able to guide their silly sister; she would have become his mistress no doubt and I should have been expected to accept that. I should have raged against them; I should have been insulted and humiliated, but I should not be in this doleful prison in the Tower.

No. I had taken a false step somewhere. All through the waiting years I had managed—with consummate skill, all would agree—to hold him at bay, to refuse him until I could take an honorable position beside him. Suppose I had not done this? Then I should now be a cast-off mistress instead of a Queen in a Tower.

I put my fingers to my throat. It was long and slender. It added an elegance to my figure. I accentuated it as I did all my assets and I disguised my defects, with success, I believe. I could almost feel the sword there.

All through the waiting years I had known I must hold him off. I knew him as the hunter and his delight in pursuit. As long as it remained the chase he was determined to succeed. But the joys of capture were brief.

I should have known. I should have realized even as the crown was placed upon my head that it was there precariously.

I knew well the man on whom my fate depended. None knew

him better. I should have realized that my life depended on one who was not to be relied on. His fancies faded as quickly as they came. I had been bemused because he had pursued me so ardently and with such persistence. The years of the chase had been long; those of possession short. When had he begun to weary? When had he begun to realize all he had done for me and to ask himself whether it had been worthwhile? What did he think now of his public quarrel with the Pope and the power of Rome—all for a woman who had ceased to interest him?

I should never have become involved with him. I should have escaped while there was time. I should have married Henry Percy. I should have died of the Sweat. Then this would never have come to pass.

Somewhere along the years the fault lay with me. Where? I would seek it. It would occupy me in my prison. It would keep my thoughts in the past, away from contemplation of the fearful future.

I would go back to those happy days at Blickling and Hever, to the glitter of the Court of France, my return to England—a young girl knowledgeable beyond her years, brought up in the most sophisticated and elegant Court in the world. That was what had made me what I was, and what I was had brought me to my present state. I wanted to recall it in detail . . . and while I waited here in my prison I would do so.

THE DEATH OF A KING

THE FIRST TIME I SAW THE KING was in the cavalcade on the way to Dover where his sister, the Princess Mary, was to embark for France and her marriage to the King of that country. To my surprise I was a member—though a very humble one—of that glorious assembly. This was the most exciting experience of my young life so far and I was in a state of constant apprehension lest I should act without due propriety and be sent home before we embarked because of some deficiency discovered in me—my youth, my inexperience or because I did not know how to behave with due decorum in the presence of the great. True, I had been assiduously schooled by my governess, Simonette, and I spoke French with a fair fluency; but I was realizing that the cocoon of safety which had enclosed me at Blickling and Hever was no longer there. I had left my childhood behind me forever.

And there I was in close proximity to the King himself. He was big—surely the biggest man I had ever seen, which was as a king should be. He was twenty-three years old then. His hair shone golden in the September sunshine and he wore it short and straight in a fashion which had come from France where, Simonette told me, all the best fashions came from. There would have been no need for any to be told that he was the King; all would have known just to look at him. He glittered. The jewels in his garments were dazzling; he laughed and joked as he rode along and the laughter of those about him seemed to punctuate every remark he made.

On one side of him rode the Queen and on the other the Princess Mary. Beside him the Queen looked almost somber—a peahen beside a glorious peacock. She had a serious, kindly face and the cross she wore about her neck called attention to that piety which we all knew was hers.

The Princess Mary bore a strong resemblance to her brother; she was strikingly beautiful, but at this time she wore a sullen expression which indicated that, however much others might be delighted by her marriage, she was not.

I thought how alarming it must be to be dispatched off to a husband whom one had never seen and who had already had two wives—the last one recently dead and the first put away because she was hump-backed, ill-favored and could not bear children. I knew this because Simonette had thought it necessary for me to know what was going on in the world about me, and as I was called precocious and Simonette said I was wise beyond my years, I listened to what I was told and remembered it.

The marriage had been arranged to indicate friendship between France and England, who had until recently been at war with each other. England's allies had been the Emperor Maximilian and Ferdinand of Spain; but Maximilian and Ferdinand had been uncertain allies and Louis of France was a wise man who saw the futility of war and sought to end it. This he did, breaking up the alliance by offering his daughter Renée as a bride for Maximilian's grandson Charles and to Ferdinand he offered Navarre on which Ferdinand had long cast covetous eyes. That left England to fight France alone; but Louis was prepared for that. Why not a friendship sealed by his marriage to Henry's sister? It must have been hard for our King to turn away such a glittering prize. His sister to be Queen of France! So, smarting from the humiliation inflicted on him by the perfidy of Maximilian and Ferdinand and knowing a good bargain when he saw one, he agreed. It was too good to be resisted, so Princess Mary was being led most reluctantly to the altar. It was small wonder that she looked sullen.

As we came into Dover the fierce wind was rising and a feeling of apprehension swept through the company. None of us looked forward to crossing that strip of water which separated us from the Continent of Europe. Storms blew up suddenly and I had heard people talk with horror of what had to be endured on a storm-tossed ship.

So we came to the castle where we should stay until the sea was calm enough for us to set out.

The great fortress loomed before us, its casements dug into the solid rock. It was known as the Gateway to England—a formidable building which could house two thousand soldiers and which had stood for centuries overlooking the sea. It was said that King Arthur of legend had inhabited the castle and that William the Conqueror had had difficulty in taking it. Of course it had changed since those days; it had been restored and added to, to make it the great fortress it was today; and here we must stay to await the King's pleasure and that of the sea.

As I lay in bed listening to the wind buffeting the walls of the castle I thought of how my life had changed so quickly. It had begun with the death of my mother two years before.

I believed I would never forget that day at Blickling. The Wyatts—Thomas and Mary—were with my own sister Mary, my brother George and myself in the garden. We saw a great deal of the Wyatts because our father and theirs had been appointed joint Constables of Norwich Castle, and when we were in Kent—they at Allington and we at Hever—we were close neighbors. We were great friends. I found Thomas exciting to be with and Mary a comfort.

Thomas was a vital person. He wrote poetry and he used to read it to us. Sometimes it made us laugh; sometimes it made us think. I was always happy to see Thomas; and his sister Mary was a girl who never said an unkind word about anyone; she was serious and quite clever. I think I liked Thomas more than anyone except my brother George, who was also a poet and a great talker. I loved to be with them both although I was expected to listen; and I was not allowed to speak for long, they being so much older than I was.

As for my sister Mary, she admitted that she never listened to what they said. Her mind would be flitting off on lighter matters such as what ribbon she would wear in her hair or whether her dress should be blue or pink. That was Mary—not so much stupid as having a lack of concentration. But she was good-hearted and we all loved her.

I was not quite six years old but I seemed much older, perhaps because my father had insisted that Mary and I should be given a better education than most girls of our station, and I profited from it, even if Mary did not. Daughters of minor aristocracy were usually sent away from home at an early age to some noble household where they would learn to read and write, to sing, to dance and play the lute, to ride side-saddle, to curtsy, to wash their hands before and after a meal, to handle a knife with grace and to dip it into the salt bowl, take a delicate portion and never pick it up with the fingers. That was not good enough for my father. So we were kept at home until the right place could be found for us, which was not easy, for his aims were high and opportunities had to be waited for.

I knew why, of course. I had heard George talking to Thomas Wyatt. We did not have to look far back into the family history to see what great progress we had made. Our great-grandfather, the founder of our fortunes, had been a mere merchant trading in silk and wool cloth. It was true he was a very special merchant, for he had acquired a title and become Lord Mayor of London. His greatest cleverness, though, was in his marriage, for his wife was the daughter of Lord Hoo—and her father's heiress at that. They had a son, William, my grandfather, who had married the daughter of the Earl of Ormond; hence more blue blood was injected into the Boleyn circulation. My father had done best of all, for he had married Elizabeth Howard, daughter of the Earl of Surrey, who in due course became the Duke of Norfolk; and the Dukes of Norfolk considered themselves—most dangerously—more royal than the Tudors.

That was the pattern, said George, and our father planned for us all to continue with it. Therefore his children must receive a special education. They must be prepared to stand equal with the highest in the land. They should therefore not only learn the social graces but have the education which was generally reserved for royal children.

Our governess, Simonette, was aware of this. She was a worldly woman with the fatalism and realism of her race. I was her favorite, which was strange because Mary was more lovable as well as being outstandingly pretty. She was hopeless with her lessons, because she would not—or could not—give her mind to them. So I supposed that was why Simonette favored me.

I must dance as the French danced, walk as they walked in France, and I must speak French as it was spoken in that country. I was fond of her because she admired me and I had always yearned to be admired. I was very conscious of being less pretty than Mary and I confessed this to Simonette.

"No, no, no," she cried. "You have the grace. You have the charm. You will be the one, little Anne. Mary . . . oh yes . . . very pretty . . . loved for a while because she is giving . . . too giving . . . and that can pall. Oh, *mon amour,* I should want to see you older . . . a little older, yes. Those eyes . . . they are *magnifique* . . . yes, *magnifique.* And I tell you this: you know how to use them. It is something you are born with . . . for I have not taught you . . . They will allure, those eyes."

I studied them critically. They were large, making the rest of my face small in comparison. They and my thick dark hair were compensation for the mole on the front of my neck and the beginning of a nail on the side of my little finger which made me think that God had intended to give me a sixth finger and changed his mind, leaving me with only the nail.

I hated it. I could not understand it. I found myself staring, fascinated, at other people's hands.

My brother George said: "Never mind. It makes you different. Who wants to be the same as everyone else?"

"I do," I said vehemently.

Simonette also tried to comfort me. "Sometimes it is more *chic* to have a little imperfection . . . more human . . . more exciting . . . more fascinating. You will see."

Then came that summer's day when we were all in the gardens. I remember so well that feeling of impending doom. I knew that something fearful was going to happen. The household was subdued. Even George and Thomas Wyatt were quiet. Mary was trying to fight off the evil as she always would by pretending that it did not exist.

But we knew that all was not well, for they had sent to my father, bringing him home from the Court, and that would be something no one would dare do unless it was very important.

My mother was dying. This was not just another of those yearly illnesses which beset her. This was not what they called "another disappointment." This went beyond that. The doctors were there with the midwife.

I thought of her. She was tender and loving to us children, but we had seen little of her. When she was well she accompanied our father to Court and it was only when he was on embassies abroad that she returned to her family. When she grew heavy with child she would be with us. Then would come the confinement and the brief rest before she joined our father. It was a pattern which seemed to go on forever.

Neither George nor Thomas Wyatt could talk as usual on that day. We had been silent, glancing every now and then at the house, waiting.

It was Simonette who came to tell us. I knew as soon as I saw her walking across the grass as though reluctant to reach us.

To lose one's mother when one is not quite six years old is not only a tragic but an illuminating experience. It teaches one that life is not as pleasantly predictable as one had thought it to be. There comes a terrible sense of aloneness and the alarming knowledge that nothing will ever be the same as it was before.

Our father went away on a mission to the Netherlands and was absent for a whole year, and when he came back there was more change in our household. He was clearly rather pleased with himself. George told us that he had had to conclude a treaty with Margaret of Savoy, Archduchess of Austria, by which the Emperor Maximilian, Pope Julius and Ferdinand of Spain should, with England, make war on France. This was the treaty which was soon to founder; but at that time my father believed that its conclusion was a great success for him. There was something else which was equally pleasing to him. My sister Mary was to go to the Court in Brussels over which Margaret reigned as Regent of the Netherlands.

George said: "This is what our father always wanted—to get his children into royal circles."

So I lost Mary and as George was soon to go to Cambridge—and Thomas Wyatt with him—our little group was much diminished and Mary Wyatt and I did our best to console each other.

I remember well the long summer day at Hever or riding over to Allington, feeding the pigeons with Mary Wyatt. I was fascinated by the pigeons; they had light brown feathers, different from the ordinary gray ones. I thought the reason why they were there was so romantic. I had first heard it from Thomas, who told it so beautifully—as he did everything.

His father, Sir Henry, had been the prisoner of Richard III because he had not supported his accession to the throne, and on account of this had been thrown into the Tower. There he was severely tortured and when he had fainted with the agony, mustard and vinegar had been forced down his throat to revive him. When he refused to give way, he was put into a cell and left to starve.

Sir Henry had thought his end was near but one day he saw a cat on the windowsill. He staggered to the window, delighted to have contact with some living thing; he put his hand through the bars to stroke the cat's fur. Instead of repulsing him the cat had purred. He felt the better for it. The cat went away but shortly afterward came back with a pigeon it had caught and killed. The pigeon was for Sir Henry. It was food and he was almost dead of starvation. He ate the pigeon.

The next day, the cat appeared again with another pigeon, and thus did that cat keep Sir Henry alive all through the time of his captivity. So he lived to see the defeat of Richard at Bosworth Field and the arrival of Henry Tudor, who, wishing to reward him for his fidelity to the House of Lancaster, immediately freed him and restored his estate to him.

Sir Henry never forgot. Whenever I saw him at Allington it was with a cat . . . not the same one which had kept him alive, but a descendant of that cat; his cat was like a faithful hound; it followed him wherever he went, slept on his bed and was constantly in his company; and to remind himself of how he had been saved, he had pigeons brought to Allington and he said they would be there as long as there were Wyatts in the castle. And the strange thing was that the cat and the pigeons of Allington were friends. They lived together amicably in the castle—symbols of Sir Henry's survival to serve with loyalty the Tudor Kings.

So Mary Wyatt and I were often together at Allington or Hever until I heard that I was to go to France in the service of the King's sister.

So here I was about to embark on this great adventure.

Read Jean Plaidy's
Queens of England series
in historical order:

The Courts of Love
The Story of Eleanor of Aquitaine

AVAILABLE NOW FROM
THREE RIVERS PRESS

1

The Queen's Secret
The Story of Queen Katherine

AVAILABLE FROM
THREE RIVERS PRESS
IN SPRING '07

2

The Reluctant Queen
The Story of Anne of York

AVAILABLE FROM
THREE RIVERS PRESS
IN SUMMER '07

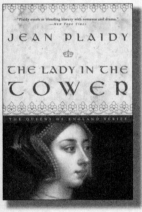

The Lady in the Tower
The Story of Anne Boleyn

AVAILABLE NOW FROM
THREE RIVERS PRESS

The Rose Without a Thorn
The Story of Katherine Howard

AVAILABLE NOW FROM
THREE RIVERS PRESS

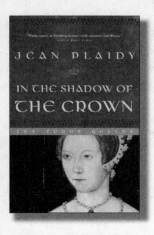

The Merry Monarch's Wife
The Story of Catherine
of Braganza

previously published as
The Pleasures of Love
AVAILABLE FROM
THREE RIVERS PRESS
IN SPRING '08

The Queen's Devotion
Princess Mary of York,
Daughter of James II,
Wife of William of Orange

previously published as
William's Wife
AVAILABLE FROM
THREE RIVERS PRESS
IN SUMMER '08

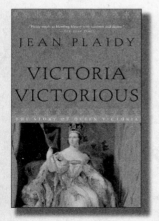

Victoria Victorious
Memoir of Queen Victoria
AVAILABLE NOW FROM
THREE RIVERS PRESS